MW00852515

THE SECRETS WE BURY

MARY BUSH

Copyright © 2021 Mary Bush

The right of Mary Bush to be identified as the Author of the Work has been asserted by her in accordance to the Copyright, Designs and Patents Act 1988.

First published in 2021 by Bloodhound Books.

Apart from any use permitted under UK copyright law, this publication may only be reproduced, stored, or transmitted, in any form, or by any means, with prior permission in writing of the publisher or, in the case of reprographic production, in accordance with the terms of licences issued by the Copyright Licensing Agency.

All characters in this publication are fictitious and any resemblance to real persons, living or dead, is purely coincidental.

www.bloodhoundbooks.com

Print ISBN 978-1-913942-61-8

ALSO BY MARY BUSH

A Simple Lie

For Ray — my dear friend, colleague and partner in our forensic dental team.

1

Valentina Knight stepped around the altar. She estimated its size to be about ten feet across and two feet in width. Bright lights above, set up by crime scene technicians, illuminated the bodies lying on top, making it seem like heaven was shining down and at any moment angels would come to collect them. Prayer—this was all that was left for the young mother and her son, especially after they died like *that*.

Three cops huddled together in stunned silence as the technicians quietly moved around the church scouring for evidence. No one had any words right now. Val couldn't help but feel an uncomfortable stillness in the air, as if those fortunate to be alive, those spared death, were waiting to exhale in relief... *This wasn't my family. This isn't my nightmare. Thank God.*

The team had started at the altar. Now that the victims had been photographed, and a search for hair, fibers, fingerprints, completed and documented, it was up to Val to do a preliminary exam for cause and manner of death before sealing up the boy and his mother and transporting them to the morgue.

Val shivered as she looked at the odd placement of the bodies. Their heads were at either end of the altar, feet pointed together, like mirror images. Each had died in a very different way, though.

"Jesus, I've never seen anything like this before," Officer Powell said, his face ashen. He held a document, which Val guessed was the missing person's report. Computer printout photos were paper-clipped to the front. "The priest found them this morning, though he can't say how long they've been here. He hasn't been in the church since services last Sunday." Officer Powell was the first responder and would be in charge until homicide detectives Mitchell Gavin and Alexander Warren arrived.

This was Val's first opportunity to even get a briefing on the case from him. The lead crime scene tech, though, had provided her with a summary of the findings and also let her know that the names of the victims were Gabrielle Morgan and her son Adam.

"Sunday? That's three days ago. There's no way these people have been dead for three days. There isn't enough decomposition for that," Val said and then nodded towards the officer's document. "Do we know how long they'd been missing for?"

"About a week. Six days to be exact." Officer Powell handed Val the report. "This was filed on Monday."

Val looked at the victims and then back at the pictures attached to the file. This was them. No doubt. She glanced through the narrative.

Last Friday, January 24th, Gabrielle Morgan, age thirty-one, left her house in Amherst NY, a suburb northeast of Buffalo, at roughly 7:40am. This is the time she usually leaves to drop her eight-year-old son off at school, which is less than a half mile away from their home, before heading to work. This was confirmed by one of her neighbors, a Mrs. Jennifer Ballard who lives next door. Mrs. Ballard saw Gabrielle and waved. Gabrielle waved back. Adam kept his head down, opened the door and got inside the car. He did not wave to Mrs. Ballard, but that was not unusual as the boy often appeared preoccupied. Though Gabrielle seemed to be in a hurry, Mrs. Ballard stated Gabrielle did not look distraught. Gabrielle then got into the car and drove away. That was the last time anyone saw her alive. She did not report to work that morning and no one had seen or heard from her until the discovery of her body today.

On the day Gabrielle disappeared, Adam arrived at school by 8:15am, which was twenty minutes later than usual. Adam's teacher took note of this because he was always seated at his desk by 7:55. Class started at 8am and Adam was never late. Adam gave no answer for his tardiness and his teacher did not press—everyone has an off-day.

At this moment, she was not aware that Gabrielle had left home at their usual time. No one could confirm that Gabrielle was the one who dropped Adam off. By 8:15, all students and teachers were in the building. Shortly thereafter, Adam started acting as if something was bothering him. He had trouble concentrating, made sharp remarks, lashing out at his teacher, which was uncharacteristic, and later, fell down twice. After about two hours he complained of stomach pain and went to the nurse's office where he vomited. Multiple attempts were made to contact Gabrielle about her son but all were unsuccessful. The number she had given for an emergency contact, a Ms. Bethany Arias, was not in service.

The boy stayed with the nurse for several hours at which time he stated that he felt better and wanted to go back to class. At 3pm he left school and immediately started walking down the sidewalk.

A number of his classmates confirmed this as many were outside, preparing to go home themselves. They noticed only because Adam was usually picked up by his mother. If she wasn't on time, he waited. He commented to one classmate that his mother didn't like him walking home from school, although home was well within walking distance. Her rule was she picked him up. Adam always followed the rules. His teacher verified this trait. "Model student" she called him. That day, he walked away without hesitation. He didn't wait, he didn't look around for his mother. He simply started walking.

He, also, was not seen again until the discovery of his body this morning.

Though Val would get a better estimate for time of death once she finished her exam, by the condition of the bodies, she guessed they'd been dead only about a day. What had happened to Gabrielle Morgan and her son Adam from the time they disappeared until now? *Jesus, what happened right after they left their house? There's twenty minutes unaccounted for.*

Val opened her mouth to speak but before she could say anything, one of the crime scene techs motioned to Officer Powell, and he quickly ran over. Val held her breath as she watched their interaction. *Did they find something new?* She waited, but then slowly exhaled. It seemed the technicians had finished collecting evidence in the last section of the church and he was asking for directions on where to go, what to do next.

As Val turned her attention back to the bodies, she pulled her wool hat down to cover her ears. Outside, the wind gusted, rattling the windows. Snow was building quickly on the bottom of the sills; about a half inch from the time she'd gotten there, thirty minutes ago. The storm all the news stations predicted had arrived as promised.

It was late January in Clarence, New York, a suburb ten miles east of Buffalo. The temperature had hovered at twenty degrees Fahrenheit throughout the morning but had dropped steadily as the storm approached. Val checked her phone. The outside temperature was now five degrees. No blizzard warnings, yet.

She quickly scrolled through her messages. Nothing new. Frustrated, she shoved the phone back in her pocket.

Val glanced at the church door often, anxiously waiting for the homicide detectives to arrive. Where in the hell were they? She'd been postponing her exam until they got there. Mitchell Gavin, who would be the lead homicide detective, had sent her a text right after she walked through the doors of the church. All he said was: "I'll be there soon. Wait for me before you start." Something big was going on with this case. She glanced at the bodies again and wasn't surprised.

Val tried hard to keep an emotional distance from the scene that lay before her. She was a death scene investigator with the Erie County Medical Examiner's office in Buffalo NY. The name said it all. Death was her job. As such, she was to respond to unexpected, suspicious or violent death as a representative of the medical examiner's office. Her primary responsibility was to document the circumstances of the fatality and do a preliminary examination of the bodies. Basically, collect anything that would help Dr. Richard Maddox, the new chief medical examiner for Erie County, determine cause and manner of death. Val's charge was to focus on the victims. The cops' emphasis was on the crime. Fine lines blurred the two roles and a cordial weaving of skills often came into play to get the case solved.

In cases of homicide, especially those that have happened under unusual circumstances, she would be the liaison between the medical examiner's office and law enforcement. That was certainly going to be the case here.

Shifting her weight several times, Val tried to find a comfortable position to stand as she waited. The chilly bite in the air was taking its toll on her legs, particularly the right one, which was starting to feel numb. The doctors had told her the injury would be sensitive to temperature changes. *But damn it, it's been eight months already.* As she fidgeted, she tried hard to

5

not think about why these people died—particularly about the boy. She wondered if his mother had killed him—then taken her own life. *Or did someone else murder both of them?*

Val took a deep breath and looked at her surroundings, then pulled out her phone again to check the time and her messages again. Where in the hell was Detective Gavin? She put the phone back in her pocket, wondering *how* this place was chosen for Gabrielle Morgan and her son to die. What was the significance? The décor in this building screamed anything but *peaceful*. Maybe that was the point.

The small church had four columns of pews, about twelve rows long on each side. Many of the windows were stained glass depicting the stations of the cross—the crucifixion—a gruesome reminder of our violent nature, one that never would be eradicated through evolution, conditioning, therapy. This trait is one that survived and only strengthened over time. Growing to be a little more concealed, a little more calculated; maturing strategically into an innate skill, honed to methodically plan, execute, and take down another human being masterfully.

The windows seemed in perfect harmony with the back wall of the church where a large mural of heaven and hell was painted. It had a medieval quality to it. The top half of the painting replicated heaven, where the blessed and righteous were given eternal life. The bottom half depicted hell. Val winced at the gruesome portrayal of people being beheaded or thrown by pitchforks into flames. Humans can be ruthless and savage, and cunningly veiled. Your closest, your most loved, most loyal, can quickly and silently, in a snap before your eyes, become your most feared. Hence a dead mother and her boy.

Val's gaze quickly reverted to the altar, and her mind to Gabrielle Morgan. *Murder and then suicide? Or double murder?*

The sound of the church door opening made Val look up.

Finally, she thought as she let out a sigh of relief. Detective Mitchell Gavin entered. He brushed snow from his long black coat as he walked toward Officer Powell. Gavin was a striking man. He stood slightly over six feet and had silver-streaked brown hair. His partner Alexander Warren was right behind him. Warren was a few inches shorter than Gavin. He shaved his head to remove what little hair he had left. Val hadn't seen him in a while and was surprised that his characteristic goatee had transformed to a tightly cropped beard and mustache, giving him that stubbly, unshaven look.

Though Warren was his partner, Gavin would be in charge of this case. He was in charge of any high-profile case in the county and it wasn't the first time Val had worked with him.

The detectives spent some time talking to Officer Powell before he turned and pointed at Val. A few minutes later the detectives came towards her. Val limped forward to greet them.

"Just when you think you've seen it all, the latest and greatest version of crazy appears," Warren said.

"Sacrifice?" Gavin asked, pointing to the boy.

"At this point, anything is possible," Val said.

"She's certainly dressed for some type of..." Warren hesitated and appeared to be searching for the right words as he spoke of the mother. "Ceremony."

She certainly was. The mother wore a long white plain satin gown. White satin ballet flat shoes were on her feet. Her long blonde hair was parted in the middle, which hung loosely around her face and shoulders. She held what appeared to be fir tree branches in each hand. These lay at either side of her body and were secured in her grasp with duct tape. Duct tape also covered her mouth. No obvious sign of trauma or cause of death could be seen.

The boy, though, had his throat slashed. Arced blood spatter patterns plastered the ground to the left and right of him and a large pool of blood congealed on the floor beneath his head and neck.

"Odd that he isn't dressed up in *some* way too," Warren said. Val did note that the boy wore jeans with a beige pullover sweater. Snow boots were on his feet. He looked like a regular kid who just came in from outside, apart from his gaping throat and blood-soaked clothes.

"No winter coats?" Gavin asked, looking around.

"No. None were found in the church. The mother's car was discovered in the back of the parking lot here. No coats in there either." Val was sure the boy at least, was alive when he came into the church; the evidence was obvious for that. Did his mother bring them both here without coats, or did someone else take them away?

"The murder weapon for the boy?" Gavin asked, glancing around. "Is that here?"

"Yes. After it was used, it was placed on the pulpit behind the altar." Val pointed to a large wooden lectern with a simple cross engraved on the front. "It's bagged for evidence, and in box three, if you want to take a look."

Gavin walked over to a row of cardboard evidence boxes, which were clearly numbered. He pulled the lid off "three" and removed a sealed plastic bag holding a large knife with a bright red handle and a long intimidating silver blade.

As he turned the bag around, Val said, "It looks like some kind of hunting knife, the kind you get from an outdoors store."

"That's exactly what it is. It's a fillet knife. And it's used to cut up everything from fish to large game," he said. "These are typically razor sharp because they're meant to slice through bone."

"Jesus, that blade has to be about nine inches in length," Warren remarked. "You think something like this belonged to the mother?"

"If she was looking for an instrument to do the job, then it's likely," Gavin said.

"Hopefully we'll get fingerprints, or DNA off the handle," Val said.

"I don't think that will tell us much," Gavin responded.

"What do you mean?" Val asked, surprised.

"If this knife belonged to the mother and she used it, we'd expect her fingerprints and DNA to be all over it." Gavin put the bagged knife back in the box. "A killer would have known we were expecting it too, and would have placed them all over it."

"That would be a smart killer. And someone who knew the victim. The ceremonial aspects have to have some significance for her," Warren said, shaking his head. "Mitch, you can't be thinking this isn't anything but a murder–suicide. It's far too dramatic for anything but that."

"Alex, I don't want to jump to conclusions. The knife was left here. So now, we really only have two options. We either have a mother who killed her son and herself and the knife was left behind because she herself was about to die, or a smart killer with a connection to the victims, who left the knife to implicate Gabrielle. Those are our only two options. And there's nothing I like better than taking down some damn asshole who thinks he's a smart killer," Gavin said. "No one is *that* smart."

"And if you don't have DNA from the mother on the knife?" Val asked, though a random killing like this seemed pretty unlikely.

"Then we have some crazy psycho loose on the streets," Gavin answered. "And nothing so far points to that. No this..." Gavin circled around. Val could see that his gaze was held on the mother. "This was planned."

"Do you know if she left a suicide note at her home?" Val couldn't help a gnawing feeling that this wasn't a cut and dry murder–suicide. Not because of the evidence at this scene. No, the evidence at this scene was almost textbook for a murder–suicide. There was something about the actions of the victims on the day they disappeared, and the daily habits of Gabrielle Morgan which were spelled out in the missing person's report that bothered Val. "No note was found in the church."

"We're checking her residence for that." Gavin glanced at his watch. "A forensics team is there now processing the entire place for evidence."

"Do you need anything more before I continue with my preliminary external exam, then?" Val asked, eager to get a look at the victims close up.

Gavin motioned to Officer Powell who quickly came over. "We'd like to begin examination of the bodies. All documentation complete?"

"We're good to go on that," Powell confirmed.

Val limped forward, shaking her numb leg to awaken it. She put on a white disposable Tyvek jumpsuit, and booties on her shoes, then placed a surgical bonnet over her hair, so that she wouldn't contaminate the evidence. A surgical mask went over her nose and mouth. Lastly, she slipped on a set of latex gloves and moved closer to the altar, towards the dead boy, wincing at the gruesome scene. Blood has a nauseatingly sweet, sharply metallic odor and there has to be enough of it to detect it simply by inhaling. Though Val recognized the characteristic scent when she walked into the church, it was much more powerful here, next to the body, even with the protection of her mask.

"The boy had his throat cut as he lay on the altar." Val's skin prickled. Though she knew what she was about to say next— hell she knew from the first moment she saw the crime scene— nothing prepares you to utter these words. "He was alive when it happened."

"Are you sure?" Gavin asked, coming forward, careful to step away from the pools of blood.

"No doubt." Val pointed to varying blood patterns on the ground. "Those spurts in an arcing pattern show arterial spray. If his heart wasn't beating that wouldn't have happened. That can only occur if blood was still pumping through his system, and at full force. See how some arcs are very big and some are small. You'll get a different pattern with each beat of the heart. As the blood pressure drops, as he's losing his blood supply, the patterns get smaller. Then after his heart stopped, he simply bled out as seen by the large amount of blood that seeped down the side of the altar creating the massive pool beneath him."

"All of that blood is from him? He's just a kid," Warren said.

"We'll double check the DNA to see if anything got mixed, but there's 1.2 to 1.5 gallons of blood in a human body. By the age of six, children have the same amount as an adult," Val said.

Officer Powell pointed to the mother. "There's very little blood on her dress. If she's the one who killed him, wouldn't she have been covered in it? There's no way it wouldn't have splashed on her." Powell was right. The gown was almost pristine.

Val positioned herself near the boy's head. "If she's the one who cut his throat and she did it while standing behind him, she could have missed most of the spray, especially if she stood back far enough after the cut. If she stepped back, I wouldn't expect much, if anything, to have gotten on her since the blood spray is localized to the sides of the body, not behind." Then Val added, "*Anyone* who cut his throat in this manner would have avoided becoming a bloody mess."

"Any blood in her car in the parking lot?" Warren asked, directing the question to Officer Powell. "She also could have slashed his throat, gone somewhere, and then returned in her white gown."

"Some. The crime scene techs found a small amount on the front driver's side and the rear passenger seat," he said. "But it was no greater than if someone had a minor cut or had a bloody nose. Nothing to account for something like this."

Gavin paced silently for a few moments, as if taking everything in. "Val, I think we're ready for you to go ahead and start the exam of the mother. Gabrielle's body will have far more to tell us about this crime than her son. He's the only one at this moment that we can confirm is a victim."

Val moved to the mother and began inspecting that body, happy that Gavin was keeping a double murder option open, at least for now. "No obvious sign of trauma." She looked up at both detectives. "Honestly, she looks like she's sleeping."

"Can you roll her over a little? I want to see the back of the gown," Gavin said.

Val took hold of the body and pulled it forward. Smeared blood patterns were evident on her back.

"It's all simple transfer," Warren said. It's consistent with what's already on the altar."

Gavin crossed his arms. "The fact that the blood was there first is important. What we know is that she was either placed there or got up on the altar *after* her son died. At this point, Gabrielle Morgan is still either a victim or a murderer."

"The altar is only about three feet high," Warren commented as he came closer. Val watched his eyes travel from mother to son. "I have a bad feeling about this one, Mitch. I hate to say it, but my gut is screaming Mom was looking to end it all and decided to take her kid with her. Really, as far as suicide goes, there's nothing about the condition of the body that she couldn't have done to herself. She easily could have gotten up here, then placed the duct tape over her own mouth and then duct taped the branches to her hands."

"She certainly could have," Gavin said. "Val, can you preserve the tape so we can check for fingerprints and trace evidence on the underside. We also need to see how the tape was wound around her hands, if she could have done it herself."

Val nodded and pulled out a roll of clear plastic wrap to seal the victim's hands and head. The plastic would keep the evidence contained and uncompromised during transport. Val moved to the head first, then suddenly stopped. Something wasn't right. The mother's cheeks appeared full. Val took a pair of tweezers out of her supply bag and teased the duct tape back, then grabbed a small flashlight. Parting the woman's lips, she shone the light inside. Val shot back, shocked, then parted the lips again and inched in as close as she could. "There's something in here."

"In her mouth? Something's in her mouth?" Gavin said as he and Warren moved closer too, making sure to stay away from the bloody spurts around the altar. "What is it?"

"Looks like...*seeds*." Val said, almost as a question.

"Seeds?" Warren said as if he didn't hear right.

"That's what they look like," Val said, stunned. "Do you want to see for yourself. I have another set of booties in my bag."

Gavin grabbed a pair, placed them over his boots, and came closer. He took the flashlight from Val and as she held back Gabrielle Morgan's lips, he glanced inside Gabrielle's mouth. "Holy crap. My guess is that those are seeds too."

"Jesus, and I didn't think this case could get any more bizarre," Warren remarked.

Val shook her head in disbelief and replaced the duct tape back over Gabrielle's mouth, then sealed Gabrielle's head tightly in plastic wrap to prevent anything from escaping. Val moved to the hands next.

"Fingerprints," Gavin said, causing Val to stop mid unravel with her plastic wrap. "Val, can you get her fingerprints before you wrap her hands?" Gavin asked.

"I think so." Val surveyed Gabrielle's hands, which were

clenched. Luckily, Val was able to loosen the tape and pry the stiff fingertips free without disrupting the tree branches. She took an inkpad and a fingerprint card from her supply bag and pressed the tips on the pad, and then rolled them on a card. The fact that Gabrielle was thought to have killed her son would certainly be cause for Gavin to run her prints, to see if she had any past crimes.

When Val was finished, she wrapped the hands in plastic. It would all be removed and examined far more thoroughly once back in the morgue, where they'd have more control in collecting the evidence. Val rolled the body onto its side to examine the skin on the back, hoping to get an estimate for time of death. "She's in full rigor." Val pushed a gloved finger into purple discoloration. "No blanching. Lividity is fixed. It's consistent with her lying on her back since she died. She hasn't been moved. So, rigor indicates death happened about eight to thirty-six hours ago. Lividity suggests she's been dead at least twelve hours."

"It's freezing in here. That's going to change things," Gavin said.

"Cold will affect rigor mortis, and algor mortis which is the cooling of the body. They both slow down a lot in weather like this," Val said. "Algor is so unreliable in cold temps, that I'm not going to put much into it. Lividity, which is the pooling of blood in the lowest point of the body, usually the parts in contact with the surface the body's lying on, isn't affected that much by temperature. This is dependent on when the heart stops beating and there's no more blood pressure."

Next, Val pulled back the woman's eyelid and shone the flashlight beam on the eye. "There's a film that develops on the corneal surface after death, it's called corneal cloudiness. If the eyes of the victim remained open, this occurs in a couple of hours. These are closed which can delay corneal cloudiness from happening for as much as twenty-four hours. Cloudiness is just beginning, and that's not temperature dependent either. She hasn't started to decompose yet, but she's getting there. That starts at about twenty-four hours, but that *is* temperature dependent. Given all of this, I'm going to say she's been dead about twenty-four hours."

"Don't people die with their eyes open?" Warren asked. "Wouldn't someone had to have closed them for her?"

"No. If she closed them herself, maybe in preparation for death they would have stayed closed when she died." Val pointed to the boy, hesitating for a second, sick to her stomach with what she was about to say. "Her son's eyes are open. He saw what was about to happen to him."

"I can't imagine the terror of that," Gavin said.

"Neither can I," Val said, stepping back from both bodies. "I'm going with the same time of death for Adam as well. I can't do any better here. We'll have to wait for Dr. Maddox to make his analysis at the morgue to hopefully get a more precise estimate."

"How's the new chief medical examiner working out so far?" Warren asked. "We haven't had a lot of interaction with the guy."

"He's all right," Val said of Dr. Maddox. "A little strict with protocol but seems to know his stuff."

Another half hour passed as she pored over the victims, finally becoming confident there was nothing more she could do at the crime site. "I'm done. Is there anything more that you need before I bag them up for transport?" Val asked.

"No," Gavin answered. He jotted down a few notes. "I want the information about the tree branches and seeds kept confidential. This isn't to be released to the media." The significance was clear. If this was a double homicide only the killer would know about this oddity. Keeping the detail back would help rule out crazy people who usually come forward to claim that they've committed a murder they've had nothing to do with.

Val pulled off her Tyvek suit, booties and gloves. These would be bagged with the body. All of her protective clothing possibly contained transferred evidence, and would need to be examined by the crime lab as well. Next, she took out her phone and sent a text to Dr. Maddox, letting him know she'd be leaving soon. Val looked around at the crime scene. With the bodies packed up and ready to go, this wasn't an ending. No, this was only just beginning.

2

Val arrived back at the morgue by 6pm, and after placing Adam Morgan in the cooler, quickly wheeled his mother, clad in a white body bag, down the corridor to autopsy room one, the morgue's private autopsy suite. Gabrielle would be first, Adam next. Dr. Maddox planned on finishing both post-mortems tonight. Val would stay to assist Dr. Maddox, of course. She frequently helped him out. In his short seven months at the medical examiner's office, Val had become one of Dr. Maddox's most sought-after assistants.

The position of death investigator called for attention to detail and medical knowledge; but death investigators are not doctors. Val was thankful for that, though she had been a doctor once. Well, sort of. In her previous occupation, she had been a dentist but one of her patients, Mr. Tate, a suspected serial killer, ended that career by mangling her left hand. Val had been helping the cops collect evidence against him by getting molds of his teeth—bitemarks had been left on the victims' bodies. He attacked Val in a brief moment when she let her guard down. Val would never do that again.

This case became her initiation into a criminal world. It had ignited her desire to help catch murderers and was a vibrant reminder of the dangers and demands of doing so. A hand and now a leg. There were occupational hazards with crime fighting. Val was convinced that she'd be in a wheelchair before retirement if she kept this up. Or she'd have to get better at crime fighting.

God, how long ago was the hand incident now? Val couldn't believe it had almost been two years—and two years since she'd practiced dentistry. Forced to find a new profession at the age of thirty-five, she was lost for what to do next, and after nearly a year unemployed, with bills piling along with foreclosure notices threatening her home, Val grew desperate. In a defining moment during her interview for this job, her death investigator job, she told a simple lie. That's how she landed it. Then skill, and a little luck, let her keep it.

Val rarely thought about the hand incident anymore. Her left hand could function quite well, just not well enough for dentistry. But unfortunately she would be forced to relive the event. Mr. Tate's trial date was finally coming up. Val would have to testify and she was dreading it. She checked her phone; the prosecuting attorney for the case had been badgering her. He needed to start prepping her for the stand soon, and was trying to make sure Val wasn't getting cold feet. Jesus, the mere thought of testifying made her nauseous. Thank God her inbox was quiet, well, except for some recent texts from Dr. Maddox.

Let me know when you're ready to set up.

As she walked, Val was pleased to find that being back in a building with sufficient heat, her leg felt pretty normal again and her limp was just about gone. She opened the autopsy room door and then looked at her watch. Gavin and Warren should be arriving at any minute. A voice down the hall made Val turn her head.

"I was wondering when you'd get here. I've been following the story on the news," Gwen Carmondy said, quickly running forward. Gwen was Val's fellow death investigator. But she was more than a co-worker, she was Val's friend. The two became roommates just last week. Val had an extra bedroom in her house and Gwen needed a place to stay. So far the arrangement had been good.

Val looked up at Gwen, who was five feet nine, a good seven inches taller than Val. She had deep blue eyes and long curly dark auburn hair that Val would have killed for. Her own long black hair was poker straight. This, coupled with dark eyes gave Val a distinct Mediterranean appearance. Attractive? Attention from the opposite sex said yes, but that's all Val had to go on. "This case is crazy." Val wheeled the gurney into the autopsy suite. "Want to help me set up?"

"Absolutely." Gwen grabbed the gurney and wheeled it into place.

Val texted Dr. Maddox, letting him know she was in the autopsy suite and that she'd be ready for him in a few minutes. Val's stomach growled. When was the last time she'd eaten? Breakfast maybe? Adrenaline pushed her forward. There was no way she'd be home before midnight tonight. She didn't care. She wouldn't be able to sleep and food was not on her mind.

Val put on latex gloves, walked over to the gurney and unzipped the white body bag just as Dr. Richard Maddox entered. He stood about six feet and had dark hair cropped short. His steel-blue eyes had an intensity that gave him a commanding, uncompromising appearance. Val often thought that if his edges were softened even just a little he'd be a very handsome man.

As she pulled the bag open and away from the body,

exposing Gabrielle Morgan, Val gave him a summary of the crime scene and her findings at the church, ending with the fact that the victim had tree branches in her duct taped hands and seeds in her taped mouth. All of this could easily be seen through the clear plastic enclosure and being wrapped in plastic gave Gabrielle an even more macabre appearance.

"They didn't report the branches and seeds on the news," Dr. Maddox said, coming closer to get a better look.

"Detective Gavin doesn't want that fact released to the public."

Dr. Maddox put on latex gloves and inspected the body briefly in the opened bag. "Val, Gwen, can you lift her out? We'll unwrap her on the exam table."

Gwen took hold of Gabrielle Morgan's shoulders, while Val held her ankles, and the two moved the body to a stainless-steel table where the autopsy would be conducted. Dr. Maddox placed a metal tray under each of Gabrielle's hands, making sure it extended up her forearm, then he carefully took off the plastic wrap. "Looks like these branches belong to a fir tree. Val, start with photography and then we'll get them out of her hands. We'll need to find out exactly what kind of tree these belong to, might have some relevance to the case. We'll have to identify the seeds, too."

Val nodded, taking mental notes of Dr. Maddox's instructions. He was right. The kind of tree and seeds should have some significance to Gabrielle. Val pulled out the camera as Detectives Gavin and Warren walked through the door. "Any more news?" she immediately asked.

"Yes, big news... Gabrielle Morgan is the daughter of James and Rachel Morgan, of Morgan Foods."

Val's jaw dropped open and everyone in the room suddenly stopped, stunned. All heads turned towards Gavin.

"She was one of *the* Morgans?" Gwen finally broke the silence.

"Yes." Gavin took off his coat and placed it on a counter by the door.

"That fact isn't listed anywhere in the missing person's report," Val said. Hell, nothing in that report, nothing about how Gabrielle lived, hinted that she was part of this family. Plus, Morgan was such a common name that Val wouldn't have even suspected this connection.

Morgan Foods manufactured packaged bread, whole-wheat crackers, and breakfast cereal. Almost every supermarket in the country carried Morgan Foods products. The company was started in Buffalo and dated back to the late 1800s when the family ventured into the lucrative grain industry that was skyrocketing in the area. Val knew this because the history of the family business was printed on every package.

Val was Buffalo born and raised, migrating for only ten years to practice dentistry in Clearwater, Florida, leaving behind snow and skiing for sun and beaches. She returned home when her dental career was cut short. This city was in her blood, and with nothing to keep her in Florida the choice to come back to Buffalo was an easy one. The community was tight-knit, friendly, welcoming. Everyone helped everyone, the rich included, some more so than others.

The Morgans donated to many charities and organizations. And after their daughter and grandson died like this, the pressure would be on the police and medical examiner's office to solve this case quickly and to their satisfaction. Hell, it was an oversight no one standing in this morgue wanted to have. It would be a career-ending move if anything went wrong. Or if the Morgans perceived that anything had gone wrong. Stress? Yes, this just upped the stress level with this case. It was already high-profile because of the nature of the deaths but the involvement of the Morgans just catapulted it to another level.

"Her parents weren't the ones to file the report." Warren also removed his coat and placed it next to Gavin's. "One of her co-workers did."

"What?" Val stared at him.

"Gabrielle and her parents were estranged. It seems there was a falling out several years ago, and she moved out on her own and cut off all ties with them. They didn't even know she'd gone missing," Gavin said.

"How did you find out who her family was, then?" Dr. Maddox asked.

"After we ran her fingerprints, we got a hit. About ten years ago, she was arrested twice for DWI. Back when those happened, the address for the Morgans' estate was listed as her place of residence. We sent a couple officers to inform her parents. After the shock, they managed to give a preliminary account of their relationship with their daughter. Seems that Gabrielle was a bit of a handful when she was younger, hence the arrests. Her parents have agreed to help in any way they can, which is reassuring for now," Gavin said. "Warren and I are planning on talking with them tomorrow."

"Take that hospitality when you can get it because who knows how long it will last," Dr. Maddox said sarcastically.

Val said, "Can I tag along when you talk to the parents? I'll have to speak with them anyway. It might be easier for them if we do this all in one shot rather than two." With her job as a death investigator Val had to question relatives, acquaintances, neighbors, really anyone who knew of the deceased and could give her information to help Dr. Maddox determine cause and manner of death. Parents of victims were always tough. They'd have to relive the death of their child when the cops talked with them, then again when Val did it. The second time around was always more difficult than the first. It only rubbed salt in wounds, and Val guessed that rubbing salt in the Morgans' wounds was employment suicide.

Gavin nodded. "Sure. We have an appointment with them at ten tomorrow morning."

"I'll be ready." Val pointed the camera at Gabrielle's hands and began taking pictures of the tree branches duct taped in place. "Did the crime scene techs find anything of forensic value in Gabrielle's house?"

"There were no signs of any struggle. Nothing looks out of place. It's as if these two simply walked out and never came back," Gavin said.

"Suicide note?" Dr. Maddox asked, before Val could do so.

"No," Gavin said. "They found a laptop and took that for analysis. So we'll see if anything was written, or deleted. Though she has a cell phone, we didn't find it in her home, her car. Or in the church. Her cell phone carrier tried pinging it for us. They got nothing." Val knew what Gavin was talking about. The cell phone carrier will send a signal to the phone to check its location.

"They went missing six days ago and more than likely, died sometime yesterday. They had to have been somewhere, alive, for all that time. You have to have another crime scene," Val said.

"Staying somewhere, or *kept* somewhere. We don't know that answer yet," Gavin stressed.

Dr. Maddox came over to Val's side. "Gwen, why don't you take over with the photography. Get pictures of Gabrielle's mouth next, then start the full body photos. Val, let's start getting the duct tape off so we can get the branches out of her hands. Be careful with the tape. We'll want to preserve it."

Gwen took the camera as Dr. Maddox started dictating the external exam. Val picked up a pair of forceps and slowly, teased the tape open. Luckily, she was able to unwind it in one piece.

The inside of the tape, the part wound around itself and not in contact with the victim, was the most important. If Gabrielle taped herself, her DNA would be all over the inside. Trace evidence also could be stuck to the inner part.

Most of the branches stayed in place. Val wasn't surprised. With the amount of rigor in the body, Gabrielle's hands were locked in place. With some prying of the fingers, Val managed to remove the branches. The tape and branches each went into separate evidence bags.

Next, Val pulled off the duct tape from Gabrielle's mouth and placed that into its own evidence bag. Carefully she parted the lips. Once opened enough, she grabbed a small metal scoop and a flashlight, then pulled the seeds out, placing them in an evidence container. "I can't tell if I got them all." She peered back into the mouth again.

"I plan on doing a thorough dissection of the oral cavity and throat to see if anything else is in there. So, don't worry about it," said Dr. Maddox. "Let's prepare for the internal exam."

After the victim was unclothed, Dr. Maddox made the Y incision. Val picked up a set of long handled garden loppers. Starting under the bottom of the last rib on the left side she placed the blade around the bone and cut up. She repeated the motion on the right. One of the first things she learned at the medical examiner's office was that other than the skull, which required a Stryker saw, most bone removal was done with the loppers. Cheap. Easy. No mess.

"What kind of job did she have?" Val asked of Gabrielle Morgan.

"She was a fundraising manager for The Next Step, a non-profit organization that helps those recovering from drug and alcohol addiction," Gavin said.

Val set the loppers down and lifted off the rib cage. It detached in one piece. "And no one she worked with knew who she was? Her background? Her parents are known for donating to all the major charities. They're philanthropists." She set the ribs on the counter. Gabrielle's organs were now fully exposed.

Warren took a step back from the body, his face, pale. "Gabrielle lived in a modest house in the Buffalo suburb of Amherst, and evidently told no one—not even co-workers or neighbors—about her background. They wouldn't describe her as secretive. She just didn't talk about herself that much and never volunteered information when asked. No one suspected she was part of *that* Morgan family."

"None who admitted it, you mean?" Val said.

"Not so hard to believe, Val," Gavin said. "Morgan is a common name and there is no online presence for a Gabrielle Morgan. No pictures, no stories. No mention of her in the media makes no obvious connection to her wealthy family. Plus, she's estranged from her parents. They didn't talk about her."

"I'm not surprised that she didn't tell anyone who she was." Dr. Maddox came over to the body, scalpel in hand, and began removing organs. "Maybe she didn't want *a label* of where she came from to complicate her new life. Coming from an extremely wealthy, prominent family wouldn't have helped her at all while she lived in a middle-income suburbia. In fact, it would have worked against if she was trying to fit in." Dr. Maddox placed Gabrielle's heart and spleen on a metal table, then moved to the lungs. "She was estranged from her parents. No sense in bragging about them to those who are far, and I do mean far, out of her *milieu*. It would've killed her socially, or made her very vulnerable to unwanted attention. She would have lost all the way around."

"That's just it. We don't think she was trying to fit in, at all." Warren continued to stay back from the autopsy table. "So, we can rule out attempting to fill her social calendar. According to her neighbors, she waved when she saw them, but that was all.

The boy rarely came outside and when he did, she was with him. They never saw friends of the child at the house. Gabrielle had mentioned on more than one occasion, when pressed, that he was sick a lot and had allergies. That was her excuse. They didn't buy it. It became neighborhood gossip that Gabrielle was a hypochondriac because of the way she acted with her son. Anyway, this is what the neighbors told the responding officers. We'll be interviewing them too in more detail over the next several days."

"He was sick the day he disappeared," Val reminded them. "He fell down and then went to the nurse's office and vomited."

"And that fact," Gavin said, "is concerning."

"The mother's actions, now that I've heard all of that, have the hallmarks of a possible abusive household." Dr. Maddox stopped removing organs and looked up. "Rich or poor, however you look at it, abuse happens everywhere. The fact that he was sick is raising my red flags."

"You're right," Warren said. "They're either hiding from someone, or she doesn't want anyone to know what she's doing to her kid. Or planning to do to her kid."

"We hope to interview the boy's teachers and classmates soon. He might have confided in one of them if something wasn't right at home," Gavin said.

Dr. Maddox continued with the autopsy. Now that Gabrielle's organs had been weighed, he moved to sectioning them. "This is odd. Her lungs are edematous. There's fluid in them." He tilted his head, peering at the contents. "She had pretty strong congestion at the end. I'll test for any pathogens to find out what she had."

"How sick was she?" Gavin asked.

"Hard to say. People react differently to physical ailments. What might make one person want to lie in bed all day, would only make another go to work and struggle through it. Some people just tough it out more. Could she have functioned with this amount of congestion? Yes."

Dr. Maddox moved on to the other organs, cutting through each. The specimens would have samples prepared and these would be sent to the histology lab to check for any abnormalities. Others would go to the toxicology lab to investigate for drugs or poisons. He stopped mid slice with Gabrielle's liver. "Would you look at that!"

Val noticed the problem immediately. And the significance.

"What's that?" Gavin asked.

"That's a tumor," Dr. Maddox said.

"She had liver cancer?" Gavin asked, coming closer to get a better look.

"More than likely this is not liver cancer," Dr. Maddox answered.

Gavin took his eyes off the liver and looked up at Maddox. "I'm not following."

"Just because Gabrielle had a tumor in her liver doesn't mean that she had liver cancer. Roughly two percent of all cancers in the liver are true liver cancers, in other words, cancer which has the liver as the primary site. Cancer that spreads to the liver is far more common than cancer that begins in the liver. If this started somewhere else, let's say the breast, the breast would be the primary site and what we're seeing here would be breast cancer in her liver. Once cancer develops in one organ and travels elsewhere, it's a metastasis. It's still the same cancer but in a different organ. It can be a death sentence when it spreads."

"Was she terminal?" Gavin questioned.

"Again, hard to tell at this point. I'll need to get more samples tested to be sure. All depends on if this is a metastasis or not. We'll have to follow up with her doctor too." Dr. Maddox shook his head, puzzled. "I've seen no other tumors so far in any of her organs and there's no sign of any surgery where she might have had any removed. Honestly, I'm surprised, because it would be so damn rare for her to have true liver cancer."

"If it spread and she was terminal, that would be an excellent motive for suicide and murder," Warren said.

Dr. Maddox nodded, agreeing. "If she was terminal... I would guess it was still early in the progression though. She was a normal weight and she appears nourished, definitely not in the late stages of cancer. Which also tells us for the last six days, she wasn't starved. I'll check stomach contents, but that'll only tell us what she ate, if anything, in the last couple of hours before her death. There are also no signs of dehydration. All points to the fact that she was eating and drinking normally at the end."

"Jesus," Gavin said. "The cancer... I mean this has to be a suicide that involves a ritual of some kind. A ritual that needed five days to complete, because she was dead for the sixth day... how could it not be... especially with the white dress, tree branches and seeds. It's what my gut is saying."

It wasn't what Val's gut was saying. At one point in their professional relationship, she would have agreed with anything Gavin said. She'd been attracted to him, and honestly probably still was. It wasn't something that was planned or intended. Val had flirted once with him, momentarily, no longer than a blink of an eye, as she felt that undeniable flutter, the one that says there's something special about the person you're speaking with. She had felt the chemistry that brings on the giddy, odd, nervousness raw desire generates. Then, well before she was able to make a move and embarrass herself, she'd found out Gavin was married.

Thankfully. End of story.

But the twinge was still there. The tremble in her chest—she couldn't deny it. *Get over it*, she told herself. All crushes like this cause pain in the end, even more so if they mature to affairs. Val had decided to keep her distance.

But this case... no it wasn't that neat and tidy. Why send Adam to school on a day that Gabrielle had decided that both of them were going to die? Why did he not wait for his mother outside the school? Why didn't she pick him up there?

Dr. Maddox's voice snapped her out of her reverie. "I agree that suicide is the most likely cause here, but we'll need to rule out homicide before it's official," he said. "Val, I want more detailed sections of the other organs. Maybe we missed something. Histology will be able to tell us what other organs had cancer. Cause and manner of death will remain unknown at this point, pending the results of the tests. It still could be suicide or homicide, depending on the outcome of the investigation." Dr. Maddox continued with his summary. "I'm leaning towards cardiac arrest or respiratory failure, secondary to some other event for cause since I see nothing else at this point. She must have had a poison in her system, or a drug overdose. Whether it was self-administered or not is anyone's guess. So, Val, have Zoe do a full toxicological screen on the tissue samples too. I want updates until I can rule on Gabrielle Morgan's cause and manner of death."

Val nodded. Zoe Beauchamp was the toxicologist for the medical examiners' office. There was no doubt that this case was going to keep her busy for a while. Val was thrilled that Dr. Maddox was letting her investigate this, that he was keeping an open mind, but her nerves quickly grew wary. Screw-ups with this kind of case would be a career downfall. *Suicide and murder versus double murder.* Gut feeling is one thing. Evidence another.

Once Val finished with Gabrielle's organ sections, she pushed the exam table to the side and went to get Adam from the cooler. When she returned to the autopsy suite, they started the examination. The procedure was exactly as that for his mother, with one exception. Adam Morgan was X-rayed, full body. With the possibility of a history of child abuse in this case, there was a need to check for healed fractures. Since the radiographs were digital, images immediately appeared on a computer screen. Dr. Maddox placed his face close to the monitor, examining them in detail. "No broken bones in this kid's lifetime."

"That doesn't rule out abuse," Warren said.

"No, it certainly doesn't." Dr. Maddox stepped back from the screen.

After the external exam was completed, the boy was undressed. Val used a hose to clean the body of the copious amount of blood covering it. As the blood washed away, and flushed down the drains, Val was able to finally see the damage to Adam Morgan's throat. He was nearly decapitated.

Gavin circled the table as Val finished rinsing the body. "We need to find out if there are any death rituals that involve tree branches, seeds, and—"

"Throat slashing?" Warren finished the sentence.

"I just can't imagine a mother killing her son like that," Val said. "It's way too aggressive."

"Aggressive or necessary. Depends on the mind of the killer," Warren said.

"Some make hesitation cuts, to build up the courage to carry out the act. Others just get the job done," Gavin added.

"This killer didn't hesitate," Dr. Maddox said. "Whoever did this, made one confident cut and that cut was deep and effective."

Dr. Maddox inspected the body and then took hold of the boy's head, tipping it back so that he could examine the wounds. "I don't see any other obvious cause of death than the cut throat. Both left and right carotids are lacerated. Cut clean through. He bled out. There are no defensive wounds on his hands. So, while still alive, he didn't fight back."

Gavin took a step forward. "Didn't or couldn't. That's important to know."

"Val will have Zoe check his tissue samples too for any drugs that might have been in his system. I'm guessing he was sedated. He had to have been."

"Or restrained and then the restraints removed," Warren said.

Dr. Maddox picked up the boy's hands. "I see no ligature marks on his wrists, so if he was restrained, he didn't fight against them. And that would be expected if someone was coming at you with a large knife. You'd be wringing your hands together to loosen the binds, creating deep gashes and brush burns. He had to have been sedated."

"If he were awake, it would have been terrifying and painful to die like that. I think we can all agree on that," Val said. *A mother doing this to her son?* She couldn't get the thought out of her mind.

"The terror leading up to the event would have been worse than the event itself." Dr. Maddox stripped off his gloves. "He probably became unconscious about five seconds after the cut was made. With about 100ml of blood traveling through the heart and a heart rate of a 120 to 150 beats per minute under a terrifying ordeal like this, that's about how long it would have taken for enough blood to leave his body and his blood pressure to drop, making him unconscious, and for his heart to stop as death occurred. Once he was unconscious, it was over."

"Still, five seconds is a long time to suffer." Val knew the cue with Dr. Maddox taking off his gloves. The autopsy on Adam Morgan was finished.

"Yes, it is," Dr. Maddox said. "Abuse is going to have a big impact on this case because it would have been a lot easier for his mother to hurt him now if she's done so in the past. I see no obvious signs of abuse with this child, but that doesn't mean much. You'll want to follow up with his physician and hospital emergency rooms, though. See if Mother was a frequent visitor. Check with his school for behavioral problems."

"We certainly plan on doing that," Gavin said.

"I plan on keeping both bodies for a few days, in case there's any more tests we want to run, or want to follow up with any new leads," Dr. Maddox said. "I was pretty thorough with tissue collection. So, if her parents protest that I'm holding on to their daughter and grandson too long, and I'm forced to give them up prematurely, I've covered our bases. I can't imagine what more we may need."

"Thanks, Richard," Mitchell Gavin said.

Dr. Richard Maddox extended his hand. "I'm going to say goodnight then, Mitch. I'm exhausted."

Val knew it was time to go too and as Dr. Maddox walked out of the room, she said to Gavin, "Mitch, I have some more questions."

"What are they?" he asked.

"If her son never walked home from school, if he always waited for his mother, why did he break that rule? Where was he going and who picked him up?"

"Maybe his mother picked him up at a different location," he said.

"But why? Why not just follow the normal routine? Here's my last two questions, why send Adam to school on a day that she had decided that both of them were going to disappear and die. And why drop him off twenty minutes late?"

3

It was 1:30am when Val and Gwen arrived home. Val struggled to get through the door. Tired or hungry. Bed or food? Which would win?

"Do you think Jack is still up?" Gwen asked, following Val in. A colleague of theirs, Jack Styles, a Brit who now lived in Boston, had arrived in Buffalo that afternoon, luckily just before the winter storm, which had now tapered off to minor flurries. Val told him the spare key was under the doormat, and to let himself in.

Jack's reaction hadn't surprised Val. "Key under the mat. What are you thinking?" He was recalling her last mishap with the person who caused the injuries to her leg, nearly taking her life in the process. Jack had worked that case with Val and though she referred to him as her colleague, he had grown on her to become a friend as well.

She had responded with, "Jack, if I didn't leave the damn key under the mat, you'd have to wait outside until I came home."

There had been no retort. From Jack? Maybe the snowstorm, and the need for warm shelter had created a well-won *touché*.

"If he is," Val said to Gwen, "I'm sure he'll hear us and come downstairs if he's up for socializing."

If Val's occupation dealt with death and the occasional depravity, Jack's focussed more on depravity. He and his partner, Thomas Hayden, worked as private detectives. All their cases were high-profile, media-worthy events. True crime TV and radio shows regularly featured them. The more heinous and more hopeless for the defendant, the better. That's how the TV stations liked it—for ratings, of course.

When Jack called and said he wanted to come to Buffalo to see her she jumped at the opportunity, though at that time, no death investigations were on the planned excursions. She couldn't wait to tell him about the latest that just landed in her lap. Val opened the refrigerator door and pulled out leftovers from last night's dinner: Mexican food, which she had made herself: chicken enchiladas, refried beans, salsa, cheese. She grabbed it all. It was official. She was ravenous. Val also pulled out a carton of sour cream. Yes, sour cream was definitely needed, too. "Do you want any of this?" she said, her focus still on the contents in the fridge.

"I'd love some," Jack answered.

Val heard the familiar British accent and quickly turned around. Gwen turned too. Val set the food down and ran towards Jack, giving him a huge hug. "Oh my God, I'm so glad you're here." This was the first time she'd seen him since their last case together.

Though it had been a while, she hadn't forgotten how attractive Jack was. With dark hair and dark eyes he had a devilish quality to him, maybe even more so with his just out of bed appearance. He had to bend down to hug Val. She only came up to just above his chest. "I've missed you!"

"I've missed you too," he said.

Once Val let go, Gwen snatched a hug from Jack. "Our gang rides again!"

"I told you we'd get together again soon," Jack reminded them.

Val put her hands on her hips. "You promised that nearly eight months ago." Though it had been more than half a year, with Jack in her home, the familiarity of being around him again, it was as if time had stood still. It seemed like only eight hours had passed. *Jesus, had it really been eight months?*

"I can't believe how quickly time goes," he said. "A blink of an eye and we're here, today. It seems like yesterday we were catching Buffalo's newest psychopath. Not many cities get more than one of that kind of caliber. Have you developed a reputation?"

"Let's get the food ready and we'll fill you in on the latest," Val said.

Jack looked confused, his gaze traveling from Val to Gwen and back to Val. "What have the two of you got yourselves into now? The case when I was here last spring was bad enough."

"Go sit, and we'll talk." Val's skin crawled. She refused to think about the lunatic from last spring that Jack was referring to.

The other psychopath he mentioned... Well the other was just as bad, though that one had been almost thirty years ago. Val herself had been a child at the time. A man was raping and murdering women, abducting them along secluded bike paths and the media had given him a nickname, "The Bike Path Killer." One path in particular, the University at Buffalo bike path, was one that Val had been on many times in recent years. And as she cycled along its long stretches of quiet, desolate, insulated trails she felt an eerie reminder of "what could happen"—how someone could be snatched without warning, with no one witnessing it. No one to help. The signs advising "do not bike alone" still existed today. Fear had run rampant through the city back then, so Val had been told. The warnings to "not go anywhere by yourself and keep doors locked," and the questions about who would be next, then seeing the *next* on the news all created the reality that *I* could be next. And someone was always next until the murderer is caught. "The Bike Path Killer was over thirty years ago." Val shuddered: terror and fear are the same no matter the era.

"And the wrongfully convicted man released from prison twenty years after," Gwen reminded.

"Yes, thankfully he was." The thought sent additional chills down Val's spine. An innocent man had spent two decades in jail for a crime he did not commit. Val didn't want to think of this right now. She was going through her own emotional rollercoaster with Mr. Tate, the patient who bit her. Though he ended her dental career, the evidence the prosecutors had to convict him on serial murder was shaky at best, and she knew it. Of course, what he did to her was unmistakable. He sunk his teeth into her hand, violently.

But was he a serial killer? Val's stomach churned. Mr. Tate was facing the death penalty. Val's testimony could decide his life and she didn't feel confident enough to point an almighty finger at that fate; not with what the prosecutors were telling her anyway, though by their accounts, it was all ironclad.

Val microwaved the food and brought the dishes into her living room, placing them on the coffee table in front of the couch. Gwen and Jack sat on the floor. Val joined them, and they filled their plates.

Val took a few bites before speaking. She needed to, before she passed out from hunger. "A mother and her son are dead."

In between more bites, Val explained the aspects of the case that she knew so far—the tree branches, the seeds, the slashed throat; the fact that Gabrielle Morgan, of *the* Morgan family, appeared to be an overprotective mother, one that didn't socialize with her neighbors. Oh, and the cancer. Gabrielle had cancer.

Jack scooped salsa onto his enchilada. "That's certainly one of the most bizarre I've heard about in a long time."

Val took another bite. "So much of this case points to a murder and then suicide, but there are things that just raise red flags. Like, why would a mother kill her son this way? So violently. *Could* she have cut his throat so deep, with one swift slash? With a *hunting* knife? Why would she even own such a thing?"

"One swift slash? That concerns me. The kind of knife, not so much. A tool to do the job is simply that, a tool to do the job," Jack said. "Unless there are signs of child abuse, which, Val, you'll have to look into, I'd think a mother slicing her child's throat would have hesitation marks, even if it was for a ritual. If she was hurting him for the first time, she'd be new at this. Confidence wouldn't have been there. And confidence would have been required for one effective gash, regardless of the type of knife."

Val nodded, agreeing with Jack on this point. Even those who chose to end their life by slicing their wrists have hesitation marks. It's telltale for *I'm not sure.* Causing harm to oneself or another human being is never faultless the first time around.

"Dr. Maddox and Detective Gavin *are* suspicious of child abuse," Gwen said. "They plan on looking into it further."

"Good. This case hinges on it." Jack grabbed another enchilada. "If she never hurt the child before, she wouldn't have been able to hurt him now, this way. Plus, the kid would have been terrified. Screaming even. Fighting her off."

"He had no defensive wounds on his hands so it looks like he didn't or couldn't fight back. We're testing for drugs in his system," Val said.

Jack sat back and crossed his arms. "A mother who might have sedated him, now that's interesting. A mother who may have drugged him is an entirely different breed."

"What do you mean?" Val asked.

"An abusive mother wouldn't have drugged him to kill him in a humane way. Nor would have a random killer."

"What about killing him in a *quieter* way?" Val asked.

"I was thinking the same thing myself," Gwen said.

"Now," Jack smiled, "you're both thinking like smashingly good experts in crime."

"Well, I guess all we can say at this point is Gabrielle wasn't your average mother." Gwen reached for the sour cream. "Not with her odd behavior."

"And that leads to my biggest concern," Val said. "Gabrielle Morgan always picked her son up from school. She had a rule that he wasn't allowed to walk home. A rule which he broke on the day they both disappeared. According to witnesses, he didn't even look around for her. He just started walking. What happened that day? Why drop him off at all? And twenty minutes late to boot. Plus, this kid was sick enough to fall down and vomit. Was he abused, or did he simply know what was going to happen to him?"

Jack wiped his mouth with his napkin. "There's always an event that sets a case in motion. So, let's look at this case in detail. See where all the puzzle pieces want to go in. If they all don't fit then your picture is all wrong. The fact that they disappeared is incidental. By the time they vanished, the outcome was already determined that they were going to die— by whatever means and by whoever's hands. The day you're talking about, Val, is the one that begins the *process* of their death, but something preceded this. For what reason should these two people be dead?"

"The cops are the ones who look for motive, Jack. My job is

providing information to Dr. Maddox so he can rule on *how* they died."

"Screw that. You'll never solve a case like this without determining motive. Motive dictates actions, and I think your tree branches and seeds are the starting point," Jack said. "That's what your killer, or person committing suicide, wants us to know about. The ritual, if that's what this is, is what you need to look at first. And the fact that this was only found for Gabrielle, and not her son, means something." Jack pushed his plate away. "Val, Gabrielle's cancer is another starting point. Don't lose sight of that, because it's a big one."

"I won't," Val said. Jack was right. Everything in this case pointed to murder–suicide, but not all those puzzle pieces Jack spoke of fit within this jigsaw. "The tree branches are a fir of some kind. The seeds, I haven't a clue what they are."

Jack shrugged. "I know of nothing offhand that uses this practice. We'll need to find an arborist, a tree specialist, who can tell you what kind of branches she was holding. This person should be able to help with the seed identification too."

"*We'll*? Does this mean you'll help with this case?" Val said, excited, knowing that there was something that aroused Jack's suspicions too.

"Of course. I find it fascinating. Plus, there's a lot I can teach you in the process. You two will be top criminalists in no time."

"That's awesome!" Gwen exclaimed, then her expression changed, becoming worried. "What about Thomas? Will he be happy that you're part of this?"

While Jack and Thomas Hayden were partners, Thomas was the star investigator, almost akin to Jack's boss. In the criminalistics world, his word was gospel. To work with these two was a career game changer—a catapult upwards, and to learn from either of them, well that was unheard of, especially a second time around. Would he let Jack do this?

"I'll keep Thomas informed. It has enough to keep him engaged," Jack said.

"Great!" Val said. "I'll look for the arborist in the next day or two. Tomorrow, I'm going with Detective Gavin to talk to the victim's parents." Val sat up straight. "Oh, Jack, sorry! I won't be able to spend time with you until later on."

"That's okay. I can take care of myself tomorrow. There are things you need to learn from her parents. She was estranged from them. Why?"

4

Gavin pulled up to the Morgans' estate on Lincoln Parkway in the city of Buffalo. Warren sat next to him. From the rear passenger side window of the car, Val couldn't help but stare at the sheer magnificence of the place. The house was Beaux Arts Classical, a dominant design of the early 1900s. Val only knew this because she had found a newspaper write-up from last spring about the Morgans' home. It was featured on the annual Buffalo garden walk. Before today's visit, Val googled what she could about this family. This article was prominent. Other than the surprisingly sparse reporting about the death of Gabrielle and her son, their names were conspicuously missing from any media or online sources.

The use of symmetry in the architecture was obvious. The red-brick structure had large, white centered columns framing a wide veranda. Tall windows were equidistant on each side. Elaborate white glazed terracotta and wrought-iron accents dominated the architecture.

The street itself was composed of one early twentieth century mansion after the other. Buffalo was home to some of the wealthiest families in that time period—the booming grain and steel industry drove them here—and this street, along with Delaware Avenue, was one of the top choices of where the elite, uber rich wanted to build their homes. Though Delaware Avenue was described as a millionaire's row, many of the original houses there had been torn down or converted into commercial property. Lincoln Parkway remained residential. "How much do you think that goes for?" she asked.

"More than I'll make in a lifetime," Gavin replied.

"At our salary, maybe a few lifetimes," Warren added.

Val, Gavin and Warren got out of the car, trudged through the snow, and climbed the stone steps to the front door. Gavin rang the doorbell. They waited for a couple of minutes. Gavin put his finger on the bell to ring a second time when the door opened and an attractive woman in a tailored black dress answered. She had a pale pink cardigan on her shoulders and was wearing black high heels. Very nice, expensive high heels.

"Yes?" the woman asked with a polite smile as she pulled back the door in a welcoming manner. She had a neat and precise way about her. Opening the door for guests was an orchestrated event, which she played out effortlessly. Her ash blonde hair was just past her shoulders in length. Bangs were angled to the side with a deliberate style to them. Val couldn't help but notice the woman's deep blue eyes. Delicate fine lines could be seen on her face as she smiled a welcome to the group standing on her doorstep. Val guessed her age to be early fifties. Everything about her appeared to be, in one simple term, perfect.

Jesus, I bet this woman was drop dead gorgeous her entire life, thought Val. The dress hugged the body of a stunning woman who went to the gym, and probably always had.

Gavin held out his hand. "I'm Detective Gavin from the homicide department. This is my partner Detective Warren, and this is Valentina Knight. She's a death scene investigator with the

Erie County Medical Examiner's office. We're here regarding the death of Gabrielle Morgan and her son Adam."

The woman took Gavin's hand, shaking it. "I'm Claudia Flynn, the Morgans' household manager." She then held out her hand for Warren and Val. "Please, come in. Mr. and Mrs. Morgan are expecting you."

Household manager? Val couldn't believe this woman was the housekeeper.

"It's so tragic about Gabrielle and Adam. It's been such a shock for all of us," Claudia said as Gavin, Warren and Val entered a two-story, marble-floored foyer. Val turned her gaze in all directions to simply absorb the vastness of the place. A large crystal chandelier hung above. Straight ahead was a curved grand stairway leading to the next level.

"I'm sorry about Gabrielle and Adam," Gavin said, his voice echoing in the cavernous space.

"Thank you, detective. I'll take your coats."

Gavin slipped his wool coat off and gave it to Claudia who placed it over her arm. Warren and Val followed, doing the same with their parkas. "How long have you worked for the Morgans?" Val asked.

"A little over thirty-three years now." Claudia pointed to a large mat by a bench, strategically placed so guests could sit while removing their shoes. "You can leave your boots there. I can bring you something to cover your feet if you wish."

Val quickly did the math. With Gabrielle dying at the age of thirty-one, Claudia was working in this house before Gabrielle herself arrived.

"Oh no, we'll be fine," Gavin, Warren and Val almost said in unison. The three were well accustomed to walking into people's homes in the winter. While Warren and Gavin assured Claudia that they were more than comfortable in their heavy socks, Val pulled out a pair of soft soled fleece slippers from her bag.

Claudia nodded, opened a closet and hung the coats. "Please, come with me. I'll take you to Mr. and Mrs. Morgan."

"Were you close with Gabrielle?" Val asked Claudia as they followed her down the hallway.

Claudia halted for a split second before continuing. She seemed surprised by the question. Her jaw tensed. "Of course I was. I was her nanny. I was nanny to all the Morgan children, until they were too old to require one. Gabrielle was like my own."

Nanny? To *all* of the Morgan children. Val shot a look to Gavin, who raised his eyebrows. Nowhere in any of her internet searches did it mention the Morgans had other children. Not even in the sparingly written reports about Gabrielle's death was there a hint of siblings. Val wondered how much influence the Morgans had to hush Gabrielle, who was a scandal for them. But why hide the children?

Val was about to ask more but Claudia turned into a parlor where a man and a woman sat on a dark red brocade sofa. Behind them, a full wall of windows, an easy ten feet in height and probably thirty in length, displayed a snow-covered garden. The couple stood when the group entered. The woman had to do so with the aid of a cane. Val noticed her ankle was wrapped in an elastic ace bandage. Val's own leg twinged a little bit. She had good days and bad days with it. Today wasn't so bad. The man spoke first. "I'm James Morgan and this is my wife, Rachel."

James Morgan had short, gray hair and wore a crisp white button-down shirt, the sleeves adorned with gold cufflinks; a blue tie with gold stripes; and neatly tailored blue suit pants. Mr. Morgan certainly did workout. His clothes stretched across him like a well fitted glove, accentuating broad shoulders, well defined arms, flat stomach, and trim waist. He was somewhere around sixty. Mrs. Morgan was a bit younger, maybe mid-fifties. She had large brown eyes and her brown hair was cut into a short bob. While pretty, she wasn't as striking as Claudia, or even her husband. They all shook hands.

Mrs. Morgan smiled and motioned for all of them to sit. "Claudia, can you bring us all some coffee?"

"Of course," said the household manager, and exited the room.

"We're sorry about the loss of your daughter and grandson," Gavin said, addressing both Mr. and Mrs. Morgan.

There was an odd moment of hesitation, Val saw Rachel Morgan move—just a small flicker—towards her husband.

"Thank you, detective. What can we help you with?" Mr. Morgan's tone was all business and Val wondered if he was remarkably reserved or if there was another reason for this cool, almost sterile response.

"What can you tell us about your daughter?" Gavin asked.

Mr. Morgan shrugged. "I'm afraid not very much that may be relevant. Up until about a month ago we hadn't seen or heard from her in some time, probably a couple of years."

"Up until a month ago?" Gavin raised his eyebrows. "She made contact with you recently?"

"She wanted to reconcile. We were happy to talk about it and end this nonsense," Mr. Morgan said.

"Can I ask what caused the estrangement to begin with?" Gavin pressed.

Again, Val could see a sharp flash of a movement from Mrs. Morgan to her husband.

"I guess you could call it a game of hers. Who'd break first. Gabrielle liked to get her way, and would do anything to ensure that she got it. A time came when we had to put our foot down. That made her angry. Cutting us out of her life was her way of punishing us. She wanted us to give in, and her weapon was not letting us see our grandson. Gabrielle was pretty good at not flinching first." Mr. Morgan locked his gaze on Gavin's. "But I am better."

"What did she want?" Warren asked, causing Mr. Morgan to sharply turn his head.

"To marry an unemployed musician who loved my money more than he loved her."

"James!" Rachel Morgan's eyes went wide. "That's unfair."

"I'm sorry to be so blunt. Please understand, being straight forward is just my way. You don't get very far in life if you don't do, and say, things that are necessary, even if they are unpleasant." James Morgan shifted his position on the couch, his back poker straight. "Gabrielle went ahead and did it anyway, married him. He divorced her two months later, after I'd cut her off financially. After a couple of years of the silent treatment, out of the blue, she contacted us again. I think Gabrielle finally realized that she needed my money."

"James, she said she looked forward to fixing things with us. She wanted her parents back in her life," Mrs. Morgan offered to her husband. Her eyes appeared glassy as if she was getting ready to cry. Val felt sorry for Rachel Morgan. The heartache of losing her daughter, not once but twice, was apparent.

Mr. Morgan didn't even bother to look at his wife after she spoke.

Val asked sympathetically, "Was it about her cancer? Is that why she wanted to put any differences aside?" Dr. Maddox said that it was possible that Gabrielle was in early stages of cancer and may not have known about it. Val wanted to find out if Gabrielle did know, and telling her parents, and wanting a reconciliation, may indicate that.

"What cancer?" Rachel snapped her head towards Val, alarm in her voice. She gripped her cane hard and it appeared she was trying to stand. "Gabi had cancer? James, did you know about this?" Mrs. Morgan was practically shouting.

"She didn't tell you?" Val asked, her voice calm, though she'd already guessed the answer.

"No. There were many things she didn't tell us." Mr. Morgan just looked irritated rather than worried, certainly no alarm was apparent in his face. His daughter had cancer. He didn't know until this moment, and Val could tell that he didn't even care. There was no remorse. He continued to ignore his wife.

But there was one more thing Val needed to ask. "Maybe this is what she was planning to tell you, then? Maybe waiting for the right moment?" Val addressed Mrs. Morgan specifically.

"What kind of cancer did she have?" Mrs. Morgan sat back, resigned, her gaze focussed straight ahead.

"Liver, that we can tell so far. We're checking to see if another cancer metastasized there, that it spread," Val said softly.

"How far along was it? Was she dying?" Mrs. Morgan ran one sentence quickly after the other. She locked her eyes on Val's, searching for answers. Mrs. Morgan's desperation to grab any information about her daughter was palpable.

"We're waiting to see what the tests show. We're also trying to track down her doctors. Anyone who would be treating her. We have the name of a primary care physician. Do you know who else she might have been seeing, though?" Val asked.

"I can tell you who her doctor was when Adam was born but that would be about it. Honestly, I don't know that much about my daughter anymore," Mrs. Morgan said, her eyes cast downward now. *My* not *our*, Val caught that.

The group stopped talking as Claudia brought in a tray with coffee, cups, and a dish of assorted bite-sized fruit tarts. She set out the cups and filled each, placing a small plate and napkin next to each guest for the tarts, then quietly exited the room.

How well-trained, Val thought. She watched Mrs. Morgan's reactions to Claudia. Other than a smile of gratitude, nothing more.

"Please help yourself. They're homemade." Mr. Morgan picked up his cup and pointed to the tarts. "My Rachel is quite the *baker*, and *gardener*. The berries are from your own plants, aren't they? The preserves are from last summer as I recall." It sounded slightly knowledgeable yet derogatory, as if this high-powered man didn't want his wife to engage in activities that were designated for the hired help.

Asshole. "They look delicious." Val picked up a pastry, raspberry, it looked like. There was no way that she was going to let Mr. Morgan bully his wife, who seemed to care more about their dead daughter than he did, or maybe only at the level that he would allow. Val wondered what Mrs. Morgan would say if her husband wasn't around. "Mrs. Morgan, I garden too. Tomatoes, cilantro, cucumbers and a lone watermelon plant last year. I might have to pick your brain for tips." Val took a bite and chewed. "This is fantastic."

"Thank you." Mrs. Morgan smiled. "Anytime you want to know something please don't hesitate to ask." It all came out automatic. The lady of the house giving a polite response to a guest.

"I'll certainly do that," Val said, wiping her fingers on a napkin, taking a moment before carefully asking the next question. "Do you have any other children besides Gabrielle?" Val held her breath. Claudia mentioned that she had been the nanny to *all* the Morgan children. Sometimes siblings have a better understanding, deeper knowledge of each other than parents. Maybe speaking to one of them might help with piecing together the kind of person Gabrielle was.

"We have another daughter, Bridget. She's two years older than Gabrielle," Mrs. Morgan said.

"Can we get her contact information?" Gavin took his phone from his pocket, ready to enter the details. Val sat forward too.

"She lives with us," Mr. Morgan answered plainly. For the

first time he did not look at Gavin when he spoke. James Morgan kept his eyes down.

Gavin straightened in his chair. "Can we speak with her, then?"

Mr. Morgan also straightened. "Today is not a good day. She's taking Gabrielle's death hard. She's been given a sedative to help her calm down."

"Did Gabrielle maintain contact with her sister during the time you were estranged?" Gavin asked.

"No." Mr. Morgan set his cup down hard enough to clank the saucer. The noise made Mrs. Morgan jump.

"No?" Gavin raised his eyebrows. "I'm not understanding. You said Bridget took Gabrielle's death hard."

"You'll have to forgive me for not fully explaining," Mr. Morgan said, his demeanor politely softening. "Bridget has developmental disabilities. I refuse to put her in a situation that she is not capable of handling. She loved her sister Gabrielle dearly, and when Gabrielle cut us off, Bridget deteriorated to a level I had not seen before. Being subjected to questions regarding her sister's death is not something Bridget will be able to tolerate. I'm sure you understand, Detective Gavin."

Val could see the body language between Mrs. Morgan and her husband. The uncomfortable shifting and sideways glancing. "Any other kids?" Val asked, throwing her fishing line out one more time. She reached for another fruit tart, blueberry this time.

"We had a set of twins, a boy and a girl." Mr. Morgan picked up his cup again, seeming eager to move this conversation on.

"Had?" Gavin asked. Val nearly spat out her tart. Not reporting their other children in news articles was one thing, but the Morgans wouldn't be able to hide them from the police. Mr. Morgan had no choice but to answer Gavin's questions.

Again, a strong movement from Rachel Morgan towards her husband.

"They died in a swimming accident in our pool," Mr. Morgan said with no emotion. "It was many years ago."

"They died together?" Gavin asked, the surprise evident in his voice.

"They were six at the time, they shouldn't have been in the pool at all, left alone unattended. Gabrielle was supposed to have been watching them," Mr. Morgan said, his jaw taut. "It was Claudia's day off."

The pain that spread across Mrs. Morgan's face was heart-wrenching. It was as if the children had died today. Val winced. She thought Mrs. Morgan couldn't be hurt any further by the revelations coming out today, but Val was wrong. She was reliving tragedy, old wounds were being ripped open.

Mrs. Morgan glanced at her husband, then back to Gavin, as if waiting to get his approval, before proceeding. She finally spoke without waiting for it. "We never blamed Gabrielle for this. This was our fault for not having a better supervisor look after the twins. Gabrielle was barely more than a child herself."

"She was sixteen, Rachel." Mr. Morgan's voice came out sharp, cutting to the point.

Another look passed between the Morgans. And too long a moment of uncomfortable silence before Mr. Morgan spoke. "Detective, please don't get us wrong." Mr. Morgan cast his head down, shaking it regretfully. After a few seconds, he rose his gaze to those in the room. "We loved our daughter very much. We loved—and continue to love—all of our children. Every family can tell you things that are unpleasant, especially if heard out of context. Snippets of stories are no substitution for having a well-rounded account of the person you're talking about. We stayed by Gabrielle's side and supported her as best we could throughout her entire life. But there is only so much you can do.

The past is in the past but today, our grandson is dead and I want to know why. If Gabrielle was responsible, I want to know it."

Val could see no love lost between this father and his daughter. Mrs. Morgan just seemed torn apart. Though Gabrielle wasn't blamed for her brother and sister's death, it was obvious Mr. Morgan did hold her responsible. He also seemed to think Gabrielle was capable of taking her own son's life.

Val hated to press forward. Mrs. Morgan almost looked like she couldn't bear to go through any more today but there were a few more things Val wanted to know. "You said you cut Gabrielle off because she wanted to marry a musician. This wasn't Adam's father, then?" Val asked.

"No. Adam's father was a wonderful man. He died of cardiac arrest when Adam was two," Mr. Morgan said.

"That's an awfully young age to die from something like that. Did heart disease run in his family?" Gavin took over the questioning.

"Malcolm—or Max as we called him—was older than Gabrielle. We didn't mind. He was good for her. Helped her make the right decisions. He truly had her best interests at heart. Plus, he was CEO of GDA pharmaceuticals." Everyone grimaced at the name. Mr. Morgan obviously saw the reaction. "At the time, he didn't need my money."

"So, he died before the scandal?" Gavin asked.

"Yes. Right before, but when one of your top drugs is found to kill people, and there's an attempt to cover it up, that's bad news for the beneficiaries who inherit your stock in the company." Mr. Morgan had a cavalier way about him when talking about the people in his life, pointing out deficiencies with ease, and with such knowledgeable perception.

"But Max wasn't part of that awful mess," Mrs. Morgan said, defending her dead son-in-law.

"No, he wasn't," Mr. Morgan said confidently.

"So, I'm going to guess that Gabrielle wasn't left with much money after he died," Val said.

"No, the stock was worthless. I found out shortly after his death that my son-in-law was a bad investor; everything went back to GDA. He didn't have life insurance because he didn't think he needed it. What Gabrielle had in savings at the end went to cover legal fees. At this point she and Adam were living with us," Mr. Morgan said.

"What caused her to move out, then?" Warren asked.

"She wanted to stand on her own two feet, get her life back together. So I set her up with a monthly allowance and bought her a very nice downtown waterfront condo, complete with boat for her dock." Mr. Morgan smirked. "If you can call that standing on her own two feet."

"The musician ended this?" Warren asked.

"Yes. I don't know how she was supporting herself after I cut her off and took the condo back. I hear she got a job? She never told me what it was," Mr. Morgan said.

"She worked for The Next Step, a non-profit organization," Gavin said.

Mr. Morgan's eyebrows raised for a split second and his head made a slight cock to the side. Val wondered if this had some significance to him.

"Did Gabrielle keep her maiden name of Morgan through both of her marriages?" Warren asked.

"Not at first. Max's last name was Chandler. She was Gabrielle Chandler. She became a Morgan again after he died to distance herself from the fallout at GDA Pharmaceutical. After she married a second time she kept Morgan. I think even she knew that marriage wasn't going to last."

"Mr. Morgan, I hate to ask this but is there any chance

Gabrielle would have killed herself and her son to punish you?" Gavin asked.

Val absorbed the question. It did make sense. Maybe Gabrielle wanted to come into her parents' lives long enough to give them hope and then snatch it away. If she saw Mr. Morgan as winning, that she had to give in to him, she trumped him.

"That's totally possible," Mr. Morgan said without any hesitation, then glanced at his watch. "I'm sorry to have to cut this short but Rachel and I have to be at a fundraiser in less than an hour."

Mrs. Morgan did not protest when Val, Gavin and Warren rose. They all shook hands and Gavin thanked the couple for their time. "If we need to talk again, would that be possible?" Gavin asked Mr. Morgan.

"Of course, detective. Rachel and I will work with you on whatever you need. Touch base with Claudia and she'll set up an appointment." For some reason it seemed less than sincere and Val couldn't help but think that this was the one and only time Mr. Morgan was going to discuss his daughter under Detective Gavin's terms. Any other correspondence would be under Mr. Morgan's conditions.

5

Val's thoughts were still spinning after meeting with the Morgans. Gabrielle's life was far more complicated than Val could have imagined and each piece picked apart, exposed another. Gabrielle's own parents—well her father at least—practically confirmed she was capable of carrying out a murder and suicide.

The tree branches. The seeds. Hopefully, Val would find out what they were today. Possibly also, what meaning they might have had for Gabrielle. Or this case in general.

Val had an easy time finding an arborist. The Buffalo Botanical Gardens had two on staff. Excellent internet hit. After she called and made an appointment to meet with a Dr. Cal Delarosa, she asked Jack if he wanted to tag along for the visit. Plus, lunch at Schwabl's, a hometown favorite for roast beef sandwiches, was planned for after. No need to twist his arm.

Val hadn't been to the botanical gardens since she was a child on a school field trip. It was a shame she didn't visit more often. When you know you can experience a local marvel at any moment, how often do you ever grab the opportunity? Val had to laugh, though she lived only twelve miles from Niagara Falls, one of the wonders of the world, she couldn't remember the last time she visited that either, other than to work on the murder case last spring. Maybe crime was helping her become reacquainted with Buffalo's treasures.

As they walked from the parking lot to the door, Val admired the elegance of the stunning tri-domed conservatory. It had opened in 1900, created by a star-studded architectural team, including famed landscaping architect Fredrick Law Olmsted. Encouraged by Jack, Val had read up on the botanic gardens ahead of their visit and knew that it had been designed to resemble the Crystal Palace in England.

On this cold winter morning Val and Jack would be staying inside, rather than visiting the outdoor gardens. Inside, in the building's tropical warmth, Val happily unzipped her jacket. The pair was greeted by a staff member who wore a moss-green long-sleeved polo with the Botanical Garden logo stitched on the front. She smiled as Val approached. Val read her name tag; Alison it said.

"Admission for two adults?" Alison sat forward with a smile.

"I'm Valentina Knight. I'm from the Erie County Medical Examiner's office." Val pulled out her ID and showed it to Alison, whose eyes went wide as she glanced at it. "This is my colleague, Jack Styles. We have an appointment to see Dr. Cal Delarosa."

"Oh, he's expecting you. He's in greenhouse twelve, Florida everglades." Alison pointed to her right and handed Val a map. "Through the palm dome, and just the next greenhouse to your left. Would you like me to show you?"

"I think we can find it," Val said, wondering what Dr. Delarosa had told this woman about her visit today. It could compromise the case if he revealed sensitive information about the tree branches and seeds. Information, Val stressed when she called him, that was not to be shared with anyone.

"Take your time as you walk through. The palm dome, the first dome you'll enter, is our main dome and is sixty-seven feet high which allows us to have a fantastic assortment of palm and tropical fruit trees. Make sure you take a look. It's really quite impressive," Alison said.

"We'll certainly do that," Jack pulled out two twenty-dollar bills and placed them in a donation container, which was separate from the till for cost of admission.

"Thank you." Alison smiled.

As soon as they were out of hearing distance Jack spoke. "If we're going in for free, we should at least give something to the organization."

As they entered through the large glass enclosure, the heat and humidity grabbed Val and she removed her coat as she immediately began to sweat. Jack did the same. Val glanced around. It was as if they just stepped into the tropics. She inspected some of the placards describing the species of trees. Pondarosa lemon, chocolate tree, foxtail palm, old man palm, were just some of them. To her left was a sign stating "House Twelve." At least they didn't have to go far to find Dr. Delarosa, though Val would have happily toured more of the greenhouse.

A short way in Val spotted a thin man who wore khakis and a short-sleeve green polo shirt. He turned and looked in her direction as she and Jack approached him. Val extended her hand. "Dr. Delarosa?"

"Yes, you must be Valentina Knight." He extended his hand as well.

"Yes, and this is Jack Styles," Val said as they all shook hands. She was a little hesitant to say much more about who Jack was. It probably crossed a line with her position at the medical examiner's office to have him there with her today, but Val really wanted Jack with her for this. Val looked around, relieved that they were the only people in this greenhouse. Luckily, not that many visit the botanical gardens at 10:30am on a weekday.

"Looks like you've got an odd one on your hands. The fact that the victim was holding tree branches... Wow, I have to admit I was shocked when you told me that on the phone," Dr. Delarosa said. "And the seeds too."

"That information is not being released to the public," Val stressed. "Please make sure to keep that confidential. If this information gets out it can really mess up the case for the detectives in charge."

Dr. Delarosa's facial cringe said it all. "I have to admit, I told my wife you were coming today and I'd get to see some evidence from the murder case of Gabrielle Morgan. I didn't mention trees. *That* was okay, wasn't it?"

No, not really because what in the hell else would you be looking at? thought Val, but didn't press the issue. She put on a set of latex gloves, opened her paper evidence bag, then pulled out a sample of the branches. "We think it's a fir or spruce of some kind."

Jack let out a gasp. "It can't be..."

Val shot him a stunned glance. "You know what these are?"

His eyes opened wide, his gaze focussed on the branches. "I am nearly positive, but I'll wait for Dr. Delarosa's verdict." Jack shook his head and moved closer to the branches.

"Very interesting." Dr. Delarosa put on his own set of gloves, before taking hold of them. He turned them around and inspected the needles closely. "It's a conifer. That's a tree that has cones and needle-like leaves. It's also an evergreen."

"Aren't they one and the same?" Val asked.

"No. Minor technical difference. All conifers have cones but not all evergreens do."

"Isn't hemlock a conifer?" Val remarked. "Oh my God, is this hemlock?"

"No, it's not. And you're confusing your hemlocks. The hemlock conifer is not poison hemlock, which is an entirely different plant and the one everyone thinks of when they hear the word *hemlock*." Dr. Delarosa laughed. "The poisonous one comes from the carrot family, and its leaves can be mistaken for parsley. And sometimes are, accident or purposely, is anyone's guess. Hemlock is probably the poster child for poison. It's been used to get rid of people since ancient Greece." Dr. Delarosa signaled for Val and Jack to follow him. "Come with me. I'd like to get a better look at this in our lab."

Val decided that she was pleased with her choice of tree specialists, especially since Dr. Delarosa just displayed an impressive hair-splitting detail on conifer, evergreen, and hemlock facts. Hell, until just now, she didn't know what a conifer even was. She just hoped his ability to keep quiet about the evidence was just as strong as his knowledge.

They followed Dr. Delarosa out of the Everglades house, through the palm dome and down a long corridor, into a room lined with tall cabinets and drawers. Straight ahead was a well-lit work bench outfitted with a large magnifying glass on a retractable arm.

The doctor pulled out a stool and sat down. He positioned the magnifier and turned the light on. "Just as I thought. This is a conifer. It *is* also an evergreen. But it isn't a fir tree, as you suspected." Dr. Delarosa sat back, his eyes narrowed. He seemed puzzled, then grew concerned. He looked at Val before he spoke. "This is a yew tree. Specifically, English yew."

"I knew it," Jack said. "Yew trees are all over England, in the churchyards."

"It's not a fir?" Val said. "It looks so much like one."

"Yes, it does. These needles are commonly mistaken for fir because they're so similar. Here, let me show you." Dr. Delarosa got up and walked to one of the cabinets. He pulled out some samples and brought them back to the workbench. "These are firs. See how the needles are rounded and there are two white stripes on the bottom. But take a look here, in the sample you brought the needle is sharply pointed, with no white lines beneath it."

Val liked this guy. He knew his stuff. "What's so special about a yew tree?"

"It's the tree of the dead," Jack said.

Everyone in the room stood still. And quiet. Val's heart rate picked up a few beats. *What the hell?*

"Common misconception," Dr. Delarosa finally answered. "It used to have the reputation of the tree of the dead. Now it's thought of as the tree of rebirth. Resurrection."

"But it's highly poisonous," Jack stressed.

"That's true. All parts of the yew, except for its seed cups, which are red, fleshy, and look like a berry, contain the highly poisonous alkaloid taxine, which causes death due to cardiac arrest and respiratory failure. Only takes about thirty minutes after ingestion for this to kill someone."

"Seed cups? You mean this tree has seeds?" Val nearly shouted.

"Yes. And they're very deadly," Jack added.

Dr. Delarosa shook his head. "Depends on how you view it. The yew is an odd tree. All parts of this plant contain toxic alkaloids that can be fatal even in small amounts. Even touching this plant may cause a skin reaction in some people. Luckily, we're wearing gloves." Dr. Delarosa smiled. "To date, there is no antidote for yew poisoning. But the toxin has its up sides too. The seeds are used to make medicine for conditions such as asthma, anxiety, mania—just to name a few. The bark contains another alkaloid called taxol. It has anti-cancer properties."

"Anti-cancer!" Val exclaimed.

"Mostly for ovarian and breast cancer. The drug created

from the alkaloid was called Paclitaxel because it came from the Pacific yew." Dr. Delarosa rubbed his chin, as if stretching for a memory. "This would have been back in the late 1970s."

"Do they still use this drug today?" Val asked.

"Yes, Taxol remains one of the best plant-based cancer treatments out there for ovarian and breast cancer. But it's all synthetic production now. It has to be. The Pacific yew is slow growing, making the drug very expensive to manufacture. And the ecological cost is high—harvesting the bark kills the tree. The synthetic version is where Tamoxifen came from. You've probably heard of it. It's the oldest and most prescribed medicine for breast cancer."

Val pulled out a plastic container holding the sample of the seeds discovered in Gabrielle Morgan's mouth. "Dr. Delarosa, are these yew tree seeds?"

He opened the container carefully and used a set of tweezers to pull one out. He examined it under the lighted magnifying glass. "Yes, they are."

Val absorbed that. *Jesus, there can be little argument that Gabrielle didn't kill herself and her son. As soon as Gavin learns this, he'll probably shut the case.* But there were things that just didn't make sense, and Val couldn't let these inconsistent shards slip by. The answer, though seemingly getting sharper, was only getting murkier.

"You said the yew is a tree of rebirth. Is it because of these healing properties that you've mentioned?" Val asked.

"No. That comes from the unique way in which the tree grows. To form new stems, the existing branches grow down to the ground, then eventually bury themselves into the soil. The new stems rise up out of the ground around the ones that grew down creating linked trunks that remain separate. The new is created from the old. Death and rebirth. Druids, with their belief in reincarnation, and later Christians with their faith in the resurrection, regarded it as a natural emblem of everlasting life."

"Maybe Gabrielle wasn't trying to die," Jack said, "but trying to come back."

This is exactly what Val thought, and what precisely made her question Gabrielle's motives and actions with a murder–suicide.

Dr. Delarosa nodded. "Very possible. There have been reports of the seeds being used in an ancient mystical practice, where yew seeds were consumed when Venus and Jupiter come into alignment. Believers ate these seeds to experience the afterlife and then come back again. But yew seeds are so toxic that even eating a few would be lethal."

"Would she have been healed in this rebirth?" Val asked.

"Depends on the religious belief," Dr. Delarosa said. "There's variations. Do you know if she belonged to any druid sects, or more specifically shamanistic groups, which rely more on the spirit world and holistic medicine?"

Val thought of the white gown and ritualistic nature of Gabrielle's death.

"That might not matter in an investigation like this because there is also another group of people who might try something like this," Jack answered. "Desperate people will believe anything. My point being, Gabrielle did not have to belong to any religious affiliation to engage in its practices. An internet search could have given her all she needed to know."

Jack was right. Even those who do not subscribe to a religion may undertake its practices if they perceive they'll get what they want from it. In other words, desperate people do desperate things even if common sense dictates something entirely different. Dying people want what no one can give them. Life. Any promise is better than no promise. Hell, what do they have to lose?

"How often does this alignment occur?" Val asked.

"About every thirteen months." Dr. Delarosa pulled out his phone, tapped the screen, scrolled and then looked up. "It just happened about five days ago, on January 22. This one was unusual because it was right after the total lunar eclipse, a blood moon. The name comes from the reddish color the moon takes on. It was all a pretty big celestial event."

"Perfect timing," Jack said.

Val said, with skepticism in her voice, "*Too perfect.*"

Dr. Delarosa nodded and then turned the branches over, studying them again. "I don't know where these would have come from locally though. English Yews are not native here and won't be hardy in Buffalo weather conditions. It will survive in areas ranging from up to southern New York State and New England. So, the tree you're looking for isn't from around here, but may not be terribly far away."

The next few seconds of silence made Val realize that she had nothing more to ask of Dr. Delarosa, at least not now, and certainly not without regrouping her thoughts. "Well, Dr. Delarosa, I'd like to thank you for your help. Your knowledge is impressive. If it's not too much of an inconvenience can I call or stop by with more questions should they arise?"

"Of course. If there's nothing more, would you like a personal tour of the gardens," Dr. Delarosa asked with a smile. Val and Jack nodded eagerly.

They stayed a couple hours more as Dr. Delarosa showed them around. By the time they left both were silent again, hunger this time apparently causing the lack of discussion. Val's stomach growled: it was now after 1pm and she'd had nothing to eat all day, but she wouldn't have missed the personal tour for the world. It wasn't until they were seated at lunch, with roast beef sandwiches in front of them, that the conversation turned back towards Gabrielle Morgan.

Val spoke first. "Well, that answers our question on how she died. Eating the yew seeds would have caused either her heart to stop beating or her lungs from inhaling. Thirty minutes is the right amount of time. She wouldn't have had to lie on the altar for long."

"Everything points to suicide with hopes of reincarnation, doesn't it? Maybe a curing of her cancer in the process?" Jack said. Val couldn't help but think he was challenging her with his questions rather than stating the obvious. And Val was happy because she didn't believe it was this easy either.

She picked up a French fry and quickly set it down. "Yes, everything points to a murder-suicide, but it doesn't make sense. This is what I have a hard time believing. Why kill her son and not try to bring him back with her? If she was doing something that she believed would bring her back from the dead, maybe healed, why didn't Adam have yew tree branches in his hand. Why didn't he have seeds in his mouth. Not to mention, having him eat the seeds would have been a nicer way to kill him than slicing his throat," Val said. "Hell, why kill him at all for that matter if she thought she was coming back?"

"Bravo, Val," said Jack. "All excellent points. I have the same questions. Now that we understand the ritual to some extent, my main question is—and this is a likely possibility that we need to explore—was she sacrificing his life for hers? It all goes back to my original assumptions on this case, when I asked you if she ever hurt the child before. Was she abusing him? It would be extremely hard to hurt him now without that, even if she wanted his life in exchange for hers."

"We heard nothing about this ritual having a sacrificial element," Val said.

"Doesn't matter. Only what Gabrielle Morgan thought, believed, and would have done matters. We don't know any of the answers to those questions yet," Jack said.

"So, did she love her son, or herself more?" Val said. "Or did someone else kill them both?"

Val put her elbows on the table and placed her forehead in her palms. "Jack, please tell me now if you think this case is open and shut."

"I can't tell you that because that information isn't here. Is there reason to be skeptical of the obvious? Yes. Are you wise and prudent to examine all angles? Yes. Is this what any good criminalist would do? Yes. Honestly, Val, I'm sitting back and not asking my own questions when you're questioning people because I think you're doing one hell of a good job. You don't need help working this case. I'll jump in only when I'm needed."

Jump in only when I'm needed. Another good friend of Val's said that to her, at a defining moment in time as well. That was last spring, when she was working the case that caused the injury to her leg.

"Have the DNA and fingerprint results come back on the tape from Gabrielle's hands and mouth?" Jack asked. "That's your next piece to this puzzle."

"The results on the tape aren't in yet. But that should be ready any day now," Val said.

"Good. That will be another step in confirming if she could have done this to herself or not. That gives you plausibility and hardcore evidence that she might be the guilty person. Keep in mind, you have no evidence like that yet. Everything so far has been circumstantial."

6

Gavin had a hard time doubting that Gabrielle Morgan killed herself and her son, especially after Val had told him, in a phone call just that morning, about the yew tree. After Val finished, he filled her in on what he had learned from Adam's teachers.

All confirmed he was a quiet kid, a good student who was well liked. But they couldn't shake the feeling something wasn't right at home. He never had bruises, but he was out sick a lot. Several times he arrived at school not feeling well. They could never coax any information out of him to warrant any further investigation into his mother.

As far as locating Gabrielle's doctors, Gavin found only one. He confirmed he was not treating Gabrielle for cancer, but the last time he'd seen her was more than a year ago. A lot can happen in that timeframe.

Right now, there were a few other loose ends Gavin needed to tie up. *Never jump to a conclusion in a case*: Gavin had learned that lesson the hard way. He also knew not to discount wealthy parents who want to get involved in their child's investigation. It wasn't a matter of *if* the Morgans would get involved, but simply *when*.

They could call the shots. And, evidently, they were about to take advantage of that fact. They had no love for their second son-in-law and in a phone call this morning they had made it clear that they wanted the police to investigate him. Gavin was curious about what caused the Morgans' sudden decision. As far as he could see they suspected their daughter was behind all this. But this morning, they had changed their minds, and they gave no explanation for that.

Perry Logan, Gabrielle's ex-husband, the man of the hour, was hard to track down. Gavin finally found him living in a run-down apartment in the Allentown area of Buffalo, a trendy and artistic district where housing prices come at a premium for those who wanted to be part of the culture. Property value in the entire city was skyrocketing due to a rebirth as the city exploded into prosperity with its quickly forming medical campus corridor. Every day it seemed several high-rise buildings, expensive lofts, and hotels were being built. But as with any tired city experiencing an awakening, some places are still sleeping, and will never come to life. The place Gavin was about to enter was one of them.

"This eyesore is sitting on prime real estate. I don't know why they don't sell it so someone can tear it down and build something else." Warren looked around. "Anything else."

"Beats me. Slum lording must be pretty lucrative," Gavin said.

"How did Perry react when you told him about Gabrielle?"

"The same way all ex-husbands react. Indifferent."

As they walked through the hallway, deeper into the dark, depressed building, the scent grabbed Gavin, making him wince. Urine, mold and mildew mixed with marijuana. Lovely.

"Which one are we going to?" Warren asked.

"Number 336."

Warren glanced around the hallway, then traveled down it about twenty feet, peering around a corner at the end. "Dammit, there's no elevator," he said, irritated.

"Did you expect one? And if there was, would you want to get into it?"

Warren pursed his lips. "Point taken."

The two men climbed the steps, at the top of the third landing they turned to the right—the only way to go—and followed the numbers to the correct apartment. Gavin knocked.

"It doesn't smell much better up here." Warren dipped his nose into his scarf. "In fact, it might be worse."

"Jesus, people must be pissing in the hallway." Gavin buried his nose in his coat.

"Depending on how stoned you are, it might be hard to make it to a toilet, I guess."

They only had to knock once, thankfully, before the door opened. Gavin was taken aback. Perry Logan appeared healthier and far more clean-cut than Gavin would have expected. He was about six feet tall and clean-shaven with longish, well groomed, light brown hair. He wore khakis and a short-sleeved blue polo that read "Best Buy." Gavin introduced himself and Warren. Perry invited them in and they took a seat at his kitchen table.

Gavin noted that there were no dishes in the sink and the room was organized. A working man, who didn't live like a slob, but lives *here*. It led to Gavin's first question. "Interesting choice of a place to live." His voice upbeat, and a pleasant smile was on his face when he asked. *Act engaged and non-threatening, positive and not negative; don't put Perry on the defensive.* That would be Warren's job. The interrogation technique had worked well for them in the past. Build Perry's trust and then go at him when he's least expecting it. Easiest way to get someone to crack; don't let them see the sledgehammer coming.

Perry smirked. Gavin guessed Perry was well aware that he lived in a shitty apartment in an even shittier building. "This is where the music scene is. I work in retail to pay the rent, but the networking in this area is great for my band. I can't afford any of the other buildings." Perry shook his head. "Rent prices here have gone crazy."

"Isn't that a fact." *Be agreeable. Gain trust.* But Gavin didn't need to pretend on this one. Perry was telling the sad truth. Rent on some of the new lofts was far more than he himself could've afforded. "What's the name of your band?" Gavin asked with interest and a continual smile that Perry seemed to buy.

"The Lords of Mercy. We're alternative. Two albums are available for download and our third will be out next month. We have a pretty decent following," Perry said, proud.

"I'll have to check those out." Gavin tilted his head in an appraising, yet amused way. "You don't look very alternative."

"Come and see me about eleven tonight." Perry smiled. "Things will be different."

Gavin laughed and patted Perry on the back. The interrogation was going just as he wanted it to.

"But your music isn't paying the bills though? Right?" Warren asked. He stood up from the table and walked around the cramped kitchen, a purposeful, criticizing look. "That's why you live *here*?"

"I'm getting where I need to be," Perry said slowly, cautiously. His eyes narrowed as they followed Warren's movements around the room.

"Did you hope Gabrielle would get you there faster? Maybe finance your band?" Warren pressed. "I mean, it would be easier for you to concentrate on your music if you didn't need to take what, *a retail job*."

Perry quickly shifted his glance from Warren to Gavin. Gavin kept his gaze locked on Perry, saying nothing.

"I didn't care about the Morgans' money." The defense in Perry's voice was audible. Practiced too? Definitely. Perry has said this line before. Gavin just sat back and observed. Poor Perry, in more ways than one. This man would never be able to shed the stigma of marrying a very wealthy woman. And he knew it. Forever trapped. Forever labeled. Forever judged. He never could have married her for love, not in anyone's eyes. It was simply preposterous, that nagging question of intent always remaining. *How much was she worth?*

"I heard Gabrielle had a nice waterfront condo. With a boat parked at the dock right outside. Did you ever live there?" Warren asked, causing Perry to shift his gaze again. Gavin remained quiet, his arms crossed now, waiting for the answer.

"Briefly. Maybe a couple of months." The words said carefully again.

"Far cry from this, I'm assuming," Warren said with a knowing smirk.

Perry opened his mouth in protest and Gavin took over.

"You divorced Gabrielle shortly after her father cut her off, correct?" Gavin sat forward. The assertive pose demanded an answer, but he didn't wait for it. "Must have been hard not having that nice condo anymore." Gavin shook his head, regretfully.

Perry put his hands up in the air in a *stop* fashion. "Detective, I think we need to get one thing straight. I didn't divorce Gabi over money, or a condo." Perry's composure remained steady now. He did not waver. "I divorced her because she was insane."

Gavin opened his eyes wide. Defining moments in interrogations always come, and they either make it or break it. But this was something Gavin was not expecting and wasn't sure the best way to turn with it. Here he was, hoping to blindside Perry, yet Gavin himself just got taken by surprise. He swallowed hard and treaded carefully. "Insane? In what way?"

"I think she was bipolar. I really didn't see the signs while we were dating. Maybe she had meds then. I don't know."

"She acted differently while you dated?" Warren asked. "Let me ask, how did you meet her?"

"At one of my concerts. She started showing up every week. Kept flirting with me, buying me drinks. I couldn't get rid of her."

"Did you know who she was? That she was Gabrielle Morgan of the *Morgan* family?" Warren again.

"Not even a little bit. Honestly, she was pretty slutty... the way she was dressed with a low-cut short dress... her hands were always all over me, hell, she let me know I could have her if I wanted."

"Did you sleep with her?" Warren continued to ask the questions.

"Of course. I wasn't going to turn her down." Perry laughed. "She was slutty and she was hot."

"So, she made all the first moves. Pursued you, I guess you could call it," Warren said.

"Yes. And then we eventually started dating." Though he answered Warren, Perry kept his eyes shifting to Gavin's defensively, as if waiting for another move.

"And you dated for only a short amount of time before you married her?" Warren asked.

"Six months. I wouldn't call that short."

"Many would," Warren shot back quickly. "When did you find out who she was? That her father was James Morgan."

"The night I first slept with her," Perry said, unwavering. "But I didn't know before."

Gavin gave Perry a long, careful glance. "Did that improve your relationship with her? Maybe switch who was pursuing who?"

"No, as I said. I didn't care about the money."

"But you said that she made all the first moves, even getting you into bed was her move. Hell, you said you couldn't get rid of her. Then, after you find out who her father is, you date for only six months before asking her to marry you?" Warren asked, eyebrows close together, face taut, scrutinizing.

"Look, detective, Gabi was aggressive at first and that turned me off but then I got to know her and fell in love. I loved Adam too. She introduced me to him right away. He was a great kid. Sometimes you just know when things are right."

"Until they're not anymore," Gavin said, which caused a sharp look from Perry.

"You weren't married long either. Let's get back to that," Warren said.

"No." Perry let out an exhausted huff. "Jesus, shortly after the ceremony she changed."

"Ah yes, that's right. You said that you thought she was bipolar. Let me ask, do you have a degree in psychiatry?" Warren pressed.

"No but I do know how to look up signs and symptoms on the internet and read what's listed by reputable medical sources. I'm not diagnosing her but merely suggesting the possibility. Isn't it your job, detective, to see if this was correct or not? Maybe to follow up with those with a degree in psychiatry, as you say." Perry's snark couldn't be missed.

What a sophisticated answer from Perry, Gavin thought. He said plainly, "Then please explain for me in your own words what you experienced."

"The highs and lows became evident and then glaringly obvious. Some days, she'd be so depressed she wouldn't speak and then without warning she'd have so much energy that she wouldn't sleep. I think mental issues ran in the family. Her sister Bridget was the real nut job though."

Jesus. Gavin felt blindsided again. He remembered the

Morgans speaking about this sister. The one that Gavin was not allowed to speak with. "The Morgans said that she had developmental disabilities."

"She's a loon and they keep her locked away so that no one can see it. Gabi could at least function in front of people. Fool them." Perry laughed. "She fooled me."

"You've met her, Bridget?" Gavin watched Perry hard, waiting for the answer.

"Once. I remember she was shaky and nervous, very confused overall. I saw her on the only day I ever stepped foot in the Morgans' house. Gabi brought her down from her room to meet me. Mrs. Morgan heard the commotion. She appeared a few minutes later and yelled at Gabi. She had the maid take Bridget away and then told me to get out of her house," Perry said. "If you ask me, the whole family was messed up."

"So, they disliked you before they even met you?" Gavin asked.

"I wasn't some blueblood chosen for their daughter. I didn't need to do anything other than *not be that*."

"Was her first husband chosen for her?" asked Warren.

"I have no idea. Gabi never spoke about him and I didn't want to know. I just assumed that's how it goes with those who are stinking rich."

"Gabi defied her parents' orders and married you anyway. After they cut her off, she carried a grudge against them, didn't she? She refused to have contact with them and kept Adam away from his grandparents," Gavin said.

Perry scoffed. "The Morgans were trying to get custody of Adam. That's why she was staying away from them."

Gavin opened his eyes wide, glancing for a split second over at Warren, then shifted his gaze back to Perry. "Was this in retaliation for the two of you getting married?"

"No, by this point they'd been trying to get Adam for a while, well before I met Gabi. I think our marriage put the pressure on and gave them the ammunition that was needed. They really upped the game, calling her unfit. Several social workers came to the house but found nothing wrong with her parenting abilities. I guess money can't buy ripping a child away from his mother."

Social workers found nothing wrong? "You said Gabi had mental issues, wouldn't Adam have been better off with his grandparents, well at least until his mother got herself into a healthier place," Gavin pressed hard.

Perry shrugged. "I think this battle was a power struggle between them. Mr. Morgan wanted to control Gabi and she couldn't be controlled. But I do want to reiterate that even though Gabi and I had our differences, she loved her son."

Loved her son. Gavin repeated the words to himself. Part of this case hinged on the possibility of abuse, that Gabrielle was an abusive mother. "Outwardly loving parents can sometimes hide signs of mistreatment. Did she ever do anything with him that made you feel uncomfortable?" Gavin asked.

Perry opened his mouth to speak but then closed it, pursing his lips together.

"Did she ever do anything that made you uncomfortable?" Gavin repeated, harder this time.

"People all have different parenting strategies." Perry said nothing more.

"That's not what I asked you."

"There was one time…" Perry hesitated and shifted in his chair. "Detective, kids can sometimes push your buttons…"

"What did Gabrielle do?"

Perry took a deep breath and ran his fingers through his hair. On the exhale he spoke. "I came home from work one day to find Gabrielle passed out on the couch. I heard screaming coming from Adam's room. I went in. He was locked in the closet. He'd been in there for hours. He was so upset he'd actually vomited in there. When I confronted Gabi she said she couldn't take it anymore. He was crying and carrying on. She just needed him to shut up."

"Did you do something about this?" Gavin challenged. "She crossed a line here."

"I tried." Perry sat back on the chair. He took a second before he answered. "She said she'd never do this again..." Perry took a deep breath. "One thing about Gabi that you have to understand... she was vindictive. She didn't like being challenged..."

Gavin was about to ask his next question but stopped, something about Perry's hesitant demeanor caught his attention. "Were you afraid of Gabrielle?"

"No." Perry diverted his eye contact for a brief second.

Gavin wasn't convinced. "Perry, let me ask this next question —and it is total speculation but I want you to think about it. Would Gabrielle have killed Adam to make sure the Morgans could never have him?" Gavin held Perry's gaze. "Was she vindictive enough to get revenge on her parents by killing Adam?"

"That wouldn't have been a typical vindictive move from the Gabi I knew. When Gabi was getting revenge, she wanted you to know she was the one doing it. She wanted to see the results of her plan. There'd be no thrill for her if she was dead, because there'd be no way to see you suffer." Perry checked his watch, which Gavin noted was an iWatch. "I'm sorry, detectives, but I have to end this meeting. I need to be at work soon."

The three men rose. As Perry walked them to the door Gavin asked, "Did you talk to Gabrielle after the divorce? Did you maintain any contact with her, or Adam?"

"No. I just told you she was vindictive. When I left, I became her enemy," Perry said. "She made sure she saw me suffer."

"By doing what?" Gavin narrowed his eyes.

"She started small by trashing my band online. Then she went further. I think she contacted some big vendors in the city. I lost a huge gig playing at Canalside last Labor Day. It was a daylong event of free concerts and my band was one of twenty that was supposed to play. We won the spot in a contest and when they uninvited us, that was a big loss. Thousands of people attend the event. Though we weren't making any money for playing, the exposure would have been tremendous." Perry checked his iWatch again. "I really do have to go."

Gavin placed his hand on the door handle, and then stopped. "One more thing. I'll make it quick. Gabrielle had a brother and sister, twins who drowned when she herself was a teenager. Gabrielle was supposed to have been watching them."

"Gabi only talked to me once about that. All she said was, 'I wish I could have done something more, but it wasn't possible.' She didn't elaborate on what 'more' was and I didn't press her." Perry looked at his iWatch, getting impatient. It was obvious he wanted to wrap this up. "It didn't come up again."

When they were back outside Warren asked, "What do you think?"

"I think he didn't ask his ex-wife enough personal questions to get to know her before, and after, he married her."

"Maybe he didn't care about anything other than the money."

"I agree. And it seems like he ended up with a rich, spoiled, vindictive woman who controlled the household. Locking her son up was either a meltdown for Gabrielle or a pattern of abuse, or a psychotic episode." Gavin tightened his scarf and shoved his hands into his pockets. "Also, I think that man's not stupid, he knows what to say to us... and dammit, Alex, I think he has a watch that's too expensive for him."

Warren pulled out his phone and began checking his

messages. "An iWatch is not like having a Rolex, Mitch. Get with the times. The guy works at Best Buy. Could have gotten an employee discount on one."

Gavin smirked, and let out a deep breath, which immediately became visible in the frigid air. "Jesus, what's the temperature out here?" He was so pumped he didn't feel the cold.

"Has to be less than ten degrees."

Gavin's phone vibrated and he pulled it out of his pocket to see who was calling. It was the Erie County Crime Lab. Gavin quickly answered. The DNA results on the tape wrapped around Gabrielle Morgan's hands and that on her mouth were completed. The knife too.

After a couple of minutes he said, "Any holy water in the church?" Causing Warren to raise his eyebrows. Gavin listened for a few more minutes before hanging up.

"Where does holy water come into all of this?" Warren asked.

"Before I explain, first let me say only Gabrielle's DNA is on the tape. Only her fingerprints are on the inside of it, along with more of her DNA. Her fingerprints and DNA are all over the knife too."

"And we thought all along her DNA would be all over the knife, either planted or real. But she taped herself. This means she killed herself and her son. The case is shut, Mitch."

"Maybe not."

"Care to explain?"

"A small amount of cornstarch powder was also found on the inside of the tape. The same type of powder used inside latex gloves."

There was a few seconds of silence. Gavin knew Warren sensed the significance, but his face told Gavin that he wasn't convinced.

"You want to hang everything we know about this case so far on *that*? It's pretty weak and could have come from anywhere." Warren sighed and looked up at the sky, like he was contemplating, thinking. "Mitch, the only way that could have happened is if the killer wore gloves and then for some reason, changed them. Or wore two sets of gloves, and removed one. It's the only way the powder from the inside of one set would have transferred to the outside of a new pair. The only way powder would have been on the *outside* of the gloves and transferred to the tape."

"Exactly. Manufacturers only put powder on the inside. And..." Gavin hesitated on the *and*. "If someone changed his or her gloves, there's no way he or she could have washed their hands in that church. There's no bathroom. It's a Protestant church so they don't put holy water out in little receptacles like the Catholics do."

"That's why you asked about holy water," Warren said.

"Yes. Even if someone wiped their hands on a cloth it wouldn't have eliminated all of the powder."

Warren shook his head. "It's a possible scenario, changing the gloves, but, Mitch, I'm not buying it because it would be so rare."

"Maybe not so rare." Gavin put his hands in his pockets. "Cornstarch wasn't found on the knife."

Warren raised his left eyebrow up. Gavin could tell he now understood the significance of what he was hearing.

"If someone other than Gabrielle murdered Adam—who had to have died first because his blood was underneath where Gabrielle lay—and this person used gloves to kill him, then they would have had to change the gloves otherwise Gabrielle and her white dress would have been a bloody mess."

"Jesus, Mitch. It's possible," Warren said. "People who use latex gloves are skilled at removal. Hell, we've watched Dr.

Maddox do it enough times to know they can do it without letting anything from the outside of the glove contaminate themselves. The blood wouldn't have transferred to the person's hands. What's on the inside, the powder, that's unavoidable."

"Exactly. Alex, this is making me feel uncomfortable. If Gabrielle didn't tape herself, someone did a damn good job of making it look like she did. They would have known to put her fingerprints on the *inside* of the tape. Honestly, for all practical purpose, this was the only real evidence we can use that suggests Gabrielle is responsible for her own death."

"That means someone wanted her dead and knew how to do it the right way. Smart killer, as I said at the beginning, if this is how it went down."

"And what did I tell you, there's nothing I like better than taking down some asshole who thinks he's smart. They all have a weakness, my friend, and this is how we catch them."

Warren looked at Gavin, his expression serious. "Mitch, remember one thing. If someone was setting Gabrielle up to look like murder–suicide, you can't set up cancer."

"Very true. If someone wanted her dead, they had to have known she had cancer because if this is a setup, it revolves around it." Gavin circled the car to the driver's side, his thoughts churning. Suddenly he remembered something else and he stopped in his tracks. "A co-worker of Gabrielle's filed the missing person's report. What was their name?"

Warren searched through his phone. "His name is Scott Payne."

"*His*? A male co-worker reported her missing? You know, Alex, I keep getting bothered by things here, and this is another one of those. Gabrielle was an extremely private person. She didn't socialize with her neighbors. Her son wasn't seen outside alone. She didn't even let him come home from school on his own. But this person happened to have pictures of Gabrielle *and*

Adam that he supplied for the missing person's report. How did he get those?"

"Seems awfully friendly to me."

Gavin tucked his hands in his pockets. "Alex, I think we need to pay Mr. Payne a visit."

7

The organization Gabrielle Morgan worked for, The Next Step, was located on Ellicott Street in downtown Buffalo. The goal of the not-for-profit was to provide job counseling, training opportunities, and help finding housing for those recovering from long-term alcohol and drug abuse. Many of those who took advantage of the program had been in in-house rehab and now that the substance abuse was under control, they needed to take the *next step* and enter the world again. Gavin commended these people, on both ends. Many do fall off the wagon: it's a constant struggle to stay sober when for the majority of your life you weren't. What's the incentive to do so now? The Next Step sought to provide this. It was selfless work for those who strive to make the lives of others better. It gave support. Hope.

Gavin had called Val, and let her know about the cornstarch. He also let her know where he was going today. Did she want to join him? Val wished she could, but she was on duty at the medical examiner's office and had two dental IDs to do.

Such is the life of a death scene investigator. New cases

always popped up that must be intermingled with the old, the ongoing. Could she catch up with him later?

Gavin agreed. Could he make reservations for dinner?

Val accepted.

Gavin had to admit that his thoughts drifted to Val often. And he finally made up his mind. Tonight, he planned to discuss more than the case with her. He wanted to take their relationship in a more personal direction. He'd been wanting to do this for a long time. And God, he was nervous. Val had never acted in any other way than professional and he had no idea what she thought of him. She knew he was married though. What would she say if she found out he was getting a divorce? His stomach twisted in knots as he made the reservations, hoping he wasn't doing the wrong thing.

~

"Hello, my name is Aaron. I'm 836 days sober. What can I do for you?" a red-headed man said with a welcoming smile. He wore blue slacks and a blue and green checked button-down shirt.

"Aaron, that is a commendable achievement. My name is Detective Gavin. I'm with the Buffalo homicide division and this is my partner Detective Warren. We're looking into the death of Gabrielle Morgan." Gavin held a large brown envelope containing evidence discovered just last night. And he couldn't wait to ask Scott Payne about it. Who, Gavin also learned, was Gabrielle's boss, not co-worker. Scott, in addition, had chosen not to respond to any of Gavin's requests for a meeting, pissing Gavin off to no end.

"Oh my God, poor Gabrielle. We can't believe what happened to her and Adam."

"No clue she was part of the Morgan family?" Gavin looked straight at Aaron.

Aaron's eyes went wide. Stunned. "Detective, no. None at all. It was such a shock to hear it on the news."

"Did she ever seem suicidal to you?" Warren asked.

"Stressed, yes. But not even anything close to suicidal." Aaron shook his head in regret. "But, detective, you never know what goes on under the smiling face, the façade people put on. Many hide their pain, and they do it really well. It blinds people around them to their disease, their demon. Some try to erase it with drugs and alcohol. That never works. People who are depressed need to express their feelings, not hide them. We can't help if we don't know something is wrong. Unfortunately, some are masters at hiding it. You have to want help, detective."

"Well, Aaron, I'll admit *I* need help, but in a different way. I need to find out what happened to Gabrielle," Gavin said, his face sympathetic, searching.

"Of course. I'll do anything that I can." Aaron's eager eyes shifted from one detective to another.

"Well, we were looking at her missing person report and I see that a Scott Payne filed it. Is Scott here today?" Gavin asked. "Can we talk to him?"

"Yes, he's here." Aaron took out his phone. "Let me text him to see if he's free."

Gavin stopped Aaron mid text. "Scott hasn't responded to any of the messages I left for him earlier. I was hoping to catch him in person, to speak to him informally." Gavin grinned and added. "I wouldn't want to have pull him into our headquarters for questioning, now. Can you let him know that in your text?"

Aaron nodded, wide-eyed. "Of course. Scott is a busy man, detective." He typed the message. "I'm sure this was an oversight on his part."

"I'm a busy man too," Gavin said, choosing not to say anything more on Scott Payne's *busy-ness*. Gavin would go after

Scott one-on-one soon enough. "Aaron, while we're waiting can I ask you another question."

"Of course, detective." Aaron set the phone down on the desk in front of him. "Shouldn't be long. Scott usually gets back to me right away when I text."

"What can you tell us about Gabrielle Morgan in general? What type of person was she?" Gavin asked.

Aaron smiled. "She was a great co-worker." He hesitated after he finished the sentence, seeming reluctant to say more.

"I almost feel a 'but' in your description," Gavin said, pressing Aaron a little bit.

"I'm sorry, I didn't mean to do that." Aaron tilted his head down, but then slowly looked up. "You see, there was something about her that I just can't put my finger on and I don't want to speculate because that wouldn't be right at all. Everyone is entitled to have their space and our understanding. Not our gossip."

Gavin could tell that Aaron was struggling with loyalty versus honesty. Many close witnesses, those who know the victim well, do this too. He wouldn't have pegged Aaron as a *close witness*; it could just be the counselor side of Aaron shining through. Either way, Gavin needed to find out what he could about Gabrielle, and it seemed Aaron knew more than expected. "That's very commendable, but I am a detective, Aaron, and I see speculation and gossip differently than most. Speculation, many times in my profession, helps to find a killer. Aaron, we need to know about Gabrielle, all about her. Though something may not be flattering, it might help us to find out what happened to her and her son. We're not judging her. We're trying to find closure for her family. And justice for her and Adam."

Aaron nodded. "Don't get me wrong with what I'm about to say." He hesitated again, as if trying to get his words right.

"Gabrielle was friendly and nice, but there was a very private side to her. You could only get so close. A lot of us would get together after work and she always had an excuse to not come along. It was always Adam. She had no one to watch him and she wouldn't leave him with a babysitter."

"Did you find that odd? That she had no one to watch him, I mean. No family or friends that could do it?" Gavin asked.

"That's just it. We didn't see *that* as odd, not in the beginning anyway. She just seemed like an overprotective mother—that she wouldn't let anyone *else* look after him. She was young, he was her only child, that's not uncommon... then she started taking a lot of time off work." Aaron stopped speaking, as if he just said the wrong thing.

"Was Gabrielle sick?" Gavin thought of Gabrielle's cancer; maybe she had symptoms. Even if she didn't know about it, she could have had symptoms. Gavin needed to find out what Gabrielle knew. Felt. What she told people.

"No, Adam was the one sick."

"Adam?" Gavin's eyes flew wide open. He couldn't help it. Adam's teachers also confirmed he was sick a lot. "How soon before her disappearance was she taking time off to care for him?"

"A few months, I'd say." Aaron sighed. "We were sorry for her, of course, and wanted to help, but then we grew concerned because she wouldn't let anyone help her."

"How often did you yourself ask to help her out?" Warren said with a smile.

"Oh, all the time," Aaron said.

"Maybe one time too many?" Warren's lips became a straight line. The implication clear.

Aaron's face went blank and Gavin shot Warren a look signaling to hold off on pressuring this man. Now wasn't the time. Gavin jumped in quickly. He didn't want Aaron on the defensive with them, not at this point. *Aaron knows more then he's letting on and he seems to be a credible, though hesitant, witness. No, Aaron needs to feel comfortable around us, let his guard down. So far, he's been doing that.* "As you've said, Aaron, sometimes it's hard to accept help," Gavin offered with compassion, and a darting glance to Warren to let up. "It can be frustrating if you are asked too many times *if you need help* even if you need it desperately. I think that's what my partner was suggesting."

Aaron quickly turned towards Gavin. "True, detective. Though she was taking time off a few months before she disappeared, she was still the same Gabrielle. But a couple of weeks before, I saw a dramatic change. We all did."

"What kind of change?" Gavin asked.

"She started to appear more stressed than usual. She wasn't herself." Aaron put his hands to his face again, fingers outstretched on his cheeks, gaze cast downwards, like he was remembering a moment in life that he wished he could rewind. Or forget. "We knew she was going through a tough time. And no one wanted to intrude on her any more than we were already doing." Aaron shook his head, regrettably. "Detective, she was a rock of strength. Until she wasn't anymore. Like I said, some people hide pain so well. I can't help but feel we missed the signs. Those of us who are not supposed to."

"Thank you, Aaron, for your honesty." Gavin heard a chime and pointed towards Aaron's phone. "Is Scott available to speak to us now?"

Aaron looked down at the device. "Yes, detective, you can go right in to his office. It's the first door down the hall on the left."

"Your assistance today was much appreciated. I know that was hard for you. But we all need to do everything we can for Gabrielle. This isn't about us anymore, it's about her."

"Thank you, detective, but as I've said, you have to want help. That's the key." Aaron nodded at his own comment as if trying to convince himself of the mantra.

Everything Gavin just heard would fit with Gabrielle learning she had cancer. *A rock of strength until she wasn't anymore.* A diagnosis of cancer crumbles everyone. She knew the protocol. How to hide things that were troubling her.

All alarming things.

Maybe even the possibility that someone might want her dead.

Gavin and Warren entered Scott Payne's office. Gavin held the envelope with evidence and he unclipped it as he and Warren walked in.

Scott was roughly six foot two, with blond hair and brown eyes. Maybe about forty to forty-five years old, Gavin guessed. His gray suit fit him well. In fact, he was nicely dressed, stylish with an in-charge appearance. Good clothes make a statement. Gavin needed to figure out Scott's. This was a non-profit organization.

Scott approached Gavin and Warren immediately with an outstretched hand, and a sympathetic face. "I'm so sorry I didn't respond to your phone calls, detective. Since the news about Gabrielle Morgan came out, things have been so hectic I can't keep up with real requests versus spam. Whatever I can do to help Gabrielle, please let me know."

Spam? Scott Payne thought the Buffalo homicide department was spamming him? Gavin decided to let Mr. Payne's poor judgment slide for now. Gavin was pissed, but as with Aaron, Gavin didn't want this man on the defensive. No, not yet. "Mr. Payne, what's your role in this organization?" The detectives took the two chairs in front of Scott's desk.

Scott perched himself on the edge of the desk, right in front of Gavin and Warren. He casually crossed his arms and tilted his head attentively, ready to absorb any news and give his thoughts. "I'm the director. I coordinate fundraising, budgeting and community outreach for the entire organization." Scott's voice had a pleasant ring and his mannerisms indicated this man was engaged, not aggressive and not defensive. "My biggest job, though, is to go out into the community and get the money from potential wealthy donors. It's how we survive, from donations."

Gavin sized Scott up one more time. *Okay, the nice clothing is because he speaks to wealthy donors. He has to look the part to fit in. And the humble persona allows him to be heard. Grovel when necessary. Good clothes with a kiss-ass, smooth talker wearing them. Yes. This is why Scott is the boss here.* Gavin could already tell Scott excelled at this. "And what was Gabrielle's position?" Gavin asked.

"She was a project manager. She'd manage individual projects that I assigned to her."

"Was she a good employee?" Warren asked.

"She was great." Scott hesitated, tilting his head in careful consideration. "When she was up for it."

"Care to elaborate?" Warren asked.

"Gabrielle had a lot of personal issues, mostly with her son. He was sick a lot and then he started to have disciplinary issues. Not uncommon for an eight-year-old. Kids rebel. I cut her some slack. She needed time off to deal with these problems at home."

An interrogation is often like creating a sculpture from a block of stone, as each bit gets whittled away, a shape takes form. Sometimes it's brilliant, unexpected, and other times it amounts to nothing more than sheer crap. Gavin narrowed his eyes. Was Adam a handful that Gabrielle had a hard time parenting? "I have to be honest, Mr. Payne, we've heard he was a good kid who did what he was told."

Scott laughed. "Yes, he was a good kid. But he had grown to the age where he didn't always want to do what his mother told him to do. Gabrielle struggled. There were fights, slammed doors, comic books and video games taken away. Unsuccessful time outs... I still remember Gabrielle telling me that he demanded his own smartphone. She refused, of course: he was eight. The result was a temper tantrum that lasted for days. Parenting a young child in this day and age is hard. I don't know how anyone does it anymore."

"I hear you, man. My five-year-old wants a phone," Warren said. "But let me ask this. Could Adam have been rebelling because he wasn't feeling well? Sick kids can be very irritable too," he suggested.

"Detective, I'm not a doctor and I don't have any children of my own, but that sounds..." Scott shrugged, "plausible."

"We heard Gabrielle was private and somewhat protective of her son," Gavin said.

"Yes, she was. Maybe overly protective would be correct." Scott had a faint, knowing smile.

"You seem to know a lot about them," Gavin said, reclining casually in his chair. "Seems a strong association, and you were what... just her boss." Gavin slid out photos from his envelope, but kept them out of Scott's view.

"Yes," Scott said slowly, glancing at what Gavin had in his hands.

"Mr. Payne, you were the one to report Gabrielle and Adam missing. You submitted photos to the police." Gavin handed Scott the photos. "Were these taken from your phone?"

Scott nodded. He didn't seem bothered by the question. "Yes, I took those."

"I had the crime lab blow up the images to produce these."

Gavin pulled out another set from the envelope and handed them to Scott.

Scott took them and shrugged. "Looks pixelated to me. Why would you want to use these, detective?"

"These are not to use in any report. It's for us to know a little more about the photo itself. To study its contents." Gavin pointed to a spot on the image. "It's what's in the far right-hand side that I'm concerned with. Can you see this, sir?"

Scott did, because his face went white.

Gavin continued, "That's Gabrielle's refrigerator. This was taken in her kitchen. In her home. Can you tell me how this came about?"

Scott regained his composure and smiled politely, shifting his position on the desk. "Gabrielle was missing a lot of work due to Adam." Scott nodded as if the picture jarred his memory. "Yes, now I remember. Adam *was* sick. I stopped by her home to make sure they were both okay. I had a care package of food, all made from the employees at the office. When I entered her home, she seemed simply exhausted. But then Adam came out of nowhere in his pajamas and was all smiles. One of the containers held chocolate chip cookies and he wanted one. Gabrielle was thrilled because it looked like Adam was feeling better. It was such a happy moment that I snapped a few pictures before I left, for Gabrielle of course. I sent these to her so she'd have them. Little did I know a few weeks later that I would send these to police to help find them after they'd gone missing." He handed the printouts back to Gavin and shifted his position on the desk again.

"Scott, how often did you visit Gabrielle in her home?" Gavin asked.

"Only that once."

"You didn't erase the photos from your phone after you sent them to her?" Warren asked.

"Do you know how many pictures that are on my phone that I need to erase?" Scott laughed. It was a jovial, non-confrontational remark. Regardless, Gavin was pissed at the candor. Scott was lying to him.

"Can you take a look at this other photo." Gavin pulled out another from the envelope.

"Sure." Scott took the picture.

"Can you tell me what's different in this one? Specifically, right there." Gavin pointed again to a spot in the image.

Scott sensed a problem. He swallowed hard and stared, Gavin could see him trying to stay one step ahead as he saw what Gavin was pointing at. It was no use. He'd already buried himself.

Gavin spoke. "The clock. Look at the clock on the wall." Though pixelated it could easily be seen. "In the picture with Adam, you can see the clock and it reads six o'clock. Perfectly in line with your story. But the one with Gabrielle reads ten. AM or PM is anyone's guess, but that's a substantial difference in time. These are head shots, sir. What I can't tell is if this was a different day."

Warren remarked, more of a statement than a question, "You stayed longer than you thought? Or were there more visits than you admitted to?"

Scott got up from the desk and paced. After a few seconds he shook his head. "Detectives, I think you already suspect the truth... that Gabrielle and I had a work-related romance. We did. Short-lived. It was a poor decision to get involved with an employee, especially one so much younger than myself, and I regret it. But it wasn't something that would stop me from filing the missing person's report. I do the right thing. You need to know that about me."

"Care to elaborate on *short-lived*?" Warren asked.

Scott shook his head again, regretfully. "Our relationship

came out of nowhere. Gabrielle kissed me one day and I kissed her back. One thing led to another and we were in bed before I knew it. The sex was hot. She was hot. We dated secretly for a few weeks. But there was really nothing more between us to keep the relationship going. I think we both knew it was over when it finally ended."

"Did she take the break-up well?" Warren asked.

"Very well." Scott gave a laugh. "I don't think she had any sleepless nights after I was gone."

"Was she ever vindictive?" Gavin asked.

"Vindictive? No. I didn't see her socially anymore and when it came to our work environment, Gabrielle and I always maintained a professional demeanor during, and after. Hell, no one even suspected anything was going on between us here."

So, Perry Logan describes Gabrielle as vindictive but Scott Payne does not, thought Gavin. "Thank you, Mr. Payne. Anything more you care to add?"

"I can't think of anything." The caution in Scott's voice was evident.

"How was Gabrielle dealing with her cancer?" Gavin purposely asked this out of nowhere to get Scott's honest reaction.

"What?" Scott's eyes went wide and he looked from Gavin to Warren, searching for an answer. "*Cancer?* Did I hear you right? Gabrielle *had cancer?*"

"She didn't say anything to you about it?" Gavin remained calm.

Scott's reaction was of true shock. He didn't know. "No, not a word." Scott walked over to his desk chair and sank down into it. "My God, poor Gabrielle."

Gavin looked at Warren, who shook his head, signaling neither had anything more to ask Scott at this time. "If you can think of anything, can you give me a call?" Gavin rose and held out a card with his number on it.

Scott took the card. "Of course."

Once they were in the hallway Gavin's phone vibrated. He pulled it out and took a quick look at the screen. It was the crime lab. They had found something odd with regard to Gabrielle Morgan's body. Specifically, her hair.

8

Val sat in the bar at the Buffalo Chop House. She swirled her glass of Malbec as she waited for Detective Gavin to arrive. She had to admit she was surprised by his choice of restaurant. A top steakhouse in Buffalo? His treat? Gavin either had good news and wanted to celebrate or... Val laughed. This was not a date. Though she had put on her best, and sexiest, black dress and four-inch black-and-white snakeskin pumps.

Thank God Jack was out of the house with Gwen doing some shopping when Val left for her *meeting* tonight. How would she have explained to Jack why she was going to see Detective Gavin, *dressed like this?* Now Val asked herself that question. Jesus, what in the hell was she doing? She was hiding her intentions from Jack and meeting a married man, in this outfit. No good comes from circumstances such as these. Val tugged at the skirt of her dress attempting to lengthen it and then adjusted the V of her slightly plunging neckline, hoping to close it.

Fidgeting on her high bar chair, Val's thoughts circled to Jack again. She was fond of him but he didn't arouse the kind of feelings in her that Gavin did. Maybe it was all because Gavin wasn't attainable. Deep down inside, Val thought she could have Jack if she wanted him. *You always want what you can't have.* Val took a big sip of her wine. Success with men wasn't her strong suite. *Follow your heart*, she told herself, but maybe her heart was screwing with her. It always did. She brought the glass to her lips again. Regardless, she'd never go after a married man. Mitchell Gavin was off limits.

She nearly jumped when she set her glass down. Gavin was standing right beside her. "What are you drinking?"

"Malbec." Val's heart pounded and her face felt hot. She picked up the glass again and took another sip. Why was she so nervous?

"Any good?"

"Uh huh." Val nodded.

Gavin motioned for the bartender and then pointed towards Val's glass. "Ready for another?"

Crap, Val hadn't even realized she had finished the contents. Her eyes lingered on Gavin as he ordered their drinks. He wore dark slacks, blazer, shirt and tie. *Damn, he looks good tonight.* "I really shouldn't." Val's gaze traveled over Gavin again. *Holy crap, she really shouldn't.*

"You'll be okay. If you need a ride, I'll take you home."

Val tried hard to not read into that response. *Professional.* This was a professional meeting with a colleague. He was joking. Of course, she could handle a second glass; the question was could she handle a second glass with Gavin. Val crossed her legs and casually put her elbow on the bar. Then placed the arm down, crossing both arms now in as serious a pose as she could. She needed to look serious. And concerned. *And hopefully not tipsy and silly.* Her second glass of wine arrived. As did Gavin's first. At least the alcohol was helping ease the stiffness in her bad leg. Today was a good day for it overall, otherwise Val would have never been able to walk in her four-inch heels.

"So, what did you find out today from Gabrielle's boss?" Val asked, focussing her thoughts as best she could.

"He was seeing Gabrielle romantically." Gavin picked up the glass and swirled the contents. "And hiding it."

Val raised her eyebrows, shocked by the first statement, not the second. "He was her boss. Not uncommon to hide it. Anything else between them?"

"Not that he's admitting to."

"Do you believe him?"

"The guy rubs me the wrong way." Gavin put both elbows on the bar and leaned forward and sighed. "But I have nothing on him, other than this relationship."

"Didn't you pressure him to tell you more?"

"I let him know that I wasn't going to be fooled by him. But no, I didn't eviscerate him. I need him cooperative and talkative... and feeling somewhat comfortable. People make mistakes when their guard is down."

"Sir, your table is ready."

Val glanced at the hostess, who gave a whole new meaning to sexy black dress. This five-foot ten, twenty-year-old, model-like, red-haired creature held menus in her arms. "Are you ready to be seated?"

"Yes, I think we are?" Gavin posed it as a question to Val.

"I'm ready." Val picked up her glass and stood. Yes, the wine had done wonders for her bad leg.

"Great, then please follow me," the hostess said with a charming smile.

Once seated and the hostess gone, Val resumed the conversation. "Any pings on Gabrielle's cell phone?"

"None. We think it's turned off."

"I thought a turned off phone could still be tracked." Val sat forward, both arms on the table.

Gavin laughed and took a sip of his wine. "The National

Security Agency, aka the NSA, can do that. Local police departments cannot. And the location of Gabrielle's cell phone is not a case of national security, so the NSA probably will not help us out. What we can do is track its last location before it was turned off and that was at Gabrielle's house on the day she disappeared. And it was right before she left her home at 7:30am. So, Gabrielle didn't want to be tracked."

"Or someone else didn't want her to be tracked."

"Why not just leave the phone at her home, then?" Gavin grinned knowingly about the answer.

"Because this way Gabrielle can still be the number-one suspect in her own death as well as that of her son. She would have taken her phone with her. Especially since she and her son were missing and alive five days prior to their deaths on day six."

"I like the way you're learning to think about crime, Val." Gavin smiled and grabbed her hand in a warm embrace. He held on for a second or two before slowly releasing, his thumb sliding across her palm. Val's pulse exploded. His smile, she'd seen it more than once in their conversations. But the touch, that was different. And deliberate. "Some days I'm convinced you rival the best."

"I'm learning from the best." Val's chest flipped with a prickly, hot upsurge of the emotions that lead to desire. She'd become pretty good at pushing her feelings for Gavin to the side, but every now and then he'd do or say something that reminded her how she felt and how hard she had to work to keep him out of her personal thoughts, and in her professional world. This man was not hers for the taking and she sat back, composing herself. *He's a colleague not a potential boyfriend, and especially not a fling for the night.* Val swallowed hard, thinking of something to say because Gavin was sitting back casually swirling his glass, smiling at her. It all made her lose her train of thought.

Something sensible finally popped into her mind, breaking the spell. "Hey, what about Bridget Morgan, Gabrielle's sister. Have you heard anything more about her?" Val blurted out, exhaling, thankful that she found something, anything to say.

Gavin picked up his glass, which was now almost empty. "Perry Logan, Gabrielle's ex-husband, has his own opinion about Bridget Morgan and it's very different than what we heard from Mr. and Mrs. Morgan. Sorry I didn't tell you this earlier."

"Welcome to The Chop House. How are you two doing this evening?" the waiter said. "I'm Aiden and will be taking care of you tonight."

Both Val and Gavin awkwardly turned their attention towards this man as he told them about the specials. She took another sip of wine and set down the glass, which was almost gone. "Can I get you another drink while you decide?" Aiden asked.

"Sure. We're both having the Malbec," Gavin said before Val had a chance to protest.

"Can we order some appetizers now?" Val managed to get out before Aiden could dash off to another table. Food, Val definitely needed some form of food.

"Of course," Aiden said.

Val ordered. "I'll have the mussels in white wine sauce."

"Make that a double order." Gavin laughed, like he was thinking about a personal joke. "I was eyeing the same thing. I'll tell you why later."

Val wondered what was so funny. And what the mystery was. All she could think about was oysters and libido... do mussels count too? *Get your mind back to professional issues*, she told herself.

"Excellent choice. I'll get that in while you look over the menu," Aiden said.

As soon as Aiden left Val cleared her thoughts, preferring not to press Gavin about the mussels, at least not now, and said, "What did Perry Logan have to say about Bridget Morgan?"

"There's a discrepancy between the Morgans' accounts of their daughter Bridget and what Perry told us about her. Perry said she was crazy, not developmentally disabled."

"Holy crap, Mitch." Val's eyes went wide, stunned by what she just heard. "Should we see for ourselves?"

"That's going to be tough. Our attempt to meet with Bridget was politely declined by Mr. and Mrs. Morgan, stating Bridget's *mental well-being* and that *she's not up for something like that*, remember. I could try to put some pressure on, but I have no cause for a warrant so all that's going to do is piss them off and get us no further than where we were at the beginning. Unless they change their minds, she's off limits."

"I can understand. This family has all but one child dead. Of course they're protecting her." Val sat back in her chair. "I know how we can get a better handle on Bridget Morgan's mental state. The funeral for Gabrielle and Adam is Monday morning. I'm sure Bridget will be there. Gwen and I were planning on attending."

"Dr. Maddox released the bodies?" Gavin looked stunned and his voice had a sharpness to it. "I didn't hear about this."

"He had no choice. The Morgans were pressuring him. A lot. Plus, Dr. Maddox was officially finished with both autopsies. Tissue samples had been collected and toxicology was still running all necessary tests. It will take a couple more days to find out what, if any, foreign substances Gabrielle and Adam had in their system." Val wondered why Gavin was worried about the bodies being released. Dr. Maddox told him himself right after the autopsies that he collected all he could, even more than he should, really, in case he had to release the bodies prematurely. There was nothing more for the medical examiner's office to do that required Gabrielle and Adam in person and after considerable pressure from the Morgans, Dr. Maddox agreed to release the remains of their daughter and grandson for burial.

"Did he save hair samples?" Gavin said, anxious for the answer.

They both stopped talking as Aiden placed a bowl of mussels in front of them, along with a plate of beautifully toasted bread and refills of their wine.

"Yes," Val said to Gavin.

"Hope you enjoy. Is there anything more I can get you right now?" Aiden said.

"I'm ready to order dinner." Val looked at Gavin waiting for a response.

Gavin sat back and picked up his glass, he seemed to relax a little. "So am I. Go for it."

"I'll have the fillet, medium rare and the mashed potatoes." Hell, they were in a steakhouse. Was there anything other than steak to order?

"Excellent choice, and for you, sir." Aiden turned towards Gavin.

"Porterhouse rare, with a baked potato. Sour cream on the side."

"Perfect. Enjoy the appetizers and then I'll get these in."

As soon as Aiden left, Val reached for a piece of bread and dipped into the white wine sauce, which was heavenly. Wiping her mouth on her napkin she said, "We took hair samples so that Zoe could do a toxicology screen on them to check for drugs. Hair can maintain a very nice calendar of intake for some drugs and testing hair is standard practice in a case like this."

"Can she check for more than just drugs?"

Val narrowed her eyes, scrutinizing. "Not sure I'm following?" She picked up a mussel and speared the contents with her fork.

"A number of strands were stuck on to the duct tape covering her mouth. The crime lab found traces of crushed pearls on them. I'm not sure where pearls could have come, maybe it was part of the ritual. But wherever it came from, it was superficial, on the surface of the strand. Is this some woman hair thing that I don't know about? Do women put crushed pearls in their hair?"

"Is this where your desire for mussels came from. You said you'd let me know why you were eyeing them on the menu." Pearls are formed in all mollusks.

"You have me." He smiled.

See, a G-rated explanation, Val told herself, somewhat disappointed. "No reason to use crushed pearls that I know of. I can ask Zoe to do a further analysis with this." Val pulled out her phone and googled pearls and hair. A number of hairstyles showed up on the screen. Pearls weaved into braids, dotting buns, intricate wedding coiffures. She showed the phone to Gavin.

"I got the same kind of thing on my search. There were no pearls in Gabrielle's hair, though. Unless they were removed. But these were crushed. In powder form."

"Would that have been possible then if the pearls were placed whole in her hair? To find them crushed?"

"Pearls are one of the softer gems and they do break easily." Sounded like Gavin was stretching for his answer.

On a hunch Val typed pearls and hair products and bingo! "Hey, would you look at this. They put crushed pearls in expensive shampoos to make hair shiny. Particularly to make blonde hair shiny." Val scrolled through the screen. "Holy moly! Look at what some of this stuff costs. Varies dramatically on the brand but none are cheap. Here's one that's nearly 300 a bottle. Absolute Blonde it's called. Zoe will definitely have to follow up on this." Val picked up her glass of wine, intending to milk it until the end of the evening. "So, Gabrielle Morgan disappeared from her home five days before she died, and in this time, she shampooed her hair with a pricey, specialty product for blondes?"

"I knew I was right when I said you were rivaling the best with your crime skills." Gavin picked up a mussel, but kept his eyes on Val.

Val laughed. "Be careful how you say that!" She couldn't help but think Gavin had something on his mind, something else he wanted to tell her. Shy smiles were intertwined with long devouring looks. What was it? It seemed like he was waiting for the right moment to pounce. Or was Val's judgment clouded by the wine. *Professional. This was a professional dinner.* "What about DNA on the tape?"

"Only Gabrielle's. Minor, salivary, no more than from touching her lips and epithelials from her skin. All points to Gabrielle. But..."

"But?"

"Cornstarch powder was also found. Like that used on the inside of latex gloves." Gavin explained the findings to Val.

"Jesus, Mitch. Though everything points to murder–suicide, small things come up that make it crumble."

The next hour slipped by easily. Dinner arrived and the steak was magnificent. The conversation ebbed and then flowed away from Gabrielle Morgan. Gavin's gaze was growing more intense as he looked at Val. Dessert menus came.

As they sat looking at the choices Gavin said, "Val, there's one more thing I want to talk about." He sat forward and held her gaze. A shy smile spread across his lips. Val looked at him, eager to hear what he had to say, her pulse pounded. Gavin had been flirting with her all night. Should she flirt back, let him know if things were different... he not married... suddenly her phone chimed and she instinctively looked down. Val's eyebrows knitted together and she tapped the screen to read the text she'd received.

"Something wrong?" Gavin asked.

"Jack asked if we knew yet if Gabrielle had yew poison in her system." Val was about to text *No* but another text from Jack popped up. She kept her eyes down, reading.

We need to talk with the Ballards.

"Jack? Jack Styles? From the case last spring? He's texting you about *this* case?" Gavin's gaze on Val now intent.

Val stared at Gavin with a loss of words. *Oh no, I've screwed up big time.* Jack was not officially part of this case and giving him any information, particularly confidential information such as anything about the yew trees, allowing him to be part of the investigation, could possibly get Val in trouble and maybe even fired. Val held her breath, Gavin would yell at her, of course he would. *That's what he's going to do now.* But he wouldn't tell Dr. Maddox. Val was confident of that... well, maybe not so much now, because Gavin looked really upset.

She scrambled with her excuse. "Jack's in Buffalo. Visiting. I simply asked him a few *English* things—about yew trees," Val said, trying to make it all sound innocent, but then she stopped, hesitating. She couldn't say anything more, even about Jack in general. Gavin would blow a gasket. On top of the firing issue, these two men did not get along.

Judging by Gavin's expression, Val knew she was right. The way Gavin was looking at her... no... the way Gavin was looking at her was all wrong, it wasn't like he was going to reprimand her about Jack, about protocol. Professionalism. *How a proper investigation is conducted.* He was blank... well no, that wasn't it either. Honestly if Val wasn't still clouded a little from the alcohol she would have said *disappointed*.

"*He's visiting?*" Gavin quickly looked at his watch. "It's getting late. I think we should call it a night."

9

Val set her phone down. No texts. Nothing from Gavin since their dinner Friday night. She finally relinquished. *Why would there be?*

As Val sat at her desk in the medical examiner's office Monday morning, pen in hand, she jotted down a few notes about the Gabrielle Morgan case. She couldn't keep her mind from wandering, circling back again, reliving dinner with Gavin, dissecting details. Had she misread Gavin all night? Of course she had. That night was not a date and everything that happened, the looks the signals, were no more than alcohol-influenced errors in judgment.

God, am I ever relieved I didn't say or do anything I shouldn't have, thought Val. Now, after having two days to collect her thoughts, she was happy she hadn't made a fool of herself. *What in the hell was I thinking?* If Gavin was flirting with her, well then screw him. He was a married man. Val could rest assured that she did nothing wrong, other than maybe let her guard down. A little overly friendly? Yes. A slut? No. *Thank God.*

Gavin's demeanor had changed suddenly after the text from Jack. It had snapped both of them to attention and led Gavin away from making a wine-fueled adulterous move and Val from just being, well... stupid.

Jack... the events of that night created a crack, one large enough for Val to see him differently. Her attraction to Gavin was only wasting her time. Val wasn't getting any younger and she was pushing away men far better suited for her. Jack was available. He was attractive... well no, that wasn't correct. He was downright one of the sexiest men Val had ever seen in person.

He had taken her breath away the first time she saw him, even though she had also hated him then. He was so arrogant. *Hell, he still is arrogant.* Would he tear at her heart though? Like Gavin did.

Jack had been waiting for her when she got home after dinner with Gavin. He teased her about her choice of clothing and asked where she'd been.

'I went for dinner with Gavin,' she told him.

Jack's only response had been to say, "We need to talk with the Ballards."

"The who?" Val had questioned. The name didn't immediately ring a bell.

"Gabrielle Morgan's next-door neighbors. The wife was the last person to see Gabrielle alive." Jack raised his eyebrows, as if he were surprised Val didn't know this. "Val, when investigating a case, you ought to know who your witnesses are—"

Val had cut him off. She was in no mood for his pontificating. "I know the neighbor was the last person to see Gabrielle alive. I just didn't remember the name was Ballard. What about them? Does the husband know something too? You said *Ballards.* Plural." Val made a point to show she had caught the distinction.

"Mr. Ballard tended to be left home alone—a lot—while his wife worked late-night shifts. The neighbor across the street told me that. The neighbor across the street also told me that

Gabrielle Morgan's lights seemed to be on later than usual on those nights. Could be neighborhood gossip but I think we should look into it. Anyway, it's late. I'm heading to bed. We'll talk about it tomorrow."

Val had just stared at Jack as he climbed the staircase. He kept his gaze forward, not looking back at her. "By the way," he had said, "I should have mentioned it earlier, but that dress looks great on you."

~

"Val, we need to go!" Gwen poked her head into their office.

Val eyed Gwen's dark suit and checked her watch. She herself needed to change out of the scrubs she was wearing. "Give me five minutes."

"I'll be in the car."

Val jumped up. *Holy crap how did I lose track of time?* Val and Gwen's shift, which had started at 6am, had flown by. The funeral services for Gabrielle and Adam Morgan began at 9am and Val and Gwen planned on attending. Now Val had another purpose: to see Gabrielle's sister, Bridget, in person. She rushed to the women's changing room, pulled off her scrubs and put on a pair of navy slacks, beige blouse, and finished with the matching blazer for the pants. She slipped on her boots, grabbed her knee-length black wool trench coat and ran to the parking ramp to meet Gwen, who was already sitting behind the wheel in her car. "We should just make it," Gwen said.

Ten minutes later they were circling around the funeral home. Val squinted. The sky was a cloudless, bright blue, and the sun reflected starkly off the white snow, creating an intense sheen. Val had to shield her eyes from the glare as she looked out of the window. "There must be several hundred mourners here." She noted all the cars, and the number of people trying to get into the funeral home, where it was warm. The blue sky was very deceiving. The outside temperature teetered at ten degrees Fahrenheit.

"Jesus, there's nowhere to even park," Gwen said.

"When your name is Morgan, you draw a crowd." Val turned her head in all directions. The reporters certainly weren't missing the event. Every local station was here. Val saw two national ones, too.

Gwen spun the wheel, taking them down a side street which was parked bumper to bumper. After going up and down several streets, they eventually got a spot in the lot of a small strip plaza about three blocks away.

It took a full five minutes to walk over snow-covered sidewalks back to the funeral home, but there was no way they were going inside yet. The line to even get to the door was snaking around the building. Val was limping as she and Gwen got in place behind a young woman with long blonde hair. Her bad leg was at its worst in cold weather and that walk just about tested its limits. Val looked at her watch. "It's 9:10. We're missing it."

The blonde, who was about Gwen's height, turned around. "The Morgans' receiving line starts at nine. The service, at eleven."

Val's eyebrows shot up, surprised. She'd never been to a funeral with a receiving line before. Its etiquettes and customs were something beyond her comprehension but it made sense with this many people coming to pay their respects. "Thanks for letting us know."

"No problem." The blonde turned back around. Though the woman was helpful Val didn't feel comfortable with the fact that she had no problem listening to her conversation, and signaled to Gwen to say nothing sensitive.

Forty-five minutes passed before Val and Gwen entered the

building, and shed coats, which they now held over their arms. They were finally close enough to see only Mr. and Mrs. Morgan. And the single casket. Something wasn't right. *There was only one casket? And where was Bridget? Or a female who could be Bridget?* Val looked all around. *Where in the hell was the other daughter? The only child left alive?* Val and Gwen kept inching forward, Val's leg getting better now that she was in the warmth of the building.

After several more people addressed the Morgans and expressed sympathies, the blonde in front of Gwen and Val was next and as soon as the space opened up, she quickly moved towards Mrs. Morgan, placing her arms around her as she sobbed.

"Bethany, I'm so glad you came." Mrs. Morgan held Bethany in a tight grasp. "Gabrielle would be so happy to know you're here."

Bethany? Val's ears perked up. A Bethany Arias was Gabrielle's emergency contact for Adam. The one who couldn't be reached the day he wasn't well at school, the day he disappeared. *Holy shit, was this that Bethany Arias?* It must be. How many Bethanys could Gabrielle have known? Val could kick herself now for not talking to this woman more. *They were right behind her in line for a damn forty-five minutes!*

"Please, if there's anything I can do." Bethany pulled back from the embrace and gripped Mrs. Morgan's hands. Both women held tight.

Bethany then turned to Mr. Morgan, her hands still holding Mrs. Morgan's. "I can't believe they're gone."

"She's at peace," Mr. Morgan said. He made no physical contact. No hug, no shake of the hand. The sterility was clear. Val wondered what Bethany had done to piss Mr. Morgan off, especially after seeing such a warm reception from his wife. But maybe, this simply was how Mr. Morgan was.

Bethany said a few more things to the Morgans: somber regrets about not keeping up correspondences, and sympathetic offerings to help in any way that she could. After a few moments, Bethany left and Val and Gwen moved up to their place in front of the Morgans.

Val noted this couple was definitely alone. No female that could be Bridget was anywhere near them. It wasn't the time or place to ask the Morgans about it though. "I'm so sorry for your loss, Mr. and Mrs. Morgan. This is my co-worker Gwen Carmondy."

"I'm terribly sorry," Gwen said.

"Thank you, Valentina, Gwen," Mr. Morgan said. All Mrs. Morgan could do was wipe away tears and nod. Mr. Morgan's gaze left theirs and Val knew to keep moving along in the funeral line.

As they walked away, Val kept her sights on Bethany and followed her to their next stop, in front of the single casket which was closed. Bethany's hand rested on top, her eyes also closed, lips moving but no words coming out. Val could read the lips speaking in prayer. *Hail Mary full of grace...*

Val looked around, whispering the obvious to Gwen, "There's only one?" she said of the casket.

"They're both in there." Bethany opened her eyes, suddenly awake from prayer, and turned towards Val, startling her. "Gabi would never want to be separated from her son. They had to close the casket because of Adam. Poor boy." This woman, yet again, eavesdropped on Val's conversation and answered Val's question. Val was not going to miss another opportunity to talk to Bethany but before she could say anything more, several people moved closer to the casket and it became apparent that the three of them were backing up the line. Bethany walked away and went towards a large poster board covered with pictures of Gabrielle and Adam. Val and Gwen quickly trailed after her.

"Bethany?" Val asked.

Bethany looked at Val, perhaps confused as to how Val knew her name. "Yes?"

Val gave a somber smile. "I overheard Mrs. Morgan call you Bethany. I just wanted to say thank you for all of your help this morning, letting me know the time of the service and that both Gabrielle and Adam were in the same coffin."

"You're welcome," Bethany said. Her attention went back to the photos. Silence now, and Val thought quickly of her next question.

"I don't mean to intrude in your time of grief but can I ask how you knew Gabrielle?" Val asked.

"We were best friends growing up." Bethany pointed to one of the photographs on the poster board. "Here we are. God, we must have been ten years old in this one." Bethany shook her head with a *smile?* Val had a hard time reading the expression. No, it was really a smirk on Bethany's face as she relived the memory.

Both girls in the photo looked... well, they looked uncomfortable. Val wondered why Bethany reacted the way she did to *this* memory. There were several other pictures tacked up on the board that Bethany could have chosen to point to. In those, the girls looked a lot happier. "What a lovely picture," Val lied. "What was the occasion?"

"It's the day we met Melinda. She was our age and had just moved next door to Gabi. The three of us eventually became inseparable."

"Did you also live close to Gabi?" Val chose to use the nickname Bethany did.

"My family lived next door on the other side. Gabi and I were friends since we could walk and talk." Bethany turned her body fully now so that she could look at Val straight on. She narrowed her eyes. "Can I ask how *you* knew Gabi."

"I'm so sorry I didn't mention this before. I'm a death scene investigator with the medical examiner's office. This is my colleague Gwen. We're here today to pay our respects to the family. Would it be possible to talk with you some other time about her? Anything you might recall could help us with determining what happened to them."

"Oh my God, of course, I'll do anything to help Gabi and Adam." Bethany's eyes welled up and she reached into her bag and pulled out a tissue. "Sorry. You have to excuse me. I know they're dead but what you've just said, makes it seems much more *real*. It makes me think of how they died. I'm so sorry," Bethany reiterated as she tried to stop tears from streaming down her cheeks. "The news was pretty graphic about it."

"I'm the one who should be sorry. I didn't mean to startle you." Val knew she had to be diplomatic when describing her position, especially to family and friends of the victims. She put a loved one's death up front and center for the survivors, but the news was usually far more upfront than Val could ever be.

"Don't worry, I'm not that delicate. Contrary to what you're seeing right now, I can handle the truth." Bethany dabbed her eyes and straightened her back, pulling herself together. "I'm afraid I don't know much about her recently, though. As I've said, we were best friends growing up. We grew apart after she married her second husband. She became very private after that."

This second marriage seemed to cause a lot of dissent in Gabrielle's life. But there was one more important piece of information. If Bethany and Gabrielle grew apart after Gabrielle's second marriage why on earth did Gabrielle list Bethany as an emergency contact for her son recently. Now was not the time for Val to delve into Bethany's admission, though.

Val was at a funeral. Instead, she asked something else. "Can you tell me if Gabrielle's sister is here. Bridget?"

Bethany turned her head in all directions. "No, I don't see her but I wouldn't expect Bridget to be here."

"She wouldn't be at her sister and nephew's funeral?" Val questioned.

"It's just that Bridget isn't good with crowds like this. Quiet places are best for her."

"Quiet places?" Val pressed a little more.

"Bridget has some type of disability. It worsened as we were growing up." Bethany shook her head. "We all used to play together when we were kids. Then one day Bridget no longer played with us. In my opinion, I think she needed to be institutionalized but the Morgans refused to do that." Bethany crossed her arms. "I still remember seeing Bridget, medicated out of her mind. I always felt sorry for her, that maybe she would have been better off at an institution."

Val opened her mouth to speak but Bethany cut her off.

"Oh, please don't get me wrong, the Morgans are wonderful parents but they didn't know how to care for Bridget. And neither did Claudia, her nanny." Bethany curled her upper lip up as she said Claudia's name. "Anyway, I think the Morgans thought if they kept Bridget at home, they kept her *normal*. At least to them."

"Could you guess what kind of disability..." Val trailed off on the sentence, really not knowing what to say here. Perry Logan said Bridget was insane and Val was wondering how to ask this question in a roundabout way without herself looking insane for bringing such a thing up at a funeral.

"Sorry, I'm not sure what she had exactly. Gabrielle didn't talk about it and neither did the Morgans. There was a time that Bridget at least could function somewhat, but after the death of the twins..." Bethany's eyes shot up as if she just said something she shouldn't have.

"It's okay, the Morgans told me about them," Val said.

"They did?" Bethany sounded surprised.

Val nodded, wondering why Bethany was shocked by this.

"...anyway, after the twins died, I only saw Bridget on a few occasions. As I said, Gabrielle never talked about her and when I brought Bridget up, Gabi changed the subject." Bethany tensed. "She really hated talking about Bridget. So, I stopped talking about her too."

"Bethany, oh my God, I can't believe it." A young, tall, very attractive woman with long, wavy blonde hair, green eyes, and black fitted suit came up to Bethany and hugged her. Once the tall woman pulled back, she glanced from Bethany to Val and then to Gwen, as if she just realized that Bethany had been speaking to other people. Her gaze narrowed as she scrutinized the two strangers standing before her. Val felt like she was in high school again and the queen bee was judging whether to accept her into the clique.

"Melinda Holbright, this is Valentina Knight."

Val's attention shot straight up as she stared at Melinda. Melinda Holbright... the person that Bethany named in the photo. "And Gwen... I'm sorry, I don't remember your last name. They work for the medical examiner's office. They're trying to figure out what happened to Gabi."

Melinda extended her hand in a lukewarm, barely engaged, obligatory manner. Val and Gwen worked at the medical examiner's office. They weren't in the right income bracket and social circle. No acceptance to the clique here. They didn't belong. Polite courtesy only. "Pleased to meet you." It was obvious she wasn't pleased at all.

"Mel was the third in our little trio that I told you about.

God, we were inseparable back then, weren't we? Time is an awful beast that really does come between people, doesn't it?"

"It certainly does." Melinda straightened her purse on her shoulder.

"God, how long has it been?" Bethany asked.

"Too long!" Melinda looked at Val, then Gwen again. "Beth, I don't mean to be rude to your *acquaintances* here, but some of our high school friends have gathered in the foyer. I told them that I've come to retrieve you. They're dying to hear what you've been up to. Plus, we're planning a celebration to honor Gabi tonight. Should be like old times." Melinda put her hand on Bethany's arm. "Sean is here. So sad about his mother." Melinda leaned in to whisper in Bethany's ear.

Val couldn't make out what Melinda said, but she watched Bethany's reaction to Melinda. Bethany's lips curled up slightly. The private conversation had such an air of familiarity, of knowing... of orchestration, that Val couldn't help but feel this wasn't the first time Bethany and Melinda had gotten together recently, nor did Sean really have anything sad happen with his mother. A reunion between these women happened before today. They knew how to act around one another. For one another.

Bethany turned and looked at Val in a way that you do when you're ready to move on from a conversation.

Val spoke up quickly before they walked off. "I'm still hoping that we can meet at another time to discuss this further? Any information you can give me might help Gabrielle and Adam." Val handed Bethany a card with her contact information and then locked eyes on Melinda. "I'd like to speak with both of you, if possible."

"Of course," Bethany said. Melinda's hand was on her arm, coaxing her to walk away.

"I'd be happy to talk to you too," Melinda said and quickly

snatched her own card as Val handed her one. With that she grabbed Bethany's arm tighter and pulled her away.

Val quickly glanced over at the photographs on the board. None were recent shots of Gabrielle and Adam. Val wasn't surprised. The Morgans hadn't had a strong relationship with their daughter in several years. No photo opportunities for this family. But there were no photos of any little girl, or teenager, that could have been Melinda either. All of the childhood photos, right through early womanhood, were of Gabrielle with only one other girl, Bethany. Looks like the Morgans had no problem expelling Melinda from their lives.

All conversation stopped as a bell chimed several times. Val looked towards the sound, to the casket. A priest stood in front of it, a Bible open in his hands. Val glanced at her watch. Eleven o'clock on the nose. "We'd better get seated. The priest is ready to start the service."

Val's phone vibrated. She took a look at who was texting her. Zoe Beauchamp, the toxicologist for the medical examiner's office wanted to see Val as soon as she got back to the office. Zoe had finished the drug testing on Gabrielle and Adam Morgan.

10

"So, when did you do that?" Val asked Zoe.

"Last night. What do you think?" Zoe Beauchamp turned around so that Val could get a good look at her platinum blonde hair. It was cut short, cropped with long angled bangs, purposely maintaining black roots. The low-lighting effect was pretty cool. Since Val had known Zoe, she always styled her hair in a jet-black bob. Its color was a nice contrast to her pale skin and watery blue eyes. Zoe didn't need a *look,* though, to define herself, especially not at work. When it came to drug analysis, Zoe was brilliant. With her PhD, numerous awards, articles in journals, and invited presentations about how drugs work, Zoe simply made the medical examiner's office shine.

"I love it!" Val then squinted and pointed to Zoe's eyebrow, getting closer to inspect the small silver braided ring. "The piercing is new too?"

"Glad you noticed. No one else did today." Zoe laughed. "I'm glad you're at least happy with my appearance because you're not going to be happy with the news I have for you."

"Oh no." Val cringed and sat back in the chair, bracing herself. "Give it to me."

Zoe's face straightened, serious now. She picked up a pair of glasses that sat on the counter and put them on. "First, Adam Morgan has no drugs in his system that I can find, so he wasn't sedated before his throat was slashed. This kid was wide awake when this happened."

"Holy crap! How do you hold an eight-year-old down and cut his throat, then? He should have fought like hell."

"I agree, but maybe he didn't see it coming?" Zoe tried.

"Possible. If he was lying on the altar and someone was behind him, he might not have known what was about to happen." Val just shook her head, though plausible, it was just unlikely. "What about Gabrielle. Was she poisoned?"

"You're not going to like this even more."

Val cringed a second time. "Give it to me too."

Zoe picked up several reports which were strewn on her table, sorted through them, and selected the one she wanted. "There is no yew poison in Gabrielle Morgan's system."

Val stood up. "That's impossible. She had the seeds in her mouth."

"Yes, the seeds were in her mouth, but they're not toxic in this form—as whole seeds. They need to be chewed, or digested by stomach acids, to release the poison. She had no seeds in her stomach according to Dr. Maddox's report, which I have right here." Zoe held up the papers.

Val opened her mouth to speak but Zoe put one finger in the air, signaling for her to stop.

"Hear me out." Zoe pointed to one paragraph in the report. "The majority of the seeds were in her mouth and a small amount were behind the soft palate. There is no evidence that she swallowed." Zoe looked up at Val. "This is an important line. Not that she didn't digest any of the seeds or swallow any of the seeds. But that she swallowed at all."

Val saw the obvious and slid back down into her chair.

"There's no way she wouldn't have had an urge to swallow with those seeds in her mouth. The amount of saliva generated from them simply being in her oral cavity would have done it. If she didn't swallow, she would have salivated all over herself."

"Yes, she would have and I took a look at the report from the crime lab. The tape across her mouth had minimal saliva on it," Zoe said plainly.

The significance was clear. Val absorbed the news, overwhelmed and excited by a bit of true evidence that pointed to the likelihood of Gabrielle Morgan committing suicide as pure and utter crap. "This is all consistent with the seeds being placed in her mouth after death and gravity took a few down the upper part of the oropharynx, but she didn't swallow so none entered the esophagus. How did she die, then?"

"According to Dr. Maddox, cause of death is more than likely cardiac or respiratory arrest secondary to some other event—meaning either of these happened after something else caused it. There were no pathological findings, other than the cancer and that wasn't advanced enough for the tumor to start causing organ failure. So, in my opinion, a drug caused her death, I just don't know which one yet. The one thing I can tell you is that yew poison was not the culprit."

"Jesus, where do we start?"

Zoe let out a long exhale. "There are only about a hundred common drugs and poisons that are routinely tested for at autopsy. And there are literally thousands of things that can cause death. It's intuition that sets me on the hunt for this *something else*. Many poisons mimic the effects of natural symptoms or a medication overdose. For example, strychnine poisoning and a tetanus infection mimic each other. The signs of oleander poisoning replicate the effect of a digitalis overdose, a drug that helps the heart beat stronger. So, I'll look for poisons that could have imitated her possible causes of death. You said she was missing for several days before she was discovered, right?"

"Yes, she was alive for five days before her death."

"My next guess is that she was given something that took that amount of time to do its job. I'll start with drugs or poisons that don't take effect immediately."

Val narrowed her eyes. "Do you think she was held somewhere purposely in order to poison her?"

"Possibly. Val, the trick with poisons is to make sure they do their job slowly—that irreversible damage is done which eventually leads to death after several days, while the drug itself dissipates from the body during the process because the person is still alive to metabolize it. An expert poisoner can avoid detection every time if they just remain patient. As I said, most poisons replicate natural symptoms and ailments. They get confused for these. And if you've administered your poison the right way, over the right time. Bingo! Dead person. Looks natural. No poisons can be detected since the body eliminated them, and you go free. It's so perfect it's beautiful."

"Are there common poisons that people use?"

"Yes, and some become *en vogue*," Zoe scoffed. "Honestly, I can spot those a mile away. Ethylene glycol, or antifreeze, is the number-one poison in the US right now. Buying it doesn't raise suspicions, especially in winter. Plus, it has a sweet taste. You can put it into anything that's already sweet and your victim can't taste it. Let me tell you that it's a nasty, nasty way to go. It forms calcium oxalate crystals which are pretty sharp. Once those crystals go through your system and arrive at your kidneys, they shred them apart. But this is all common knowledge amongst toxicologists. No one who knows what they're doing, does this kind of basic 101 poisoning. As I've said, a *skilled poisoner* knows how to do it right, in the right amounts and is patient during all of it. That's the triumvirate of skills of a master poisoner."

"Remind me never to make you angry!" Val laughed and wheeled a few feet back from Zoe. "I need to keep a safe distance."

"Hey, we all have our strengths. I have to at least claim something someone can inscribe on my gravestone."

"Ha, I'm still looking for mine!" Val got up to leave, she had her hand on the door when she turned to Zoe. "If the seeds weren't meant to kill her, why do you think they were placed in Gabrielle's mouth?"

"If the seeds are a distraction, decoy, or part of a ritual, I don't know. Either way, someone knew what they were doing with them. That was intentional."

11

It was late in the afternoon now and Val sat in her office looking over Dr. Maddox's autopsy notes, getting more and more frustrated with each flip of the page.

He reported the fact that Gabrielle didn't have seeds in her throat any further than the back of her soft palette, that none were in her stomach, and that he felt Gabrielle never swallowed once the seeds were placed in her mouth. But Val read no hard proof Gabrielle was dead before this.

"Not swallowing" doesn't indicate death. Circumstantial evidence yet again on this case.

Crap, Val threw down her pen. Circumstantial evidence usually makes a case take incidental turns. That's why they call it circumstantial. It relies on an extrapolation of the facts. What Val needed was another motive. From someone other than Gabrielle. But who would want to kill Gabrielle and Adam if Gabrielle was already potentially dying from cancer? If her cancer hadn't progressed, and this wasn't a metastasis, maybe this was a way to ensure the woman died. *Why though?* Val glanced at her watch. She and Jack were due to speak with the

Ballards, Gabrielle Morgan's next-door neighbors, in about an hour.

"Did you prepare your thoughts on the candidates for Dr. Maddox's interviews tomorrow morning?" Gwen asked as she entered their shared office and pulled up a stool next to Val. "He's wondering where it is."

Val grabbed a folder that held several résumés of those applying for the positions that had come available after the staffing upheaval eight months ago. Luckily Dr. Maddox came on board shortly after as chief. Now all they needed was a deputy medical examiner and another death scene investigator to fill the void. Dr. Maddox asked Val to give an opinion on the applicants for both jobs, though tomorrow he was only interviewing for the deputy position.

Inside her folder she had a torn piece of notebook paper listing her opinion of the candidates, which was not as detailed as she would have liked. Or even presentable. Val glanced at her watch. Damn! She didn't have much time before she had to meet Jack. No way her analysis of applicants was going to get any better before that.

"Next will be the search for our new fellow death investigator. With Howie gone too, we've been operating with a skeleton crew," Gwen said. "Did you get a chance to look through those applications yet?"

"It's next on my list." Truth was Val really couldn't bring herself to do it. Howie had been Val's partner in death scene investigation when she first arrived and he was the one who taught her everything she knew about this job. His sudden departure from the medical examiner's office was painful and she had to admit that she missed her work friend. She didn't want to deal with replacing him now. *Why can't Dr. Maddox review his own damn candidates?*

Gwen put her elbow on the counter, palm on the side of her

cheek. Wary. "It'll be nice to have some free time again. I clocked nearly seventy hours last week."

"Well I have nearly eighty." It came out a little sharp and Val immediately regretted it. Val knew Gwen was fully aware of Val's stress with this issue, but her reaction was uncalled for. "Sorry."

"Really, it's okay, Val. I know what you're going through." Gwen's hand went to Val's, reassuring.

She smiled at her friend and held her hand tightly. Val's phone vibrated and she looked down to see who had left a message. Her stomach dropped.

"What is it?" Gwen shot up. "You've gone pale."

Val didn't pick her head up from the screen. "It's the prosecutor from Clearwater, Florida. The one who's handling the case of the man who bit me, the suspected serial killer." The moment Val had been dreading, the moment she had pushed as far away from her as she could, was here. And as she remained glued to the phone she wished it to not be true. The prosecutor left a simple text:

We're going forward next month. We need to start prepping you for the stand. Now.

Val's hands were shaking. "Gwen, I don't know if I can do this. I don't want to look at him again." Val hated to feel like this—a victim. After her attack, she hid away from everything. Her job at the medical examiner's office had been a rebirth of sorts for her. And she just wanted to put that part of her life behind her and not relive it. Jesus, Val understood why victims don't want to confront their attackers. But Val also had her other reason for not wanting to testify. While she was a victim of Mr. Tate, he bit her and he ended her dental career, Val just wasn't sure he was a murderer. "Gwen, I wasn't convinced by the dental evidence I collected. What if he didn't kill those women? This is a capital case. It's not a jail sentence. It's life or death."

"That's the question this trial will answer." Gwen placed her hands on Val's shoulders. "You have to do this. There's a lot riding on this case. Val, you're one of the strongest women I know for going through all that you have. You can stand up to this guy, as well as the judicial system. Hell, I've seen how you stand up to people and it's not pretty for them. I don't want to be in the way of a Valentina Knight wrath."

Val smiled. The woman she once was shone through at times. This other one, though, the victim, made her want to cower in the corner. That victim reared her head less and less these days. "You do know you've just put a lot on my plate. Serve justice and conquer its ills all in one swoop."

"And not mess up your hair in the process." Gwen laughed, and then her face became serious. "All joking aside. You need to do this."

"You're right." Val stood up. "You know, I think my problem is I'm just a magnet for psychos."

"Aren't we all at some point in our lives?" Gwen said wryly. "Anyway, I'm here for you through this. Remember that. And I plan on being on that plane with you when you go to Florida to testify. So, look through those applications so we can hire someone. We both can't be away from this place without some help to cover for us."

"Thanks." Val meant it. Gwen was a good friend and she couldn't believe how lucky she was to have her.

"Now, if you want to give me that sad-looking torn sheet of paper with your candidate opinions, I'll type it up and make something presentable before I give it to Dr. Maddox for you." Gwen curled her fingers in a "hand it over" motion which Val complied with. "Now, you need to contact the prosecutor." Gwen shut the door as she left.

Val hit reply quickly before she lost the courage to do so. Every ounce of her willed the voicemail to come on. No such luck.

"Valentina, how are you doing? The new job going well for you?" the prosecutor, Haywood Sinclair sang in his unmistakable southern drawl. Though he's the district attorney for Clearwater, Florida, he's originally from Mississippi. Val cringed. He had this annoying habit of calling her now ten-month-old job, *the new job*, every single damn time she spoke to him.

"Yes, things are fine."

"Val, Dennis Tate is finally coming up for trial and we need *you* to testify. You *are* my star witness, you know."

Hayward also liked calling Val "my star witness" too, and in a way that implied no other witnesses existed. Val was convinced this was his method of persuading all those who were reluctant to take to the stand. *I need you and only you can do this.* Jesus, this guy didn't get to be a district attorney for nothing. And it did work. Val had to admit she immediately felt guilty for wanting to bag out, because she now felt obligated to join the crusade.

She had to remind herself, *I don't want to do this.* "Any chance that you can go forward without me?"

"None. Look, Val, this man robbed you of your career. He stole the lives of several women and you have the ability to see that he pays for it. *Your* voice can speak for those who can't. We need you, Val. I have to admit my case hinges on your testimony. Without you, a killer *can* go free. And I know you are too strong and too courageous to let that happen. You alone have a chance to make a difference."

Bravo Hayward. Who in the hell says no to that?

Haywood was a master at this "reeling a witness in" crap. Though Val was being lulled into donning armor, raising her sword and saying an eager *YES*, she still resisted.

The shaky, unreliable, evidence made her hesitate. A man could die if she said the wrong thing, or got led to say the wrong thing by a skilled attorney. "How is that possible? You have other witnesses, bitemark experts."

There was the briefest of pauses and then a small sigh. Hayward was just building momentum for a point he now needed to make. Val had been down this road with him before.

"Four highly respected bitemark experts said that he was a match and another three, who were not of the other experts' stature, said 'absolutely not.'" Hayward sighed again, and there was contempt in the huff. "These charlatans will confuse a jury. To add to that, a set of bitemark researchers, a husband and wife, said that it was scientifically impossible to make a match. This is new information.

"Val, what the defense is doing is trying to muddy the waters, create doubt in a juror's mind. Confuse them into acquitting. That's all they have. Without *your* testimony, which is ironclad and firsthand, told from a survivor, we have a chance of losing this case. *I know you don't want that.*" The way Hayward said the last sentence made Val herself seem she'd be guilty of the crime if she didn't testify.

"Scientifically impossible?" Val said, picking up on these words through the rhetoric. "How am I supposed to outdo that?"

"Don't worry about the science, Val, the husband and wife are not bitemark experts. They've not looked at real world cases, neither of them. Only the experts know what to look at, how to read a bitemark. You've had direct confrontation with this man. You know what he's capable of. Don't forget that. That will outweigh any *scientific* evidence. You're a dentist too, just like all of our respected experts—who can compare his teeth to a wound and a victim of his. Your testimony matters more than any other."

Val knew Haywood was right. Her testimony would mean

more. The most, really. She had been bitten by this man. Who in the hell cares about science that's saying you really can't compare a bite in skin to the set of teeth that created it, when you have that? A man's life hung in the balance, though, and Val would be the deciding factor. She hated Mr. Tate, she freely and fully admitted to that. But what Val had in her grasp was the balance to decide if he lived or died. Maybe this was her biggest quandary. Everyone has to look in the mirror at the end of the day and accept what they've done, their decisions, actions. Could Val wield truth here? The real truth. Could the law? Was Mr. Tate a serial killer or just a crazy man who bit her.

Val hadn't been listening to Hayward, because she had been lost in her own thoughts in the last minute or two. Her silence must have weighed on him because he started to go into new arm-twisting territory. "This man can't be loose on the streets. Look at what he did to *you*. If those cops weren't outside your door the day of the attack..."

Val still didn't respond. Hayward's remarks only opened old wounds. Those cops brought this man to her office to begin with. They left him alone with her while they took a call. Cause and effect do not erase cause alone. They weren't her saviors. They caused the problem. And had to *correct* it afterwards.

"Val, proper cross-examination will always bring out the faults in science."

Val wasn't that naive. Cross-examination is not about the truth, but about who argues better. There is no correction here. No righting of wrongs. The most convincing side wins, not the most righteous. Because, in the end, it is never about the truth but rather, who tells the most persuasive story. *Isn't it always?*

Val was still silent. She didn't want to do this and yet she couldn't say no.

"Val, you won't be there alone. My entire firm is rooting for you and my team will be in the courtroom with you. Along with the cameras. This is going to make the national news. Honestly, it already has. Take a look at the papers. I've made sure they've mentioned you as *the star witness*." Val could feel the hook come firmly into her mouth on the sentence.

Great. National news. They'll all congratulate Val for putting a serial killer behind bars. No one will pat her on the back for letting a potential one go by not testifying. She was definitely stuck between the rock and hard place. "Just tell me what I have to do."

She listened for her instructions, then hung up. Haywood would start prepping Val for the stand in the next couple of weeks. He'd send her the questions he'd ask on direct examination; she'd give her answers; and then Haywood would run her through a mock cross-examination. They'd practice as many times as Val needed. Her stomach twisted. This was real and there was no turning back.

She pushed all this from her mind. She had to. Jack was waiting for her. The trial for Dennis Tate may be next month but the Gabrielle Morgan case was in full swing right now. Val quickly ran to the women's changing room to get out of her scrubs. Jack was picking her up in fifteen minutes. She was eager to hear what the Ballards, Gabrielle Morgan's next-door neighbors, had to say.

12

It was just past 6pm and already dark when Val and Jack parked in front of the house Gabrielle Morgan owned in Amherst, NY. The street consisted of small Cape Cod and ranch-style homes. It was a normal middle-income neighborhood and the suburb had been voted for a number of years as one of the safest in the country. The fact that Gabrielle and her son died in Clarence, less than fifteen miles away, and not at her home in Amherst helped to maintain that record.

"This is a far cry from the place she grew up in," Val said.

"Certainly is," Jack said. "I drove by her parents' place a couple of days ago. Pretty impressive. Beats the two-story brick detached house I grew up in back in the UK. In Surrey."

Val eyed the tiny ranch Gabrielle was living in. "So, she gave up money... lots of money... for..." Val struggled for the answer. "Love? For Perry?"

"When facts in a case don't make sense, they're usually not *facts* but rather fallacies instead." Jack shook his head. "No. I don't buy the love angle. Giving up profound wealth for love only works in story books. In real life, we bite off our noses to spite our faces for something like revenge. Not true love."

"What if the person isn't mentally balanced? Facts won't make sense either," Val stressed. "Perry, her ex-husband, said Gabrielle had mental issues."

"Don't forget that we only have his account of Gabrielle's mental state. And that he was a person she was trying to screw over too." Jack looked at his watch. "We'd better go in. I told Mrs. Ballard that we'd be here by six. It's ten past, and I've seen the window curtains open twice since we've parked."

As Val opened the car door, her stomach knotted, as if she just realized what she was about to do was wrong. She knew she was stepping over her job description boundaries here. Yes, Val could interview people, in fact she was expected to, but only those who could help determine cause and manner of death for any case that she was investigating. Since Gabrielle disappeared and died six days after Jennifer Ballard saw her, this neighbor really couldn't add anything for Val. This was Gavin's witness, not hers. Nonetheless, she desperately wanted to walk this fine line to gather any information she could. Gavin usually never yelled at her for overstepping, especially when she brought him useful information, something he couldn't get from a witness. Small female, non-threatening, this described Val. People let their guard down around her, and she used this to her advantage. Since Jack was a private investigator, they spoke with him of their own free will. Many were happy to do so. To gossip. To tell their story. To feel important.

To maybe sway a case in the wrong direction? Val knew that was a possibility too, but they'd have to be smart enough, not to mention *ballsy*, to do that. Few are good enough to pull it off, so Jack had told her.

They got out of the car and walked up the driveway to the front door. It opened before they had a chance to knock. A tall, thin woman in dark-washed skinny jeans, light brown Ugg boots, and white turtle-neck sweater stood in the doorway. She had long straight blonde hair, parted in the middle, and dark brown eyes. Val guessed her age to be late twenties, early thirties at a stretch. A small boy about six or seven years old stood behind her. "You must be Jack Styles and Valentina Knight. I've been waiting for you."

Jack smiled. "Yes, we are. Mrs. Ballard?"

"Jennifer. Please call me Jennifer." She smiled too and opened the door wide. "Come in." Jennifer stepped aside, pulling the boy with her as Jack and Val entered. "Just leave your coats on the coat rack." She pointed to the wooden structure already holding one too many parkas, and closed the door. "I still can't believe what happened. It's such a tragedy," Jennifer said. The boy wiggled, trying to get free of his mother's grasp. She held hard, smiling. "This little kiddo is my son, Toby." She tousled the boy's hair. "My husband, Ron, is still at work, he got held up, but should be home soon. I know you wanted to talk with him too."

With her coat off, boots on a mat by the door, Val rubbed her hands together, warming them from the cold outside. "We can chat with you for now, if that's okay."

Jennifer nodded and led them all into the kitchen. Each took a seat around the table. Toby stuck to his mother's side, trying to get on her lap. "Why don't you go watch a cartoon, Toby. Mommy needs to talk with these people." Toby finally did what his mother said and as soon as he was out of the room, Jack began.

"How long had Gabrielle lived next door?"

"She was here when we moved in, so at least a year."

"Did you know her well?" Jack asked.

"Not as well as most next-door neighbors would know each other. She was pleasant but not outwardly friendly. We waved and said hello but that was about it. I invited her in for coffee once but she refused." Jennifer shrugged. "I've never set foot in her house or she in mine. It's a shame because I thought our kids could play together. Toby's a little younger than Adam was but at this age range it doesn't matter. It's not until they get into their tweens that they care." She let out a sigh. "Gabrielle tended to not let Adam out of her sight. It's not healthy for a child to have such an overprotective parent."

"Did you ever get a chance to talk to Adam without his mother around?" Val asked.

Jennifer shook her head. "Never."

"What about Toby?" The little boy was in the next room, sitting on the couch, remote control in hand. Cartoon character voices, totally unfamiliar to Val, were singing in the background. "Did he ever talk to Adam?"

"A couple of times, when Gabrielle and I bumped into each other and chatted in the driveway."

"How did she appear the morning she disappeared?" Jack asked.

"She seemed to be in a hurry, but she could have been moving fast because it was pretty cold that day. Adam had his head down and got into the passenger side. He didn't look up when I yelled hello and waved."

"Gabrielle *did* wave back?" Val remembered what the missing person's report documented.

"Well, as good as she could." Jennifer laughed. "It was pretty blustery. She raised one hand up but she grabbed her hood with the other to hold it in place. I even yelled a joke about the crappy weather. I only remember because my own hood blew off right after that."

"She wore a hood?" Val asked.

The door opened and a sandy-haired man entered. He stopped in the doorway, staring at the people sitting around his kitchen table. This must be Ron.

"Daddy!" Toby came running and jumped into the man's arms.

"Hey, buddy," the man said as he picked up his son.

"Ron." Jennifer stood up. "This is Valentina Knight and Jack Styles. The ones I told you were coming tonight. They're investigating what happened to Gabrielle, from next door."

"What can we help you with?" Ron set Toby down and took off his coat. He wore a V-neck gray sweater with a work logo over a white button-down shirt, and navy slacks. He must have been around five foot eight or nine. He was the same height as his wife, but was spread out around the middle. Honestly, Val didn't see Jennifer and Ron as a couple. She was attractive and he was... well, he was rather plain and stocky. Val immediately hated herself for having such a superficial, judgmental response to this poor man. Toby clung to his father's side.

"We're looking for any information that can help in determining the circumstances surrounding Gabrielle Morgan's death," Jack said. "So really, anything you tell us might be useful."

"Toby, why don't you go back to the living room, honey," Jennifer said. He looked at his mother, hesitating, and then glanced at his father.

"Do what your mother says." This time Toby obeyed, running off to watch his cartoons again.

Ron pulled out a chair and sat at the table, shrugging. "There's nothing to tell. She was quiet and didn't socialize much. We invited her over a few times but she never accepted the invitation. Finally, you get the hint and stop asking."

"Did you have any idea she was *a Morgan*?" Jack asked.

"Oh God no!" Jennifer jumped forward, giddy by the fact. "Morgan is such a common name, but in Buffalo with that kind of Morgan... It was a shocker when we found out on the news that someone that rich was living right next door, wasn't it,

Ron?" Jennifer opened her eyes up wide. "You really don't know who your neighbors are, do you?"

Val glanced over to get Ron's reaction, he crossed his arms, frowning slightly. Val couldn't help but feel that the news reports weren't the first time he learned who his neighbor really was. Suddenly he changed his expression. Val sensed that he had caught her watching him.

"It's funny how you can live right next door to someone for so long and know nothing about them. I used to comment to Jennifer all the time that something wasn't right with that woman. Honestly, I'm not surprised by what happened," he said. "Being so secretive and all. But one of those Morgans. Wow! That floored us."

"Did she get much company?" Jack asked.

Jennifer immediately shook her head but her husband hesitated in his reaction. "No." It took him a second to say it.

Val chimed in. "Gabrielle might have had a couple of friends stop by... two blonde-haired women?" Val thought of Bethany and Melinda.

Both Ballards heads shook in unison this time.

"Mrs. Ballard, do you work?" Jack asked. Val's ears perked up. The reason she and Jack were here tonight was to find out about Jennifer Ballard's work schedule. The neighbor across the street commented that the nights Jennifer worked late, Gabrielle's lights tended to stay on longer than usual.

"Yes, part-time. Tuesday and Thursday nights from 4pm until 11pm at Route 5. I bartend. Then every other Saturday 10pm to close at the Old Pink in Allentown."

"Close is 4am," Val said. She had been to the Old Pink enough times in her early twenties to have had the distinction of being a *regular*. Jesus, the mention of the name brought memories flooding back. Dark bar, pounding alternative music, bottled beer, tequila shots, people dressed in black, questionable bathroom, and the overall sense that you were beyond cool for hanging out there. "That must be tough."

"Yeah, but the money is great," Jennifer said.

"Do you have a babysitter for Toby on the weekdays?" Jack asked.

"No, Ron's home by three on those days and Toby's with him."

Jack gave Ron a nod. "My nephew used to have fits the nights his mother worked late. I still remember my brother saying that getting the boy to sleep was nearly impossible."

"We don't have a problem at bedtime," Ron responded plainly. "Dinner, a few cartoons and he's just about out by eight."

"Any secrets I can pass on to my brother? My niece is starting to do the same thing." Jack smiled.

Ron shrugged. "We've never had an issue getting our son to go to sleep. We set rules and he follows them."

Val had to admit that this was a very well-behaved little boy. He'd been sitting quietly watching his cartoons since she and Jack arrived, only momentarily being a little defiant when Ron came home. But then he immediately did as his father told him.

"Children tend to grow out of those kind of things," Jennifer chimed in.

"You're right, I guess my brother might have some hope after all... in a few years." Jack laughed and turned his attention back to Mrs. Ballard. "Jennifer, seeing that you work late on Thursday nights, how did it come to be that you were outside at 7:40am on the day Gabrielle disappeared? That would have been a Friday morning, right after a late-night shift."

"Oh, I'm always up. I need to be. I have to put Toby on the school bus at 7:30. I went out to the grocery store after that. Since I don't work on Fridays, I found it's a great time to shop. Not many people at the store at that hour. Gabrielle was running out to her car as I got into mine."

"Adam didn't take the bus?" Jack asked.

"No, Gabrielle always drove him."

Given Gabrielle's habits with her son, Val already knew this fact, but there was one thing that did shock her. "You don't park in the garage? *Gabrielle* either?" Val looked out the window and pointed, smiling politely. "It's winter out there. Would have helped on those blustery mornings."

"We have a single car detached. Gabrielle has the same thing. I'm not sure why she parked outside but there's no way we're getting a car into ours. Not with all of the stuff we store in there." Jennifer laughed. "I don't think we'd be able to get another bicycle in there let alone a car."

"Fair enough!" Val laughed too. "Seems everything I try to discard ends up in my garage instead. I don't use it for my car either."

Jennifer Ballard chuckled, but Ron smirked. He shifted in his seat, and glanced at his watch. It was only then that Val realized they had been in the home for nearly an hour.

"If there's nothing more, we should be starting dinner." Ron Ballard took another look at his watch, then glanced at the clock on the wall, to emphasize the time.

Jennifer nodded in agreement. "It is getting late. If I don't start some food soon, the quiet little boy in the next room won't be so quiet anymore."

"Well, thank you both for meeting with us. This has been most helpful." Val rose from her chair. "If we can think of anything else, any other questions, would it be okay to give you a call?"

"Of course," Jennifer said. Ron nodded.

After Val had her coat on, she looked at Ron, specifically the logo on his shirt, and asked one final question. "I'm sorry, Mr. Ballard, to be so rude as to not have asked this earlier. What kind of work do you do?"

"I sell cars. High-end resales at Exclusive Auto. BMWs, Audis, Mercedes." Ron reached into his pocket and pulled out a card. "Call me if you're ever in the market." Val took the card and glanced at the front before politely putting it in her pocket. A high-end auto was not on her shopping list.

Once outside Jack said, "He was without his wife three evenings out of the week. Confirmed."

"You think Gabrielle and Ron were having an affair? Why?"

"Why do I think so? Isn't it obvious?" Jack lingered on the words like a dare.

"I mean why *Ron*?"

13

———

Val sighed. "Plus, what would they have done with the kids? How would Toby not have at least mentioned to his mother that his father was having a *friend over*. Plus, how did they get from one person's house to the other without someone seeing. The neighbor commented only on Gabrielle Morgan's lights being on, not witnessing one of them traipsing over to the other's house, Jack. Though Ron seems to know more about Gabrielle than he's letting on, the logistics of an affair don't make sense."

"Toby's six and Adam was eight. They would have been in bed somewhere between eight and 9pm at the latest. If Gabrielle and Ron hooked up then, that's plenty of time before Jennifer Ballard gets home from work," Jack said. "Getting back to your question of *why Ron*, let's try this; Ron Ballard knew something about Gabrielle, and he was blackmailing her. The payment was sex, because what else could she really give him, especially if he thought she was a poor, single mother living in the house next door. Then he finds out she was a bajillionaire and kicks himself in the ass for wanting sex and not money. You could see it on his face, Val, he knew about the money. Too late for him, though."

Jack laughed. "The man's a damn salesman. He convinces people to spend more cash on a car than they probably can afford. And couldn't manage to put a penny in his own pocket with Gabrielle, but he probably did manage to put his—"

Val held her hand up in the air. "Okay. Enough." She stood still and let out a breath in the frigid night air, a cloud of condensation forming around her. "Jack, I think your mind works in devious ways."

He put his arm around Val's shoulder. "My dear Val, you have to think like a deviant to catch one. That's why I'm so successful."

"Ha! What about Jennifer, then. What are your thoughts on her?"

"Did she know her husband was possibly shagging the neighbor, is that the question?" Jack stopped and put his hands in his pockets. "If Gabrielle Morgan didn't take her own life, then someone she knew *very well* killed her. By all accounts, Jennifer barely knew her at all."

"The fact that she didn't know Jennifer very well was only reported by Jennifer." Val smiled, remembering Jack's comment about Perry Logan. *Only Perry reported Gabrielle had mental issues.*

"Ron and Jennifer confirmed separately that as a couple they hardly knew Gabrielle at all. There's a difference."

"Yes, but there are long stretches of the day when Jennifer is home without Ron; her social activities could have changed at any time. Same goes for Ron. And if he's shagging the neighbor, he's certainly not going to be comparing notes with his wife about her."

"Now who's thinking like a deviant?" Jack smirked.

"I'll add one more deviant detail. All of Gabrielle's friends have been pretty blondes, like herself. Bethany, Melinda. Jennifer could have easily fit into that clique."

"Excellent observation, Val," Jack said. "But if that's the case, why is *she* with Ron? The used car salesman. And living with him in a modest house."

"Gabrielle also ended up living in a modest house," Val reminded him.

"That she did. I'm teaching you very well now, aren't I?" Jack said. "Your thought process is amazing."

"I aim to impress."

They continued to walk towards the car but then Jack stopped outside Gabrielle's house. The front porch light was on, as well as a few lights in the house. *Probably all on a timer*, Val thought.

"Val, have you been in there at all?"

"No. I really don't have a reason to. This is not where she died. There's no one to question living in the house. The crime scene techs have already gone through it and found nothing unusual. I don't know what more I can add." Val looked at the driveway and noted wooden posts on each side of it, from the street up to the front of the house. Markers for a snowplow service. The markers ended at the house making it obvious that Gabrielle didn't have her driveway plowed further down, to where the garage was. This is why she didn't park in her garage. She couldn't. But why not just plow the entire driveway and use the damn garage?

"Maybe we should take a look. Examining crime scenes is *my* specialty."

"Jack, that's called breaking and entering. I thought you just said *think* like a deviant, not *act* like one."

Jack pointed. "It has a lock box on the door. Do you have the combination?"

The lock box would open with a combination, and inside would be a key to the house. The same system is used by real estate agents. It's so that anyone wanting to enter the residence will have the means.

"Yes. I typically get them for all cases I'm part of," Val said slowly, sensing what was coming next.

"Then that's not breaking and entering." Jack smiled. "Val, when you have legitimate means to access a residence or establishment then nothing you're doing, when you enter, is criminal. I seem to remember pointing this out to you before."

He did. On another case. Nonetheless, Val hesitated. Having the ability to go in still doesn't make it right. "Because I can doesn't mean I should."

"Come on, I know you *want* to do it," Jack tempted. "A *want* overrules a *should*."

She did want to. A lot. At least the crime scene tape had been removed, making it look a little less wrong to enter. "Jack, one day you're going to get me fired, or arrested."

"Neither has happened yet."

"Yah, I keep spinning the bullet in that revolver." Val pulled out her phone. "The combination should be listed in the report. Let's see if it's here." She scrolled for a few seconds. "There it is."

She punched in the correct numbers and the box opened. She pulled out the key. "Once we're inside, keep your gloves on."

Jack smiled. "I'm pretty familiar with the drill. I do know how to not get my fingerprints on anything."

Val ignored him and slipped in the key. Her heart pounded as the two entered the parlor. No foyer, just right into the parlor, which was typical in these small homes. The shoe mat was next to the door. She looked around quickly. A lone lamp illuminated the room. Just as she thought: it was plugged into a timer in the wall socket. Another light came from a room down the hall. The kitchen maybe?

"Now Dr. Knight, tell me what you see as you walk through this house. Then, I'll tell you what I see, what you missed. Should be educational for you."

"Not my first time at the rodeo. I plan on getting an A on this test." Val slipped off her boots. Jack did the same.

"Then earn one."

"Maybe, as we go through this, I'll point out what you missed." Val gave him a sharp, sideways glance.

"Of course you might." Jack smiled, patting her on the arm. "Now, tell me what you see. The first thing you notice."

Val hesitated.

"Quickly now. What's your gut instinct?" Jack pressed.

"This house is clean and neat," Val said. It certainly was, well besides the obvious signs the crime scene crew had come through here—fingerprint powder still stained most of the surfaces anyone would have touched. In the parlor sat a beige couch, two navy chairs and a console with a flat screen TV. No toys, no mess or disorder... hell it looked like no one ever used this room.

"Gabrielle was a single mother living with a young boy. She worked a full-time job. Should this house be clean and neat?"

Val thought for a minute. "Let's look at the kitchen. And then Adam's room. That will tell us just how truly neat and clean this house is."

"Slippery move, Val. Get some more information before you commit yourself to a wrong answer." Jack smiled again.

"Wrong answer? Ha! I don't think so. Never underestimate your student, Jack."

Val moved to the kitchen. Jack was right behind her. A small light gave some illumination but overall the room was dim. Val pulled out her phone and used the flashlight feature. There were no dishes in the sink. Not even a coffee cup.

"On the morning they disappeared, Gabrielle had time to clean up any breakfast dishes?" Jack asked.

"Maybe she did. Or maybe they didn't eat."

"Or maybe she cleaned up because she knew she wasn't

coming back?" Jack said. "For all the circumstantial evidence found so far, murder and then suicide in this case is still highly probable, Val, you can't lose sight of that."

Val knew Jack was right. She glanced around and then opened the fridge. "Oh my, would you look at that."

Jack looked over her shoulder.

"The refrigerator is full." Val sniffed. "Doesn't seem to be anything spoiled in here." She picked up a container of milk. The expiration date was tomorrow and the carton was unopened. "She must have bought all of this just before she disappeared. If she was planning on disappearing and killing both of them, why fill the fridge?"

Jack stepped back. "Excellent point. No dishes in a sink we can explain with many plausible answers. A full fridge is not so easy. But..."

"But?"

"Minor facts like this need to accumulate. You have to have a number of them to create some reason to pursue an investigative course that lies at odds with bigger facts that exist in the case. I'll stress again, Val, your evidence is overwhelming that Gabrielle committed suicide and took her son to the great beyond with her. We have tidbits that point otherwise. Two steps forward and three back, only takes you back. Now, let's check out Adam's room, let's see if more small facts exist and I say 'small' because if there was a smoking gun in this house, your *friend* Detective Gavin would have found it." Jack turned his back and walked down the hall.

Val caught the sarcasm in his voice and decided to leave the comment about her *friend* the detective alone. But the minor facts in this case *were* adding up

Jack stood in the doorway to Adam's room and said, "Tell me what you see in here. This is your next test." He stepped aside to let her enter.

The first thing Val noticed, other than the fingerprint powder and signs the crime scene crew had been through here, was that the bed had been made. Part of the bedding had been moved away, suggesting the crew looked under the mattress. "Either he made his own bed before leaving for school the morning he disappeared or Gabrielle did it before she left the house for work." Val glanced around. There was a desk in the corner. Books lined three shelves to the right of the desk. *Harry Potter, Goosebumps, Diary of a Wimpy Kid, The Fault in Our Stars*. Posters on the wall were of Spiderman, The Avengers; bedding was simple blue checked. Val pulled open drawers and looked in the closet. Everything was just as tidy as the living room. But it was more than that. This room was organized. "He was a neat kid. Not all of them are messy, Jack."

"I agree. So, I vote that he made his own bed. Maybe he was the one to keep the house in order too?" Jack asked. "Depressed mother, bipolar according to her ex-husband Perry; the son keeps the household together."

"Of course, that's possible." Val searched around a few more times, a little upset she didn't see the obvious Jack just pointed out.

"Anything else?"

Val crossed her arms, and walked around the room, examining everything carefully. Dammit, she saw nothing. But she knew Jack did.

After a few moments, Jack sighed. "There's a lot to take notice of here, and not just a neat kid with a made bed, who may have been taking care of his suicidal, bipolar mother."

"Then what is it, Jack?" Val couldn't help but snap.

"Val, you have to look at this room not only for evidence but also as a means to illustrate who your victim was. You have to look for things that allow you to understand what your victims would have cared about. That will tell you a lot about a person.

Or child. Understand what people do. How they live their lives. People are all different but there are trends in commonality. For example, an eight-year-old, like Adam, would have been developing social and physical skills. What type of kid was he? Artistic? Athletic? Studious? What do you see here that exemplifies these things with him?"

"He liked books. So, he was a loner?"

"No." Jack's words were clipped. "That's not what this tells us. Take a look at his schoolwork. He has some of it over there." Jack pointed to the desk and walked over to it. "At this age, eight, children like to be part of a group, so they either love school because this gives them what they need or they hate it if they're being bullied. He has old homework assignments stacked on his desk." Jack pulled out some papers. "He has A grades written on all of these." Jack's finger traced a paper calendar taped to the wall. "But more importantly, this is a school calendar and he's placed circles around the events. There's an exclamation point next to the three of them and multiple exclamation points next to the science fair and a soccer game being held in the gym. Grade three versus grade four. This tells me he liked going to school. So, he had friends there. His mother kept him isolated here, but at school, he had freedom."

"His teachers liked him," Val remembered. "He lashed out on his last day."

"Something set him off." Jack circled around. "There's one more fact here. A little one, but like I said earlier, little ones build."

At this point all Val could do was guess. She was failing Jack's test miserably. "There's no sports equipment here, and nothing is sports-themed in the room, but he's happy about a soccer game."

"Well spotted, Val, but that's not it. Let's take another look at one of the novels he was reading. *The Fault in Our Stars*. Eight-year-old children tend to be in a more imaginative mind frame. They like complex games and middle grade books that deal with issues common to them, that's why it's important that our eight-year-old has this young adult novel on his bookshelf, which makes me think he was more advanced for his years and the subject matter appealed to him. It deals with kids with cancer. Maybe he knew his mother had cancer—which meant she knew she had it—and this is why he wanted to read it—or maybe because it was highly popular with a movie and all. It's a small fact that I don't plan on discounting. You shouldn't either."

"That might be the only clue so far that points to maybe Gabrielle knowing about her cancer. Anything else I missed?"

"Let's see, an eight-year-old is also developing cognitive ability, they're learning to ask questions and draw conclusions. This means he has the ability to notice things, maybe things he shouldn't have noticed, like our neighbor Ron Ballard *wanting to have time alone with Mommy*."

"Do you think he'd talk about things like this with the kids at school?"

"If he had a good social network there, he might have become vocal, but only to those he trusted and felt comfortable with."

"Jack, how do you know so much about eight-year-old children?"

"I knew our victim was eight, so I read into it. Every age category has its psychological definitions. It's helpful to understand them, Val, if even what you learn is rudimentary." Jack glanced around and took a few steps towards the closet. "Now, thirty-seven year-old unmarried childless women, such as yourself, might be feeling very broody and possibly depressed over the likelihood of becoming an old maid. But don't worry, there's still hope for you. You're holding up well for your years." He patted Val on the cheek and grinned.

"Holding up well!" she yelled. "And what about yourself."

"*Bachelor* has a positive ring at any age. *Spinster* does not."

"I am not a spinster!"

"Of course not, dear. Now, untwist your knickers so we can get a good look in here." Jack opened the closet. "Anything obviously important was taken by the crime scene techs and the homicide detectives of course, but it never hurts to check for yourself for something they could have missed. But honestly, I see nothing more here."

Jack walked out of Adam's bedroom. Val followed him across the hall into Gabrielle's.

"By looking at this room, what can you tell me about Gabrielle?" he asked as he stood to the side of the doorway.

Val stopped dead before entering. She had to admit that she wasn't expecting to see it in such disarray. "Well, Gabrielle definitely wasn't the neat one." Jack called that one right after they inspected Adam's room. Her bed wasn't made and dirty laundry lay piled on the floor. Val walked around the clothing being careful not to step on anything. It's possible the crime scene techs created some of the chaos when going through the house looking for any evidence but they wouldn't have thrown laundry on the floor. Actually, they probably moved it out of their way so this is more than likely neater than it was.

"Yes, there is a considerable amount of disorganization here. Adam was our organized one." Jack repeated the process of checking all the dresser drawers and closet.

Val circled the pile of clothes on the floor. As she did, she noticed something shiny and bent down to inspect it. A small chain had slipped out of the pocket of a pair of jeans. Val pulled on it, tugging it out of the pocket. Once freed, a key swung from the chain. It wasn't a typical house key, it looked like a flat, short skeleton key but a little fatter, and there were several rectangular cuts in the shaft.

"Now that's interesting." Jack stood at the bedroom window, glancing out.

"What is it?" Val came to his side. The Ballards' back porch light was on, illuminating the rear yard. "I don't see anything." The key was still in her hand and she was about to show it to Jack when she saw what he had noticed. "Jesus, the fence."

"Yes. Look at how the two slats are on an angle, causing them to separate. Looks like they're loose and eventually got stuck apart in the snow as it piled up." Jack quickly headed out of the room. "Only one way to know for sure."

"Jack!" Val followed close behind. She was out of the room and down the hall before she realized she still had the key. "Jack, slow down. We're not going out there, are we?"

"You don't want to?" He was already slipping on his boots.

Val had to think of her job description and how she was already crossing over several lines, lines that could get her fired. Jack was right though. She wanted to see this. Just like coming into this house. Plus checking out a back fence outside was probably the least of her worries. She still held the key. "What kind of lock do you think this belongs to?"

Jack squinted. "Where did you get that from."

"The chain was poking out from a pocket in a pair of jeans in the laundry pile on Gabrielle's floor."

"Looks like it belongs to some type of lock box."

"What should we do with it?"

"Put it back."

"What do you mean put it back?" Val looked at Jack, dumbfounded. "Maybe I should give it to Detective Gavin." Val winced at that thought. Then she'd have to tell him she was in the house.

"No need. If there was a lock box in this house, Detective Gavin would have confiscated it and he wouldn't need the key to open it. They'd break the lock. Plus, why would Gabrielle put any kind of important key in her pocket. Then take off the piece of clothing and discard it in a laundry pile?"

Val felt relieved at those thoughts. "Okay, give me a second." She ran back to the bedroom and was about to slip the key back into the jeans pocket when she hesitated. *I can always come back and return the key in the next day or two if I have to.* Right now, she just wanted to know what it belonged to and having the key itself would help with an internet search. She put the key in her own pocket and ran back to Jack, quickly putting her boots and coat on. "I kept the key," she said as they exited.

Jack laughed. "That was my next test. It's exactly what I would have done."

"Do I get an A for today, then?"

"We're not finished yet."

Once outside, they walked along the side of the house, up the driveway, which had not been plowed, again making Val wonder why. She eyed the detached garage, which was about twenty feet behind the house. "Jack, stop."

He came to a halt. They were both ankle-deep in snow and the drifts going to the garage were only worse. "What is it?"

"Gabrielle didn't use the garage. I want to see why, what's in it." Val trudged through the snow to the side of the garage, no problem in her knee-high Cougar Canada, waterproof, thermal snow boots. Nonetheless, being outside, especially in the snow, she knew she only had a short amount of time before her leg would start to bother her and she picked up the pace. Jack was moving a little faster too. His boots were trendy leather lace-ups, barely higher on his leg than ordinary shoes. His feet must be soaking by now. There was a window on the garage wall and she placed her gloved hand around her eyes so that she could peer in. "I can't see anything."

Jack turned the handle on a door next to the window, which

opened easily. "There's no lock. When there's no lock, you should always try the door."

Val held her tongue as she stepped inside. Her jaw dropped open. "Drywall? Lots of drywall. Why would she have drywall stacked inside the garage?"

"There's lumber in here too. Framing wood. Building or redoing a room in her home? That's what it looks like."

"A home renovation? Is that the something someone contemplating suicide would do?"

"Small fact, Val. They keep adding up," Jack said. "Do you know what kind of car Gabrielle drove?"

"Good question. She left it, or someone left it, in the church parking lot where she and her son were found." Val pulled her phone back out. I'll see if it's in the report. After a few seconds, Val had her answer. She nearly dropped her phone. "Mercedes GLE."

"High-end Mercedes SUV?" Jack said. "Wonder where she got it from." His last sentence had a sarcastic ring.

"Daddy could have gotten it for her. Or maybe she walked into the dealer and bought one with her own money..." Val smiled.

"Or she got it from Exclusive Auto from her neighbor, Ron?" Jack grinned. "Is Jennifer Ballard the only witness to see Gabrielle the morning she disappeared?"

"Yes."

"Is she the only one to give an account of what happened that morning?"

"Yes, again."

They shut the garage door and plodded through the snow to the fence. Val again, was happy to be wearing her thermal boots and she used her right foot to clear away some of the snow. As soon as she did the slat swung back into place. She repeated for the next slat. Both were now straight and appeared as if nothing was wrong. "The storm the other day must have blown these out of place and then they got stuck in the drifting snow. They swung open pretty readily."

Val took a long hard look at what she was seeing. Through the open slats she had a pretty good view of the Ballards' back door.

Jack inspected the pieces. "These didn't come loose by accident. The screws are missing from the bottom. These top ones have been loosened, allowing this to swing open." He illustrated the movement by sliding them left to right, and then back again. "Val, this is why it's important to see the home where a victim lived, even if they weren't killed in the home. It tells you a lot about them and their way of living. This was deliberate. It's just enough space for someone to slip through and it certainly wouldn't have been seen by anyone since it's at the back of the house. No neighbors would have seen who's coming or going through this."

14

The next morning was crazy, and though Val wanted to run with everything she discovered last night, she couldn't right now. Four bodies had come in overnight and as Dr. Maddox worked on the autopsies, Val was called out to a crime scene at Regency Hotel on the waterfront. The maid found a man hanging from the shower head in the bathroom. Not very creative—he tied the bedsheet around his neck to do it.

And Gwen had her own case to attend to: a woman had been stabbed to death by another woman in her West Side home. A knife duel, it seemed. The winner would get the man; a drug dealer prize no one ever should have wanted.

Val read her report as she entered room 1404 at the Regency Hotel. The maid had vacuumed the rugs and changed the sheets before going out to her cart in the hallway to retrieve a bucket and scrub brushes to clean the bathroom. She entered the bathroom and immediately called the manager. The maid didn't appear distraught as she spoke to police now. Evidently a naked guy swinging from the shower was not the most disturbing thing she'd found on her cleaning rounds.

Val peered into the shower. The chair that he used to stand

on was kicked away inside the large walk-in stall and a suicide note was laid on the counter. No signs of foul play were found in the room and the surveillance camera showed no one other than this man going into the room. Open and shut, just how Val had liked them.

Val took photographs and thought if this guy were a couple of inches taller, he'd have had to find another way to do this. He only cleared the floor by that much. She then got on a chair herself and with the help of two officers, cut the man loose. There was no way she was untying the tightly wound sheet. She did a preliminary exam, reviewed lividity and rigor, then got a liver temperature. She estimated he had died between 2 and 4am.

"We can bag him to go," she told one officer. Her cell phone chimed. She knew the sound. It was Detective Gavin. His text read:

Can you meet for lunch?

Val was a little stunned. This was the first time she'd heard from him since their dinner at The Chop House. And, as with all of her past experiences with Gavin, any negative feeling she'd had towards him that night had dissolved and she looked forward to seeing him again. *God, I'm a glutton for punishment*, Val thought.

She checked the time and then quickly reviewed the paperwork for the body she was transporting before texting Gavin to agree with his suggestion of noon at the Anchor Bar.

Gavin texted back:

Got the police and autopsy report from Gabrielle's twin brother and sister, the ones who drowned in the family pool. We'll discuss when we meet.

~

When Val walked into the Anchor Bar she couldn't help but feel déjà vu. It was the Anchor Bar where she had had her first meeting with Gavin to talk about a case. That night, back then, was also the first time she realized her feelings for him.

Val had to push past the crowd of people waiting to be seated. *Jesus, it's going to take forever to get food*, she thought. Gavin was waving at her from a table. "What time did you get here?" she asked as she sat.

"About twenty minutes ago, otherwise we'd have never gotten a seat."

"Smart move." Val laughed. Menus were already on the table and an almost empty glass of what looked like Coke sat in front of Gavin. She was happy when the waitress came right over for her drink order. She asked for an iced tea and then said, "I'm ready to order if you are, Mitch."

"Go for it."

"I'll have chicken wings." She had to get them: this place was famous for them. In 1964, Teressa Bellissimo, who owned the Anchor Bar at the time, along with her husband Frank, created the "buffalo wing," which became a world-wide phenomenon. Any good Buffalonian knows how to make the sauce, and many have their own recipes for it. Buffalonians also tend to be wing snobs.

"You were reading my mind with the wings," Gavin said. "Make that two orders."

"I'll put this right in," the waitress said.

"So! You got the reports about the twins. Give me the details!" Val couldn't wait another minute.

"Yes, I finally got a copy of the police report, and the autopsy report. The Morgans worked hard to bury these back then. They weren't easy to come by," Gavin said.

"And?"

"It goes all the way from the 911 call to the final autopsy notes." Gavin pulled a packet of papers from his bag. "A call came into emergency dispatch at 2:28pm the afternoon of June 26th 2006...

Dispatcher: 911, what's your emergency?

Young female voice (Screaming): Help! My brother and sister are in the pool! They can't swim! (Sobbing) They're not moving! (More screaming)

Dispatcher: Miss, stay calm, I'm sending help (Pause— dispatcher is tracing the call). Can you tell me your name?

Young female voice: (gasps) Gabrielle.

Dispatcher: Gabrielle, how old are you?

Young female voice: Sixteen. What the hell does this have to do with anything! I need help! Now!

Dispatcher: Gabrielle, help is on the way. Can you reach them without going into the water yourself? (Call has been traced. Emergency crews and police have been dispatched.)

Young female voice: I... I don't know. But they're not moving! Oh my God! I don't know what to do! They're not moving!

Dispatcher: An ambulance will be at your house in less than two minutes...

Young female voice: No! (sobs)

Dispatcher: Gabrielle? Gabrielle!

Line goes dead.

Gavin looked up. "At this point, it's assumed Gabrielle threw the phone down, and it turned off, or she disconnected, because she did get her brother and sister out of the pool." He continued. "At 2:36pm emergency responder arrived at 130 Lincoln Parkway where they found two children, a six-year-old boy and girl unresponsive, not breathing with no pulse, on the concrete patio just outside the inground pool. Resuscitative attempts were started at the scene, continued in the ambulance, and in the hospital emergency department. CPR was given for nearly thirty minutes before being aborted. The children were pronounced dead at 3:08pm. The emergency room physician stated that he felt they had been unresponsive for some time, prior to their arrival in the ER. Autopsies of the children determined cause of death was drowning. The need for toxicological screening, and any tissue sectioning other than the lungs was deemed unnecessary."

Gavin set the report down on the table. His eyes were on Val's. He wasn't reading anymore. "Any further attempts to question Gabrielle about that day was halted by the Morgans. The only thing emphasized in this report is that Gabrielle did acknowledge she was babysitting the twins since it was the nanny's day off. She got lost in a game she was playing and when she went to check on them, they weren't in their room, where she'd left them and told them to stay until she returned. After searching the house, she went outside and found them in the pool."

"The Morgans are rich. Didn't they have other staff in the house that day?" Val couldn't believe this. "There must have been some other adults in the house."

"No, the kids were alone." Gavin exhaled deeply. "The Morgans aren't as wealthy as we think they are. They're not poor by any means but the Morgan company has had its problems. They filed for bankruptcy protection twice."

"Jesus, I didn't know that."

"Not many do."

"So for Gabrielle, a kid gets lost in a game and forgets the time. A tragedy occurs..." Val said. "Could be why she was so protective of Adam. Why she wouldn't let him out of her sight. The twins drowned because Gabrielle wasn't watching them. She doesn't make that mistake again," Val said. "Mourning, pain, and regret all last a lifetime."

Gavin's pause told Val otherwise. "There's one more thing that's important about the 911 call." His eyes were on Val.

"What's that?"

"Gabrielle was lying."

"Holy shit! About what?" Several other diners glared at Val with her outburst and she mumbled quick apologies.

Gavin picked up the report and began reading again. "It is of interest to add the suspected time of death is estimated to be up to an hour *before* the 911 call. This was based on liver temperatures." Gavin looked up. "At an hour after death there was no rigor yet, so there was no reason to doubt Gabrielle that the accident recently occurred. Could be why emergency crews even attempted CPR."

"If Gabrielle found them after they had been floating for a while she might not have known how long they were in the water," Val tried.

"That's not what she lied about," Gavin's gaze remained locked on Val. "The twins were already out of the water when she called 911. Probably about thirty minutes out of the water by that time."

Val's eyes opened wide. "Are you sure?"

"Yes. The responding officer noted concerns in his report because the children's clothes weren't soaked, but damp, which was inconsistent for only a less than eight-minute time span from receiving the call to arriving on scene, even with the warm weather which was eighty-two degrees that day. Certainly not hot enough to start drying the clothes in that length of time, suggesting the children were out of the water for a much longer time span than Gabrielle claimed. Gabrielle denied any discrepancies in time, though. The officer did say that she was traumatized, and it was hard to get a timeline of events from her, as questioning was difficult."

"Two orders of wings," the waitress sang and dropped

baskets in front of both Val and Gavin. Gavin picked up a wing, dipped an end in blue cheese and took a bite. Val did the same.

"Dammit, Mitch. This case doesn't make sense. Everything that goes in one direction ends up traveling down a different path."

"That it does."

Val licked hot sauce from her fingers. "I met two of her childhood friends at the funeral, one was Bethany Arias, Gabrielle's emergency contact for Adam."

Gavin's eyebrows shot up. It was at this moment that Val realized she had never filled Gavin in on what she learned and proceeded to give him a summary of Bethany and Melinda, and also the fact that Bridget was not there. And why.

"Bethany at least, has a pretty good feeling of what Gabrielle was like, before and after the twins died. I'm planning on talking with these women soon."

"Good. I want you to do that ASAP."

"You know, Mitch, I'm convinced they were still seeing each recently, though they aren't admitting to it." Val took another wing. "This is what concerns me... Gabrielle was using Bethany as an emergency contact but the number was old and not in service. Since the number wasn't updated, this tells us they did lose touch. But I think something brought them back together. It was obvious at the funeral that Melinda and Bethany were familiar with each other, that Melinda was trying to get Bethany away from me. I think Gabrielle fits in here somewhere with them, and this is why Melinda and Bethany are trying so hard to make it look like they've been estranged this whole time. Because unless something was going on between all three of them, there's no reason to make it look like they had nothing to do with each other. There's something that the two living ones don't want us to know about."

"I'm glad you're talking to them because they might open up to you more than they would with me."

Val thought of Jennifer Ballard, another pretty blonde. Did she fit in here as well? But how to mention it to Gavin that she had spoken to the Ballards and been in Gabrielle's house so that he wouldn't blow a gasket? Honestly, he'd only blow a gasket if he knew Jack had been with her. Sometimes the best way to get something out in the open is to simply come clean.

"I met the Ballards last night," she said bluntly, purposely leaving Jack out of the story. "I got a lead, so did some digging."

"You did?" Gavin raised his eyebrows. Val could see that he was trying to read into this, and she held her breath. "What did you think of them? The Ballards."

She exhaled, relieved he didn't press further on why she would do this. "I got the feeling the husband knew Gabrielle more than he's saying. He might have been having an affair with her." Val stretched the truth here by omitting that this was Jack's assumption.

"What made you think that?" He set down his next wing and wiped his hands on his napkin.

Val explained about Ron Ballard's reaction to the questions and also about the detached wooden slats in the back fence. "I have an odd feeling about Jennifer Ballard, too."

"In what way?"

"She's the only witness that saw Gabrielle the morning she disappeared." Val went further into the discussion, maybe out on a limb, when she finally disclosed how all of Gabrielle's friends were pretty blondes and Jennifer could have easily fit into this group. Val expected Gavin to laugh at her for such a wild assumption, but he pulled a small notebook out of his coat pocket and jotted something down. Val saw that it said Jennifer Ballard. Gavin drew a circle around her name.

"I'll run a background check on Jennifer. Maiden name,

where she attended high school, college and so forth." Gavin still had his head down, writing notes on his pad.

"There's more." Now how to tell Gavin about the key she found in Gabrielle's house? Sometimes it's just best to keep coming clean. Or as clean as you can.

Gavin stopped mid scrawl.

"I took a look in Gabrielle Morgan's house too."

Gavin held his gaze on Val's. "Why?"

Here it comes. He let the Ballards *why* slip by but not this one. At this moment Val wished she had a stiff drink to take refuge in. The rest of the conversation was going to be painful.

Gavin raised his eyebrows even further, cocked his head, and then pursed his lips. "*Val...*"

"I know. I know. What I did was wrong. But I had a tip that I wanted to follow."

"How did you come by this *tip*? After the *lead*. Both of which you decided not to share with *me*."

Val looked around, straightened a wrinkle in the tablecloth, and repositioned the napkin on her lap. Twice. "I'd rather not say."

"Dammit, Val." Gavin shot back in his chair and shook his head. After a second or two he came forward again and curled his finger for Val to sit forward too, to come closer, to listen to what he had to say. "There's a proper way to conduct an investigation. You work for the medical examiner's office, not the damn Hardy Boys."

He knew about Jack, that he was behind this. It was obvious. Val cringed, but came forward and met Gavin's eyes. There was something she had to get out, put out in the open between them. "Mitch, you normally don't have a problem when I investigate leads. What gives now?" She knew this was personal for Gavin. Would he admit to it?

Gavin took a breath. "What did you find? You must have

found something otherwise we wouldn't be having this conversation."

Val also took a deep breath. "I found a key."

Val mentioned nothing about *keeping* the key.

As far as Gavin was concerned, she left it in Gabrielle's pocket. He did, however, confirm that no lock box was confiscated from Gabrielle's house.

15

The first thing Val did the next day was leave voicemail messages for both Bethany Arias and Melinda Holbright asking them to meet with her as soon as possible.

Now, Val sat in her office, reviewing the police and autopsy reports from fifteen years ago, from the twins drowning. Gavin gave her a copy of both. If Dr. Maddox also saw the post-mortem results, he didn't share his opinions with Val. There was good reason for it, because there really was nothing to be gained. What was done back then fit in line with the most rudimentary of autopsies she'd ever read about. Basically, this report said nothing beyond the obvious. The twins drowned. End of story. This autopsy was an orchestrated formality so that the ugly incident could be swept under the rug for the wealthy Morgan family, so that their daughter wouldn't be dragged over hot coals. Gabrielle was supposed to be watching the twins and she screwed up.

The question now was just how much.

The timeframe in the police report was the big question. Gabrielle, or someone else, removed the children from the water about thirty minutes before the 911 call. There was no way they were still floating when Gabrielle made that call. Scared kid, not knowing what to do? Plausible, but the more Val read, the more she realized the entire call was nothing more than theatrics. Which was not innocent. Suggesting Gabrielle knew exactly what she was doing. Or what she thought she should do. She was only sixteen after all. But at the age of sixteen, Gabrielle attempted a cover-up.

As Val googled, searching for any news at the time, Gabrielle's name, the Morgan name, was noticeably missing. There was simply nothing about this tragedy out there. The story of Gabrielle's life, apart from maybe a few rare moments, was not on the internet.

Val's fingers clicked through the posts quickly, scrolling from page to page. At the end of each one she swore this would be the last. Wasting her time, that's what she was doing. One news source, ten pages deep in Val's query caused her fingers to pause, the cursor hovering over the text, at the article headline: *Gabrielle Morgan, Daughter of John Morgan, of Morgan Foods, Was Not Alone at the Family Home When her Brother and Sister Drowned.* Val frowned. Seemed like a muddled, crappy, non-reliable news post from a rag of a publication that had gone out of business not long after this story came out. Then Val saw two names. Bethany Arias and Melinda Holbright—confirmed to be at the house the day of the drownings. Val's heart pounded. She read further.

The maid from the house next door was in front of the kitchen window doing the dishes and saw the girls running from the Morgans' back door, which was the servant's entrance. Not long after, she heard ambulance sirens. The maid, Ingrid Gruber, said there was only about a ten-minute lag in time between the girls running out and the sirens blaring. She knew because she had something cooking in the oven and was using the timer.

Val clicked through the photos in the article and shot back from the screen on the third one. The pictures taken back then, of the maid, of Ingrid... holy crap, she was the spitting image of Jennifer Ballard now.

Val now typed Ingrid Gruber and Jennifer Gruber. Nothing came up. Val's next search, Ingrid Gruber and Gabrielle Morgan. Several articles popped up, all describing Ingrid as an unreliable witness with an unreliable story. She had a documented drug and alcohol problem and made multiple attempts to blackmail the Morgans before being committed to a rehab facility, where she later died. Seems she fell and cut her leg while in the facility. The wound became gangrenous and she died from sepsis.

"Are you almost done?" Gwen said as she entered their shared office. "Want to grab some lunch?"

"Almost," Val said, her eyes glued to the story about Ingrid Gruber.

"I can go for Thai. Sound good?" Gwen leaned against the wall.

"Sure... Gwen, you have to see all of this." Val motioned for her colleague to look at the screen.

Gwen peered over Val's shoulder. As she did, Val's phone buzzed and she looked to see who was calling. She nearly dropped the device.

"Who is it?" Gwen asked. She must have seen Val's reaction.

"It's Bethany Arias." Val let the message go to voicemail, so she could have time to digest this with everything else she just learned. She waited a second and then replayed, letting Gwen listen with her.

"Hi, it's Bethany Arias. I'm returning your call." The voice had a singsong, nonchalant quality to it. "Yes, I agree we should talk. There are a few things that my friend Melinda and I would like to chat with you about. Can you meet for lunch tomorrow at my house?" At this point, the tone became a little less laid-back.

"We thought a private meeting would be better than a restaurant."

Hell yes. Val asked Gwen, "Can you do tomorrow?"

Gwen nodded.

Val's fingers typed and then hovered over the keypad.

I can meet tomorrow. My partner Gwen is available too. What time? Where?

It only took seconds for the answer to show up on Val's screen.

Noon, 36 Waterfront Circle, unit 501

"That's perfect for me," Gwen said.

Val typed in *See you then*, but hesitated. She deleted that and sent off:

Can we make it 1:30 instead?

"Why are you changing the time?" Gwen asked, irritated. "I said twelve was perfect. I can't do 1:30. Why didn't you ask me? 1:30 isn't even lunchtime."

Val held up her hand, signaling for Gwen to stop. "Just wait."

It took a few seconds longer this time for a response, but it still came quickly.

That will work.

"Won't work for me," Gwen said.

"Exactly. How did Bethany know the change in time would work for Melinda? She responded too quickly for a text or phone call."

"Your point?"

"They're together typing this, just like we are," Val said, then responded to the text.

On second thoughts twelve is much better, see you at the original time.

16

Thirty-six Waterfront Circle happened to be a five-story luxury building directly on Buffalo's waterfront. Bethany's condo, unit 501, was the top floor, the penthouse. Val remembered that at one time, Gabrielle also had a waterfront condo.

"Wonder what she does to afford this?" Val said as she and Gwen stood outside. Val turned her head to the side to protect her face as the wind gusted with razor-sharp intensity. Small pellets of loose icy snow smacked her hard, and she winced.

"Her family is wealthy, Val. She doesn't need to do anything." Gwen tightened her scarf and put a hand up to shield her eyes. Both women rushed to the door. Val pushed the button on an intercom for unit 501 and waited until a bell sounded and a woman's voice said, "Please come in."

Once inside the voice on the intercom came on again. "Please take the last elevator at the end of the hall. The one with the green door. It goes directly to unit number 501. I'll take care of everything once you're inside." The voice was cheery. Val and Gwen made their way down the hallway.

There were no buttons for the elevator, nothing other than a keyhole. Val traced her fingers over it, wondering what kind of key would fit in here. Suddenly, the doors opened, and Gwen and Val stepped inside. Though the thought of getting into an elevator with someone else at the controls, going to God knows where made Val feel a little uneasy.

Once the doors shut, Val glanced around. There was another slot for a key, obviously for the owner to control it themselves. For all others, someone from inside the condo had to let them in. *And out*, she presumed.

The doors opened on to a marble entrance hallway to the residence which took up the entire fifth floor. A woman, obviously the housekeeper, was waiting for them. "I'm Louise. Please come in. I'll take your things." Louise was dressed in typical maid garb. Light gray dress down to her knees with white collar and white trim, buttons from waist up. Her dark hair was pulled back in a chignon. Val guessed her age to be a little older than Bethany's. Mid-thirties, maybe?

Val and Gwen took off their coats and boots and followed Louise in. The expansive unit was all open-concept. High ceilings with skylights and windows everywhere made it seem as if they were standing outside. Furnishing and accents were sparse but bold. A portrait of Marilyn Monroe in stark contrasting colors, very reminiscent of Andy Warhol's work, hung on the wall over the marble fireplace. Everything else in the room was white or gray, with careful strikes of red, purple and yellow. Though it should have been cold and uninviting, Val had to admit this wasn't the case. Oddly, it almost pulled you in. A surreal modernistic interior, pitted against a primal exterior.

Bethany Arias and Melinda Holbright sat on a plush white couch. Behind them, and to their left and right, walls of windows allowed for a panoramic view of the water. The picture of Lake Erie through the floor-to-ceiling windows was breathtaking, with all variations of grays, whites and blues. The dark slate colored sky signaled the next round of snow ready to hit the area. A storm coming in off the water was an amazing sight. Nature's fury unleashed, unstoppable. This condo also gave an impression of "unstoppable;" a well-matched rival. Maybe this was what Bethany was going for.

The two women giggled and appeared engaged in a discussion as Louise brought Val and Gwen over to them.

"I'm so sorry. Mel and I were just catching up." Bethany rose and extended both hands, taking Val's in a warm, interlocking grasp. She did the same with Gwen. "So good to see you both again. I hope you're hungry. I have pan-seared salmon being prepared for lunch, with a vegan choice if necessary?" she ended in a question.

"Salmon is fine for both of us," Val answered for herself and Gwen. Gwen nodded.

"Great! the hors d'oeuvres should be ready in a few minutes." Bethany held up a bottle of wine. "Can I get you something to drink?"

"Unfortunately, we have to get back to work when we're done," Val said.

"Iced tea, soda?" Bethany tried again.

"Iced tea for me," Gwen answered.

"Make that two," Val added.

"Louise, can you get two glasses of iced tea. Please bring the pitcher as well," Bethany asked.

Louise nodded and turned away to fulfill the request.

Melinda crossed her legs and picked up a glass of white wine that sat before her. "Thank you for agreeing to meet with us this afternoon," she addressed Val and Gwen and then nodded her glass towards Bethany. "And a thank you to you Bethany, for the offer of lunch."

"Yes, thank you, Bethany," Gwen said.

"My pleasure." Bethany filled her glass with wine.

"You have a beautiful home," Gwen said.

"Now it's my turn to say thank you. I have a dual master's degree in art history and fine arts, concentrating on painting and sculpting. I designed everything in here and made that Warhol knockoff myself." Bethany pointed to the Marilyn Monroe painting above the fireplace.

"Wow, I'm impressed," Gwen said, getting a little closer for a better look. "This is fantastic."

Bethany gave a modest smile.

"You're certainly talented," Val said, admiring the painting and then walking over to the windows to glance outside at Lake Erie, frozen in time. Thick ice covered the shoreline but the water broke free about a hundred yards out. Waves rocked back and forth as the wind gusted, loose snow from piled drifts blew in a frenzied haze, creating clouds of white, momentarily obscuring Val's view before it settled. "You definitely know how to complement your home with the outside. Balance it, that is."

"So glad you noticed." Bethany joined Val. Her tone had a faint hint of surprise to it, making Val feel that maybe Bethany didn't get too many people who understood her artistic expression. "Color says so much about a person, don't you think, and how it's used evokes our emotions. For example, yellow is such a happy color—bright and warm, but it also causes frustration and anger. Babies tend to cry more in yellow rooms." Bethany pointed to the sparse yellow accents in the room, then shifted her finger towards the plum-colored ones. "Purple is connected to power, nobility, luxury, wisdom... spirituality. But use it too much and it can also cause frustration. Some actually say its overuse is a sign of arrogance." Bethany smiled wryly as if she just told Val a joke.

"What's the psychology of red?" Val asked, looking at the stabs of it in the room.

"Ah, red is considered the warmest yet most contradictory of the colors. In fact, this hue has more opposing emotional associations than any other. Strength and power, aggression and dominance. Passion and love. Danger. Everything from valentine hearts to stop signs are symbolized by red." Bethany laughed. "Anyway—it's all in the eye of the beholder. That's my goal here. My home speaks, gives you what you wish from it."

"All very interesting," Val said.

"You said you see balance. I find *that* interesting."

"How so?" Val asked.

"We all want to have our lives in *balance*, but few do what's necessary to place themselves there. I don't blame them. Chaos is easy but balance is a challenge. That's because you have to have control to have balance. To gain control, Val, you compete with everything," Bethany smiled politely, "and you must fight hard. So, in my opinion, balance is won. Come now, let's join Mel and Gwen. The hors d'oeuvres are out."

"Bethany, you'll have to give me the name of your cook. If this all tastes half as good as it looks, I'm stealing this person!" Melinda had walked over to the buffet. With a dish in hand she choose a few items.

It did look great. Val eyed at the spread before them. Warm Brie, hard cheeses, baguette, mini quiche, assorted crudités, and prosciutto. Room for salmon after this?

Once everyone was satisfied with their choices, they took a seat in the living room. Bethany and Melinda back on the couch and Gwen and Val on oppositely placed chairs.

"You're probably wondering why Beth and I decided to meet *here* today, privately." Melinda scooped some olive tapenade onto a baguette round.

"That did cross our minds." Val tried to sound friendly and not flippant. It was a loaded question because really, what could she say? By the smiles on everyone's faces, they all accepted *friendly.*

"Sorry for procrastinating, it's just not an easy topic to start. In fact, I don't know where to begin." Bethany looked at Melinda for help.

"Oh, Beth, just say it." Melinda set down her dish and wiped her lips with her napkin. "We were with Gabrielle the day her brother and sister died."

Val also set down her plate, and calmly held her gaze on Melinda, who seemed fairly shocked by the lack of any reaction from Val. "I have to admit that I saw an old news report on the internet about that."

"We knew that *someone* would eventually see that. And now with Gabrielle dead... well, this was going to resurface again." Melinda crossed her legs and casually leaned forward. "We didn't want this to lead to any rumors."

"Mel's right. We wanted to let you know the truth. And that we're not hiding anything," Bethany added. "We were there, Gabrielle didn't watch the twins, and a horrible accident occurred."

"The Morgans made all of this worse by trying to bury this fact back then. To protect Gabrielle. They didn't want everyone to know that Gabrielle was hanging out with us instead of keeping an eye on her brother and sister," Melinda said.

"Do you mind if I ask why you were there that day?" Val asked.

Bethany picked up her glass. "We weren't supposed to have been. Gabi was being punished for skipping school again and wasn't allowed to have friends over. It was Claudia's day off and Mr. and Mrs. Morgan had to go to a charity luncheon at the art museum. So, Gabi was babysitting. She was supposed to have been watching her sister Bridget, too."

"The Morgans didn't have a staff member who could watch the children?" Val asked, still surprised by this fact.

"No. Only Claudia was allowed to do that," Bethany answered.

"Gabrielle wasn't worried one of the other staff members would see you in the house?" This time Gwen posed the question.

Bethany glanced at Melinda before she answered. "No hired help was there that day."

"None?" Val said. Though Gavin had told her the children were alone, she wanted confirmation from Bethany and Melinda.

"The Morgans didn't have help in the house at all times," Melinda said. "Claudia was the only one who lived there."

Bethany laughed. "Our parents had money but we didn't live like those families you see on TV, Val. We had people who cleaned the house, tended the garden. But they had days off because really, they didn't need to clean the house every day, nor all day."

Val got it. "Did Gabi skip school often?" she asked, moving to a different line of questioning.

"Oh, all the time. We all did," Melinda said offhandedly, which caused Val to raise her eyebrows.

"If you think skipping school was bad, then I hesitate to tell you some of the other things we did as teenagers." Melinda laughed with a bit of scorn and looked at Val as if Val was a goody two shoes.

"Mel, we weren't *that* bad. We did stupid kid stuff," Bethany said. "Val, you just have to understand, Gabi always did what she wanted to do. The more you told her not to, the more she wanted to do it. We followed her. We did what she said. When we were young, it was fun, fun to be rebellious."

Val had been under the impression that Melinda was the alpha in the group. But maybe that was Gabrielle?

"But that day wasn't fun?" Val asked. "Or at least I'm assuming it wasn't."

"It's been my nightmare since it's happened. I can't tell you how glad I am to get it off my chest now," Bethany said.

"Me too," Melinda added. "The Morgans thought they were protecting all of us by making it go away, I can't fault them for that. They thought they were doing the right thing."

Hard to bury a secret when at least one other person knows the truth, Val thought. Risky questions sometime come up in an investigation but Val thought she needed to go out on a limb. "Your family's maid, Ingrid, saw you that day, didn't she, Melinda? And she was fired after that?" Val tried to sound non-accusatory but it came out a little stronger than she wanted.

Melinda's lips formed a straight line. "Ingrid was fired for her drug and alcohol problem. And the awful lies she said to try to blackmail the Morgans to support that problem. My parents had no hesitation getting rid of her. Honestly, what she was saying was so absurd that it was laughable."

"What did she say?" Val asked.

"That we helped Gabrielle cover up a crime." Melinda rolled her eyes and leaned back on the couch.

Val fought hard to keep her emotions calm, and her face straight, after that admission. She was speechless, trying to find her next words. "How did she come up with that conclusion?" she finally asked.

"Exactly," Melinda said sarcastically. "No window from our house even overlooked the Morgans' pool for Christ's sake. The back of the Morgans' house had two wings on each end that formed a square-shaped U. The pool was tucked inside the U. So, Ingrid didn't see anything, not that there was much to see other than three scared girls finding two children floating in the water." Melinda sat forward and locked her gaze on Val, in what Val saw as a challenging pose. "Ingrid's story was complete and utter bullshit. She did see Beth and me running across the lawn to the side of the house after the twins were found, which was true. The rest she made up."

Val leaned in too, moving closer to Melinda, and did not divert her stare. Val was not backing down. "Did Ingrid have a daughter?"

"Not one that I recall." Melinda picked up her wine glass and drained what was left of the contents. "I don't socialize with the help, so I wouldn't have known."

"Lunch is ready." Louise's voice echoed in the room. Val hadn't even seen her enter.

The four women rose and went into the dining room. Each took a seat and Louise brought plates of salmon, wilted spinach and fingerling potatoes. Val could smell the lemon caper sauce drizzled over the fish. It all looked spectacular and as soon as plates were before all of them, she picked up her fork and took a bite. It was heavenly. She took a few more bites before speaking again. "Weren't you concerned that Gabrielle wasn't watching her siblings that day?" she asked. "They were pretty young to be left unattended."

"No. We were over there because she had no intention of watching them to begin with. She was pissed with her parents for punishing her," Melinda said. "I think this was our biggest regret. She didn't keep an eye on them; we also didn't care about them; and then something tragic happened." Melinda's words had no emotion.

"Weren't you worried at all that someone would have told the Morgans you were there? I know you said that the staff wasn't there, but the twins would have seen you enter the house. They could have told their parents, if they had lived," Val said.

Melinda had an icy stare on Val and Val waited for her response. But the answer came in Bethany's voice. "We snuck in through the servants' entrance in the back of the house, and went up the servants' stairs to Gabi's room. We saw no one. Never did when we went in this way. Never saw anyone on the way out either. The day the twins drowned was the only time that was witnessed," Bethany said.

"Well, the only time you know someone witnessed it, right?" Val asked. "I mean the only reason Ingrid came forward was because of the death of the twins, but on an ordinary day would someone have cared which door they saw you come out of?"

Bethany glanced at Melinda, but Melinda would not divert her gaze from Val. "I guess you're right. Well, then we might not have been as crafty as we thought we were back then."

"I understand a servant's entrance but servant's stairs?" Gwen asked.

"The house has a set of back stairways for the servants to use. When the house was first built, servants could come and go without being seen on the main staircases or in the hallways. This is how they got to their quarters or to where they were working. The stairs were behind doors that looked like they belonged to a bedroom or linen closet. Back in those days, servants were seen only when necessary, so when serving guests dinner, answering doors, taking coats. Never roaming through the house," Bethany said. "My house had the same kind of thing."

"Mine too," Melinda said.

"Had?" Val caught the word from Bethany.

"My parents moved about ten years ago," Bethany said.

"My mother's still in our house but my father lives in Brussels." Melinda picked up the wine bottle and filled her glass. She nodded it towards Val. "Sure you don't want some? It's delicious."

Val shook her head. "How long have they been divorced?"

Melinda laughed. "They're not. It's just better for them this way. Living in separate houses has really helped their marriage."

"Speaking of parents, can I ask what were the Morgans like?" Gwen asked.

Melinda shrugged. "They were okay. A little odd, but what parents aren't?"

"Odd in what way?" Gwen asked again.

"Odd in a good way." Melinda's eyes took on a glassy appearance as she swallowed more wine. "Look, my own mother was drunk half the time when I was growing up, most of the time now. And my father was rarely home. Now that he's in another country I haven't seen him in over three years. I think the only reason they haven't divorced is because they've figured out how much each would lose in the deal. The Morgans were at least parent-like."

"Mel is being kind in her description of her parents," Bethany said. Val raised her eyebrows at Bethany's remark wondering what *unkind* would sound like. "I'll admit that my mother was a downright bitch. The Morgans' house was my safe place. From what I remember back then, Mr. Morgan was strict. But Mrs. Morgan tried so hard to bond with Gabi but Gabi wanted to be closer to her father than her mother, so she went out of her way to distance herself from her mother. It was cruel. So, I befriended Mrs. Morgan and became her 'daughter.' Maybe we each needed the other but Gabi became furious with me for it."

"Oh, Beth, you are so right." Melinda slurred a little. "As a kid, I would have killed to have Mrs. Morgan be my mother." Melinda put both elbows on the table and let her glass dangle from her right hand. "I remember one huge fight I had with my own mother about my boyfriend, this was a couple of years after the twins died. I was supposed to be home by eleven but things got *intimate* and I lost track of time. No, I didn't sleep with him, that's why he dumped me, and when he dropped me off at home around 1am, we were through. I cried my eyes out.

"The next morning my mother wouldn't let it go. Called me a whore. I ran to Gabi's house to get away from it all. Gabi wasn't there but Mrs. Morgan was. She listened... really listened to me." Melinda shook her head with a tight-lipped smile. "And she tried to give me advice about boys. I could tell she was uncomfortable, but there was something about that day... Mrs. Morgan was enjoying being a mom and I don't think she got that opportunity much. Gabi used to get jealous of the time I spent with her mother too. She forced me to choose at one point. So, I backed away from Mrs. Morgan. I think that hurt Mrs. Morgan quite a bit."

Bethany nodded in agreement. "It was a mistake back then, to let Gabi call the shots, but I can speak for myself when I say I was a teenager, I was all kinds of stupid and let bad judgment direct me. As an adult, I've been in contact with Mrs. Morgan. Sometimes you have to right the wrong and thankfully, I as an adult got the opportunity to fix something stupid and regrettable that I did as a kid. How often does that happen?"

"It's fantastic when do-overs come back around," Gwen said.

"Awesome for you, Beth," Melinda said, with a mock clap of the hands. It had a jealousy component to it that made Val think that the *friendship* between these girls was nothing more than a competition. Val wondered how badly Melinda lost. There were no pictures of her on the poster board at Gabrielle's funeral. Fences weren't mended between Melinda and Mrs. Morgan. *A competition*...Val said the word to herself. Maybe this is what Bethany was trying to say with her condo and its color palette. *Competition. 'To gain control, Val, you compete with everything.'* Bethany's words rang in Val's ears.

Bethany shot a look back at Melinda. She had obviously caught the jab. She sat poised, composed, her hands on her lap and a pleasant smile crept across her face. "It certainly is."

"The death of the twins destroyed the family, they fell apart after that. Mr. and Mrs. Morgan weren't the same with each other, Gabi became more defiant," Melinda glared back at Bethany, "and we saw less of Bridget."

There was several moments of silence. Finally, Bethany spoke. "There's something more we need to tell you about that day."

"What is that?" Val slowly asked.

Bethany held her gaze on Val. "We were texting a couple of guys from our class..." Bethany laughed. "That was on our flip phones back then... When all of a sudden Gabi stopped and ran to the window. She insisted someone had come home, that she heard a door slamming in the driveway. She told us to run upstairs and hide so we wouldn't get in to trouble."

"Gabi was convinced it was her father. Her parents had a terrible argument that morning and she thought maybe the argument continued and he left her mother at the art museum and came home. So, we hid," Melinda said.

"Where did you go?" Val asked.

"Gabi's room has a stairway that leads to the third floor and right into another room. This used to be the nanny's bedroom. The layout was so the nanny could have access to the children. There was another exit up there that went down to Bridget's room."

"Was this upstairs bedroom Claudia's room?" Gwen asked.

"Yes. Once the twins were born, Claudia moved next to them so she could be closer. This left the third floor vacant. So, we were pretty free up there," Bethany said.

Secret staircases and rooms where no one can see you enter or leave. *This must have been a teenager's dream*, Val thought. "How long were you in the nanny's old room?"

Melinda shrugged. "Not long. We kept an eye out for either Mr. or Mrs. Morgan coming in or going out. When we thought it was safe, we came out of the room, and left the same way we came in, through the servant stairway and out the back door. The pool was right there, in the back of the house. The first thing we saw were the twins floating in the water. We screamed and Gabi came running out."

"What happened next?" Val asked.

"Gabi called 911. We jumped in and got the twins out but they weren't breathing. We left right after that."

Val knew this was a lie. The twins were out of the water at least a half hour before Gabrielle called 911.

"Look, we feel terrible about this. I live every day with guilt. Maybe we could have prevented this." Bethany put her elbows on the table and used both hands to pull her hair from her face. She shook her head back and forth. "But here's the thing I think you should know. The twins wouldn't have gone into the pool alone."

"They were only six. It's good that they knew not to go into the water unattended," Val said.

There was silence. Val didn't know what to say next.

"That's not it." Bethany finally spoke. "They were afraid of the water."

"Afraid of the water? Why?" Val asked.

"I don't know. They loved to go in and splash when we were all swimming, but wouldn't go near it unless someone else was there," Bethany said and then took a deep breath. "While we were upstairs in Claudia's room, we don't know if someone came home that day or not. After we found the twins, what we do know is no one was there at that time."

Melinda looked at Bethany again. She was holding something back.

"What is it?" Val asked of Melinda.

"Bridget was also in the house that day and no one knows where she was," Melinda blurted.

"Mel!" Bethany yelled.

Val narrowed her eyes, confused. "Could Bridget have managed to get to the pool on her own?"

"If she was having a good day and was coherent, she might have. Back then she wasn't as bad as she is now," Melinda said. "Bridget loved the pool, so it's a possibility. I always thought the twins must have seen someone they knew by the water."

"Wouldn't she have called for help if something happened to them while she was there?" Gwen asked.

"She could have been scared. Gabi looked for her after Melinda and I found the twins, she couldn't find her. It wasn't like her to hide, though," Bethany said.

"I thought you said Gabi called the police after you found the twins. You jumped in the water got the twins out. The two of you left after that. At what point did Gabrielle check on Bridget during all of this?"

Melinda sat composed and took a second before she answered. "I think she went to check on Bridget as we went to the servants' stairs to leave. It happened so long ago and the bad memory is such a blur now."

And there was lie number two? "I don't recall a mention of Bridget in the police report," Val said. There was no documentation of another person in the house that day. Maybe the Morgans' influence had something to do with that omission, but somehow Val thought she had been told another lie by these women. The sequence of events just didn't add up.

"We left right after the twins came out of the water. So we have no knowledge what the police did," Melinda said plainly.

"Well, there you have it," Bethany said. "It was a horrible mistake. One I regret every day of my life. I hope we've cleared the air."

Between odd small talk, the women finished their lunch. Once Louise cleared the plates, it became obvious Bethany was done hosting for the afternoon, and Val took the hint.

"We have to thank you for this lovely afternoon and delicious lunch." Val and Gwen stood. "I hate to ask this but from what you knew of Gabrielle, could she have killed herself and her son?"

"I'm afraid I didn't know her very well at the end. We lost contact some time ago," Bethany said.

"Same with me," Melinda added.

"When was the last time either of you saw Gabrielle before she died?"

"*Saw her?*" Bethany thought for a second. "After she met Perry the musician, but before she married him. In fact, she wasn't even engaged then. So, I'd say at least a couple of years. We bumped into each other at Starbucks and did the obligatory two minute catch-up for the last two years of your life as each of us held a cup of to-go coffee."

Melinda laughed. "God, it's way longer than that for me."

"Bethany, weren't you Gabrielle's emergency contact for Adam?" Val asked.

"I *was*, yes." Bethany emphasized the *was* and offered nothing further.

"What caused the estrangement between you? I mean you were childhood friends," Val said.

"Val, not all friendships last forever," Bethany said plainly.

Bullshit, Val thought. These girls have been pretending to not know each other as much as they currently do. They're also hiding the truth of something that happened fifteen years ago. Jesus, it seemed like they were hanging out together now not because they wanted to, but because they had to. Something brought them back together.

17

Val was making lasagna. Jack leaned against the counter and crossed his arms. "I'd wish you'd let me help you more. I know how to stay invisible and out of the radar of Detective Gavin and subsequently, Dr. Maddox."

Val couldn't risk having Jack do much more with this case. That was clear. Her job could be on the line if anyone found out he was involved with it, and as such Jack had to sit on the sidelines. He helped, but now as *quietly* as he could. "Have a seat in the living room and once I get this in the oven, Gwen and I will tell you about Gabrielle's two best friends."

"Deal. That lasagna looks fantastic." Jack grabbed three glasses and a bottle of Chianti. "I'll get this opened," he said holding up the bottle.

Val finished alternating the wide flat pasta, a layer of ricotta cheese, mozzarella and ground beef, spooning on tomato sauce and then repeating. Once the dish was assembled, she slipped the pan into the oven and joined the group.

Jack and Gwen sat around her coffee table, the police report from the day the twins were discovered in the pool before them.

Jack had opened the Chianti and poured three glasses. After clanking the glasses Val took a healthy swallow.

"Those two women know more about the death of the twins then they're telling. Boy, did they trip over their fifteen-year-old story," Gwen said.

"Orchestrated and yet disjointed, that's what happens to a lie over time," Jack said. "No one gets it right that many years after. But what it does tell me is that they rehearsed recently. I think the Bridget addition might be new; she wasn't part of the original story because there's no mention of her in this report." Jack handed the pages to Val.

"Kind of odd, don't you think?" Val said, thumbing through the papers. "There's mention of everything the police did once they arrived and after the twins were put in the ambulance. Jesus, they called the Morgans, who were both still at the charity event, but there's nothing about another kid being in the house —if only to report she was alive and well."

"The Morgans worked hard to hide this tragedy from reporters. Could they have had enough influence to get Bridget's name omitted from the reports?" Gwen suggested.

"Possibly," Val said.

"So, Gabrielle was supposed to have been watching two six-year-olds and a developmentally disabled eighteen-year-old. If you were the parents of this reportedly defiant teenage girl, would you have let this happen?" Jack asked.

It was exactly what Val had been thinking. Bethany and Melinda said Bridget was in the house but neither of them reported actually seeing her. "Someone in that house that day knows the truth about what happened to the twins. Two children afraid of the water aren't going to go for a fun dip in the pool while their parents are gone."

"Six kids were there that afternoon. Three are dead. Two are telling the current story, and one is not able to speak about it." Gwen finished what was in her glass and refilled.

"There's always the possibility someone else was there in the house," Jack said.

"Or someone else saw more than they're reporting. Like the maid who saw the girls running across the lawn," Gwen said.

"Melinda told us that no window from her house overlooked the Morgans' pool." Val pulled out her phone. "I looked at Google Maps which shows close-up satellite views of the properties and it looks like the pool probably *was* tucked inside this U shape of the back of the house, exactly as Melinda described. There is no pool now, so it seems the Morgans' filled it in. Not surprising after what happened." Val showed Jack and Gwen the image. "But look at the yard. The yard extends out far enough beyond the house so that if someone was standing at the far corner of the fence of the property next door, Melinda's home, they might have seen something."

Gwen enlarged the picture. "You're right, Val, but it's hard to judge because it's not clear at this magnification. There are a lot of green images in this aerial shot that are probably trees, lots of trees. Though fifteen years ago, who knows what this looked like."

"Those do look like trees, fully mature trees. Given the age of the house, my guess is those have been there a long time. And that's a good thing with what I'm thinking... because that makes a good hiding place," Val said.

"You don't think a maid was standing in a mini forest watching children swim in a pool?" Gwen handed the phone back to Val. "That looks like a lot of foliage someone might have had to wade through to have gotten a peek from."

"I'm not thinking of the maid," Val said.

Gwen's gaze shot up. The alarm buzzed signaling dinner was ready and Val got up to get the pan out of the oven. The smell of tomato sauce was fantastic. "If the maid had a daughter, she might have looked through the trees at the yard next door, at children her own age playing. Privileged children, where the maid's daughter was not allowed to be. Not allowed to join in. Maybe she watched often and then one day saw something she wasn't supposed to."

"Do you think there's a possibility of Jennifer Ballard being involved in this? That she was Ingrid Gruber's daughter?" Gwen asked.

"The resemblance is uncanny," Val said.

"If that's the case, how did she come to live right next door to Gabrielle?"

"Good question... speaking of Gabrielle's house... the key. I have to put the key back. The one I found in Gabrielle's pocket."

"Did you find out what it belongs to?" Jack asked.

"I've researched it online and found several things it might open. I took plenty of pictures so I can investigate it more but I really can't keep it any longer. Honestly, the damn thing is making me nervous holding on to it for this long. I think I'll feel better once I put it back. Gwen, care to go with me after dinner to do that?" Gwen was a better choice than Jack. There was a risk that they'd be seen going into the house. If caught, she'd never be able to justify why Jack was there with her. She'd be fired immediately.

"Sure. What do you think the key opens?" Gwen asked

"A safe deposit box. If that's the case, the Morgans might start looking for their daughter's key. Gavin knows I found one. And it can't be in my possession if anyone starts asking about it."

18

It was 9pm. Val and Gwen sat outside of Gabrielle's house. Val's pulse pounded hard: she was worried about someone seeing them go into the house. She glanced over to the Ballards' home. Lights could be seen in the front room window, flickers suggesting someone was watching a TV. She looked over at the other houses. Most were similar, with TV lights flashing. A quiet night, families watching a movie. Hopefully no one was looking out of their window.

"Did Detective Gavin mention a safe deposit box?" Gwen asked as they continued to sit in the car.

"No. Doesn't mean that he didn't find it. He just never mentioned it if he did."

"A review of Gabrielle's bank statements would have shown a fee for a safe deposit box."

"I *know* that. That's what I'm kind of worried about. If one exists, the Morgans will certainly find out about it."

"Okay, let's just quickly go in and get this over with, then," Gwen said. "How do you want to do this?"

Val knew Gwen was asking how they were planning to get to Gabrielle's door, and not be spotted by any of the neighbors.

"Once we're out of the car, we'll walk up the block, then come back down. If anyone hears our car doors shut and looks out of a window, they'll just see two women walking on the sidewalk, probably company going to someone's home, and then hopefully retreat back to their TV." Val wore a knit hat with a pom-pom. Gwen had one too. Each wore puffer jackets and knee-high snow boots. "We look innocent. And hence boring for anyone watching us."

"Please tell me you didn't stay up all night thinking of this one? I was wondering why you wanted me to wear this silly hat." Gwen tugged on the bottom, adjusting it over her ears. "It is warm though. But I want you to know I'll get hat hair from this. And static. Don't even get me started on static." Gwen, like Val, grew up in a cold weather climate. Both knew the pros and cons of hat wearing. Warm, cute when you have it on, but taking it off was hair kiss of death.

"It looks good on you," Val said, appraising Gwen.

"Thanks. This jolly pom-pom probably takes about ten years off my age." Gwen laughed.

There was silence for a few seconds before Val said with a deep breath, "Okay, let's go." She opened the door and stepped outside.

Following the plan, Val and Gwen walked up the block, about six houses, then circled back. This was all Val's bad leg could take before going numb. On their way back, Val glanced into the window of the Ballards' home. She stopped dead in her tracks.

"Val, aren't you coming?" Gwen, who had walked a couple of feet ahead, turned around. "Val!" She said with a loud whisper.

"Did you see that?" Val's gaze was locked on the Ballards' front window.

"See what? I was looking straight ahead. Let's go. Before someone sees *us*."

"I thought I saw a dark-haired woman in the Ballards' house. Jennifer is blonde." Val continued staring at the window, her feet not moving, her gaze glued to the opening.

"Maybe they have company. Let's go!"

"Not *they*, Gwen. *He.* It's Thursday. Jennifer Ballard works late tonight. She's not home."

"Well, if you suspect that he screws other women, this isn't going to prove anything because I doubt he's going to rip off her clothes in front of an open window. Now come on. We need to get out of sight and in that house." Gwen pointed to Gabrielle's home.

Gwen was right. They needed to go before someone saw them. The two hurried to Gabrielle's door. Val remembered the lock box code. She typed it in, opened the box and took out the house key, then slipped it into the door. After stepping inside, both women exhaled. "Well, we're in. Do you think you can put the key back without using any light?"

"I should be okay." Val waited for her eyes to adjust to the darkness before venturing much further. She squinted because something wasn't right. Then it all came into focus. What happened to the lights? The lights that were on the last time she was here? "Holy shit! It can't be."

"What can't be? Val... what can't be?" Gwen said loudly the second time.

Val ignored Gwen and quickly walked into the home, limping in circles in the front room, where she and Jack stood just days ago. The reality of what she was seeing grabbing and taking hold. "The furniture! It's all gone! *Holy crap, that means...* Val ran from the room and down the hallway with Gwen trailing behind her. Val stood in the doorway to Gabrielle's bedroom lost for what to do next. "Oh my God, the entire place is empty."

"Someone must have taken her belongings. I'd guess her parents sent someone to do it."

Val just continued to stare into the empty space, her heart pounding as she looked at the nightmare problem in front of her. "How could they do this that fast?"

"Money gets things done quickly."

"Gwen, what do I do?" Val pulled the key out of her pocket. It dangled from her hand. "What do I do with this?"

Gwen took a moment before responding and Val wondered what she was going to say. What could she say? Val was screwed. "You could tell Detective Gavin what you did, and then he tells the Morgans what you did when he gives them back their daughter's key, and then we see how angry they get."

Val sat down on the floor. If she didn't sit, she'd fall. "I can't do that."

"No, you can't. Dr. Maddox will have grounds to fire you, especially if the Morgans are pissed." Gwen crossed her arms and circled the room.

"Gwen, this is horrible. I feel horrible." Val put her hands up to her forehead, trying to grab a rational thought. "I thought I had plenty of time to return the key. It's only been three days!"

"Val, I'm only going to advise you to do what I'm going to say next because I'm your friend."

"Hand in my resignation?"

Gwen sighed. "Hold on to the damn thing and keep quiet. If you hear that Detective Gavin is looking for a key, well, that's when you come forward. He knows that you found one. Just not that you kept one."

Val shook her head. "The longer I wait the worse this looks. What's my excuse then?"

"You forgot about it. But the need to find this key jogged your memory. Keep it as simple as that."

"Thank you, Gwen, but that makes me sound guilty *and* stupid."

"Dr. Maddox will have to fire you no matter the excuse if the

Morgans are pissed. But Detective Gavin will still have a slim chance of respecting you, and helping you, especially if you give him evidence that helps with his case. Val, you'll only have to give this key up if it's important. And then he won't care if you sound stupid or guilty, he'll want the key. And he'll be happy you have it. If nothing comes of it, throw the damn thing in the garbage."

19

The next morning Val walked into the police headquarters and into Mitch Gavin's office. His secretary said he'd be a few minutes, and to take a seat in his office and wait. Val nodded and let herself in, grabbing one of the two chairs in front of Gavin's desk. He'd asked for this meeting and honestly it could be about anything, but all Val could focus on was the key.

After a few minutes Val glanced up as Gavin entered, carrying several folders.

"You look exhausted," she said. He did. His tie was loosened, top button undone. Circles had formed under his eyes. A pang in Val's chest, reminded her of how she felt about Gavin. She wasn't only attracted to him, she cared about him. Maybe too much.

"I am. This case should have been over and done within a week. Strange, but open and shut. Every time I go to close a door another swings opens. This last one, I was not expecting."

Val sat back in her chair. "I'm ready for it."

"I did some digging into Gabrielle's friends." Gavin opened one of the folders and pulled documents out. "The Arias lost a lot of their money in the 2008 recession. They managed to stay afloat but things just kept going downhill with poor business choices, bad investments. Everything finally bottomed out and they liquidated the company to pay outstanding debts." Gavin looked up. "That was about ten years ago. Mr. Arias died of a heart attack back then. Mrs. Arias sold the house on Lincoln Parkway and moved in with her brother who's in Florida."

"How is Bethany affording the waterfront condo, then?" Val asked. The look on Gavin's face made it obvious that he had an unpleasant answer and Val braced herself for it.

Gavin took a second before he spoke, letting out an exhale. "It's owned by Mr. Morgan."

Val's eyes opened wide. "Was he helping her out? Maybe replacing his estranged daughter?"

"I don't think so." Again, Gavin hesitated.

"Mitch, what are you trying to tell me?"

"He spent the night there a number of times. Security cameras in the parking lot caught it all—when he arrived and when he left. What we don't know are the details of what happened once he was inside, but I think we can guess." Gavin cast a glance at Val.

Val shifted uncomfortably in her chair. "You think he was screwing his daughter's friend?" she said, repulsed.

"I don't think he was giving this condo away for free."

"Jesus, Mitch. I'm not even sure what to do with that information." Val tried hard to wrap her head around what she was hearing. Mr. Morgan appeared so cold and distant towards Bethany at Gabrielle's funeral. *Jesus, it was all an act.*

"Ask me where on the waterfront Gabrielle once lived?" Gavin smirked.

Val, shook her head in disbelief. "It can't be."

"It is. This very place."

"Oh my God. My skin wants to get up and crawl away. He gave his daughter's condo to her friend."

"Looks like it. Probably didn't strengthen the friendship," Gavin said sarcastically. "What we don't know is if the friendship was already on its way out because of something else. So this could have caused it or cinched it."

Val sat back in her chair and exhaled deeply. She opted for cinching it. It wasn't so much that Bethany was given the condo but how she described it while she and Gwen were there for lunch. The condo was a statement of power for Bethany, Val felt it the moment she entered. "What about Melinda, anything on her?"

"Nothing yet."

Val's phone vibrated and she looked to see who was calling. "Holy crap."

"Who is it?"

"Mrs. Morgan."

20

"Answer it," Gavin said. He quickly rose from his chair.

Val's fingers fumbled to accept the call. She put her phone on speaker so that Gavin could hear. "Hello?"

"Valentina, it's Mrs. Morgan. I heard that you met with Melinda and Bethany the other day." Mrs. Morgan's voice sounded cordial, but there was an odd undertone to it. "I was hoping that you could stop by, maybe this afternoon. I have a few things I'd like to discuss with you."

Val looked at Gavin. He was at her side nodding for her to say "yes." Val's pulse raced. How did Mrs. Morgan know that she met with Gabrielle's friends? Bethany must have told her. "Of course. What time would be good for you?"

"James will be home around five. Why don't you come over before then?"

Val raised her eyebrows at Gavin. Mrs. Morgan wants a private discussion without her husband around. Val had hoped for this at the beginning, when she first met the Morgans. She didn't need to see Gavin nodding again before she responded. "Is two all right?"

"Perfect."

"Then I'll see you later." Mrs. Morgan said nothing more before Val heard the click of the phone call ending.

"Val, I want you to wear a wire. She might tell you more about Bethany and Melinda that will help this investigation, especially if she's alone." Gavin looked at his watch. "It's 10am now, why don't you come back around 12:30 and we'll get you hooked up. I'll run through how it all works."

"Of course." Val could feel sweat developing on her brow and on the back of her neck. Suddenly, she felt queasy and lightheaded.

Gavin knelt in front of her chair and put his hand on her forehead. "Are you okay? You've gone pale. Val, you don't have to do this."

Val stood. "No really, I'm fine. Mitch, I want to do it." She laughed. "Not sure what came over me. I have no problem questioning people about murder and death, but messed up friendships and grieving mothers, and a husband who's screwing one of those friends... I don't want to say or do anything to hurt Mrs. Morgan."

"You can help her learn the truth about her daughter's friends, especially since she seems to be on good terms with the one who's screwing her husband."

At 1:59pm, Val rang the bell at the Morgans' front door wearing the wire. The damn thing was disguised as a decorative pin and placed on her suit jacket. It could have been even smaller and more discreet if Gavin, at the last minute, didn't decide to get one with a camera.

Jesus, Val felt self-conscious. Hell, the fact that she was being recorded made her aware of every action. When you know someone is watching your moves, listening to your words to dissect later, being natural is impossible. "Forget it's there," Gavin had said. *Yeah, right!*

"Mrs. Morgan," Val said, her heart pounding. "I wasn't expecting you to open the door."

"It's just myself, Claudia and Bridget today and Claudia is keeping an eye on Bridget. Please come in." She pulled the door open, her face hard to read. Val wished she had asked more on the phone, like what this meeting would be about but honestly, it was hard to think logically at the time.

Val entered and glanced at Mrs. Morgan's ankle. "You don't have your ace bandage anymore?" It was only at this moment she realized Mrs. Morgan also didn't have her cane.

"That came off the other day and I can't tell you how happy I am to be rid of the thing." Mrs. Morgan smiled and Val relaxed a little.

Val took off her coat and boots and followed Mrs. Morgan into the kitchen. "Please have a seat." She pointed to the chairs around a table laid for two. Coffee and a platter of small yellow and pink cakes sat in the middle of the table. The decorative icing, in the shape of vines and flowers, was beautiful. Val wondered what pastry shop they came from.

Mrs. Morgan picked up the coffee pot and poured two cups. "Thank you for coming today. Bethany called me after your lunch."

Val nodded. *Ah, so Bethany did call Mrs. Morgan. But for what reason?*

"She told me about your meeting." Mrs. Morgan shook her head. "Bethany has been like another daughter to me. I honestly don't know what I would have done without her support after Gabrielle..." Mrs. Morgan took a deep breath. "I'm so sorry. It's just so hard to say the words."

"I understand completely, please take your time," Val said sympathetically. If Bethany was paying Mr. Morgan for the condo with sex, Mrs. Morgan didn't seem to know about it. In fact, Bethany had her completely fooled.

"Please help yourself." Mrs. Morgan pointed towards the platter, to the cakes. "They're lemon and raspberry."

"Thank you. They look amazing." Val marveled at the intricate icing design. "These are too beautiful to eat."

Mrs. Morgan laughed. "My Bridget decorated them. They are lovely, aren't they?"

"Bridget?" Val tried to keep the shock out of her voice.

"She is quite an artist. Her disability might have taken her mind but not her talent. She always could paint and draw." Mrs. Morgan beamed like a proud parent.

"I have to try one." Val transferred one to her plate. "Can I ask what disability Bridget has?"

"She has autism." Mrs. Morgan said it bluntly.

Val raised her eyebrows, wondering why neither Morgan said this before. Why the hush about it?

Mrs. Morgan gave a guilty look. She must have known Val's reaction well, seen it a thousand times. "Mr. Morgan has always had a hard time coming to terms with Bridget's diagnosis. He doesn't like to say it. Or hear it." Mrs. Morgan's eyes went wide at what she just said. "Oh, please don't think badly of him. Mr. Morgan likes perfection, and he tries to compensate... to correct." She tipped her head down and shook it in regret. "No, there's no excuse. James is James. That's the best way I can explain it. He loves Bridget. He just wants her to be something she's not."

Val took a bite of cake. "I understand. Sometimes, the people we love the most are the ones we make excuses for the most. We want the best for them. It doesn't come from hate, but loving too much."

Though Mrs. Morgan smiled politely, her face showed a sadness that couldn't be hidden. "We both love her very much.

We loved all of our children. That's why I needed to talk to you today. I don't want you to listen to gossip that's fifteen years old."

"About Bridget?" Val suspected Mrs. Morgan knew Melinda's version of the story.

Mrs. Morgan nodded. "The day our twins died, Bridget was home too. There was always speculation that Bridget led them outside. Gabi denied it but Melinda and Bethany fueled the rumor and people tended to believe it."

So, Bridget was home, and it was obvious the Morgans buried this fact. "The police reports mentioned nothing of Bridget," Val stated.

"I know. That's how we wanted it," Mrs. Morgan responded with a tight face. "We had our reasons."

So, the Morgans' influence did get this erased from the police report, but Val felt there was something more, something deeper, below the surface. "I heard the twins were afraid of the water."

"They were, but they would go in if they had the right companion to play with, and there were only a few people who they liked. One of those was Bridget. Gabrielle was another..." Mrs. Morgan's voiced trailed suggesting at least one more individual was on that list.

Val took a stab. "I'm assuming Bethany was another?"

"No. Bethany couldn't swim. Melinda was the third. And the last."

"Do you think it was Melinda that day that led them into the water?"

"I know it wasn't Bridget."

"How can you be sure."

Mrs. Morgan let out a deep breath. She held her coffee cup between both hands and stared at the contents while she answered. "James and I were going to be gone for the afternoon. I gave Bridget a sedative to make her sleep." Mrs.

Morgan looked up with wide eyes, suggesting she needed to explain. "Gabrielle wouldn't have done anything to hurt her siblings but she is not the most responsible person. Bridget can be a handful at times. It was just best to have her calm."

Val understood and it made sense now why Bridget was never mentioned in the reports. "How do you know it wasn't Gabrielle that led the twins to the water?"

"She denied it. She was my daughter and I believed her. I also don't blame her for whatever happened."

"Blaming, believing and knowing are different things." Val couldn't help but sense Mrs. Morgan was not at peace with her decision.

"I'll be honest. I don't know what happened that afternoon." Mrs. Morgan hung her head for a moment before looking back up at Val. "The story has changed slightly over the years. I have my own suspicions and that's all."

"Mrs. Morgan, can I ask a delicate question?"

"Let me hear it first. I don't break easily but some things are still painful after all of these years."

"I noticed at Gabrielle's funeral that there were no pictures of Melinda on the remembrance board, is it because you feel she had something to do with the death of your children?"

"No, I forgave both Bethany and Melinda for that day a long time ago—for whatever role they had, if they even had a role. I think we made a poor choice in having a pool. It's too tempting for kids to want to play, accidents happen. I had James fill it in. I'll never have another pool again."

"Then why did you omit Melinda?"

"She tried to seduce my husband."

Val nearly fell off her chair.

"Sorry, I didn't mean to startle you." Mrs. Morgan sat forward and put a hand on Val's shoulder. "I caught her in my bedroom, lying on my bed, wearing nothing but a thong. She thought James was coming home, but surprise, it was me."

"How long ago was that? My God, was she a teenager?" Val rambled the sentences together, trying to keep the shock out of her voice.

"No. This happened when Gabi and Adam were living here, so a few years ago. I'm not sure how she got in without anyone noticing, but she left with everyone in the vicinity seeing her because I kicked her out the same way I found her lying on my bed. Wearing only a thong."

Val laughed out loud as she pictured Mrs. Morgan chasing a practically naked Melinda out of the house. Mrs. Morgan laughed too, then composed herself.

"Of course she came to Gabi and Adam's funeral to pay her respects and I wouldn't begrudge anyone that. Nor would I have created a scene. Melinda and I stay away from each other. And she stays away from James. Sorry if I don't feel the need to display pictures of her... anywhere."

"She said you were like a mother to her." Val shook her head. How could Melinda have betrayed Mrs. Morgan like that?

"I was. That's why this hurts so much. But I don't think she wanted me to be her mother as much as she simply wanted to win over James."

"Why would she do something like that?" Val couldn't help but sound disgusted.

"Melinda's home life was bad. Wealthy parents don't always make good parents. I let Gabrielle be friends with Melinda even though I knew Melinda had some problems. I regret that decision now. I just thought that maybe providing a welcoming environment would help her, but I was wrong. Some *bad* in people can't be changed. It's who they are."

"*Bad*?" Val couldn't help notice Mrs. Morgan's emphasis on the word.

"Melinda had done some things that were concerning back then, when she was young. The problem is she's doing concerning things now. It's why I wanted you to come today."

"Concerning in what way?" Val inched a little closer to Mrs. Morgan, eager to hear what she had to say.

"At the beginning, stupid things really, like stealing trinkets from the house. The things she took weren't of any value so I thought she was just trying to get attention. But as she got older, what she started to do became more mean-spirited. She seemed to like to do things that caused harm to people. She actually appeared to get joy out of it."

"Do you think she has anything to do with Gabrielle's death?"

"That's what I want to know. Three of my four children are dead. My grandchild is dead. James has accepted that Gabrielle committed suicide, taking Adam with her. He feels that if we cover up any more tragedies with our family we'll be ruined. The public can be very judgmental, you know. They think we covered for Gabrielle fifteen years ago and they think we're doing it again. You should see the decline in value of Morgan Foods stock. James wants the cards on the table so he can move on. Re-establish the brand. But I can't have that—trade my family for the company. I don't want any more regrets. You see, I'm not so sure Gabi killed herself and Adam."

Mrs. Morgan took a deep breath before she continued. "Gabrielle had problems with Melinda in the past. I hadn't spoken to my daughter in some time when she contacted James and myself, wanting to reconcile. It wasn't like Gabi to cave in first. James was right when he said she'd hold out until we flinched. Something made her contact us. I think she was afraid of something. Or someone?"

Melinda is trying to blame Bridget for the day the twins drowned. Bethany is warning Mrs. Morgan about it. Melinda tried to screw Mr.

Morgan, but Bethany may be actually doing it. Bethany is in Gabrielle's condo. These girls have been competing with each other for years. And they all know what happened the day the twins died. One is now dead. So is her son.

There's no statute of limitations for murder in New York. Though the girls were sixteen at the time they could still be charged. The questions tumbled in Val's mind, almost tripping over each other. One other person knows what happened in the house that day.

"Would it be possible to see Bridget today? I'd really like to meet her, especially after eating this beautifully decorated cake." Val expected Mrs. Morgan to say no, but she had to try.

"Of course, Val, if you want to see Bridget I'll introduce you. She doesn't do well with crowds of any size but I don't think you alone will be upsetting to her." Mrs. Morgan stood. "Come now, I'll introduce you to her."

21

Val followed Mrs. Morgan out of the kitchen through the main hallway and up the massive front staircase. Val turned to the left and right so the camera in her wire would get a good view. Gavin was right, it was easy after some time to forget it was there.

An easy five feet across, the stairs curved gently upwards. At the top of the landing they turned right. Val and Mrs. Morgan traveled down the corridor.

Val turned her neck, looking in all directions. "This house has a third floor. Where are the rest of the stairs?"

"It has four floors, if you count the attic. The top floors were for the servants, back in the days servants used to live in the house they used a different staircase. It continues behind the door to your left over there." Mrs. Morgan pointed.

Val remembered what Bethany had said about the servants' stairs. This must be how Melinda snuck in to try to have a romp with Mr. Morgan, but why? Money? Was she trying to screw Mr. Morgan or screw over Gabrielle? Or Bethany?

They stopped at the second-to-last door on the left and entered a large bedroom. Holy crap. The entire downstairs of

Val's house—and then some—would fit in here. Val could see why it needed to be so big. This was Bridget's world. A bed, sitting area with couch, large-screen TV, adjoining bathroom and a table and chairs completed the layout.

A young blonde-haired woman, Bridget, was sitting at the table with a small canvas in front of her and a smattering of paints to her side. She held the brush, and dipped it into several colors, mixing them on a pad before applying it to the canvas.

As Mrs. Morgan entered, Claudia stood from the rocking chair in the corner where she had been reading a book. She said hello to Val and gave a lukewarm smile. Then she glanced at Mrs. Morgan, uncomfortable that Val had been brought in the room. Bridget probably didn't get many visitors.

"How is she doing?" Mrs. Morgan asked of her daughter.

"Very well today," Claudia answered. She smoothed out the form-fitting skirt of her dress and adjusted the cardigan on her shoulders.

"Claudia is still Bridget's main nanny. We don't tell very many people. Bridget does need constant care, even though she's thirty-three."

"Main nanny?"

"She has two more. They come on Claudia's days off and when Claudia is assigned other duties." Mrs. Morgan walked over to her daughter and stroked the young woman's hair. "Watercolors," Mrs. Morgan said. "She loves watercolors. It's good therapy for her. Some people thought we should have put her in an institution, that we couldn't provide the kind of care she needed." She glanced at Val, her hand still on Bridget's hair. "My daughter will never set foot in an institution."

Val walked closer to the table, to Bridget to get a look at what she was painting. It was a garden; complete with trees, flowers, branches. Similar pictures decorated the walls, all obviously painted by Bridget. Bridget seemed unaware anyone was in the room with her. She appeared content to dab paints and apply them to her evolving creation. Suddenly, Bridget stopped her brush strokes and slowly turned her head towards Val. She had no facial expression.

Val smiled and said, "Hello, Bridget, it's nice to meet you."

"Bridget, this is Val," Mrs. Morgan said as she tucked a strand of Bridget's hair behind her ear. "Would you like to say hello to her?"

Bridget turned her head to her mother. She said nothing, only staring at her with a blank face.

"It's all right, sweetheart, Val knows you're saying hello your way. You can paint again if you like."

As if a switch was turned, Bridget focussed on her canvas again, resuming dabbing the brush in the paints.

"Mrs. Morgan, is it all right if I step aside for a moment," Claudia asked.

"Of course, Claudia. Take your time, I can manage."

"Thank you. I'll only be a moment if you need something." Claudia walked through an open door into an adjoining bedroom.

Val's gaze traveled to some framed pictures of children that sat on a shelf next to Bridget's table, and Val picked one up.

"That's William and Iris, my twins. They were named after James' grandfather and my grandmother, both on our father's side." Mrs. Morgan pointed to another photo. "And that's Gabi with Bridget. Gabi was about ten in the picture. These are Bridget's favorites. There a few more on her bedside table but she likes these with her. They'll be transferred to the bedside table tonight when she goes to sleep." Mrs. Morgan smiled. "She talks to them every now and then."

"What does she say?" Val asked.

"I'm not sure, gibberish really. Bridget hasn't spoken much

since the twins died. She was very close with them. She was close with Gabi too, back then anyway."

Val put the picture back down and then watched this young woman dip the brush in her paints, making her creation, life as she knew it coming from her hands. Life told in pictures and Bridget's were of flowers. Maybe in a mad, ugly world, beauty is what Bridget sees. Watching Bridget was all Val needed, hell, it was all she was going to get. Val knew talking to her would be out of the question. There was one more thing Val wanted to see in this house before she left and hoped Mrs. Morgan would allow it. She wanted to get a peek at everything she could so her hidden camera would record as much as possible. "Would it be possible to take a look in Gabrielle's old room?"

"If you'd like to, of course." Mrs. Morgan walked to the doorway of the adjoining room. "Claudia, we're leaving now."

Val moved closer, too: she also wanted to get a look inside Claudia's room. Most of the décor was yellow and white, the furniture a dark mahogany. Yellow flowers in a purple vase sitting on the bedside table caught her eye. It was at that moment Val realized the flowers in the vase were the same type of flowers Bridget had painted on her canvas. "Those flowers are lovely. I have no idea what they are," she said to Mrs. Morgan.

"I think they're some type of lily."

"Looks like they need water, they're drooping." The buds were hanging down.

"I think they're beyond watering. They might need to be thrown out." Mrs. Morgan laughed and walked away. "Come on now. Gabrielle's bedroom is down the hall."

Val followed Mrs. Morgan again. They stopped in front of a closed door. Mrs. Morgan turned the handle and the two women went inside. There was a king-size bed and matching dressers. Everything was gray or white and very modern in design. It had such a sleek elegance, reminding Val of Bethany's décor in the condo. This room was lacking one effect that Bethany managed to achieve. Power. "This definitely is not the décor of a teenage girl."

"We had it redecorated to Gabrielle's liking when she moved back with us after Max, her first husband, died. Gabrielle took all of her belongings when she moved out so other than the furniture there's nothing in here."

"Where did Adam stay?"

"The room next door. You're welcome to look in there too, but that's pretty much empty also, except for furniture."

Val saw no need to see the room. With no personal belongings, there really wasn't much to investigate. Gabrielle's room did, however, have something Val wanted to see. There was a single door to her right and two sets of double doors to her left. Val took a stab at the single door and pointed. Is that a closet?" Val hoped it wasn't.

"It's the staircase that goes to the nanny's—well Claudia's—old room."

Bingo! This is where Melinda and Bethany say they all hid fifteen years ago. "Is it all right if I go up there?"

Mrs. Morgan shrugged. "If you really want to. I hope you won't mind if I stay down here though. That particular staircase is awfully narrow and my ankle is not one hundred percent yet."

"Understood." Val opened the door and took a look up, wondering how much of a problem her own leg would have climbing these stairs. "Where else do these go?"

"They open directly into Claudia's old room but from that you can exit to the entire floor. And then to the attic floor from there. As I said earlier, it's not in use much. Claudia is our only live-in help. We do maintain the upper floors, but honestly have no use for them." Mrs. Morgan laughed. "If this house wasn't built by James' great grandfather and hadn't been in his family for so long. I would have moved out of here years ago. He won't give it up."

"You don't love a grand house like this?" Val questioned.

Mrs. Morgan laughed. "No. A penthouse in Manhattan is more to my liking. Not a 130-year-old mansion. It's beautiful but full of quirks."

"Some would call that old-world charm."

"I call it a pain in my ass. It's a historically preserved house. I sit on the preservation society, so I have to be extra diligent," Mrs. Morgan said. "Oh do take a look at the furnishings when you go up. I think I've done my society proud with historical accuracy in that section of the house."

"Does the third floor have stairways to all of the children's rooms, like this one does?"

"Yes, it was so the nanny or nannies, could get to them at any time, older children that is. The younger ones had the nanny right next door. But there are exits to the rest of the house up there. These were for the maids and the household staff to move about."

Val nodded and then climbed the narrow, steep stairs, surprised by how well her leg handled it, and opened the door at the top of the staircase to enter Claudia's old quarters. The room had floral wallpaper so pristine that it appeared to have been hung yesterday. The furniture was all dark wood, with plush velvet cushions, and intricate stitched rugs. *Jesus, the place is like a museum.* Val walked over to the window and looked out.

Odd, there is no view of the driveway or garage from here. So anyone hiding in this room would have no way of knowing if someone exited or entered the house. Melinda and Bethany reported that they came up here because Gabrielle thought one of her parents had come home, but if they wanted to keep a watch on that, this room wasn't going to allow for it. Another lie.

So, these girls either weren't here, or they went somewhere else on this floor. Or the rest of the house.

Val exited the room and as she walked down the corridor, the floorboards creaked but other than that, everything was eerily quiet. Another four small bedrooms were here on the third floor, all decorated with late nineteenth-century furnishings, so that it felt like stepping back in time. Two of the rooms had doors opening to stairways going down, presumably to either a child's bedroom or another section of the house. The hallway itself had a set of stairs going down. So far, nothing went up to the attic floor.

Val could see how teenage girls could use this system to sneak in and out of this mansion. Just where did they go that day? They would have access to the twins and Bridget from here. Did something happen before they went to the pool?

Straight ahead, there was one last door, which did not look like a door to a room. It was a little wider and had no door handle. Val felt around the frame for any mechanism to indicate how it could possibly open but found nothing. How odd! And where are the stairs going up to the attic? How did anyone get to that floor? Since nothing was obvious, there was only one way to find out.

Val went down the stairs that led back to Gabrielle's room. To Mrs. Morgan. "The door at the end of the hall, the one without a knob, what's that for?"

"We had a new heating and air conditioning system placed about ten years ago. The access to the unit, to the part that services the third and fourth floors is behind that entry. James had the contractor make it look inconspicuous. The maintenance people know how to get in but I have no idea."

"How do you get to the fourth floor?"

"Didn't you find the stairwell?"

"No."

"I'm sorry but it's been so long since I've been up there." Mrs. Morgan shook her head, at a loss. "I can ask Claudia to help, if you like. I really don't know all that much about the fourth floor. But honestly it's just an attic now."

"No need to bother Claudia." Val saw no reason for it, she'd seen all she needed to.

Mrs. Morgan put her hand on Val's shoulder and with a big smile said, "Well then, before you leave I must show you the greenhouse. It's quite beautiful and I've been starting my new fruit garden. I think I finally have some seedlings sprouting."

Val quickly tried to think of a polite excuse but Mrs. Morgan had been kind enough to let her snoop around the house and it would be terribly rude at this point not to complete the tour. "I would love to see your greenhouse."

"Oh it's not *my* greenhouse."

Val narrowed her eyes.

"It really belongs to Claudia. My husband had the greenhouse built in gratitude for her service to our family. Claudia is the true gardener and horticulturist. Her green thumb is amazing."

He built it for Claudia? That information Val found interesting. She followed Mrs. Morgan back downstairs, through the kitchen and down a hallway. They entered a large glass structure. "It's remarkable, isn't it?" Mrs. Morgan said.

It really was. Slate floors, arched glass walls, and wrought-iron tables and chairs, created a welcoming and serene environment. To the side there were rows of tables for seedlings. They held plants at various stages of growth.

"Most of these belong to Claudia. She starts the flowers for the garden in here." Mrs. Morgan pointed to a row of pots right next to them. It's January so she plants daffodils, tulips and hyacinths," Mrs. Morgan said. "She planted the irises last month. Claudia plants irises every year because of my daughter,

Iris." Mrs. Morgan smiled and walked over to some clay pots that held dirt only, and examined them. "Looks like these pots are ready for February. I have no idea what's going on in here."

Mrs. Morgan motioned for Val to follow her. "I commandeered the far corner for my own garden. Claudia was so gracious to let me have it. I have to admit, James wasn't too thrilled about me doing this, though."

Maybe this is why Mr. Morgan didn't like his wife to garden. The greenhouse is for Claudia. If Mr. Morgan is having an affair with his daughter's friend, why not also have one with the nanny too?

Tucked away, on their own were about a dozen pots holding several varieties of berries. Val read the labels. Blueberry, strawberry, raspberry. Mrs. Morgan began talking about berries and times of the year they needed to be planted, but Val wasn't paying attention, her mind elsewhere.

Both Mr. and Mrs. Morgan stated that Gabrielle liked to have the upper hand, she didn't flinch. But she wanted to reconcile. It seemed as if she was giving in to them. Maybe Gabrielle was worried about someone, and wanted her parents' protection. But the other option; if Gabrielle knew about her father's affairs, at least with Bethany, maybe she was threatening him. Maybe Gabrielle wasn't flinching, but throwing a punch.

22

Monday morning, Val sat in her office, she had her phone pressed to her ear listening to everything Gavin was saying. He had thoroughly reviewed the video and audio feed from the wire.

"I'm checking Claudia's background," he said. "I'll let you know what I find."

"What about Jennifer Ballard, Gabrielle Morgan's next-door neighbor. Do we know who her parents were yet? Her maiden name?"

Val could hear the shuffling of papers. "So far, I only have her marriage license. Maiden name was Manning, not Gruber. Still waiting for a birth certificate to see who her parents were. It's possible the child was given the father's last name. Or Ingrid remarried." Gavin didn't sound optimistic and Val knew why. They were grasping at straws here.

Val sat back, and looked at her doorway to see Dr. Maddox leaning against the frame. "Mitch, can you hold a second." Val quickly pushed mute. "Yes, Dr. Maddox?"

"Can you meet me in my office in a few minutes?" he said.

"Of course."

He turned and walked away without saying anything more. Val wondered what this was about. "Mitch, I have to run."

"I've got to run too. I have my own meeting with Gabrielle's bank manager," he said.

Val's stomach knotted. "Bank manager?"

"Yeah. We were going through a few of her statements and I have some questions about one of the charges on them. Catch up with you later?"

"Absolutely." Val quickly added, "What kind of charges?" Her mind went to Gabrielle's key she still had in her possession, the one she felt belonged to a safe deposit box.

"Not sure yet. I'll let you know what I find out."

"Okay." Val hung up and ran down the hallway to Dr. Maddox's office. *Jesus, what is this about?*

When she arrived he pointed to a chair for her to sit, which she quickly did. "The histology reports are back on the sections we took from Gabrielle Morgan's organs," he said.

Val held her breath. "And?" she asked.

"She had hepatocellular carcinoma, in other words liver cancer. So true liver cancer; this is not a metastasis."

Val's eyebrows shot up at the mention of the diagnosis. "I don't think anyone would have guessed that."

"This certainly is a big surprise, and I'll get to more of that later. It hadn't spread, all her other organs were negative. I can't guess if she knew she had it. One of her physicians confirmed that he himself did not know. The last time she saw him she wasn't exhibiting any symptoms and the last round of blood work he did was normal, but that was over a year ago."

"*One* of her physicians?" Val questioned. "You found another?"

"Yes, I did locate another doctor she was seeing. I talked to him just this morning."

"That's fantastic. How did you find him? Did he come forward?"

"No. The crime scene techs discovered several medications in her home. They were all over the counter, vitamin supplements, but she had one prescription bottle and I followed up with the doctor who prescribed it. It took him a while to call me back."

"What was she on?"

"Allopurinol," Dr. Maddox said plainly.

"Allopurinol? She had gout?" Val said the words, stunned. "Isn't she kind of young for that?" When Val practiced dentistry, several of her older patients suffered from gout, a type of arthritis that's horribly painful when it flares up. The body produces elevated levels of uric acid that form urate crystals. These settle in the joints, particularly the big toe. It's reported to be so excruciating that sufferers would do anything, even cut off the toe themselves to stop the pain.

"Gabrielle had kidney damage, likely influenced by a past chronic infection of some sort. Having kidney damage can lead to gout." Dr. Maddox reclined in his chair. "But, Val, gout's not my oddest finding with Gabrielle. That's not why I brought you to my office." Dr. Maddox sat forward. "Her *type* of cancer is the problem."

"What do you mean?"

"Gabrielle had something called aflatoxin B1-induced hepatocellular carcinoma. Because of the highly unusual nature of this, I ran the tests twice to be sure," Dr. Maddox said.

Val narrowed her eyebrows. "What's aflatoxin B1?"

"A potent carcinogen produced by certain molds, namely *Aspergillus flavus* and *Aspergillus parasiticus*. These molds grow in soil where there are rotting vegetables or grains. The molds then show up in the foods planted in that soil. Corn, rice and wheat are the most affected."

"Sounds common. Why is this so unusual?"

"We don't normally see this in developed nations and the FDA and the Department of Agriculture routinely monitor for this on imported food. Now, don't get me wrong, we do ingest aflatoxin, it's unavoidable, but the small amounts that we consume pose little risk. What Gabrielle had was long-term high exposure."

"How does food cause cancer?" Val tried to wrap her head around this information.

"Aflatoxin causes DNA damage; when this happens the DNA mutates. This is how any cancers start. As a dentist you know DNA is the chemical in each of our cells that makes up our genes. The genes are the instructions for how our cells function. Some genes control when cells grow, divide, and ultimately die. Oncogenes tell a cell to grow and divide. Tumor suppression genes slow down cell division and cause cells to die at the right time. They keep our system in balance. But aflatoxin damages these tumor suppression genes."

"Wow!" Val sat back, needing a moment to comprehend this. "She was ingesting something contaminated? Something that led to her developing cancer? How... how do you make this kind of mistake... how—" Val stopped mid-sentence. She was at a loss for words.

"Val... let me say that I don't think this was accidental."

"Dr. Maddox, if this wasn't an accident what this all means..." Val practically jumped off her chair, "is that she didn't *develop* cancer. Someone *gave* her cancer!"

Dr. Maddox sat back and crossed his arms and Val couldn't help but think there was something else. "What is it?" she asked.

"We can't rule out the possibility that she did this to herself."

"She gave herself cancer?" Val nearly choked at the thought. "Isn't that kind of absurd?"

"Not necessarily. In my discussion with her doctor, the one

who prescribed the allopurinol, he confided that he thought Gabrielle might have had Munchausen's syndrome."

Val knew what Munchausen's syndrome was. A person acts as if they have a physical or mental illness when they themselves purposely caused the symptoms. Val shook her head in disbelief. "Dr. Maddox, with all due respect—"

Dr. Maddox waved his hand, cutting her off. "Gabrielle visited her doctor many times with odd symptoms, symptoms he could find no cause for. He stated more than once in his notes that he thought these were self-induced."

"Oh my God." Val still couldn't believe it. "But giving herself cancer?"

"Val, you have to realize that Munchausen's is a mental illness. A person will act like they're sick even when they're not. They want sympathy and attention so much that they'll even cause harm to themselves to bring on the symptoms. It stems from severe emotional disorders, like a childhood trauma and we know through talking with Gabrielle's family that she had this. She was indirectly responsible for the death of her brother and sister, that was obvious from the police report Detective Gavin gave us. Plus, when patients who feel their doctor isn't giving them enough attention, or running enough tests, they'll seek out other doctors to confirm what they want to hear, or diagnose what they know they've given themselves. She might have more physicians. Other ones we don't know about. This will make our job harder."

Val thought of Adam. *Jesus, this fits even more. There's also Munchausen-by-proxy. Everyone is sorry for a sick child, and the parent. This is what the parent wants. The sympathy.*

"Everything fits for suicide, and a Munchausen's diagnosis for Gabrielle. Even the ritual with the tree branches is Gabrielle Morgan trying to get attention, for herself." Dr. Maddox sat forward and placed his arms on his desk. "I have to rule on manner of death and I am going to go with suicide for Gabrielle and homicide for Adam. Cause is exsanguination for Adam and for Gabrielle, I've left that pending, though it's more than likely respiratory or cardiac failure caused by some drug."

"Dr. Maddox, there are a few things that don't make sense. I think we need to examine these first. For instance—"

He raised his hand up again, stopping her, signaling to let him continue. "I understand that, but sometimes we can't explain why people with mental disorders do the things they do. Gabrielle fits this mold for about ninety-nine percent of this."

"There's one percent not accounted for." Val thought of the tape that wound around Gabrielle's hands. The cornstarch powder, possibly from latex gloves. Bethany, Melinda... the twins drowning. She could go on with these small pieces of the puzzle that did not fit at all. When all the pieces don't fit the picture is wrong.

"Val, in a phone call I had with the Morgans just this morning they stated in no uncertain terms that they want this case over. They've accepted the fact that Gabrielle killed their grandson and then herself."

So that explains it. The Morgans are putting the pressure on. Val still couldn't believe it. "Why did they want Detective Gavin to check out Perry Logan, Gabrielle's ex-husband then?"

"They've been very open-minded so far and I can't criticize the Morgans for their support in this case. They understood the importance of not jumping to conclusions. And they wanted to rule out this long shot, to be of help to us. Gavin's report of his interview with Perry confirmed what they suspected of their daughter, her mental state, and the Morgans want this completed now. And I can't emphasize enough the NOW. They've protected Gabrielle her whole life and they realize they can't do it anymore."

Val sat back in her chair. She was shocked, Mrs. Morgan

wanted to know who was responsible for this. If she was caving in it was because her husband was making her. "Dr. Maddox, I don't think it's this easy. I don't want to hurt the Morgans by dragging this out, but it's possible someone killed their daughter and grandson."

Dr. Maddox took off his glasses and rubbed his eyes. "Val, that's why I'm going to let you follow through with some of the leads you have. There *are* things that don't make sense, as you've said. I think at the end of the day we'll all sleep better if we know that we covered all our bases. I'll give you one week and then this assignment is over. My ruling on manner of death will be final."

Val was thrilled that Dr. Maddox gave her this latitude, but a week? How was she going to finish this in a week? She stood up to leave, but Dr. Maddox put his hand up in the air, signaling *wait a minute*. "Gabrielle was a troubled young woman, don't forget that. I'm letting you explore, but don't go crazy. The Morgans are not a family that you want to mess with. They've said to stop and this is defying that wish. If you open the wounds, give them false hope that Gabrielle may be innocent, you'll turn them into your worst enemies and I won't be able to save you. No one can. This is the same for your job and mine. Val, screwing up on a big case is a career-ending move."

These words chilled Val. She stood on her own. Though Dr. Maddox said her job and his, she was convinced that if push came to shove, she'd be sacrificed, especially if Dr. Maddox needed to save his own ass. "Don't worry. I have no intention of screwing up."

23

Munchausen's? Val was skeptical. But it was a burning question and the best person to answer that was Gabrielle's doctor, the one who thought she had this disorder. After several phone calls and no response from the doctor, Val decided she needed to be more persuasive.

Later the next afternoon, Val pulled right up to the front door of Dr. Quinlan's medical practice. She opened the door of her official medical examiner's van, with "Erie County Medical Examiner" written on all sides, and got out wearing her official work jacket, with big yellow letters, back and front, stating "medical examiner's office," and walked into the waiting room. Every eye was on her as she entered.

"Can I help you?" The receptionist shot up from her desk, which was behind a plexiglass window.

"I'm here to see Dr. Quinlan," Val said loudly, looking around the waiting room. Every eye was on her.

"Do you have an appointment?" the receptionist stammered.

"No, this is official business."

There was a visible swallow and an audible intake of breath on the receptionist's part.

"Can I speak to Dr. Quinlan?" Val said plainly.

"Is this an immediate need?" the receptionist whispered.

Val tried hard not to smile, because everyone must have been wondering if she was here to pick up a dead body, hence a dead patient. "No, I can wait." She then lowered her voice so only the receptionist could hear. "No one died here. I just need to talk to the doctor."

"Of course... can— can you come back after our last appointment at 5pm?" The receptionist's gaze shifted from Val to the patients in the waiting room, who all continued to stare at Val.

"I'd be happy to." And with that Val turned and walked out the door. In the doorway, she turned back to the receptionist. "I hope he *is* available at five. I wouldn't want to have to come back tomorrow and sit here until he *can* see me."

The receptionist said with an uncomfortable, polite smile, "I'll make sure he will see you."

Of course she would. Having someone from the medical examiner's office enter a medical practice with live patients waiting to see the doctor is bad for business. They would have agreed to anything to get her quickly out of the door, and not to come back again with patients here.

"Thank you for agreeing to meet with me, Dr. Quinlan." Val sat in the doctor's private office, he on one side of a large oak desk and she on the other. This time Val omitted the medical office jacket, choosing her wool coat instead.

"Of course, anything I can do to help." Dr. Quinlan wore a white lab coat over a striped button-down shirt and tie. He had thinning brown hair. He seemed indifferent to Val's presence, and she guessed he was only answering her questions to simply be rid of her. "I *did* think I explained everything thoroughly to Dr. Maddox."

"Yes... yes of course, but he asked me to follow up on a few things. Would that be all right?" Val knew she stretched the truth a bit here, but it was a risk she was willing to take.

The doctor nodded.

"Can I ask what were you treating Gabrielle for?" Val asked.

"I was her primary physician for her overall health, so everything." He crossed his arms and reclined casually in his chair.

Val nodded politely. Gabrielle did have another primary care doctor, the one she saw over a year ago. For some reason she chose another. *Someone with Munchausen's will seek out other doctors.* "You prescribed allopurinol, so she had gout."

"Yes, I also gave her colchicine for flare-ups but it seemed the allopurinol had it under control."

"Wasn't she kind of young to get this?"

He shook his head. "No. It's not so uncommon in someone her age. Diet is a big cause. We have the usual offenders of meat and alcohol, but sugar and fatty food cause it too. We've seen a rise in gout in young millennials because of alcohol and sugar consumption."

Val took her time, trying to phrase the next question correctly. The doctor shifted in his chair, beginning to grow impatient and Val quickly spoke. "If she had a chronic kidney infection would this have increased her likelihood of developing gout too?" Val thought of Dr. Maddox's suspicions on what caused the gout.

Dr. Quinlan narrowed his eyes. "Of course, and although she complained of multiple ailments and presumed infections, a kidney infection wasn't one of them."

Val caught a bit of self-defense and irritation in the doctor's voice. She smiled a little, hoping he didn't think she was accusing him of missing a diagnosis. "Dr. Maddox told me that you suspected that she might have had Munchausen's syndrome." Maybe he didn't miss Gabrielle's symptoms, but ignored them.

Dr. Quinlan tented his fingers and pursed his lips. "Gabrielle reported multiple symptoms and ailments that I could find no cause for. She had specific knowledge of what she wanted me to test for and became angry when the tests were all negative and I refused to run more. This is all a red flag for Munchausen's."

"Like what kind of ailments?" Val pressed.

"Let me say the gout was real. When she first became my patient, her complaints were all consistent for gout, and the tests confirmed she had it. Then things escalated." The doctor reclined back in his chair and looked at the ceiling. "She reported respiratory problems, muscle cramps, she felt that she had heart palpitations, achy joints and thought she had arthritis. Recurrent infections were a big one for a while. So were digestive problems. There was also diarrhea, nausea, tingling in her feet, chills." He sat forward and focussed his gaze on Val. "Many of the symptoms were unclear, inconsistent, were not controllable, and according to her, did not respond to treatment. Blood tests revealed nothing wrong with her. More involved tests revealed nothing either. She then came to me with relapses that seemed to spark new symptoms that she wanted me to test for. And she had the names of these tests at the tip of her tongue. Again, it's all a red flag for Munchausen's."

"I see." Dr. Quinlan's description was pretty convincing. "Can you tell me what causes this syndrome?"

"Causes are not clear. Childhood trauma and abuse are the common culprits. The likely sufferers are women age twenty to forty, which Gabrielle fit. They also typically have some knowledge of the medical field, and are very cunning. Why do they do this? They want sympathy. Some sources say they enjoy the satisfaction in deceiving important and powerful people, such as doctors."

Val nodded, listening to what the doctor was saying. Dr. Maddox had said almost the same thing. This certainly fit Gabrielle.

"Munchausen's is a psychiatric condition," Val stated. "Is it possible that Gabrielle was also bipolar? Could this have caused it too?" Perry Logan, Gabrielle's first husband suspected this and Val wanted to know what a healthcare professional thought.

Dr. Quinlan sat back again and appeared to think about the possibility. "Personality disorders *are* common in people with Munchausen's. A diagnosis of bipolar depression is usually based on reporting of symptoms by the patient, and a psychiatric evaluation. Though, out of the multiple symptoms Gabrielle complained of, none were consistent with this."

"What about liver cancer," Val asked. "Anything consistent with that?"

"Liver cancer? Yes, Dr. Maddox did mention that she had it, but no, she never complained of symptoms consistent with any kind of cancer."

It was Val's turn to sit back and think. The doctor was treating Gabrielle for gout. A real ailment. But Gabrielle reported no issues with her kidneys, though she had signs of past kidney damage. And she might really have had bipolar. Again, not reported.

And Jesus, if she wanted to give herself cancer and knew that she had it, or thought that she had it, why not invent likely symptoms. Why not tell her doctor that she thought she had it? Have him test for it. Wouldn't that be what she wanted if she had Munchausen's?

24

Val sighed. "It doesn't make sense, Gwen. If she gave herself cancer because she had Munchausen's, why didn't she report any liver cancer symptoms to her doctor? Hell, why didn't she tell *anyone* she thought she had it. No one seemed to know about it."

"No one who admitted it, Val," Gwen responded. "You have to keep that in mind."

"Very true." Val shook her head and looked up at Zoe, the toxicologist who was standing in her doorway. "This case keeps getting more bizarre," Val said to Zoe as her pulse picked up. The only time Zoe ever came to her office was when she had something important to tell. Val took a deep breath. "What did you find?"

Zoe grabbed a chair and sat down. "I took a look at your video from the Morgans' house. Those yellow flowers in Claudia's room, they're not lilies. They're angel's trumpets."

"Angel's trumpets?" Val was unfamiliar with the name.

Zoe held up her phone showing still pictures from the video. "See here, the yellow flowers are large and trumpet-shaped, that's where the name comes from. They're so characteristic I almost laughed out loud... anyway, they're members of the nightshade family."

"Nightshade? Do you mean *deadly* nightshade?" Gwen said.

"Not... *exactly*. Let's get our nightshades straight. *Atropa belladonna*, which earned the name deadly nightshade is what you are referring to, Gwen. It's the most common member of the family. But angel's trumpets are also very deadly. They just don't have the catchy name, though *angel's* anything is a bit of a misnomer. Anyway, your nanny has them in her room. In a vase." Zoe held up another picture on her phone from a website for angel's trumpets. "See how all of the flowers are hanging down. This is why they are so characteristic."

"I thought those flowers were dying because of how much they were drooping," Val said.

"Nope. Healthy and happy. Angel's trumpets droop down because they're said to be 'showering gifts from above,' from heaven. Though I wouldn't want to be the recipient of this gift."

Jesus. Val pulled out her own phone quickly, her fingers ready to text Gavin. He needed to hear about the nanny, and the flowers she chooses to display in her room. "What does this kind of flower do?"

"Well like most poisons—and keep in mind, most poisonous plants have a good side along with their negative—they're used to make lots of medications that treat all kinds of routine health issues from nausea to asthma to cardiac problems. But an overdose of medications made from nightshades creates something called anticholinergic toxidrome. Ingesting the plant mimics an overdose of any of these medications. And let me tell you, an overdose on the medications themselves is so common, there's a mnemonic that ER doctors use to remember the symptoms... blind as a bat, red as a beet, hot as a hare, dry as a bone, mad as a hatter, bowel and bladder lose their tone..."

"And the heart races on alone," Val finished. "I remember

that from my dental school pharmacology course. The mnemonic defines..." she fished through her memory, using each part of the mnemonic as a guide, "an inability to focus on near objects plus a sensitivity to light because of the dilated pupils, flushed skin, elevated temperature, dry mouth and skin, hallucinations, delirium slurred speech, confusion, urinary retention, and a racing heartbeat."

"Sounds lovely," Gwen said.

"Um, and, Val," Zoe interrupted, "the psychosis produced by this poison—the mad as a hatter part—can be profound. Plus, it can intensify existing mental issues."

Holy crap, Val saw the significance of what Zoe was saying. Gabrielle was reported to be bipolar. "How does one ingest it? Do they eat the flowers?" Val's mind circled back to Gabrielle's cancer. She was eating something contaminated. If she didn't do this herself, someone gave it to her.

"You can, but tea can be made from the roots and seeds of the plant, that's probably the easiest way."

"Did Gabrielle have this poison in her system?" Gwen asked.

Zoe pointed at Gwen with index fingers from both hands. "And there's the problem. No, Gabrielle did not die from this kind of poison. There's none of the alkaloids, namely, atropine, hyoscyamine, and scopolamine, in any of her tissues."

Val narrowed her eyes. "No yew poison, and now no nightshade alkaloids. Yet Gabrielle was holding yew branches, had seeds in her mouth, and the nanny happens to have these toxic flowers in her room?"

"Val, Gabrielle *was* poisoned with something, just not either yew or nightshade," Zoe said. "I'm still trying to find out what that *something* was. But just because a nightshade poison didn't kill her doesn't mean that she never ingested one."

Val crossed her arms. "You know, with all of those non-specific symptoms Gabrielle reported to her doctor... I wonder if she suspected she was being poisoned. Maybe she was trying to find out if she was, by getting corroboration from her doctor."

"What are the other symptoms Gabrielle complained of?" Zoe asked.

Val recited what Dr. Quinlan told her; diarrhea, nausea, tingling in her feet, chills...

"Those are all pretty common ailments but they're also classic heavy metal poisoning symptoms," Zoe said.

"Her doctor found nothing unusual in any of her blood tests," Val said.

"If he didn't specifically test for heavy metal poisoning, a regular blood test wouldn't have revealed it." All of a sudden Zoe stopped and shook her head with a smirk. "Oh my God."

"Zoe, what is it?" Val asked.

"Heavy metals could have caused her gout by creating her kidney damage. You know, if someone was poisoning Gabrielle, and this was given to her long enough ago to have caused her gout, they would have been doing it for some time."

"Zoe, can *you* test for heavy metal poisoning in the samples we kept from Gabrielle?" Val asked.

"Depends on how long ago she would have ingested it. We have her hair, bone and nail specimens, these are the structures heavy metal gets into and hangs around in. But once those structures grow out, and the poisoning has stopped, the tests will come back negative."

"But they can also provide us with a timeline of poisoning if we find them," Val said. The poison would have gotten embedded in the hair shaft at the skull and since hair grows at a certain rate this can be used as a timeline to determine when the person was poisoned. Same principle with bone and nails. "Her hair was long, so that will give us about four years. Bone remodels about every seven years. Her nails would have the shortest time frame."

"Correct on all of the above." Zoe stood up. "I'll start ASAP and see what we have." All of a sudden Zoe stopped. She looked disappointed.

"What's wrong?" Val asked.

"This is too easy." Zoe shook her head.

"For you maybe." Val laughed.

"No, for a poisoner. It's way too easy to detect heavy metals with the right tests. I think, if you have a poisoner on your hands, you have a skilled one. I think this is someone who knows what they're doing. Heavy metal? That's amateur hour."

25

*J*esus, Val thought. *Claudia had poisonous flowers in her room.* Bridget was painting pictures of them. Was Bridget trying to say something?

Val's phone rang. She looked at the screen and her stomach dropped when she saw the name of Hayward Sinclair, the lawyer from Florida. *Oh crap, I can't deal with this right now.* So much was going on with Gabrielle Morgan and the thought of going back to Clearwater to testify was a nightmare. It was a distraction she would do anything to avoid. Though the last thing she wanted to do was answer the phone, Val also knew procrastinating wouldn't solve anything. She needed to tell Haywood, once and for all, she couldn't do this.

"Hello, Val, good news! Dennis Tate pleaded guilty. Though I have no doubt we would have won this case. No jury would have set him free." Haywood practically sang the words.

"What?" Val pressed the phone to her ear, stunned. Did she hear correctly?

"He took the plea deal. We offered life without the possibility of parole. Smartest thing he could have done. He avoids the death penalty this way. Though I have to admit I personally would have loved to see this son of a bitch take a needle in the arm."

For some reason, Val didn't feel as relieved as she should have. "What changed his mind?"

"He had no chance of winning," Haywood scoffed. "Val, even his own counsel advised him to take this deal. With you testifying, someone he bit, someone who survived and could tell the horrors this man put you through, this case was over before it even began."

Oh my God, it was me. I made this decision. Val kept telling herself this was absurd. She didn't cause this. Of course he killed those women. He had just confessed to doing so. Why did she have this sick feeling in the pit of her stomach, then?

"The newspapers are comparing this case to Bundy. I think a lot of people are relieved Dennis Tate will be behind bars for the rest of his life."

Ted Bundy was also arrested in Florida and a bitemark sealed his fate too. He was convicted, sentenced to death and executed. Bundy was a win. A monster who was destroyed. Was Mr. Tate a monster? Did he kill those women? There was no other evidence linking him to the crime. Bundy had a ton of strong circumstantial evidence to go along with the bitemark. Not to mention he was on the run after escaping from prison when he murdered those women in Florida. When he broke out, he'd been serving time for kidnapping.

"What happens now?" Val asked.

"Nothing. He goes to jail for the rest of his life. Val, I can't thank you enough. As I've said all along you were my star witness. Without you—"

Val interrupted, "Well, Mr. Sinclair, I hate to cut you short but I have another call that I have to take." She did. This wasn't a lie to get rid of Haywood: she had Jack on the line, though she knew he would have waited.

"Have a good afternoon. I won't keep you," Sinclair said, and with that, the call ended.

"What are you doing tonight?" Jack asked.

"The usual. Trying to pin the tail on those who cause murder and mayhem." She laughed uncomfortably, her mind still grappling with Mr. Tate.

There was a second of silence before Jack responded. "Let's have dinner just the two of us. Text me the name of where to go and I'll meet you downtown."

There was something in his voice that sounded determined, alluring. Charming. And for some reason, scary.

Val had tried to convince herself that what happened with Mr. Tate was as it should have been. He confessed. It was over. For him, and for her. No need to testify. Yay! Why did she feel so conflicted, then? She was stressed, and in no mood to deal with very much right now, every nerve was standing on edge—pulled to its max, getting ready to break.

Val hated to ask Jack what was up, why he wanted this private meeting but she was left with no choice. Drinks, dinner and now empty dessert dishes sat before them. Other than a discussion about the Morgan case, this evening had been pretty routine. Maybe he just wanted to get together and unwind? Val was exhausted and so completely *done* after her day, that she was ready to call it a night.

She drained her water glass, and looked at her watch. It was time to go. She sat forward and placed both arms on the table. "I'm pretty beat."

Jack reached over and took her hand, and held on, his eyes on hers.

Val's stomach dropped and her heart raced. Okay, there *was* something more going on. "What is it, Jack?"

He smiled and his cheeks reddened as he sat back. All of a sudden he had a nervous quality to him. "Have you noticed that I'm staying in Buffalo longer than I should?"

"This case has been crazy, hasn't it?" *Of course this is the reason why,* Val rationalized. But then why was Jack looking at her that way?

"My staying in Buffalo has nothing to do with this case." His eyes still on hers.

Val took a deep breath. She wasn't sure if she was ready for what she thought was coming next. "Jack..."

"Let me finish."

"No, Jack. Please don't. Once you say what I think you're going to, we have to make a decision and I'm not ready to do that." Val couldn't believe those words just came out of her mouth, but it was true. And she didn't know it until this very moment. All along she questioned her feelings, and without thinking, without debating, without struggling with herself to find the truth, the answer suddenly came out.

"I see," was all he said. His eyes cast down now. The waitress walked by and Jack quickly caught her attention. "Can we have the bill, please."

As soon as she walked away Val leaned in. "Jack, I don't want it to be like this between us."

"Val, you asked me a moment ago to not say anything more. I will ask the same of you now."

Val's pulse pounded and her mind spun, trying hard to think how to fix this. But the truth was, there was no way to fix it. No words would mend the large crack that was about to split them apart. Not at this moment anyway.

Seconds later the check came and Jack placed some cash inside the pocket of the binder. "It's all set." He got up. "I'm heading back to Boston tonight. Now in fact."

Val watched his back as he walked to the door. She tried to yell out his name, to call him back, but it wouldn't come to her lips.

Give him time. That's all Val could think about as she sat alone at the table fighting back tears. She needed time, too. To take in what Jack was about to suggest. Why did she stop him from saying it? Why not let it hang in the air between them, then grab and run with it. Why not try being together?

She knew the reason. She wasn't ready to take the next step with Jack. It could only destroy their friendship and anything possible in the future. The timing was off and entering a relationship with bad timing only makes a doomed relationship. She couldn't risk that with Jack.

The bottom line was that she wasn't ready. Her feelings for Gavin were still there. She loved Jack, she did, but couldn't enter into anything romantic with him unless he was the only man in her life. She had to be free of Gavin's spell first.

When Val arrived home, Jack and his bags were gone. For a moment Val wondered if she was ever going to see him again. That's when the tears began to fall.

The next morning Val stood in Gavin's office trying to keep her emotions under control. The sadness of losing Jack last night and now she had to deal with this... This, though, wasn't sad. *This* was infuriating and made her temper simmer to the boiling point. It was moments like this that Val was actually happy she could rely on the one emotion that never failed her: anger.

"What do you mean you can't speak with Claudia?" Val tried not to shout at Gavin. She wasn't mad at him. The situation was just so damn frustrating.

"I've contacted the Morgans and they let me know that

Claudia had a family emergency. She's gone to her parents' home to help her mother take care of her father who had a stroke," Gavin stated calmly. He was so rational about it and that only made Val more irritated.

"What! Do you believe this bullshit? Jesus, Mitch, it's awfully convenient, don't you think? Why aren't you demanding she come back to town?"

"Val, calm down. There are no yew trees in the Morgans' greenhouse. No moldy vegetables or angel's trumpets either. I confirmed all of that just this morning, to the fury of Mr. Morgan. He let me take a look in the greenhouse only because Mrs. Morgan insisted on it. She's probably the only reason I still have a job right now too." Gavin let out an exhausted sigh. "Angel's trumpets are sold online. They're popular because of how attractive they are."

"What about deadly? How about they're popular because of how deadly they are?"

Gavin threw up his arms. "Christ, Val, I can buy foxgloves, which is where digitalis comes from, at most commercial home improvement stores. Having poisonous flowers is not illegal. A lot of flowers are poisonous. That's why we don't eat them. We look at them. I cannot bring Claudia in on this. When she returns we will question her." Gavin gave her a *this is the end of the conversation* look.

"If she returns," Val scoffed, she knew she was treading on thin ice after Gavin's rant but didn't care.

He took a deep breath. "Val..."

"Okay, okay. What else do you have?"

"Well, I have some other news that might make you happy," he said with a smile.

She took her own deep breath and waited.

"There wasn't much that we found in Gabrielle's house that was of forensic value. She had a laptop but it was clean... she also had a drawer filled with old mail, all standard stuff... bank statements, paid utility bills, receipts for some purchases, like her TV and her phone—the phone we haven't found yet..."

Val grew impatient. "How is this making me happy?"

"Gabrielle had a safe deposit box. The monthly rental fee for it was on one of the bank statements."

"Safe deposit box?" Her face fell and her stomach knotted.

"The key seems to be missing, though. I'm surprised because I remember you telling me that you found one in Gabrielle's house. Mr. Morgan knows about the key and can't find it amongst his daughter's belongings. I assured him it must be there. I mean if you saw it..."

Oh no. Here it was. Finally. The key, the key Val still had, the one she believed fitted a safe deposit box. And Mr. Morgan now knows she saw it. She was going to get caught. How could she not? There was nothing left to do but come clean and come clean quickly. "Mitch, if I say something will you promise to not get mad? I've been meaning to tell you but honestly it slipped my mind until right now."

"What is it?" he said cautiously.

"Well, I told you that I took a look in Gabrielle's house, *on my own*." Val lied about on her own.

Gavin sat still. Cautious. And tense. "Yes."

"I also told you that I found a key..."

"*Yes...*"

"I kept the key."

"Jesus Christ, Val! Don't tell me..." Gavin shot up from his desk chair. "Did Jack Styles have something to do with this? Because the Valentina Knight I know doesn't do shit like this."

Val just nodded. She couldn't speak.

"Shit! Shit! Shit! How many times have I spoken to you about hanging out with him? You have a job to do and he exploits that job. You are not some celebrity crime show persona, like he is.

Christ, I know how easy it can be to be swept up in something like this. But you have protocol to follow. He does not. You screw up and guilty people go free. You screw up and the guilty people he typically defends get to go free. He wins. You lose."

Val cringed and sunk back in her seat. "I'm sorry, I told you I forgot about it until now." She knew she'd feel guilty *and* stupid if she used this excuse about this and boy was it coming on hard.

Gavin exhaled and placed his hands on his hips. "I'll let this go. Mr. Morgan thinks it's lost. This gives me a little more time to get a search warrant and get to the contents before he does."

Val narrowed her eyes, trying to follow where Gavin was going with this.

"Safe deposit boxes need two keys to open them. A personal key and the guard key. The bank keeps the guard key. Neither key can open the lock alone. If the personal key is lost the bank will have to arrange for a locksmith to drill the lock. There's a whole process Mr. Morgan will need to go through with the bank before they'll drill the lock for him, and that takes time, longer than me getting a warrant, which I'm hoping for by tomorrow morning at the latest."

Val still held her gaze on Gavin, scrutinizing.

"Depending what's in that box, Mr. Morgan can bury any scandalous evidence like he's done in the past. I guarantee, if there is anything that's unfavorable for him in that box, it will be lost. Mr. Morgan might not be protecting Gabrielle anymore, but he certainly is protecting his business."

"Do *you* need the key, then?" Val eased a little.

"Val, this is one time that I am pretty happy that you did something that you weren't supposed to do. I need to open the safe deposit box before Mr. Morgan. So, Val, what I'm saying is yes, I'm happy he doesn't have the key and you do."

26

Gavin, Warren and Val stood in the bank vault waiting for the bank manager to return with the other one of the two keys that would open Gabrielle's safe deposit box. The search warrant arrived in Gavin's hands just one hour ago.

"I knew Judge Mercado would issue this quickly. The man doesn't mess around," Gavin said.

All heads turned as the door to the vault opened.

"Sorry, it just took us a little while to find this." JT Dobson, the bank manager, held up his key. Val couldn't help noticing the man looked no older than eighteen. He probably weighed all of 120 pounds, too, in his skinny pants and tight-fitting button-down shirt and tie. Val sized him up. Couldn't have been much taller than about five foot five.

Val looked at the key JT produced and frowned. It didn't resemble the one she had. But she was no expert on safe deposit box locks. Maybe the guard key is different than the personal key.

"The box will need both keys to open it. Each will fit in these locks." JT pointed to the two key holes on either side of the box. He stuck his key in and turned.

Gavin tried the one Val had. It didn't fit.

He tried again. It didn't even go halfway into the lock. Val could feel her pulse pick up a few paces. *Holy crap.*

"Can I see that?" JT asked.

Gavin pulled the key out and handed it to JT.

After a quick inspection, JT said, "This is the wrong key." JT handed it back to Gavin. "I'm sorry but this isn't even a safe deposit box key."

"If this doesn't open that box, then what does it open?" Val snapped. She couldn't believe it.

"Ma'am, I don't have a clue. It's unlike anything I've ever seen before," JT said. "Anyway, I have a locksmith service that we use. The guy usually comes within the hour. You have a warrant so we can go ahead with getting this open. Do you want me to call him?"

"JT, yes, please do," Gavin said.

JT was true to his word. A locksmith showed up in less than an hour. While they waited, Gavin had pulled Val aside and whispered in her ear. "If I keep that key I have to give it to the Morgans. Can you hold on to it for another little while?"

Val stood back, stunned and then crossed her arms. "So, you want me to do something *that's not by the book*," she teased. "I can get fired for this. Plus, I have proper protocol to follow..."

Gavin pursed his lips. "There's a difference between my *not by the book* and Jack Styles' version."

Val couldn't help but smile to herself as she took the key and put it back in her pocket. *It's not often I get one up on Gavin.*

The locksmith had the box open in under one minute. A drill bit on a cordless drill through the keyhole did it. *So, by drilling the lock, they actually meant* drilling *the lock. Why on earth did we need a locksmith for that?* Val thought.

"Will that be all?" the locksmith asked.

JT looked at both Gavin and Warren, waiting for an answer.

"Yes, that will be it," Warren said.

He packed up his drill and he moved towards the door. JT followed him. "Once a box is open we leave the owner alone with the contents. You have a warrant and I'm not sure if I need to, or should, be here," JT said.

"We'll call you when we're done, then," Warren said.

As soon as JT was out of the door, Gavin slid the lid off the box and began pulling out contents, all of which were documents. He placed everything on the countertop. "Let's go through the items one by one." First was a photocopy of multiple pieces of paper put together.

"What is that?" Val asked.

"Looks like partial receipts for the sale of GDA Pharmaceutical stock," Gavin said.

"GDA Pharmaceutical?" This was the company Gabrielle's first husband was CEO of. A company that went bankrupt due to a drug scandal. "That stock must have been practically worthless."

"Yes, it was but that wasn't such a bad thing for the person who owned *this* stock." Gavin shook his head and smirked. "Son of a bitch."

"Who would want worthless stock?" Val asked.

Gavin dropped the documents down. "These are receipts from a short sell."

"What's that?" Val asked.

"Most investors buy stocks hoping they'll increase in value. Short selling is how you make money when the prices are falling."

"I'm listening."

"It's actually a pretty simple concept. An investor borrows shares of stock from someone who owns it and then arranges a date in the future when the shares will be returned. The borrower sells the borrowed shares and pockets any profits.

Then at the later designated date, buys the stock back to return to the lender. The hope is that the price falls for the buy back. It looks like 500,000 shares of GDA stock were borrowed and sold at $200 a share. That's $100 million. Once the stock plummeted, it was rebought for $15 a share and the 500,000 shares returned to the owner. That cost $7.5 million. The profit was $92.5 million."

Val was stunned by the staggering amount made from this. "Gabrielle made a lot of money from her husband's death? I thought her father said she was poor."

"Not Gabrielle. These aren't her receipts. There's a name for a corporation but it seems to be an alias. Looks like Gabrielle was trying to find out who's behind it." Gavin picked the papers back up again. "Look at the notes in the margin."

There were handwritten notes next to dates of the transaction. There were circles around several of the notes, notably "Max gets sick," "Max dies," "stocks die," "total wipe out," and five exclamation points around the words "I will tear you apart for this."

"Looks like she has an idea of who this was," Warren remarked.

"You know, the scandal caused the problem but the death of Gabrielle's CEO husband destroyed the company. The stock value might not have dropped like it did if it wasn't for that," Gavin said.

"Are you suggesting…" Val couldn't help but speculate.

"It was a domino effect, Val. For someone to profit the way they did from this, they knew the stock was going to decline and they knew Gabrielle's husband was going to die."

"If she figured out who's behind this. That's a pretty good reason to kill her," Warren said.

"Are all of these documents about GDA stocks?" Val asked.

"No…" Gavin said slowly as he pulled out the next piece of

paper. "This is a request for exhumation... it seems Gabrielle wanted to have her twin brother and sister exhumed."

"Exhumed?" Val reached over to grab the paper so she could see for herself. "Any reason as to why?"

"None that I can find here." Gavin shuffled through the documents. "Why would Gabrielle want to bring up the past like this? A past that she was the center of and that everyone was trying to bury, keep her name away from?"

"Gabrielle knew something about that day and she's trying to get proof about it, is what I'm suspecting," Val said.

Gavin nodded his head, eyes still on the paper.

"Mitch, can you continue with the exhumation of the twins? Can we actually get this to happen?" Val asked.

"I can try. It looks like she was just waiting to hear back from her petition to the court." Gavin laughed. "I think I might get it done. Judge Mercado's name is on this."

"If you think he's going to be agreeable, it wouldn't hurt to try to get Gabrielle and Adam brought up too." Val thought of the heavy metal poisons. Dr. Maddox may need to take additional samples for Zoe to test. "They're in the same coffin so you get two for one."

"It's possible. Everything we have on the questionable circumstances surrounding her death may give me the ammunition to complete another petition." Gavin shook his head. "It's a crapshoot, though. Judge Mercado is a reasonable guy. He'll follow the law and plausible leads but I don't know how much he'll do to anger the Morgans. Being a judge is an elected position and could jeopardize his chances in the next election. Digging up the Morgans' daughter and grandson won't be something they'll likely be happy about."

"It'll anger Mr. Morgan. Mrs. Morgan wants the right thing for her family," Val said.

Gavin didn't respond. His gaze stayed glued to the next piece of paper he pulled out of the safe deposit box. "Christ, would you look at this!"

"What is it?" Warren asked.

"It seems Gabrielle was trying to get custody of her sister Bridget. She had the paperwork drawn up about a year ago," Gavin said.

"Do you think she was playing hardball with her parents, Mitch?" Warren asked. "They wanted custody of Adam and now she wanted Bridget. Maybe this was an attempt to get them to cave in."

"Possibly," Gavin said.

One last piece of paper was left in the box. This time Val reached in to take it out. It was a newspaper article. The story was about Gabrielle's second husband, Perry Logan and his band. The photo with the article is what caught her attention. It showed Perry playing on stage. Warren looked over Val's shoulder.

"She had a grudge against the guy. Looks like she was still stalking him," Warren said.

"I might know why," Val responded. The picture captured a small portion of the audience. In the front row, with a smile and her arms outstretched, her lips almost reaching a leaning Perry, stood Bethany Arias.

Then Val noticed something else.

27

"So, Perry, did you divorce Gabrielle because she was crazy or did she divorce *you* because you were screwing her friend?" Gavin decided to get right to the point. And he meant to catch Perry off guard with the sucker punch.

Perry's lips parted as if to speak and his eyes went wide. It took a few seconds before words eventually came out. "Look, my marriage to Gabi was already over by the time I hooked up with Bethany. And let me tell you that she was no *friend*. Neither was that bitch, Melinda." Perry pulled out a pack of cigarettes from his pocket and lit one up. The three men sat around his kitchen table. Perry looked remarkably at ease.

"You knew Melinda too?" Warren asked, the implication in his voice was evident.

"Yah, I did." Perry stood up and paced the small space. "All those three did was compete with each other. I couldn't keep up with the jealousy, the trying to outdo one another. What's the old saying—keep your enemies closer. Well, in this case it was frenemies." Perry smiled. "See, I have no problem being honest with you, detective."

"Thank you, Perry. So let me ask you this, since we're being honest, how did *Bethany* take it when she found out you were screwing *Gabrielle*?"

Perry froze momentarily before continuing his trek around the ten-by-ten area. He remained silent. Gavin could see Perry trying to backtrack out of this one. Trying to figure out how Gavin knew the truth.

Gavin set down the newspaper article that was found in Gabrielle's safe deposit box. "Let me show you this. Maybe it will jog your memory." He put his finger next to the picture. "This is you and Bethany?"

Perry leaned over, took a long look, and let out a held breath. "Yes."

"Take a peek here." Gavin slid his finger up to the date on the top of the article. "This picture was taken before you married Gabrielle. Actually it's about a year before, correct? Hell, that's before you even were dating Gabrielle."

Perry nodded, his eyes everywhere but on Gavin's.

"So, Gabrielle stole you from Bethany? Not the other way around?" Warren tapped his pen on the table. "Did you know that Bethany was poor and Gabrielle was loaded?"

"Poor? Bethany wasn't poor," Perry scoffed.

"Oh, yes she is. And was," Warren said.

"Well, I didn't know that." Perry sat back down and squashed his cigarette in a tray that sat on the table. "Look, detective, I'm not proud about what I did back then. Yes, I was with Bethany first. It was nothing serious. Gabrielle came on to me and I fell in love with her. I'm sorry I hurt Bethany." Perry pointed at Warren. "Gabrielle was not sorry, though. I found out later how much not. It was during one of her crazy episodes."

"Crazy episodes?" Gavin asked.

"I told you Gabrielle would have violent mood swings. She got in my face several times and told me that if it wasn't for her wanting, and I quote, to fuck me to fuck Bethany over, well I'd have my ass living in some shithouse."

Warren looked around at the kitchen. "Maybe she was right."

Perry, for a moment, looked like he was going to lunge at Warren. Warren just crossed his arms, waiting. "Look, asshole, yeah Gabrielle stole me from Bethany and I went to Bethany in the end hoping to get her to take me back."

"Because your rich wife was no longer rich after her daddy disowned her for marrying you, and you didn't know that Bethany was also poor?" Warren pressed.

Perry stood up, shoving his chair back so hard it fell over. His chest heaved as he glared at Warren.

Gavin intercepted quickly. "Did Gabrielle know Bethany's family lost their money?"

"If she did she never said anything to me." Perry spat out the words.

"I'm sure it didn't sit well with Gabrielle that you went back to Bethany," Warren said calmly.

"No. It pissed her off to no end. Look, this is the reason why she was so vindictive. She couldn't get at her, so she got at me."

"Couldn't get at her?" Gavin said, confused.

Perry placed both of his hands on the table and leaned over towards Warren. "Did you ever try to get even with someone who is stinking rich, or according to you, someone you think is stinking rich, when you're shit poor? It doesn't happen. Daddy wasn't supporting Gabrielle at this point." Perry laughed. "This proves she didn't know Bethany lost everything. So how could I have?"

No, Gabrielle's daddy was supporting Bethany. "It works when you get creative. There are some advantages money can't buy," Gavin said.

"I beg to differ." Perry picked up his chair and sat back down.

"Evidence of a crime, hard evidence against someone, always gives you an upper hand."

"You mean blackmail, don't you?"

"Yes, but not for money, for control. Once you take money out of the picture you're on an even playing field."

Perry laughed. "That doesn't give you control. That makes you dead."

"Exactly," Gavin said.

"Please, detective, I know you don't believe me but I had nothing to do with Gabrielle's death." Perry pulled out another cigarette and casually pushed his chair back from the table, giving him room to cross his legs.

"You're not with Bethany anymore. What caused the break-up a second time?" Warren asked.

"Like I told you earlier. I didn't love her. Didn't love her the second time around either. We're simply not right for each other."

Gavin decided to let that line of questioning go. Unless he found some proof, Perry would never admit what his true intentions with Bethany were. "Can you tell us about Melinda?" Gavin asked.

"Sure. There's not that much to really tell though. Melinda is the real bitch. Really competitive. She's very smart. Gabrielle and Bethany were no match for her. I think they knew this all along."

28

Val and Gavin sat in in his office, each with a cup of coffee. There was one small window behind Gavin. Val glanced outside. The snow blew sideways and she hoped it would ease up a little in time for her ride home. Gavin had his latest documents spread out before him on the desk.

"Perry isn't terribly fond of Melinda, but he really didn't elaborate much on specifics other than to say he thought she was an awful bitch. And that she seemed to have something on Gabrielle and Bethany. Just what that was, he didn't know. Neither Bethany nor Gabrielle spoke about it."

"I've met Melinda and have to say, she wasn't my favorite person," Val said with a smirk.

"I think I know, at least, what Gabrielle's issue was with her." Gavin took a sip from his coffee cup.

Val's face tightened. "I'm listening."

"The Holbright corporation filed for bankruptcy protection about five years ago. But honestly it has been teetering on the edge for a decade. They are still in the house on Lincoln Parkway, but it doesn't look like it's for much longer. They've been liquidating to pay off debts." Gavin picked up his cup and took a sip.

"Where is Melinda living now?"

"Downtown loft. Get this, the purchase price was two million." Gavin laughed. "It's worth more than Bethany's condo. And I have another bit of interesting information about it."

"Did Mr. Morgan buy it for her?" Val rolled her eyes, confident of her answer. "Looks like out of these three families, only Gabrielle's still had money. Jesus, is this the problem Gabrielle and Bethany both had with her? Mr. Morgan treated Melinda the best?" Val remembered Mrs. Morgan's story about Melinda in a thong in the Morgans' bedroom.

"Mr. Morgan has nothing to do with this. The loft is owned by WNR LLC." Gavin took another sip of coffee and help the cup between his hands, his eyes on Val, knowing smile on his face.

Val scrutinized Gavin's expression. "WNR LLC? Why do I think that's more important than Mr. Morgan screwing another one of his daughter's friends?"

"Damn important. And I'm damn proud of myself for digging enough to get this information because it was so well hidden." Gavin set down his cup, still smiling.

"Did you do something that wasn't by the book to get this information?" Val teased.

"My tactics are well guarded." Gavin crossed his arms and grinned wider.

"Pray tell, then."

"I'm pretty sure it's Melinda's corporation."

"What the f—?" Val stopped short of spitting out the word.

"I also think it's a front. It's how she hides her money. And by money I mean the stock she short-sold from GDA Pharmaceutical." Gavin flipped over the top sheet of paper and pointed to a line on the next page. "On the day the stock was to be returned, WNR LLC had the exact same amount transferred out of its holdings. Payable to, get this, Chandler Trust."

"Are you serious?"

"Very. Gabrielle's first husband, Malcom Chandler, set up the trust fund for his family. The trust manager made the deal that loaned the stock." Gavin looked up at Val. "That manager's name was Scott Payne."

"What?" Val flew up off the chair.

"There's more," Gavin said. "Scott lost his job after this transaction. Went to work at The Next Step. Where later, Gabrielle would be employed."

Val's head spun at the revelation. "Can you prove any of this about the trust?"

"I can prove the transaction occurred, but nothing is illegal about it. Stocks are borrowed all the time in this type of capacity. But someone knew this one was going to decline big in value. And obviously Melinda knew it." Gavin pursed his lips. "Why on earth would she have wanted it otherwise?"

"Gabrielle? Did she know who was involved in this transaction?"

"I'm guessing she must have had a suspicion after the fact. Unfortunately, we found nothing in her safe deposit box with evidence. I do think she was looking for it though."

"But Gabrielle was sleeping with Scott Payne," Val blurted loudly as she looked at Gavin. She couldn't get over the shock.

"I'm guessing she was probably trying to get proof of whatever wrongdoing she suspected."

"Do you think Scott realized who Gabrielle was?"

"Possibly, but keep in mind she was Gabrielle Chandler back then, not Gabrielle Morgan. There are no photos of her online. Even when the twins died, there are no pictures of a sixteen-year-old Gabrielle Morgan, or an older Gabrielle Morgan for that matter. Plus Morgan is a common name and our Morgan in question wasn't living in a mansion."

"If Scott found out what Gabrielle might have been up to its possible Melinda could have found out too."

"Would one of them have killed her, do you mean? Depends on what other information Gabrielle had on them. As I said, short selling is not illegal. Killing Max Chandler would have been. Gabrielle was digging for proof about something. Maybe it was just to get revenge on her friend. Perry said they were competitive but this takes that to a whole new level. Don't worry, though, I plan to follow through with Mr. Payne."

Val sighed and paced a few steps, frustrated.

Gavin held up another document. "But for now, I do have this."

"What's that?"

"The court order for the exhumation of the Morgan twins. But that's not all. Here's the one for Gabrielle too. This is all happening Monday morning."

"How on earth did you pull that off?"

"The twins were easy. Gabrielle had fought and won that battle already. She died before she received notification. In her petition, she stated the reason why she wanted the exhumation. She said she believed the twins were poisoned. And that someone was also doing the same thing to her. It set the stage for us to exhume her and since Adam is in the coffin with her, he comes too."

"Mitch! That's fantastic!" Finally, some proof that Gabrielle felt she was being poisoned, but Val was still confused. The twins would have been poisoned fifteen years ago.

Gavin looked down at his cell phone. "Holy shit!"

"What is it?"

Gavin was silent for a moment as he stared at the screen. "I can't believe this," he said and jumped up, grabbing his coat. He seemed dazed, lost for what to do next.

"Mitch! What is it?" Val repeated.

"Bethany Arias. She's dead. Apparent suicide. Jumped from the balcony of her penthouse."

29

Val quickly parked her medical examiner's office van, opened the door and jumped out into the snow-covered parking lot of Bethany's complex. The drifts were already midcalf, with more flurries streaming down. Flashing lights of the patrol cars lit up the sky. Not only were cops everywhere, so were reporters. Several put microphones in Val's face, and immediately began rolling question after question at her.

"No comment," Val yelled as she hurried to the back of the van to get her supply bag. She grabbed what she needed, fending off reporters, and trudged as fast as she could to the rear of the building, the side that faced the water, to where Bethany lay dead. The reporters followed but only went as far as the first line of officers would allow. Val pulled out her badge and passed through the security checkpoint. *Finally, she was free.*

A large white tent was protecting the crime scene, placed to shield the body, and evidence, from the elements and also to stop onlookers from watching the investigation from the balconies up above. Val glanced up at the one which belonged to Bethany. Several cops could be seen along with the crime scene crew, who were dusting the railing for fingerprints.

Val parted the canvas doors. Gavin and Warren were standing in the middle of the tent. Two portable heaters in the corner were making the night air almost bearable, not that Val could feel the cold with the adrenaline rush pushing her forward, though her bad leg was starting to tingle quite a bit.

A group of officers, including Gavin and Warren, formed a semi-circle around the body. Blood had pooled, making a wide crimson radius in the snow. Val quickly limped forward.

"She landed on the pavement," Gavin said. "It was just plowed about an hour ago, not that the snow would have stopped the impact of the fall."

Val glanced at the lifeless body of Bethany Arias. Her skull had fractured open on the concrete surface and her head was twisted in a way that would not be possible unless her neck was broken. Her legs spread out at odd, unnatural angles, suggesting they too were fractured in multiple places.

"Can you start the preliminary exam?" Gavin asked Val. "Everything has been documented as best we can down here. The crew is still working upstairs."

"Of course," Val said as she circled around the body. Bethany wore no coat. She had on a short red cocktail dress, suggesting she had been out at a party. One four-inch high heel shoe clung to her left foot. The right was God knows where. "Do we have any witness accounts?"

"One of the neighbors heard a loud thud, looked out from his balcony and saw Bethany lying on the concrete. He called 911 immediately. The snowplow driver confirmed no body was here when he cleared the walkway an hour ago. So we have a timeline. She's been dead less than an hour," Warren informed her. "The neighbor reported that he heard no screams."

No screams? This was important. It confirmed a suicide or an unconscious victim.

Val knelt down next to Bethany. "There's no rigor or lividity yet." Val continued to examine the body. There was only so much she could do at a crime scene with a body in this condition. Time of death was strongly established. The rest of Bethany's exam would occur at the morgue. Cause of death would be confirmed after a toxicology screen because no means, other than trauma, could be seen. No strangulation marks, stab wound or gunshot holes were present. Manner would be pending, depending on the result of the autopsy as well. "Do you really think this was a suicide?"

"We have the surveillance tapes." Gavin walked over to a table where a laptop computer sat. "Take a look. There's no other possibility, but like so much with the Gabrielle Morgan case, there's odd inconsistencies."

Val stripped off her latex gloves and quickly moved to where Gavin was standing.

He pointed at the screen. "Here we see a staggering Bethany Arias, long coat open and unbuttoned, both high heels on, walking across the plowed parking lot, she stumbles a few times and falls in a snowbank once. She finally makes it to the door and pushes the numbers on the keypad and gets through the front door." Gavin paused the footage. "She's not in the house for long before she's dead on the pavement."

Val squinted at the screen. "She seems drunk. Or drugged." This woman was definitely not in a state of sobriety before her death. "Do you know where she was before this? Who she was with?"

"We're checking on that," Warren said.

"But there's a problem here, with Bethany's arrival home." Gavin reset the video to the beginning and pressed play. "Look where she parked. It's outside of the view of the camera." He tapped the screen. "We see her staggering but we don't see her park. Her car is pretty far out there in the lot. It's a cold, snowy night. Why park so far away? There are plenty of spots right next to the building."

"She's obviously drunk or on something. Maybe she just stopped the car and got out," Val suggested.

"Possibly." Gavin didn't sound convinced. He stared at the screen. "She's fairly inebriated. I don't know how she would have driven herself anywhere."

"Okay. So someone brought her here?" Val suggested. "And knew to stay outside of the view of the camera?"

"The crime scene techs are going through her vehicle now, so we'll see if they find evidence of that. The parking lot was plowed shortly before she came home. Any tracks in the snow have been obliterated by new snowfall."

"No one follows her in?" Val asked.

"No. This is the only way in or out and she's the only one to go in, other than people who live here, and they all check out."

"Are there any other entrances. Like a service entrance?" Val remembered these wealthy people having other ways in or out for the hired help.

"No again, but there is a maintenance door on the side of the building. The door is practically hidden, that's the way it was designed. No security camera at that entrance, but the security is pretty tight there. You need a key and code to get in. It opens to a maintenance stairwell—again no cameras." His gaze went back to the footage of Bethany.

"Only someone very familiar with this condo would know that." Val raised her eyebrows at Gavin, confused as to why he would dismiss this fact. "And you're not concerned about this at all?"

"Outside of that door, there are no tracks in the eighteen inches of snow that fell today. No one has been through it all day." Gavin shut off the video and walked towards the exit of the tent, zipping his jacket up. "Are you ready to go into Bethany's condo?"

~

Val entered the condo trailing behind Gavin and Warren. As she looked around, the luncheon with Melinda and Bethany flashed in her mind. Her feeling that day was this condo exuded a sense of power. Now, it just seemed defeated. Like Bethany down on the ground.

"Can I look around, Mitch?" Val asked.

"Put your gloves on," he instructed. "And also suit up."

She didn't need to be told. Val knew the drill. After taking off her coat and grabbing a pair of latex gloves, she also put on a Tyvek suit and shoe coverings.

Val started in the kitchen. There were no glasses or dishes in the sink. If Bethany came home drunk, she didn't have anything further. Val hadn't seen the kitchen the first time she was here, and glanced around now at the white cabinets, black hardware, red accents. She went down the hall, past several crime scene techs and looked in the guest powder room. It was a fairly large space, but it consisted of a toilet and sink only. All the hardware accents were brushed silver. Tile, speckled with red flecks.

Next, she moved to Bethany's bedroom. Black and white. Val pulled out her phone and googled the significance of the colors, knowing this was something Bethany strived for in her décor. White is innocence and black is authority, sophistication and power, but it's also subservient—this is why many religious figures, such as priests wear black. Amish do it for humility. This was the only room with not one red item or accent in it. Odd. Bethany's personal space is the one area with no red. What was going on here? What was this room trying to say? Then Val sensed it.

This room had a submissive quality to it. A stark contrast to the power in the rest of the house. Maybe this was the way Mr. Morgan liked it?

Down the hall there were two spare bedrooms. The first, blue. A boy's room? Queen bed, oak. Matching dressers. Plaid comforter. Maybe this was Adam's room when he lived here with his mother? Though the rest of the house had a modernistic makeover, this room was a sharp contrast to this. It was like Bethany never touched it. Maybe she wasn't allowed to. Val traveled across the hall, to another bedroom. Again, a stark contrast. It was as if Bethany hadn't bothered with the two spare bedrooms.

There was nothing fancy in this one either. A dark wood queen-size bed and mahogany dresser. Touch of red? The walls were light yellow, almost butter. Yellow bedding. Yellow accents. The room had an abandoned feel, as if no one had been in here in some time. Louise, the maid, must not have ever come in here either because there were a few cobwebs in the corner and dust was forming on the dresser and headboard. What did Bethany say about yellow? Val pulled out her phone again. Yellow is happy and optimistic, spring and sunflowers and daffodils, *Yadda, yadda, yadda*. Val scrolled. Every light side has a dark. And here it was, cowardice, betrayal, egoism, and madness.

Suddenly, something caught Val's eye—an open door on the far left side of the room. An attached bathroom.

Odd. The bedroom didn't look used but the bathroom did. The soap dispenser was almost empty. The toilet paper roll was spun down by half. Through the glass shower door, Val saw a couple of bottles. She pulled the door open and stepped onto the tile. She picked up the first bottle. Lavender soap. She grabbed the next one and turned it around to get a look at what it was and nearly dropped it. Absolute Blonde shampoo. Number three ingredient: Pearls. "Natural," claimed the copy on the label, "not cultured." Natural pearls would have made it much more expensive than cultured, Val guessed. Who's using the guest bathroom? Or who *was* using the guest bathroom?

Gabrielle's dead. Now Bethany's dead. Both look like suicides —with solid evidence pointing towards suicides. But Gabrielle was missing for five days before her death on the sixth and in that time she stayed—or was kept—somewhere, shampooing her hair with pearl-based shampoo.

30

Bethany's autopsy revealed nothing other than trauma as cause of death. Dr. Maddox took plenty of tissue samples for drug analysis. They'd all have to wait for Zoe to complete the tests before they knew what substances Bethany had in her system, because from the video footage, it was obvious that she was either drunk or on something.

On Monday morning, Gavin looked like he was trying hard to keep a straight face when Val told him her thoughts about the yellow room and the shampoo. "I saw the room. And it was the only inviting space in that entire condo," he said.

I guess color really is subjective, she thought, preferring not to say much more on the matter. Jack would have taken a lead like this and run with it. *Jack*. Val thought about him all the time. She wished he'd call. Val ached to make things right between them again.

"As far as the shampoo goes, Val, do you think she'd put cheap shampoo in her guest bathroom?"

Val had no answer again.

Gavin patted her on the shoulder. "Well, come on now. Gabrielle, Adam and the Morgan twins are being exhumed in about an hour."

Forest Lawn cemetery is where most of the elite of Buffalo's golden age are buried. Even the thirteenth president, Millard Fillmore, is interred there. Lakes, streams, rolling hills, ornate and expansive family monuments are what make Forest Lawn a tourist destination. Trolly cars and walking tours take people around, guides pointing out the prominent and famous graves. This is where the Morgans came to spend eternity. They even had their own private mausoleum.

Val knew they all got lucky that the family wasn't buried in the ground. They'd have had to wait for the spring thaw to get them out if that was the case. Right now, she, Gavin and Warren, along with two cemetery officials, stood inside the stone and marble structure. Outside, two bronze angels stood watch at the stained-glass door. Val couldn't help but notice that they looked judgmental, rather than watchful. Maybe this is how it was planned, well over 100 years ago. Bare your sins at heaven's gate. Only the repentant can pass. Val looked around. *Hell, if these graves could talk.*

The mausoleum was big enough to hold twelve crypts, six on each side. A small bench was at the far end, under a stained-glass window depicting saints Val did not recognize. The bench was obviously placed so the living could sit while paying their respects. Val looked at the names carved in the marble wall. James Morgan Sr., who was akin to a Rockefeller or Vanderbilt in his day, lay interred on the top row. His wife, Victoria, was placed on the top row across from him. Their children, Edmond and James Jr., underneath and Elizabeth, James Jr's wife was across from him. Spots for Gabrielle's father, James III and Rachel were one more row down, marked with a birth date only. Val shuddered. She'd never want to see her name on a crypt.

Poor Edmond, though, he was here alone with his parents. Val moved closer to see his beginning and end carved in stone. The poor boy was only seventeen. No wonder why.

The twins were on the fourth row down with Gabrielle and Adam, across from them. Val stood back as the cemetery crew prepared to open the vault.

With a pull of a crowbar, Gabrielle's marble placard was removed and the coffin exposed. The twins were next.

"They're remarkably well preserved," Dr. Maddox said of the twins.

He was right. They looked like they died yesterday. The boy was in a navy-blue suit and the girl in a blue velvet dress. Her blonde hair hung in long curls. "This is what good embalming and a tightly sealed crypt will do." He stood back and looked impressed. "I can't believe even the clothing is preserved on these two."

"Maybe money does buy everything," Warren said.

"Okay, Val, let's do an autopsy," Dr. Maddox said.

Three hours later both were finished. There were no new or remarkable findings. Dr. Maddox's main goal was to collect samples for toxicology screening so that Zoe could look for poisons, something that wasn't done during the first autopsy.

Dr. Maddox stripped off his gloves. "Gabrielle and Adam are next."

Val dropped the samples off to Zoe immediately after Dr. Maddox was finished. Zoe had the testing completed by the next day. Bethany's results were still pending.

"Val, this is an easy one," Zoe said. "Almost too easy. I guessed heavy metal as a possible source of poison for Gabrielle, so I started here with the twins. I was right. The twins were being poisoned with cadmium. It's in their bones, hair and nails."

"Cadmium?"

"Out of all the heavy metals, this one is a good choice. It produces flu-like symptoms; fever, chills... so a healthcare professional will assume a routine health problem if a patient presents with it. God, it's even odorless and tasteless and dissolves readily in water. So, all is good for a poisoner in that regard but we can detect it so easily because heavy metals hang around in the body for years," Zoe said.

Val shivered, thinking of what kind of psychopath they were dealing with. "The twins would have been poisoned fifteen years ago. That's at least when it started. That leaves someone in the Morgans' household as the poisoner. Bethany or Melinda would have been too young to be poisoning people."

"Maybe not."

"A poisoner at sixteen? Could a sixteen-year-old know how to do something like this?" Val said, shocked.

"It *is* possible, Val." Zoe took a seat. "I remember a case that occurred in England. The child's name was Graham Frederick Young, and he became known as the Teacup Poisoner after he was suspected of poisoning the tea of one of his family members. At the age of fourteen he murdered his stepmother. Rather than going to prison he was sent to a mental hospital where he was released nine years later after they judged him fully cured. Subsequently, he went on to be a serial killer who used poisons. Get this, while he was in the mental hospital, he had access to medical texts which allowed him to sharpen his skills."

Jesus, talk about breeding a killer. Val shuddered at the thought. "What about Gabrielle? What did her tests show?"

"I'm convinced she was poisoned with cadmium too. This would explain where the gout came from. Unfortunately, I can't prove it."

Val's face fell in disappointment but didn't need to ask because the reason was clear. "The poisoning with cadmium was fifteen years ago. Gabrielle's hair and nails would have long since grown out."

"You're correct. Hell, even our bone re-mineralization turns every seven years. All I can tell you is that at least in the last seven years, she wasn't poisoned with cadmium, or any heavy metal for that matter."

Hair, bone, nails... suddenly Val realized they were forgetting one more place to look. "There might be one way to tell if Gabrielle was poisoned back then."

"What's that?"

"Her teeth. Bone remodels every seven years but the composition of teeth is fixed at the time of tooth development. This does not change."

"Well, Val, would you like to extract some teeth for me, then?"

"It would be my pleasure."

31

Val's one week time limit to investigate any leads in this case ended yesterday. Thankfully, with discovery of the cadmium for the twins, Dr. Maddox allowed her a few more days. "The Morgans are very angry over the exhumations. I won't be able to hold them off for long," he warned.

As Val waited for Zoe to finish up her testing on Gabrielle's teeth, she received a phone call from Gavin.

"Hey, have you had a chance to follow up with Scott Payne yet?" she asked.

"Things have been tumbling so fast with this case that I haven't had a chance yet," Gavin said. "Here's the latest. According to birth records, Ingrid Gruber, the maid to Melinda Holbright's family, the one who witnessed Melinda and Bethany running from the Morgans' house the day the twins died... well she *did* have a daughter. Her name was not Jennifer, but Johanna." Val could hear papers shuffling in the background. "Last name on the birth certificate is Manning, after the baby's father."

Val remembered that Jennifer's maiden name was Manning. "That's too close to be a coincidence," Val said.

"It's not a coincidence at all," Gavin said. "That's because Jennifer Ballard's first name was originally Johanna. She changed it when she turned eighteen. Jennifer Ballard *is* Ingrid Gruber's daughter. We're questioning her at noon today. Would you like to watch?"

~

Gavin made sure to get a subpoena to question Jennifer Ballard. He didn't have to use it. She came into police headquarters willingly. Right now, he and Warren sat with her in the interrogation room. Val stood behind two-way glass, observing everything.

"Thank you for coming in, Mrs. Ballard. We'd like to ask you some more questions about Gabrielle Morgan and a couple of her friends if that would be okay."

She nodded.

"I do need to remind you that it's your right to have counsel with you." Gavin didn't need to go through the full Miranda Rights with Jennifer since she wasn't being questioned as a suspect. He simply wanted to know her connection to Gabrielle. Depending on how this all went, Jennifer may shut down and declare her right to an attorney. Gavin would have to wait and see.

"I have nothing to hide because I've done nothing wrong," she said plainly. A lot of suspects think that forthcoming people project lack of guilt. Heaven help the truly innocent person because every investigator thinks you're hiding something, whatever your tactic.

"You were born Johanna Manning, not Jennifer?"

"Yes. I changed my name when I turned eighteen."

"Why?"

"My mother was accused of a lot of things with the Morgan scandal. It was the best way to distance myself from that."

"What kind of things was she accused of?" Though Gavin already knew the answer he wanted to hear Jennifer's interpretation of it.

"That she was a crazy drug and alcohol addict who saw nothing the day the Morgans' children drowned."

"I'm sorry, Mrs. Ballard, that must have been awful. How then, did you come to live right next door to Gabrielle Morgan, the person at the center of that scandal?" Gavin said.

"God's honest truth, it was pure coincidence." Jennifer laughed a caught-out guffaw. She must have been waiting for this question. "I never met her before that, well not face to face. My round-about connection to her was because of Melinda Holbright. My mother worked for the Holbrights, as you know, and Melinda and I used to play together when we were very young."

"Not when you got older?" Warren's eyebrows shot up, questioning.

Jennifer smirked. "She comes from money and I was the maid's daughter. The time came when we didn't hang around together anymore."

"Was that a problem for you?" Warren pressed.

Jennifer relaxed in her seat. "The last time I did anything with Melinda Holbright, detective, I was around seven or eight years old. So no, the loss of her friendship did not scar me for life." The sarcasm in Jennifer's voice was evident. "Anyway, I was happy to not be around her anymore."

"Why was that?"

"She was a mean little girl. She did horrible things."

"Like what?" Gavin asked.

"Where do you want me to start?" Jennifer scoffed. "Since you want to know, I'll give you the typical Melinda. Back when we were children the American Girl doll was huge. Every little girl wanted one. Of course Melinda had a number of them. It's all I wanted, but they were so expensive, something my mother couldn't afford. One day my mother surprised me with one. I couldn't wait to show Melinda. When I did, she was happy for me. Said the doll was beautiful. A little while later Melinda suggested we paint our nails with some new purple glittery polish she had. My doll was sitting next to me. While the nail polish bottle was open, Melinda knocked it over and it spilled all over my doll—the hair, the face. It was ruined. Melinda apologized, but I know she did it on purpose. Probably doesn't mean anything to you two but to a little girl, this was the end of the world." Jennifer crossed her arms. "That was a mild thing she did. It wasn't long after that she started tripping me or bumping into me hard. One time it was on the landing of the staircase and I went down a flight of stairs. Luckily I didn't break anything. I didn't play with her after that."

Jesus, Gavin thought.

"Did you ever live in the Holbright house?" Warren asked.

"No. Never. Not in any of them. My mother wasn't live-in help. She went to work in the morning and come home in the evening. The two of us had our own place. It wasn't much, a second-floor flat on the West Side, but it was okay."

"Just you and your mother?" Warren again.

"Yes. She never married my father. He was out of my life shortly after I was born. My mother was busy trying to put food on our table, rather than trying to fill her dating schedule," Jennifer said with a sharp bitterness.

Gavin found Jennifer to be quick and pointed in her responses. He believed she wasn't dumb, or easily fooled, either. Jennifer seemed like the type of person who would notice things. "Did you ever spend any time in the Holbright house, specifically the one on Lincoln Parkway?"

Jennifer crossed her legs. "One summer I did. I had a part-time job working for the Holbrights. I helped the gardener by weeding, planting, mulching. Basic landscaping work."

"How old were you?" Gavin asked.

"Sixteen," she said, as if she was waiting for the next question. Jennifer appeared to be staying two steps ahead of them.

"Is this how you knew Gabrielle Morgan?"

"I didn't know Gabrielle Morgan at all. I think I told you, detective. The maid's daughter did not hang out with the daughters of the Holbrights or Morgans." Jennifer hesitated for a second. "Or Arias."

"You knew *about* Gabrielle then. And Bethany too?" Gavin sensed Jennifer purposely told him about Bethany. "How did this happen?"

"The summer I worked for the Holbrights I was assigned to clean out the wooded area in the back of the house. Rake the dead leaves, cut small branches and pull weeds. I had a good view of the Morgans' property through the fence and I used to watch these three girls swim in the pool. I wondered what it would be like to be one of them. Not to have a care in the world. Instead, I shoveled dirt and raked old dead leaves from between trees. I was scratched from branches, had dirt under my nails. Sweated all day." Jennifer sat upright in her chair, proud. "I knew one of those three girls was Melinda, and later learned who the other two were."

"How did you learn this?" Warren asked.

"I asked my mother who Melinda's friends were," Jennifer said with a sarcastic tone as if Warren was stupid.

"Did you watch these girls on the day the Morgan twins drowned?" Gavin asked.

"Yes. The one thing I remember most about watching them that day, was that they were playing pretty rough with a small boy and girl, who I found out later were the Morgan twins. The children didn't want to go into the water but Melinda pulled them in. All three of them forced the kids to stay. They wouldn't let them get out of the water. The other girl was there too. The older one. Seemed like she had something wrong with her. She was terrified and they made sure they put her through hell. I couldn't tell what was happening in the water, but it looked like they were holding their heads under. Then laughing when they came up to breathe. Then they pushed their heads under again. It was horrible watching it."

"Didn't you do anything? Run to get help?" Warren asked.

"I couldn't. I don't know why, my legs were frozen. I was terrified. I wanted to scream. I don't know how much time passed before they finally pulled the boy and girl out. I thought it was over. But then the screaming started."

"Who was screaming?"

"Bethany. Bethany was screaming."

"Where were Melinda and Gabrielle?"

"They'd pulled the kids out of the water. I couldn't really see much because they were hovering over them, but it was obvious the children weren't moving. Then it got quiet and the three of them were talking. I don't know how much longer I stood in the trees before I ran."

"The older girl, was she there then, when the twins were pulled out of the water?" Gavin asked.

"No. I don't know where she went."

"So your mother never saw anything that happened in the pool. You did," Gavin stated.

"Correct. My mother only saw Melinda and Bethany run from the back of the house. I told her what I had witnessed and she told the police that it was her. To protect me. She had a feeling what was going to happen. You see, it was her account that placed those three girls at the center of a crime, not mine.

Once the Morgans heard the story they attacked her character. Finally, my mother changed her story and reported nothing more than seeing Melinda and her friend run across the lawn."

Jennifer took a deep breath before continuing. "The Morgans had a word with the Holbrights, who afterwards fired my mother. Mr. Holbright ended up saying my mother was drunk that day and had to fire her for it. Do you know how hard it is for a maid to get a job in any other household after her wealthy long-time employer calls her a drunk and a drug addict? Called her crazy too. No one would hire her. She finally got a job at a local motel."

Jennifer's face was cold and angry, but her voice remained level. "The badgering and attacks on her character were relentless. It finally drove her crazy and she landed in an institution. While there, she fell and cut her leg. It became gangrenous and she died from sepsis shortly after. So, detectives, did the Morgans ruin my life? Yes. And when my husband and I looked at our house in hopes of renting it, I saw the woman who lived in the next-door house. *Gabrielle Morgan.* I couldn't believe it. Oh my God, I had to live next to her. I had to find out about her. Other than some weird obsession to know why she was living there, I had no motive. Gabrielle didn't ruin my mother. Her father did and if she was estranged from him, her family, maybe I'd get some ammunition... for what, I don't know. Sue him, perhaps. You have to understand, I had nothing against Gabrielle. I have everything against James Morgan. Do I have a grudge against him, yes? Did I kill his daughter, his grandson? No. So either charge me or let me go."

Gavin wasn't buying it. But he'd have to let Jennifer go. There is no evidence that she committed these crimes. Nothing other than the fact that she lived right next door to Gabrielle. Although he seriously doubted Jennifer's account of *pure coincidence*. In his opinion, it made more sense that Jennifer sought out Gabrielle Morgan, maybe to get access to Bethany and Melinda too. Maybe for blackmail?

It's certainly possible Jennifer told her husband about Gabrielle Morgan and if Gabrielle had an affair with Ron Ballard, maybe he was getting payment in his own way to keep his mouth shut.

"Mrs. Ballard, one more question before you go."

She lifted her eyes in a *what is it* look.

"Your husband, did you tell him who Gabrielle Morgan really was? Does he know your history with the family?"

"No." Jennifer said nothing further but her jaw tensed and she looked away for a second before she brought her gaze back to Gavin's. She picked up her purse in a motion to go.

"I'm sorry, Mrs. Ballard, I know I said one more question. I might have two." He kept his eyes on Jennifer's. "Is your husband faithful to you?"

Her face grew taut. He could see the heat rising to her cheeks. "Very," she said between tight, unmoving lips.

"Thank you, Mrs. Ballard. That will be all."

Gavin and Warren sat in silence until Jennifer was out of the room. "What do you think, Mitch?"

"I want round the clock surveillance on her."

32

The next day, Zoe stood in her lab, practically jumping up and down. Though she was still waiting for the results on Gabrielle's teeth, the toxicology reports were back on Bethany Arias. "Val, I told you all along you're looking for a master poisoner. This was genius. But we have the same problem as with everything in this case: I can't prove anything."

All words Val didn't want to hear. *Master poisoner. Genius. Can't prove anything.* "Give me the details," she said, frustrated.

"You saw the angel's trumpets in Claudia's room. If it wasn't for that, I wouldn't have even thought of looking down this road. As I said, angel's trumpets are in the nightshade family. There are the three main alkaloids: atropine, hyoscyamine, and scopolamine. And they appear in drug form, in common medications, treating everything from Parkinson's to diarrhea."

Val nodded. Zoe had mentioned that most poisonous plants have a good side and a bad side.

"Bethany was an asthmatic and taking medication for this. She was also on a tricyclic antidepressant. Both of these drugs are made from nightshade alkaloids. Her tox results were positive for alcohol too. These meds, taken together with alcohol, will produce overdose symptoms. The amount she had in her system was far greater than I would have attributed to her meds mixed with alcohol though."

Val cocked her head.

Zoe sounded excited: she was on a roll. "I would have stopped here in my investigation and labeled this an accident anyway. An overdose causing anticholinergic toxidrome... remember our mnemonic... blind as a bat, mad as a hatter, red as a beet... but, Val, *mad as a hatter*. This is the important one. This drug overdose produces a lot of mental impairments. It produces hallucinations. Bad hallucinations."

Val's eyes went wide. "Bethany flew off a fifth-floor balcony with no apparent help from anyone else."

"She probably didn't need any," Zoe said. "But here's more to the elegance of this poisoner. Here's the skill. There are various types of nightshades; some are also edible. For example, tomatoes, potatoes, bell peppers, eggplants are all edible nightshades. But some edible nightshades can become poisonous. When potatoes are exposed to light, they turn green and increase saponin production, or scopolamine. This is a natural defense mechanism to prevent the uncovered potato from being eaten. Scopolamine is very toxic even in small quantities. I checked the results of Bethany's stomach contacts and she did ingest potato shortly before she died."

Val nodded, she understood what she was being told.

Zoe smiled. "Use these all in combination and it's impossible to detect the root cause. And let me tell you, I can't prove this was deliberate or an accident. I can't prove where it came from. Your poisoner did a good job of confusing that. I can prove you have a nightshade, but that's it. There's no angel's trumpet flowers, or any part of the plant in her stomach contents. But if she drank tea made from it, she'd have the alkaloids only in her system."

"Oh my God. How do we catch this person, then?" Val said and then looked up to see Gavin standing in her doorway.

"This person, in my opinion, can't be caught. We'll have to wait for them to make a mistake, but that's unlikely," Zoe said. "I'll say this again. You're looking for a skilled poisoner. Someone knows how to execute the perfect crime. You are not looking for an amateur. That's why the heavy metal poisoning is confusing me, because that is amateur."

Val thought for a moment. "Zoe, what about an amateur who evolved. Became more skillful over time. Fifteen years is a long time to get good at a craft."

"That is entirely possible." Zoe shrugged.

"Claudia is back in town," Gavin announced, causing both Val and Zoe to look in his direction.

"Holy shit. When did she get back?" Val said.

"Yesterday."

33

"Thank you for finally agreeing to talk to me, Claudia," Gavin said.

Two lawyers sat on either side of her, obviously paid for by Mr. Morgan. The sharp, well-fitted suits and intimidating stares were the best money could buy. Mr. Nunez wore a red tie and Mr. Cooper, the alpha attorney, wore gold. This really wasn't to protect Claudia. It was to set a tone, because Mr. Morgan would be next. He willingly agreed to speak with the detectives, in a move that Gavin could only guess held some advantage for Mr. Morgan. Gavin had his own plan for today. He had no intention of letting Mr. Morgan get the upper hand.

Gavin, Warren, Claudia and the lawyers were in Mr. Morgan's boardroom, on the top floor of Buffalo's Guaranty Building, one of Buffalo's first skyscrapers, famous for its ornate reddish-brown terracotta exterior. They sat around a large hand-carved boardroom table. Roughly twenty feet long, it had sixteen matching carved wooden chairs, all with green leather inserts. Each station at the table was outfitted with a personal drawer.

Claudia looked at both lawyers for approval before she

spoke. They nodded. She could answer. "I'd like to just get this over with," she stated.

"So would we," Warren said.

"You were the nanny for all of the Morgan children, correct?" Gavin took over the questioning.

"Yes."

"For how long?"

"Thirty-three years. I was hired to take care of Bridget, just before she was born and then the subsequent children as they came along." Claudia sat straight in her chair, legs crossed. She seemed remarkably well composed.

"You stayed in this position mainly because of Bridget?"

"Yes. I am the household manager now, but a large portion of my duties are still with Bridget. She needs a lot of care and I know how to manage her." Her hands rested on the table, fingers casually interlocked.

"Do you medicate her? Is that how you manage her?" Warren asked.

Mr. Cooper tossed his pen down. "Detective, stop with the bullshit or I'll stop this interview right now. My clients are here today as a favor to you. Have I made myself clear?"

"Bridget knows me," Claudia said calmly. "And I know her."

Gavin showed her the picture of the angel's trumpets from her bedroom. "These are pretty flowers. Mrs. Morgan told Valentina Knight that you have a greenhouse on the Morgan property."

Claudia cast her eyes down to the photograph and then looked back up at Gavin. "I didn't grow those."

"How did you get them, then?"

"I'd rather not say."

"We'd rather you did," Warren said.

Claudia shifted in the chair and glanced towards Mr. Cooper. He nodded that she could answer.

He'd better damn well nod, Gavin thought.

"They were given to me."

"By who?" Gavin asked.

"Mr. Morgan."

Gavin wasn't expecting this. He assumed an affair... the flowers, he thought for sure Claudia had them deliberately. "Why would Mr. Morgan give you angel's trumpets? Do they have some significance for you?"

"None at all. I didn't ask for them."

Maybe she didn't need to ask for them, not if he knew what kind of flowers she might have liked, Gavin thought. "Why would he give you flowers at all?"

Claudia shrugged. "He's a nice boss and he does thoughtful things."

"Like give you a greenhouse?" Gavin asked.

"It was a very kind and thoughtful gift."

What a beautifully rehearsed response. "Claudia, were you having an affair with Mr. Morgan?" Gavin asked bluntly.

Claudia did not answer. She looked at both lawyers. They glared at Gavin and he knew he was treading on very thin ice. Sometimes when questioning a suspect an unanswered question speaks volumes.

"How long were you having an affair?" he asked.

The lawyers didn't toss their pens on the table this time, they threw them against the wall. Both men rose. "We're done here. I warned you about this and I don't give second chances," Mr. Cooper said. "My clients came here in good faith, and you decided to subject them to bullshit. Without a subpoena they will not be talking to you again."

Mr. Nunez patted Gavin on the shoulder. "Good luck in getting that."

Gavin had no problem with the threat. He had gotten what he needed from this *interview* without ever hearing an answer.

Or talking with Mr. Morgan. Or having his line of questioning controlled by Mr. Morgan. Or worse yet, his investigation dictated by Mr. Morgan. After the revelations today, Mr. Morgan may not want to rock this boat.

There was little doubt in Gavin's mind that Claudia and James Morgan were having an affair. James was also having an affair with Bethany. Did Claudia know?

34

"Val! Great news," Zoe practically shouted. She and Val stood inside her toxicology lab at the medical examiner's office. "I found cadmium in some of Gabrielle's teeth."

Val's eyes went wide. "Which ones?" Val put her arms out to give Zoe a hug but Zoe backed away. Val remembered Zoe wasn't a hugger and put her arms down quickly.

"It's in her third molars, or wisdom teeth, only."

Val quickly reviewed the development times of teeth, from first stages of calcification to root completion as cadmium could have been deposited during these intervals. "Incisors first begin to develop at three months, erupt around six with root development complete as late as eleven for the lateral incisors. The span for canines is four months to fifteen years. Premolars one and half years to fifteen years, and for the molars, the first molar is from birth to ten years, the second two and a half to fifteen, and the third or wisdom tooth is seven years to twenty-five. Though there are variations, the growth of a tooth and its root formation follows a pretty standard schedule."

Val did the math. "Since cadmium was in no other teeth, and none was in her bones, as young as sixteen as old as twenty-two.

It's highly likely the twins and Gabrielle were being poisoned together."

"Yes, and I have one more fact for you. Something to take into consideration. I did some more research on nightshade poisoning, particularly on the mental impairment part of the equation. One thing it's been used for is to model conditions such as Alzheimer's, dementia, Down syndrome, and particularly fragile X syndrome in animal studies," Zoe said.

"Fragile X?" Val questioned.

"Fragile X syndrome is a genetic condition that causes a range of developmental problems. It's hugely tied to autistic traits." Zoe's implication was clear.

Oh my God, Val started to get a really bad feeling in the pit of her stomach. The twins had been poisoned. Gabrielle was poisoned around this time as well. What about Bridget?

The drowning of the twins set this case in motion. Jack had told her at the beginning that there is always an event that *sets a case in motion*. Gabrielle and the twins were poisoned by the same means. Someone continued to poison Gabrielle afterward.

What did Gabrielle know? What secret was she keeping?

Gabrielle was also trying to get custody of her sister, Bridget. Was she was trying to get her out of that house?

Or protect her from someone else?

Because Bridget is another witness to what happened the day the twins drowned.

35

Val's thoughts circled to the Morgan twins. Something more happened that day. It had to have. The last piece of the puzzle that connects this case is missing. The only two people still alive from that day are Melinda and Bridget. Who is Bridget in danger from?

Val pulled out her phone and called Gavin for the third time and for the third time it went to voicemail. With everything that she'd learned so far, for some reason Val couldn't get the shampoo bottle in Bethany's guest bathroom out of her head. Bethany had lived in a condo that Gabrielle had lived in. And Mr. Morgan owned it.

But more than the shampoo bottle, Val thought about the key she found in Gabrielle's pocket. The elevator at the condo used a key. *Dammit, this thing has to belong to something. Was this it?* Val texted:

Mitch, I'm going to Bethany's condo. Meet me there.

After trying the key, if it worked, she'd wait for Gavin to

show up and they could check out the condo together. Val definitely wanted another look inside.

Once Val arrived in the parking lot she got out of her car and hurried to the front door, searching on her phone, she looked up the police report from the night she collected Bethany's body. Val quickly found what she was looking for: the code for the front door. She punched in the numbers and entered the building.

With the key in her hand, she moved towards the elevator. As soon as she arrived at the entrance, she tried to slip it in the lock, but it wouldn't go. She tried again. And then a third time. *Son of a bitch!* It didn't fit. Val pulled it out, repositioned, and tried again. There was no way this key was going into that hole. Then she had another thought, the maintenance entrance... that also uses a key. And a code.

Val had no code, but she didn't care. At this point, she only needed to see if the damn key fit. Val trudged outside, around to the side of the building and stepped through a couple of feet of snow to get to the entrance. By this time, her leg was well on its way to becoming numb and she had a hard time walking through the drifts. She struggled to get to the door, managing to get close enough to try the key.

Again, the key only went part way in. Dammit! Val twisted and then gave up: she didn't want to break the key. This doesn't fit here either.

Val shoved the key into the pocket of her jeans and hobbled around to the front of the building. She pulled out her phone from her coat pocket and checked her messages. Nothing from Gavin. Snow began to fall a little heavier now. It was freezing outside and Val wiggled her fingers to keep the blood flowing. *I can't stay out here for much longer*, she thought. *Damn, I'll wait in my car for Gavin to respond.*

Her car sat in the lot, maybe fifty feet in front of her, snow covering the windows. She limped as fast as she could, eager to get in and turn on the heat.

All of a sudden, a sound to Val's left made her head quickly turn, her heart pounding hard as she scanned the area. Val only saw snowflakes glistening in the glow of the parking lot lights. She exhaled, trying to slow her racing pulse.

As she continued moving towards her car, she heard crunching. Boots walking in the snow? They were getting closer. To her left again? No, they weren't to her left. They were behind her. And they were growing faster. Val turned a second time. Then everything went black.

36

Val tried to move but her head exploded with pain as she tried to sit up. *Oh my God, what happened*? She tried to focus but everything was a blur. *Where am I? How long have I been here? Where is here*? Questions came in rapid succession as Val tried to grab hold of her thoughts. Her heart beat fast and she struggled to control rising panic. Taking a few deep breaths, she tried to calm down, she needed to figure out how to get out of wherever the hell she was.

The smell... the smell was the first thing Val noticed. Dry wood. Dust. Stale air. The characteristic odor of old attic was distinctive. Her eyes scanned the space—the walls were covered in blue flowered wallpaper, yellowed with age. Her gaze darted quickly to a fireplace tucked in the corner, then to a tall dark wood dresser against the far wall. A second, shorter one was on the opposite side. A mirror hung above that one. Val's hands felt a mattress beneath her. *A bedroom. I'm in a bedroom.*

A table was to her side. The dim bulb from the lamp sitting on it barely illuminated the immediate vicinity. Someone had covered her with a quilt and Val clutched at it tightly, wrapping it around herself. She began to shiver. The room was freezing.

As Val's eyes adjusted to the lighting, her gaze locked on to a shadow. Tossing the quilt aside, Val finally managed to stand up. She immediately felt nauseous as the room spun, and she fought the urge to vomit. Slumping back down, Val placed her head in her hands, waiting for the feeling to pass. Then she stood again on wobbly legs, particularly the right one, and staggered towards the shadow. As she got closer she realized what it was—a partially open door—and she hurried towards it, nearly falling as she tried to move faster.

As Val pushed the door open, white tiles could be seen on the floor. There was a sink and a toilet. *A bathroom.* Val hobbled inside, and felt for a switch on the wall. Finding one she pushed up and quickly moved to the sink. She turned on the faucet and ran the water, dipping her hands under the stream, splashing it to her face. The shock felt good and for a moment it obliterated the dizziness from the blow to the head.

Val took a look in the mirror above the sink and raised her hand to feel a large swelling in the side of her head where she had been hit. There was a large bruise on her forehead and a gash. *Jesus, what happened?* The memory flooded back. She was heading to her car. She was in Bethany's parking lot. She tried the key in the elevator door. It didn't fit. *The key? Did she still have the key?* Val felt the pocket of her jeans. It was there and she pulled it out. Well, whoever put her in here wasn't after this. *Damn piece of garbage*, she thought as she threw it into the toilet. Then Val realized something else. *My coat. Where's my coat? Someone took it before they put me in the bed. Shit! My phone... my phone is in that pocket.*

She limped out of the bathroom and took another look at her surroundings. Whose house was she in? There were two more doors on the far side. As she moved closer, away from the lamp and the glow of the bathroom, it became too dark to see detail but it was obvious one door had no handle. She felt around the molding trying to find a latch. Nothing. Val moved to the other door. This one did have a knob. With a twist it opened. She had to stand to the side as not to block the available light and blink a few times to get her eyes to adjust to what she was seeing. It was a closet. Inside, two coats. Neither was hers.

One was a woman's parka though. The second was that of a child. A boy's coat?

Holy shit, these must be Gabrielle and Adam's coats. These had to have belonged to them. *This room, this is where Gabrielle and Adam were kept!* Now, where is *this*? Val started to shiver again. The damn room was like a refrigerator. She grabbed the woman's parka, put it on and moved towards the windows, which were completely boarded shut. Val felt around the edges of the frames hoping she could pull the wood loose. She gripped her fingers underneath and pulled as hard as she could. She gritted her teeth and pulled again but no luck.

How in the hell am I going to get out of here? Val screamed internally as she pulled hard on the wood with each word. Exhausted, she stopped pulling. It was no use. These were not going to budge. Dropping her hands, Val hobbled across the room to the dressers and began opening the drawers. All empty.

She limped back to the bathroom. Pedestal sink. No medicine cabinet. There was nothing in here to use. Val grabbed the shower curtain encircling a claw foot tub. Her eyes locked on the soap and the shampoo bottle and out of sheer delirium she almost laughed out loud. She didn't need to pick up the bottle to know what it was. She had seen this brand before. Absolute Blonde. There was no doubt now, this is where Gabrielle and Adam were kept before they were killed.

Val made a fist and clenched, opening and closing repeatedly to keep blood flowing. Her fingers were so cold they hurt. And then a thought came, making her forget the pain. *How long before whoever put me in here comes back?*

She put her hands in the jacket pockets trying to keep them warm. She had to be ready to fight once her kidnapper came for her. As she moved her fingers around, Val felt a rectangular object. She gripped it, her thumb tracing the outline. *It can't be.*

She quickly pulled it from the pocket. And stared. It was! A cell phone. Gabrielle's? The one that was still missing? *It didn't make sense, why leave this here?*

The screen was black. Val's fingers fumbled as she felt for the power button, finally managing to push it. Her hands shook as she waited for some form of life to appear. *Come on. Come on, come on, please work.* Finally, the screen lit up. And it asked for the passcode. *No wonder why someone left this here, it's useless. Sadistic sick joke, that's what this is.*

"Son of a bitch." Val was ready to toss the phone against the wall but then she stopped.

This was an android. Her last two phones were androids. She had to do a hard reboot on them every now and then, mostly to get rid of any software that made the phones run slow. Hey, she never argued about doing this because it fixed the problem. Each time, it made her reset the password.

Jesus, how in the hell did I do this? The memory was a blur, but she remembered the first step. Val turned the phone back off and then pressed the volume down and the sleep/wake buttons together. *Yes, I remember, this starts a special diagnostics mode. The prompts will come on the screen.*

Once the first one came on, Val pushed the volume down button over the choices and highlighted *Recovery Mode Option*. She used the power button to select it. During this type of reboot, the touchscreen is not used. Thank God it was all working as it should. Once this step was done, she pressed and held the power and pushed the volume up to highlight the *Wipe Data/Factory Reset* option, then pressed power to select. She tapped volume down to highlight 'yes' on the next prompt as it asked her to confirm. Val pressed power one more time to complete the reboot. The status circled. And then kept circling, making no progress. *No! Please work... Please work!* Then finally it asked "Restore as new?" *Hell yes, I want to start as new.*

Next, it asked to reset a new password. *Let's go with 1, 2, 3 and 4.* Val typed it and verified. The phone opened. Bingo! I'm in. The battery was very low, less than 20%. The fact that it was turned off this whole time was probably why it still had any power left at all.

Val punched in Gavin's number. Nothing. "No signal," the phone said. *No! No! No!* She moved around the room, extending her arm, holding the phone up in all directions. She called Gavin again, and again. And again.

No signal, it mocked.

Val typed a text.

Mitch, help me. I've been kidnapped.

Sending message displayed. The status symbol twirled and twirled. It was no use. This message was never going to send.

I have to get out of here. She wanted to scream. Panic started to overwhelm Val and she threw the phone on the bed. Taking a deep breath, she tried to calm down, steady her breathing as her heart raced. *I got in somehow. There has to be a way out.*

Val went back to the only possible way in or out, the door with no handle. She pushed on it. It wobbled a bit. *But it definitely moved. Now, how does it open?* Val looked at the hinges which were held together by three long old-fashioned metal pins. Pull the damn thing off its hinges, that's what she needed to do. She staggered back to the bathroom and grabbed the shampoo bottle. *At least this expensive crap will be put to good use.*

Val put shampoo on the pins to lubricate them, then took the cap off the bottle, placing it upside down against the top portion of the pin. She turned the bottle upside down and banged the cap against the first pin, tapping the pin up. After half a dozen strikes, it moved. Then it finally slid out. She repeated with the second and as the third pulled off, the door separated. *Thank God, thank God!* Val grabbed the door and slid it open as much as she could. She was about to slip out but realized she couldn't.

What in the hell is this? Is this another sick joke? Val collapsed to the floor, exhausted, defeated. *It's another closet. I broke into a damn closet!*

She lay on her back looking up. She was partly in the empty space but there was something in the door jamb that caught her eye. Val reached out and pulled. An accordion style metal gate? What the hell? She stood up and examined the inside of the closet. There was nothing but a keyhole on the immediate side wall. *A keyhole. Metal gate. Oh my God, this is an elevator. An elevator that needs a key.*

Val ran back to the bathroom and pulled the key from the toilet and hurried back to the elevator. She slipped it in the hole. *Holy shit, it fits. How did Gabrielle have this in her pocket? How did it end up in the laundry on her floor?* Val wasn't going to question that now.

She was about to turn the key but then ran back to the bed and grabbed the phone, quickly placing it in her pocket. Once back in the elevator, she turned the key and the elevator started to move down, to the next floor. Once it stopped, she faced another door. This one, though, was unlocked. As it creaked open Val realized she was in another bedroom.

And Bridget Morgan was sitting up in bed staring at her.

37

I'm in the Morgans' house!

Bridget's mouth opened.

Val's pulse exploded. *Oh no, she's going to scream.* If she screams, I'm dead. Val smiled as calmly as she could and put a shaky finger to her mouth emphasizing *shh.*

Bridget mimicked the motion.

Val nodded and whispered, with her finger still on her lips, "Yes, shh."

Then, suddenly, Bridget tossed back the covers and got out of bed. And headed towards Val.

Val's eyes went wide and her heart banged harder. *What to do... Oh my God, what do I do?* "Bridget..." Words wouldn't come. Val put her hands up in a stop motion.

"You need to shush. Before someone hears you," Bridget said, in a low, whispered warning. She cocked her head back, looking over her shoulder at Claudia's bedroom door, then back at Val.

Val tried to comprehend what was happening. "You... you can talk?" It was all Val could manage to say as Bridget continued to grow closer.

"Yes, I can," she said in a singsong voice.

Val's gaze shifted towards Claudia's room. The door was ajar. Her gaze shot to the bedroom window. It was light outside. *Oh my God, how long have I been in this house?* She'd been hit on the head at night. But she couldn't think about that right now. Now, she needed to escape.

"Bridget, where's Claudia?" Val whispered quickly. It was at this moment she noticed Bridget's glassy eyes and lost stare.

"In there." Bridget pointed towards Claudia's door. "Don't worry. She's dead. That's not the person you're hiding from."

38

Gavin and Warren sat with Scott Payne in the interrogation room. He was a little worried that Val hadn't texted him back last night. When he arrived at Bethany's condo, Val was nowhere to be seen, albeit he was about an hour late. *She must have gone home,* he thought. But she had yet to respond.

Gavin's phone buzzed and he quickly looked down. The text was from an unknown number and he put the phone away. Though he was eagerly waiting to hear from Val, he wanted no distractions while questioning Mr. Payne.

"I had no idea Gabrielle Morgan was part of *the* Morgan family until I saw it in the news after her death. What about her life, how she lived, would have led me to believe anything like that?" He sat back with an incredulous expression, almost bordering on *how dare you question me about this.* "Keep in mind I managed the *Chandler* Trust for Malcom *Chandler* and his wife, Gabrielle *Chandler.* I never met Mrs. Chandler and never saw her while I managed the trust."

"Gabrielle came to work for you. Slept with you. She must have wanted something from *you,* Mr. Payne," Warren said.

"If she wanted some type of revenge on me, well, she never tried it. We had a good relationship, while it lasted."

"You want us to believe she didn't attempt revenge on the person who screwed her over on a stock deal?" Warren stared at Scott.

"Short selling is not screwing someone over. I had no clue what was going on with that drug. That scandal... I simply brokered a deal, which was my job."

"What about Max Chandler? The drug scandal caused a plunge, but it was his death that destroyed the value. Knowing of his impending death would have helped an investor."

"You can't be serious." Scott's eyes went wide and shifted his gaze between Gavin and Warren.

"Do you know a Melinda Holbright?" Warren asked.

"No." Scott said nothing further.

"She owns WNR LCC. This is who bought the stock," Warren said, and then smiled. "WNR, it's like she's saying winner."

"Shit, detective, we don't sit down and shake hands when stock trades occur. It happens electronically. I don't know who these people are. Or what their acronym is *trying to say*."

"Yet Melinda made a tremendous amount of money from this deal and Gabrielle lost everything. And if Max had been alive, that might not have happened," Gavin said this time.

"Are you suggesting I killed a man to make someone I don't know rich. Take a good look at me, detective, do I appear rich myself? Why on earth would I have done that? Are these the kind of things they teach you in detective school because maybe you should take a refresher course somewhere else."

A silent moment hung in the air between the three men before Gavin spoke. "Blackmail and double cross are some things they teach us too."

"I can't believe this bullshit," Scott huffed. "I'm assuming you have no proof of either, otherwise you wouldn't be on this fishing trip. Casting the line out there, aren't you? No fish in the pond, detective. I did nothing wrong and I didn't kill anyone. Let me tell you how by the record that short sale was. The maintenance margin was set at the required twenty-five percent and I called the margin once the value plummeted. I'll stress again that I had nothing to do with the continued decline of the stock value."

"And I'll stress again that some speculated it would have rebounded if Max Chandler hadn't died." Gavin locked his gaze on Scott's.

"All stock sales and purchases are speculations, detective. Some win, some don't. I brokered a deal within the parameters of the law. I'm sorry if one of those deals was unfavorable but that's the risk one takes when they trade and buy stock."

"I have to disagree with you, Mr. Payne. On brokered deals, the broker makes guaranteed money by way of the commission. The sellers and buyers are the ones who take the risk." Gavin watched Scott's eyes narrow, waiting for what Gavin was going to say next. "You did get fired after this, correct?"

"Yes. But let me tell you something, once I learned who Gabrielle Morgan was, after she died, I did some digging into this transaction, looked at my old records, maybe learn why would she have sought me out. And one thing you should know, detective: James Morgan made a large amount of money from the GDA fallout too. Rumor was, back then, Morgan Foods would have collapsed without the windfall."

39

"Who killed Claudia?" Val asked Bridget, then took a few cautious steps backwards.

Bridget stared at Val and then without warning placed each hand to her temples and shook her head violently back and forth in a *no*. Tears began to fall as she crumpled to the floor. "I was good. I was good," she said over and over.

Val maintained her distance, completely lost for what to do next. "Bridget, yes you were good. Can you tell me what happened to Claudia?"

"She was bad. When you're bad, you die." Bridget stopped crying and hissed, "Or I'll make you wish you were dead!" She started rocking back and forth. The way Bridget spoke... Val tried to understand it. It was as if Bridget was mimicking someone else's words.

"Did you kill Claudia, Bridget?"

"No," Bridget said, frightened, shaking. The rocking grew more intense.

"Did she kill herself?"

Bridget just shook her head quickly again, eyes wide, face pale.

Val sidestepped past Bridget and hurried to Claudia's room. She had to see for herself. Val pushed the door open and looked inside, then slowly moved towards Claudia who was slumped on the bed. Her face was white and her mouth hung opened as if in a contorted scream. Vomit was on the floor. Val felt for Claudia's pulse. It was no use. This woman had been dead for hours. More than likely poisoned. Val quickly moved to Claudia's exterior bedroom door, the one that exited to the hallway. *Dammit!* It was locked. There's no way out of the house of horrors.

Val quickly went back to Bridget and knelt down beside her, putting her hands on Bridget's shoulders. "Bridget, listen to me, how do we get out of here?"

"We don't," Bridget said. "The door is locked. It's always locked."

Val looked at the elevator that had just taken her down from what was, she presumed, the attic. Val pointed at the elevator door. "Where does this go?"

Bridget just stared at Val with glassy eyes.

"Where does this go?" Val said again. This time stronger.

"From the top to the bottom with a stop here." Bridget smiled.

"The bottom? The basement?"

Bridget nodded.

Val ran back to the elevator. "Come on, Bridget?"

"No," Bridget said, frightened. She crawled back to the bed and grabbed the blanket, pulling it around her, holding it tight.

"Bridget, we have to get out of here." Val wondered what was going on in the rest of the house. She strained her ears for any movement in the hallway. Someone could be coming for them at any moment.

Bridget started rocking back and forth again. "No! I'll get into trouble if I leave."

I have to get out now. I'll come back for her, Val rationalized.

This is the only way to save both of us. Val ran to the elevator and turned the key. It began to move. Down again. Once it stopped Val opened the door and stepped out into the dark space. She rapidly ran her hands along the outside frame of the elevator and found a switch, flipping it up gave a dim glow from several overhead lights. She was definitely in a cellar. Cement walls, musty odor. Racks of shelves lined either side of the vast space. Cobwebbed items sat on them. Val pulled out the phone and tried to text again. No signal. She scanned the walls, looking for a window, a way out. Nothing.

She saw several doors, and quickly swung each open. All were storage rooms. Finally, she found a door that led to a narrow staircase. The servant's stairs. *God dammit. The only way out of this house is back in.*

~

"Mr. Morgan, that's our guy," Warren said.

"That's why we're going to talk to him, Alex." Gavin pulled out his car keys. "Let's go."

"We don't have a subpoena."

"No, but my search warrant for 130 Lincoln Parkway just arrived." Gavin pulled the paper from inside his jacket pocket.

"How on earth did you get that? It's been less than an hour since we questioned Scott Payne."

"The Morgan twins were poisoned. They're dead. Gabrielle wanted them exhumed to bolster her case that she had been poisoned too. She wanted custody of her sister. I feel poor Bridget is in danger. This is probable cause to investigate the premises ASAP."

"The poisoning was fifteen years ago," Warren said skeptically. "And there is no proof Bridget is in immediate danger."

"Did I mention Judge Mercado is a reasonable guy?" Gavin smiled and placed the warrant back in his pocket.

Warren let out a sigh. "Mitch, this is a mistake. Give it some time and let's do it right. It'll mean both our jobs if we find nothing. Jesus, what do you hope to gain from this?"

"To catch the bad guy, Alex. Isn't that what our job is all about? Don't ever be afraid to do your job." Gavin looked at his phone, at the number for the missed text. He had no clue who this was and put the phone away.

Mrs. Morgan sat at the kitchen table. Stoically. Staring straight ahead. Not speaking. She'd let Gavin and Warren in nearly fifteen minutes ago. She'd been pleasant, inviting them into the kitchen, even though she'd just been served with a search warrant. But as soon as Gavin demanded to see her husband, she shut down.

"Mrs. Morgan, where's Mr. Morgan?" Gavin sat at the table across from her and leaned forward. "Mrs. Morgan, tell us where he is."

"Detective, do you know that Morgan Foods nearly collapsed twice." She put two fingers in the air to emphasize the number. "I come from a great amount of money. A lot of people don't know that. When James married me, my money saved Morgan Foods; the first time. The second saving came after the death of my son-in-law." She smiled and nodded as if she already knew Gavin was aware of this.

Gavin's phone buzzed again with another text message, same unknown number. This time he opened it. With his eyes still on the screen he stood and shouted, "Mrs. Morgan, where is your husband?"

Mrs. Morgan smiled and calmly said, "Upstairs."

Gavin pointed to two officers. "Stay here with her." He pulled his gun from the holster and looked at Warren. "Let's go. Now!"

"Mitch, what the hell?" Warren yelled. He drew his weapon too. "What is going on?"

"Val! She's in this house." Gavin took off down the hall. Gavin and Warren ran up the stairs two at a time and began opening bedroom doors. After the fourth door, he froze. Val was hovering over someone lying on the bed.

"Val! Are you okay?" Gavin lowered his weapon and rushed towards her.

"Yes," Val said, her gaze on the lifeless body of Mr. Morgan. "He's dead. Has been for a while."

Gavin pulled out his phone. "I need an ambulance and backup at 130 Lincoln Parkway."

"Claudia is dead too," Val said. "Where's Mrs. Morgan?"

"Two officers are with her." Gavin tucked his gun back in the holster and leaned over Val to get a look at James Morgan. "Double suicide?"

"No. Double murder."

Gavin's eyes went wide.

"Take a look around the corner," Val said. "In the side room."

Gavin and Warren rounded the corner.

"Holy crap, what is this place?" Gavin yelled out.

"It's another greenhouse. Of sorts. Pretty sophisticated for an indoor setup. It's complete with artificial lights and temperature control. The yew tree is in the far corner. You can see where someone cut the branches. Angel's trumpets should be to your left." There were several other varieties of plants that Val could not identify.

"Is this Mr. Morgan's greenhouse?" Gavin yelled out.

A uniformed officer burst in. "We heard you yell from downstairs and then everything went quiet."

"Where's Mrs. Morgan?" Val asked him, as she quickly stood back from Mr. Morgan.

"In the kitchen, with another officer."

"What's she doing?" Val said, alarmed.

"She wanted to make a cup of tea," the officer said.

"Did you let her?" Val demanded.

The officer looked stunned by Val's outburst. "Didn't see a reason why not."

"Holy crap." Val ran towards the door. "We have to get down there." She took off down the hall with Gavin trailing. As she arrived in the kitchen, Mrs. Morgan had the cup to her lips.

"Stop!" Val shouted.

Mrs. Morgan pulled the cup away. The look on her face was of surprise rather than defiance when she swallowed.

"Mrs. Morgan," Gavin said. "We need to ask you some questions. Your husband is dead. Claudia is dead—" Mrs. Morgan put her hand to her chest and Gavin stopped speaking as foam seeped from her mouth.

"Mrs. Morgan, are you all right?"

It only took a few seconds more for Rachel Morgan to slump and fall to the floor.

Val felt Mrs. Morgan's neck for a pulse. "No need for paramedics. She's dead too."

40

"The tea was laced with enough aconite to kill a horse," Val told Gavin. "One sip was all that was needed."

"What's aconite?"

"Deadly wolfbane, a poisonous plant in the nightshade family, like the angel's trumpets. Only these have pretty purplish-blue flowers. Death is almost instantaneous with large doses. I'm surprised she had time to put the cup down."

"Mr. Morgan? Same poison?" Gavin asked.

"Yep."

"Claudia?"

"Yep again. If you want something to take someone out quickly, this is it. And it all came from Mrs. Morgan's private greenhouse." Val shook her head, still stunned by what she'd found. Yew, nightshade and more importantly, castor beans, as she would come to find out. Castor beans left Val scratching her head initially, but for Zoe, this was a huge find. She was finally able to detect the poison that killed Gabrielle: ricin.

There are no tests that can determine its presence, though, so Zoe got creative. Ricin comes from processing caster beans for castor oil. It's part of the waste products of the procedure.

Zoe looked for castor bean DNA in Gabrielle's respiratory secretions and got a hit. "Honestly, it's the only way to test for it," Val explained. "She had to read several studies to even learn where to begin on this. Master poisoner at work."

"Bridget has been questioned at length, now that she's finally lucid enough. Her mother had been poisoning her for years. The twins and Gabrielle too."

"You think Mrs. Morgan could have had Munchausen syndrome by proxy?" Gavin asked. Val knew what he was thinking. Was she purposely making her children sick to get sympathy for herself? It was possible Gabrielle also had Munchausen's. It's not uncommon for children in this type of situation to exhibit the same mental health problem.

"Maybe. Child abuser, definitely. Some of the stories Bridget told were horrifying," Val said.

"What goes on behind closed doors, the things parents do to their own children. We can never imagine, until it's too late. It's just crazy, and scary."

"Did she kill her husband and Claudia for revenge on their affair?" Val asked.

"Probably," said Gavin. "We'll never know what her true motivation was."

"What about Bethany's death?"

"I'd have to guess she killed her for the reason she killed Claudia, but again, 'probably' is all we can say. We're hoping that Bridget may, with some time, be able to fill in some of the gaps."

Val was hopeful too. It was Bridget who told Val that the private greenhouse was Mrs. Morgan's. When Val went up the staircase in the Morgans' basement, she ended up back on the second floor, this time in the hallway. She found the Morgans' bedroom, Mr. Morgan dead on the bed, and then located the secret greenhouse as she looked for a way out. Inside the greenhouse there was a dish with keys, and after grabbing them and trying them in the locked bedroom doors on the second floor, Val found the one that opened Bridget's room. As soon as Val entered Bridget said, with her eyes on the key, "You were in mother's secret garden."

Val sighed. "But why now. Why kill them all now?"

"Gabrielle wanted the twins exhumed. The truth was going to come out," Gavin said. "She had to kill Gabrielle to silence her."

It chilled Val to hear the words. "Why kill her grandson?"

"He was a witness to Gabrielle's death."

"Max Chandler, Gabrielle's first husband. I think he needs to be exhumed so we can see what he actually died from."

"Agreed. Without his death, Morgan Foods wouldn't have been saved a second time. This benefits Mrs. Morgan as much as Mr. Morgan."

Val frowned. "There was one thing that bothers me though. It was Mrs. Morgan's expression when she drank the tea. She seemed surprised."

"Val, you never know what someone looks like when they're overcome by poison and is about to die. There's no script for that. They act as the body dictates. There was probably no time for conscious thought."

"I know, you're right." Though Val said the words, she wasn't convinced by them. She crossed her legs and sat back. "We still have one more person out there. Melinda Holbright. And she's far from innocent."

"There's no proof that she killed anyone. Even with Jennifer Ballard witnessing the drowning of the twins, and even if Bridget became lucid enough to testify, there's not enough to take this to trial."

Val knew Gavin was right. It would be Jennifer's word against Melinda's. Bridget's mental state back then meant she could not be considered a reliable witness. Melinda might have killed two children. But she, also, made a ton of money off Gabrielle's first husband's death. Mrs. Morgan wasn't the only person to profit from that.

Val's phone buzzed. She looked at the number. It was Jack. Her pulse exploded. She hadn't spoken to him since the night they went to dinner, when he wanted to talk about the future between them. Val replayed that night over and over but there was nothing she could have done differently. Jack was ready to take their relationship to the next level. And she was not.

Gavin, he was the reason why not. He had to be out of her thoughts and out of her heart before she could do anything with Jack. It wouldn't be fair to him otherwise. Three in a relationship is one too many.

"How's your case with Gabrielle Morgan?" Jack asked.

Val explained everything.

"Well, then. You are on your way to understanding poisons to a level I could only dream of."

There was a moment of awkward silence.

"Jack—"

"Val, let me say something first. I'd really like it if we could go back and be like we used to be. I miss my friend. When and if you're ready to move forward, let me know. We'll discuss it then."

"Jack, I would love that."

Val and Gavin sat in Bridget Morgan's family room. The new housekeeper had let them in. It had been one week since Val was last here, trying to escape from this house. It still sent shivers down her spine and the thought of coming back was terrifying to say the least. But hell, if Bridget could be in this house, sitting calmly, after everything she'd been through, Val could certainly do it as well.

Right now, Bridget sat next to her, blanket wrapped around her shoulders, and honestly looking as good as she could have. With a little color in her cheeks, long blonde hair pulled back in a ponytail, eyes bright and not glassy, Bridget had a serene quality to her.

Years of abuse, poisoning, medication cocktails served by her mother could never be erased though. Her speech was still a little immature, her thought process disjointed. Bridget had a fragility that made it seem as if she might break wide open at any moment.

No, Bridget would never be normal but at least she could function, and today she was coherent. She also knew, mostly, what had happened to Gabrielle and Adam. Gavin had asked Val to be the one to question Bridget, hoping Val would be far less intimidating and Bridget would open up the best she could.

"Were Gabrielle and Adam in this house for the entire five days before they died?" Val asked.

Bridget shook her head. "Gabrielle was here one more."

"One more?" Val questioned.

"Mother brought her here the day before she brought Adam. Mother stayed with Adam at Gabrielle's house. He came the next day after school." Bridget focussed on Val and put out her hand to touch her arm. "They were both locked in the upstairs room you were in. Father never went up there, to the attic. Neither did Claudia. I don't know if you tried to scream, but even if you did, as loud as you could, no one could hear you. Mother had me locked up there enough times. That's how I know."

"Did Gabrielle die upstairs?" Val asked.

"Yes, Mother had me help get Gabrielle and Adam to the church." Bridget clutched her blanket. "She told Adam his mother was sleeping. He was crying. He didn't want to go."

"And you were okay to help her?" Val wondered how this woman was able to do that.

"When Mother didn't give me too many pills or her special smoothies, I could do things. The night she killed Gabrielle and Adam she needed my help, so she didn't give me anything at all."

Val swallowed hard, trying to imagine the horrors Bridget endured in this house. "The yew tree branches, the long white gown? Why did your mother dress Gabrielle up?"

"Mother dressed Gabrielle in the gown for when Gabrielle met God. Mother didn't know about the branches. I did that later. I didn't have to tell her because it was never in the news." Bridget smiled and looked at Val as if she had a secret, something she got away with. "Mother never knew," she whispered.

"Bridget, *you* left the yew tree branches and seeds with Gabrielle?" Val asked as if she didn't hear correctly.

"Yes. After we left Gabi and Adam, I went back."

"How did you get there?" Val asked.

"Mother didn't know I took the car." Bridget cowered a little as if she just said something she was going to get in trouble for.

"You can drive?" Val said, dumbfounded.

"Claudia taught me. She was my friend." Bridget tugged at the ends of her blanket, suddenly the pulling grew more forceful. "I'm sad she's dead. That Mother killed her. But Mother was jealous of her."

"Because your father..." Val tried to find the right words.

"Yes." Bridget didn't need help deciphering the question. "I wished Father would have left Mother for Claudia and Claudia would have been my mother. But then he started spending time with Bethany." Bridget hissed the last word and scowled when she said *Bethany*.

Bridget's implication was clear. "Who killed Bethany, Bridget?"

"*That bitch is going to die!*" Bridget stared straight ahead, appearing to have mimicked someone else's words again.

"Did your mother kill Bethany?"

"Yes." Bridget snapped to attention and focussed on Val again.

"Weren't you afraid your mother would have caught you going back to the church that night?" Val wondered how Bridget even made it out of the house.

"No." She shook her head several times. "That night I knew Mother would have taken something strong, to make her sleep. She didn't wake up when she did that. It was on these nights I got to do what I wanted. Father wasn't home that night either. Neither was Claudia. My door wasn't locked. Mother forgot to lock it when we came home."

"You loved Gabrielle? Is that why you gave her the yew branches and seeds. You wanted her to come back from the dead?" Val asked.

Bridget nodded. "She was my sister. I loved her. She wanted to get custody of me. She wanted to get me out of here. I wanted her to come back so she could do that."

"Why didn't you give Adam the yew tree branches too?" Val asked.

Bridget looked down at her blanket and played with the ends for a few seconds. "He was going to a better place. He was going to be with God."

"Can you tell us what you mean by that? Was Gabrielle a bad mother?" asked Gavin.

"Our mother was trying to get custody of Adam. If he came back, he'd be in danger here. No, he was safer with God." Bridget nodded her head, emphasizing what she believed.

Val took a deep breath, there was one more topic she wanted to cover with Bridget and hoped Bridget could handle it. "Bridget, what happened the day the twins drowned?" Val asked.

Bridget's eyes flew open wide. "I'm not allowed to talk about that."

"I'm giving you permission, so it's okay," Val said softly.

Bridget looked down and then up, at Val and then away from her, skeptical. She shook her head, no.

"Please, Bridget. I won't let anyone hurt you if you tell us."

Bridget inched closer to Val and whispered cautiously, "Gabi, Bethany and Melinda wanted to play one of Mother's games."

"What was the game?"

"The pool game."

"Can you tell me how it was played?"

"Mother would take me and the twins to the pool and we would get into the water. Gabrielle would sit on the edge and watch. Mother would make us take turns holding each other's heads down. We weren't allowed to let go until Mother said so. If we did let go, she'd hold our head down for as long as she wanted. Then after we were done, we would be sent to our room, confined for days and though Claudia brought our meals, we weren't allowed to eat them. We had to scrape them into a bag Mother would bring and if she thought we ate any of it, we'd have to drink Mother's special smoothies too. *If you're hungry, I'll give you something to eat,*" Bridget said in the voice of someone she was mimicking again. "After, we'd vomit for days. The next time we went to the pool, we knew to do what we were told."

"How did Melinda know about this game?"

"Gabrielle told her." Bridget looked right at Val, tears were forming. "Melinda drowned the twins. She told everyone it was an accident but it wasn't. She said she was going to do the same with me that day but Bethany screamed."

"Did Bethany save you?"

"No, her screaming saved me because it made Melinda stop. Bethany was just as bad as Melinda. Gabi's friends were horrible. They liked to hurt me. They liked to hurt the twins. They were like Mother." Tears were now streaming down Bridget's cheeks.

"What about Gabrielle? Didn't she try to save you?" Val said softly.

"Melinda wouldn't have let her. I think that's why she didn't try. It wasn't Gabi's fault. Melinda would have hurt Gabi too."

"What's going to happen to her?" Val asked once they were outside.

"She's thirty-three years old and has been abused by her mother for that entire time. She's also rid of that mother and is very, very wealthy. She's the only surviving beneficiary to the Morgan estate. The Morgans' will specify provisions of supervision through an uncle on her father's side. So for now, Bridget will be okay. Will she make it in the long run? Well, that's anyone's guess. Is she finally free? Yes."

"So, Melinda just gets off scot-free?" Val asked, anger in her voice.

"Sorry, Val, sometimes there's nothing more you can do. Was she a horrible child that grew up to be a horrible adult? Yes. But there's no evidence that she killed the twins, let alone on purpose. The only other two witnesses are dead. Jennifer Ballard is not credible because she had no direct close observation of what actually occurred. Plus, any competent lawyer would tear her apart on the stand for living right next door to Gabrielle. I can go on and on here. No, we just have to wait for Melinda to make a mistake."

"Mitch, there is *another direct* witness still alive. And we just left her upstairs."

"And that's why I'm going to start setting up surveillance on this house. For her protection."

Gavin went around to the driver's side door of his car and Val walked to her own car. "Val," he said.

"Yes?"

"There's something I've been meaning to tell you."

"What is it?"

Gavin locked his gaze on Val's and it seemed like forever before he spoke. "I'm getting a divorce. Should be finalized sometime this week."

Val swallowed hard. She was speechless.

"I was wondering if you were free on Saturday," Gavin said.

It took a second for the words to register. "I think I just might be." Val smiled.

～

Upstairs, I watched from my bedroom window. I pulled the curtains back slightly, and stood to the side, so no one could see me if they happened to look up. The detectives got in their car. Valentina Knight followed. I waited, hidden, until they turned on to the road. It was over. Finally over. What an odd feeling, the secrets I've buried for so long have been exposed. My family is dead. I haven't felt this liberated my entire life.

I let the curtain fall back and walked to my nightstand table and grabbed several bottles of pills from the drawer. I took them to the bathroom and opened the containers, dropping the tablets into the toilet. No more of this. No more hiding the fact that I didn't take the pills but learned to act as if I did. No more hiding in general. God, what a relief.

To keep me quiet about the day the twins drowned, Gabrielle threatened to tell Mother that I drowned the twins, and that I did it on purpose. *No one will believe you and guess what Mother will do to you if I tell her otherwise?*

Gabi could be so horrible. Then one day she did tell her lie —out of spite—or maybe to prove that she could, and Mother changed my usual punishment. That's when the extra pills started and when she started locking me in the upstairs room for days on end with no food and the temperature always kept so cold.

Mother was evil. And Gabi was just like her. Gabrielle did things to make Adam sick. She liked the attention she got when she brought him to the doctor, the pity everyone showered on her. All Gabrielle ever wanted was to be the center of attention.

But it was Melinda who drowned the twins after Gabrielle *dared* her to. Gabrielle always called them brats and wanted to be rid of them and if Melinda was a true friend, she would prove it by drowning these *rats*. I don't think Gabrielle knew quite what she was dealing with in Melinda. It wasn't until after Melinda killed my brother-in-law Max that Gabrielle found out.

I looked around the bathroom, my gaze lingered on the windowsill and I smiled. They've gotten bigger. Just the other day, I placed a few containers with plants on the sill. They were small yet but starting to grow. Belladonna. *Beautiful lady.* Bridget's beautiful lady.

Gabrielle wanted the twins exhumed. She suspected she herself had been poisoned. She knew the twins were. She also suspected me as the poisoner. Mother was pretty good at it, but I grew to be better. I learned how to beat Mother at her own game. I gave her things that made her very sleepy. When Mother slept, I was free.

Why didn't Mother ever punish Gabrielle like the rest of us? Gabrielle never had to play the pool game. Never had to drink one of Mother's *smoothies.* It just wasn't fair. Gabrielle rubbed it in our faces that she was Mother's favorite. She'd pull my hair, slap my face, trip me if I walked by her, and all Mother would do was laugh. I was forced to come up with my own punishments for Gabrielle. At first, I just did things to make Gabrielle sick.

I gave her cadmium—the same thing Mother fed the twins —but when Gabrielle told me, "I know what you've done with the poison, and soon Mother will know what you've done," well, I knew what I had to do. I gave Gabrielle something that would give her cancer. I wanted her to suffer for what she did to my brother and sister, how she coaxed Melinda to drown them. For what she was doing to me.

Once I learned that Gabrielle wanted to get custody of me, and started to tell me about the *room* she was making in her basement to keep me in, I had no choice but to get rid of her quickly. When she called Mother and Father wanting to reconcile, she asked to speak with me too. This is how I knew.

I lied. Mother did not kill Gabrielle and Adam. I did.

I drugged Gabrielle and brought her here the night before she and Adam disappeared. It was actually very easy to do. When I showed up at her house it was about 11pm, she was shocked but let me in. I made sure she didn't see me as a threat. I also made sure she didn't see the syringe that I brought with me. Mother did have a lot of these lying around.

I managed to steal the key to the upstairs room and I locked Gabrielle in there. Mother was *sleeping*, Father wasn't home. And though I hated to do this, I had to make sure Claudia was *sleeping* too.

After I locked Gabrielle up, I went back to Gabrielle's house and spent the night. Adam was very surprised to see me the next morning. I told him his mother was sick and that I would be taking him to school and that I would be bringing him home. I put on Gabrielle's coat, pulled the hood up, and we left. Even waved to the neighbor.

We drove for about twenty minutes because he started to cry uncontrollably. I finally managed to calm him down. After I dropped him off at school, I went home. No one knew I was gone. I gave Mother and Claudia enough *medication* the night before to make sure they *slept in* that morning. Later, after they were *sleeping* again, I picked up Adam from school, in a location that I told him to meet me at.

After Gabrielle and Adam were dead I brought that key to the upstairs room to Gabrielle's house and placed it in one of her pockets. I never wanted Mother to have that key again. I never wanted to be locked up there again. I knew she'd never find where I put it.

It was true, what I said of Adam. If he lived, he might have ended up with my mother as his guardian. I couldn't risk that. Mother would be free to determine her choice of *child rearing*. No, death was a better option. He was in a better place now. This world is vicious, so unkind. You need tough skin to make it through. I learned how to be a good poisoner. It was my only way to survive.

The yew tree, the tree of reincarnation? No, to me it's the tree of the dead. Anyone who experiences the afterlife gets eternal punishment for their life of sin. And I hope Gabrielle is getting what she deserved.

I killed Gabrielle and Adam but Mother did kill Father, Claudia and Bethany. I told the truth about that. For some reason Mother was convinced Bethany killed Gabrielle and Adam. She didn't suspect me. Otherwise, I'd be dead.

I overheard Mother saying Valentina Knight worked with the police. This was after the day Val came to see me, in my room. When Mother brought Val here, Mother used the key Val had in her pocket to lock her upstairs. She wondered how Val had it. She thought Val stole it the day she came to our house. I brought the key back to Val. So she could escape. But Mother found out that I had gotten out of my room. I wasn't able to avoid my pills on that day.

Val told me she tried to get me to leave with her after she got out of the attic. I have no memory of that. That's what strong drugs will do. If things didn't work out with Val, I'd be worse than dead.

"Ma'am, Melinda Holbright is here," my new housekeeper called from the bedroom doorway.

I walked out of the bathroom and smiled at her. "Thank you. Just let Ms. Holbright know I'll be right down."

Melinda killed my brother-in law. She drowned my brother and sister. She would have drowned me that day too if Bethany hadn't screamed. She's here today, thinking she's going to win. She's wrong.

You know my story. I've confessed my sins. You can judge me as you see fit. I understand that. But what I hope is that you can let me live in peace. Finally. Now I do have to go. I'm about to have Gabrielle's *old friend* for *tea*.

THE END

ACKNOWLEDGEMENTS

My deepest gratitude to Bloodhound books for having faith in The Secrets We Bury and agreeing to take it on! Thank you to Betsy Reavley and Fred Freeman, Heather Fitt- for your amazing insight on the initial draft, Tara Lyons, Clare Law – editor extraordinaire, and the rest of the editorial, design and publicity team. You are awesome. I can't thank you all enough at Bloodhound for bringing The Secrets We Bury out in the world and helping me make it the best it can be.

Thank you to all who answered my questions, gave me information and advice on poisons. I tried to keep the details as accurate and real (and as safe!) as possible. Also, thank you to those who've helped me with my forensic and crime scene investigation questions. Any errors, or stretches of the imagination, are my own.

To my friends, colleagues, co-workers, former and current students at UB, the encouragement you've given is amazing. Thank you all!

To my dear friend Dr. Ray Miller, I can't thank you enough for your support, advice, and letting me bend your ear during our Friday PM chats. We've walked a long road together, and I look forward many more miles. Yes, I know, still no dog in this book – but there's always the next.

Mom, Tony and Aunt Marcia - I did it again! Thank you all for everything. Michael – you're forever in my heart. Miss you much.

Finally, to my husband Peter, who continues to believe in my writing and encourages me every day. You are my biggest cheerleader, advocate, and rock of strength when I need a push or a shoulder to lean on. Thank you for your dedication, love and support. I couldn't have done this without you!

A NOTE FROM THE PUBLISHER

Thank you for reading this book. If you enjoyed it please do consider leaving a review on Amazon to help others find it too.

We hate typos. All of our books have been rigorously edited and proofread, but sometimes mistakes do slip through. If you have spotted a typo, please do let us know and we can get it amended within hours.

info@bloodhoundbooks.com

Made in the USA
Coppell, TX
09 June 2021

57119967R00194